W9-ASV-530

The Traveler's Odyssey in

THE BOOK OF JAMAICA

"I wanted to see, to make a vision for myself; I did not want to become someone else's information, to be seen, to be inside a vision. So I would lie. Let the truth take care of itself, I decided. It's done all right on its own so far."

*   *   *

"It was as if I had slipped into an episode of *Pilgrim's Progress* and everyone I met there and every place I went to had a strictly allegorical function and no real life of its own—except for me, who, alone among the characters, was also the reader of this book."

*   *   *

"And that is why I was afraid in the way Gauguin and Forster and Dinesen were never afraid. They may not have known precisely where they were when they found themselves in Tahiti, India, or Africa, but they knew they were not in Paris, Cambridge, or Copenhagen. And that, at least, let them see more clearly than I could now where they had traveled to and who they were moving among. A white American, I was blind, and lost."

Books by Russell Banks:

SEARCHING FOR SURVIVORS
FAMILY LIFE
HAMILTON STARK
THE NEW WORLD
THE BOOK OF JAMAICA
TRAILERPARK
THE RELATION OF MY IMPRISONMENT
CONTINENTAL DRIFT

THE BOOK OF JAMAICA

Russell Banks

BALLANTINE BOOKS • NEW YORK

Library of Congress Catalog Card Number: 79-25983

ISBN 0-345-33074-9

The author is grateful for permission to quote from the song "Brand New
Beggar," by M. Cooper, S. Coore, C. Marshall (Third World). Copyright
© 1976 by Island Records Ltd., Kingston, Jamaica.

Manufactured in the United States of America

First Ballantine Books Edition: June 1986

For Lea, Caerthan, Maia, and Danis Banks
sisters of sisters

The role that causality plays in our culture has its counterpart in the role played by analogy among the Meso-Americans. Causality is open, successive, and more or less infinite: a cause produces an effect, which in turn engenders another. Analogy or correspondence, by contrast, is close and cyclical: the phenomena evolve and are repeated as in a play of mirrors. Each image changes, fuses with its contrary, disengages itself, forms another image, and in the end returns to the starting point. Rhythm is the agent of change in this case. The key expressions of change are, as in poetry, metamorphosis and mask.

OCTAVIO PAZ, Laughter and Penitence

> I thought that happiness was mine
> Dressed in silk and drinking wine.
> Now I'm face to face with me,
> I look around, and suddenly
> I've changed—yes I have—
> I'm a brand new beggar.
> I've changed—
> I'm a brand new beggar.
>
> BRAND NEW BEGGAR

Contents

Captain Blood

They were black. They spoke beautiful English.
Who were they?
   "What is this place?" I asked.
   "Jamaica. This is Kingston."
   "Jamaica?" So that was it.

ERROL FLYNN, *My Wicked, Wicked Ways*

1

THIS PART OF MY STORY BEGINS ONE EVENING EARLY IN January 1976 in Anchovy, Jamaica, a country village clinging to the hills of St. James Parish about twelve miles south and west of Montego Bay. At that time I was residing in Jamaica for a few months, ostensibly for the purpose of investigating the living conditions and habits of the Maroons, a remnant people who were the direct descendants of slaves who had escaped from their Spanish and then British masters in the seventeenth and eighteenth centuries and who afterwards from their inaccessible mountain enclaves had successfully conducted a hundred year guerrilla war against the British. When I was not actively researching the daily lives of these people, I had sufficient leisure and interest to involve myself in the daily lives of the more typical Jamaicans who lived all around me, drinking and smoking ganja with them, playing dominoes, arguing politics, and so on. As a result I formed several close friendships with a number of my neighbors.

My closest friendship, however, was with a man named Terron Musgrave who was neither a typical Jamaican nor one of my neighbors. He was a man in his mid-thirties, my own age, and a Maroon, and though during these months he spent fully half his time in Anchovy at my house, he lived in the Maroon village of Nyamkopong, forty miles and three hours' drive away.

Terron was a short man, even diminutive, but extremely muscular, and though he gave the impression of having been packed into his body under great pressure and seemed always about to explode into furious, chaotic activity, when he moved he moved slowly and gracefully with thoughtful, deliberate precision. His skin was dark brown, almost mocha-colored, and his face had been carved by genes and character into the face of a Nigerian king. Because he was a religious man and a member of the Rastafarian sect, he was bearded and wore his hair in long, matted, leonine locks called dreadlocks, and in profile he did indeed resemble a dark male lion, which was as he desired it.

Terron's greatest gift, however, his most remarkable beauty, was his voice and the language it carried. He owned a deep, resonating baritone that came directly from his chest, and his exotic blend of Jamaican English, country patois, and Rastafarian neologism, a poem in any man's mouth, in his became a song, a chanting, rolling, mahogany and birdflight song. Against his, my own voice came to sound like the random banging of oilcans, tinny, empty, erratic, and my language as flat and uninteresting as a sheet metal duct. The comparison inevitably silenced me and my silence usually brought Terron "forward," as he would say, "into speech." He told me of his childhood in Port Antonio where the banana boats of United Fruit were loaded, his youth in the ghettos of Kingston where whole large families lived in refrigerator cartons and abandoned Japanese cars, his years in the back streets of Montego Bay where he had hustled as a middleman between the ganja growers in the hills and the dealers in the Bay, and, for the last seven years, his life among his "ascendants," the Maroons of Nyamkopong, where he himself had become a ganja grower. He told me also of his religion and the experience of his conversion, when he had come "to know I," and the marvelous changes it had wrought in his interior and exterior lives, how it had merged them, made them one holy vessel, like the conversion experience of an early Christian gnostic. His political views, too, he described to me, and they were literally that, views, for he, like all true Rastafarians, was a visionary and believed in prophecy, specifically those of Marcus Garvey and the apocalyptic books of the Christian Bible. We both mistrusted the current Jamaican government, a corrupt, incompetent bunch of ambitious men and women, most of them educated in England, where they had learned to long for the power and wealth of a ruling class and to mouth the socialist rhetoric of the dispossessed masses. But while Terron saw every evidence of their corruption and incompetence as another welcome sign of the fire to come, I saw it merely as another depressing episode in the history of the New World. Evil confirmed and deepened Terron's belief in good; all it did for me was confirm and deepen my pessimism.

The differences between us, it seemed to me, were so radical and thoroughgoing, the vocabulary and syntax of our respective lives so incomprehensible to the other, that what ordinarily should have repelled us in actuality attracted us, drew us together, so that we were like a pair of magnets clamped together, opposite pole to opposite pole. A consequence of this, or so I believed, was that neither of us took the other's descriptions of reality as revealing any reality except that of the teller himself. I believed that we looked into each other, but not through each other, to the world beyond. Almost the way lovers do, each man used the other to learn only about himself. We were utterly opaque surfaces, I thought, but as a mirror is opaque. When we sat out on my terrace in the evenings, watching the sun fall behind the lush green hills, smoking ganja and talking with one another about our beliefs, I perceived only Terron Musgrave and nothing of the world his beliefs had sprung from. This, I thought, had been a deliberate decision on my part, a decision not to translate his words, not to research him, as it were, but simply to give myself over to the contemplation of his voice and language, his profound sincerity, his genuine great-heartedness and sorrow, and his spiritual optimism. I dealt with him as a phenomenon and not a referent, and thus I learned nothing from him of the Maroons, of Rastafarianism, of Jamaican peasant life, of the intricacies of the ganja trade, or even of the geography of the island, subjects he knew too intimately and unselfconsciously to make known to me without my having first to translate him, without my having to put myself into the role of researcher. Then one night, very late, Terron told me of his knowledge of Errol Flynn.

He had been circling the subject of his work as a fisherman when he was a boy in Port Antonio, lyrically describing barracudas he had speared, chunks of black coral he'd retrieved from forty feet of water, lobsters the size of full-grown goats he'd sold at the yacht club, when I suddenly realized he was describing his discovery of the remains of a human body. He had been paddling his canoe alone early one morning from the fishermen's beach on the eastern curve of Port Antonio, headed toward the Blue Hole, a hundred-and-eighty-foot-deep natural lagoon with clear water for diving and a small restaurant where there appeared occasionally a tourist or two interested in buying fresh-caught lobster for lunch. Passing the rocks and ledges of Folly Point a few hundred yards at sea, during a lull in the breeze so that the water stiffened and cleared like a pane of glass, he had peered down forty feet to the gray, pitted bottom and had seen an unnameable brown beast with a white mouth, a strange gaping eel staring up at him from a grotto, a human leg severed from the trunk. The breeze suddenly returned, breaking the skin of the water and erasing Terron's vision of the bottom. He dared not say what he had seen; he wasn't sure that he had in fact seen what he had seen. Until afterward, when he arrived at the Blue Hole and saw on the beach a half dozen boys, fellow divers, standing awkwardly around a second human leg, swollen, slickly wet from the waters of the lagoon, dark brown, almost black from foot to thigh, where it became a white thick-lipped gaping mouth.

There had been a murder. And a shocking dismember-
ment, for within a week there were found, battered and
caught among the craggy limestone cliffs from Folly
Point to the Blue Hole, first one arm, then the second,
then the torso—a woman's—and at last, rolling in the
surf by the beach of Boston Bay, the head. The torso
had revealed the sex of the victim, and the head had
shown that the person was young, but further identification, because of the hammering of the sea and rocks and
the work of the carrion eaters, was impossible.

A few days later, when all six pieces of the corpse
were being deposited together into a wooden crate in the
basement freezer of the restaurant at Frenchman's Cove
Hotel—the only place in Port Antonio at that time where
the police could store the ghastly evidence—it was observed by one of the more astute members of the con-
stabulary that the limbs and head had been severed from
the torso with exceptional precision, as if with a single
stroke of a machete, the way a skilled butcher would
cleave the legs and head from a freshly killed goat. This
was a curious development. And, according to Terron, it
was what led directly to the arrest of the butcher, De-
Vries, and his quick conviction and execution, by hanging,
in Kingston.

This was not the end of the story, however. Terron's
story, I mean. The butcher DeVries was innocent, he
told me. The dismembered woman had indeed been his
wife. The police had proved that easily. They had simply inquired after the wife and girl friend of every butcher
in town, and when only DeVries' wife was missing, they
had asked him where she was, and he had lied. He told
them she was in Kingston visiting relatives and would be
home in a few days. Why, what was the matter, had she
done something? No, nothing she'd done, they just wanted
to talk with her about a civil suit, so DeVries was to
notify them as soon as she returned from Kingston. The
police waited, they had plenty of time, the body was in
the freezer in the restaurant at Frenchman's Cove, and
three weeks later, when DeVries' wife still hadn't re-

turned, they had simply gone back and asked him again where she was.

This time, however, he did not lie. He said nothing. It was as if he had been struck dumb. The only sound he could make was a kind of caw that came from the back of his throat, like the caw of a crow or one of those Jamaican turkey buzzards called the John Crow that loop lazily against the perfect Caribbean sky day after day, endlessly drifting in concentric circles above the point of a tiny, sudden death in the dense greenery below.

The butcher DeVries, throughout his trial and right up to his execution, remained silent, except when directed to speak, when he would gulp and strain and writhe and produce the squawk that Terron said was the work of Errol Flynn. Flynn and his American doctor friend, Dr. Menotti, Terron explained, had silenced the butcher so that he could not testify against them. For the killer had not been DeVries but Dario Menotti, the adolescent son of the white physician, a boy in his late teens who was about to leave the island and his father and go to college in Massachusetts so that he too could become a doctor. Menotti, Sr.—a longtime resident of Port Antonio and drinking companion to Errol Flynn—a widower, a man remembered for his delicate manner and precise smile, loved his son and would not have wanted to see a brilliant medical career ruined before it had even a chance to begin.

This is what happened. Sometime during a late February evening, after cognac and Royal Jamaican cigars at Flynn's finca east of Port Antonio, the two older men and the boy, all three slightly drunk and exhilarated, had determined that this would be the night to initiate the boy into his life of medicine. If you are to save lives, Flynn said, it will be merely a technical skill, a mechanic's act, meaningless and insensible, unless you first know what it means to destroy a life. Everything implies its opposite, he told them, while the doctor nodded in sage agreement. The boy did not understand what this meant, but he trusted his father and he thought Flynn heroic. Both men had been with the boy when he first tasted the pleasure of coupling with a woman, both men had introduced him to the expansive intensities of ganja and cocaine, and both had instructed him in the pleasures of gambling on the outcome of violent encounters between cocks, dogs, women with knives and men without them. Through his father and his father's friend Errol Flynn, the boy had learned how to perceive himself in relation to his environment, the environment of a black peasantry in which he was the white lord of the manor.

Flynn saw DeVries pass the window, about to start for his home in town, and he bellowed and waved for the man to come into the huge, tile-floored living room. Flynn raised red poll cattle on his thousand acres of cleared seacoast and hillside, and at times he hired all the butchers in town to come out and ply their trade with their machetes. Today had been such a day, and DeVries was the last of the butchers to leave. He stepped timidly into the room, hat in hand, barefoot, wearing bloodstained trousers rolled almost to his knees and a tattered undershirt without sleeves. He was frightened. Flynn, when drunk, could get wild and say strange things that confused and hurt people. DeVries saw that the Doctor was with Flynn. The Doctor. To Jamaicans of the interior and in ports as isolated as Port Antonio the title meant witch doctor, voodoo man. It meant obeah. Flynn was evil and, because of his wealth, powerful; but the Doctor, because of his knowledge, was even more powerful than Flynn. The two men together, however, were dangerous.

The white men were drunk, waving cigars, gesturing and talking loudly in that flat, difficult speech of theirs, pointing at the boy, who sat serious and poised near the fireplace, until at last it became clear to DeVries that what the men wanted was a woman for the boy, a woman from the streets. They would pay him for procuring her, and they would pay her well too. Ah, now

DeVries understood what was going on. The boy was about to become a man. Well, he would be happy to accommodate them, yes indeed, and with immense relief and pleasure at the thought of the money he would receive tonight, he bowed and stepped from the room, then ran down the hill from the greathouse to the low barn where his meat wagon and scrawny horses were tied. He would bring them a woman, all right, but it would not be a whore from the Port, some pretty-faced brown girl who would thank him for his trouble and keep for herself whatever she could beg, earn and steal from the white men. No, he'd go to his own wife, who also was pretty-faced and brown and still slender, the way white men liked them, and in the morning he would take from her whatever they had given her. He would make money for procuring the woman, and he would have the woman's money too. He would buy a new horse.

A few hours later DeVries delivered his wife, who was named Waila after Noah's wife, to Flynn and the Doctor and his son. Flynn told DeVries to wait at the bottom of the hill with his wagon and he would pay him later, when they were through with the woman. This confused DeVries. He had expected them to pay him and send him away. Let the girl get back to the Port on her own.

But the butcher did as he was told and walked slowly down the gravel drive to the low wagon shed near the gate. It was very late, almost midnight, overcast and moonless. He smoked a cigarette, talked to his bony horses for a while, and then climbed into the back of his wagon and, curling up in a pile of burlap bags in a corner, fell asleep.

Sometime toward dawn, when the horizon was silvering into a soldered line between sea and sky, DeVries was wakened by a man's hand, Flynn's, shaking him roughly by the shoulder. He rubbed his eyes and sat up and remembered where he was and what he was doing there. Flynn growled at him, told him to follow him back up to the house, and turned and disappeared into the gloom. The butcher swiftly followed, running barefoot along the gravel drive, and arrived at the back entrance of the house just as Flynn, somehow there before him, opened the door from inside. DeVries could see the Doctor sitting in a heavy chair beside the fireplace and next to him his son, chalk-faced, staring intently into the fire.

Flynn ordered DeVries to follow him into the kitchen and stalked ahead of him, through doors and along dark corridors. When they entered the large, high ceilinged kitchen, Flynn switched on an overhead light, and the butcher saw his wife, naked, lying on a long table in the middle of the room, above her a rack of pots, pans, and skillets hanging by their handles like small carcasses. Though there were no wounds on her body that would tell him how she had died, the butcher knew that she was dead and that the Doctor and Errol Flynn and the Doctor's son had killed her. She was a beautiful woman to DeVries at that moment. It had been a long time since she had seemed beautiful to him.

That was as close to grieving as the butcher came; it was all his terror would permit him. Flynn simply told the man to get rid of the body and come back later in the morning for his pay. Throw it in the sea from Folly Point or someplace, and make sure no one can identify it, Flynn instructed him, and then he left the man alone with his wife.

Quickly he gathered her up, hitched her over his shoulder, opened a door that led directly outside, and, as the sun braised the sky and washed his face with light and warmth, he hurried down the hill to his wagon, where he wrapped the body in burlap, packed it into a corner—the same corner he had slept in—and started for Folly Point.

At his trial DeVries squawked and cawed whenever called to testify or answer for himself. Errol Flynn was in Spain and the Doctor's son was in Massachusetts. But the Doctor attended the trial every day, sitting in a front-row seat, cool and silent and crisp in his white linen suit, smiling delicately when he saw someone he knew, chatting easily later with the lawyers in the corridors, patting the policemen lightly on their bulky shoulders, and all the time, no matter what else he seemed to be doing, watching DeVries, circling over him like a turkey buzzard riding the rising currents of air, waiting for the smell of death to reach him.

2

IN FEBRUARY 1976 I MOVED OUT OF MY HOUSE IN ANCHOVY and returned to the States to resume my normal activities there. In April, however, I was obliged to come back to Jamaica to attempt to answer certain questions concerning the Maroons that had become apparent to me only from far away. I rented a car, a banged-up yellow Toyota sedan, at the airport in Montego Bay, where Terron was waiting for me, and the two of us drove into the interior to the Maroon village of Nyamkopong, where I would stay for ten days in the home of a man who was my friend and who was also the village wise man, an old man of crackling intelligence and power who functioned as his people's historian, jokester and magician, their conserver of language and rite. Terron was my guide and companion, my lightning rod in this storm, for it was that to me—a storm.

Following my ten days in Nyamkopong, I was to travel to the eastern end of the island to visit the remaining three Maroon settlements—Gordon Hall, Charles Town, and Moore Town—moving as impulse and circumstance indicated from one to the other of these tiny, isolated, mountain villages, sleeping in the back of my yellow Toyota and in huts and under the counters of crossroad shops and inns, interviewing the chiefs and old people, observing their conventions, recording their talk, learning their names for the things they lived among,

13

trying to understand how they perceived themselves. Terron, of course, accompanied me throughout this journey, and even though we were moving through people and places and spiritual events that he himself had never encountered, he nevertheless protected me and facilitated my entry into this world. He was black and I was white; he was a Jamaican and I was a foreigner; he was a Rastafarian and I a questioning skeptic; he was a Maroon and I a direct descendant of their enemies; he was articulate and I was unable to speak without first translating my thoughts into words. Yet, despite my dependence on him, on his intelligence and good will, I trusted him completely, and because of this, the people I moved among, ordinarily angry against and withdrawn from strangers, white or black, foreign or Jamaican, seemed to trust me. The storm, therefore, continued to rage.

Traveling along the coast between Gordon Hall, huddled among the vertebrae of the seven-thousand-foot-high Blue Mountains that spine the eastern end of the island, and Moore Town, a village that seemed to have been glued to the side of limestone cliffs, Terron and I passed through Port Antonio, where we stopped for a few days, for Terron had been a child and adolescent there and had not been back since then, and he wished to visit a brother who still lived there and to walk through some of the rooms and along some of the streets of his childhood. After a few queries in bars along the waterfront, we learned that Terron's younger brother Holmes was now living with a man named Evan Smith in Smith's house on the edge of town.

I was exhausted by the time we reached Smith's house. The demands on my attention during the past three weeks began to leave me at the end of the day too exhausted to recover fully by morning, resulting in a kind of entropy. I was running down. That very morning, in the shade of a breadfruit tree in Gordon Hall, an old man with lines crawling over his face like snakes as he talked and hands holding sunlight like delicately woven baskets had revealed to me how the Africans, as he called himself and his people, had come to Jamaica. His tale had taken the form of a test. First a question, How did the Africans come to Jamaica? and my answer, I don't know, the only correct answer, and then his answer, They flew over, followed by another question, Where did they land? Again, my answer, I don't know, the only correct answer, with his, Over there on that hill. Another question, Where on that hill? and my confession of ignorance again, I don't know, and his answer, On a tree. What kind of tree? I don't know. A cashew tree. And why that tree? I don't know. Because they were hungry when they arrived. And what was the name of this place then? I don't know. Cashew Town. And who was here to greet them? I don't know. Nonny the Warrior Queen and her brother Cudjoe. And who were her other brothers? I don't know. Nyamkopong, Johnny, Quao, and Cuffee were the four brothers. And why are there four Maroon villages? I don't know. Because there were four brothers, one village ruled by each brother. And so on, for hours, until at last, breaking, I found myself weeping, and the men in the room, the old man telling the story and my friend Terron and two younger men from the village, reached out and touched me and smiled into my eyes.

Now, after a supper of gungo peas, rice and chicken wings cooked up by Holmes, I was sitting at Smith's rickety Formica-topped table with Smith across from me and a bottle of over-proof white rum between us. Holmes and Terron had gone out, apparently to visit old girl friends, cousins, aunts and uncles. Because of my exhaustion and because I liked this man Smith, I had declined their invitation to join them. Smith was in his early sixties, a man with a broad smiling face, a shovel-shaped beard speckled with gray, and a rasping, hurried voice. He was an intelligent man, one of the managers of the Port Antonio higglers market, but also an eccentric who lived alone, except for Holmes, who exchanged housekeeping and cooking for room and board. Smith had built his two-room cabin atop one of the bluffs that stick up like bony knees on the western end of the Port, had built it, evidently with Holmes' help, shortly after his wife had gone to the States to live with her two daughters and grandchildren in the Bronx. He could have joined them, he said, but he had chosen to stay in Port Antonio. That was his chief eccentricity. He explained it by pointing out that his wife's daughters were not his, though he had raised them as a father would, and that here in Port Antonio he was a man with many friends. I guessed that this smiling man's wife was probably a strong-willed and demanding woman and that he might have a lady friend here in Port Antonio.

From the bluff I could peer out the open, curtainless window all the way down to the Port, could see its curve from Folly Point to Bryan's Bay, with Navy Island in the middle, guarding the Port like a huge sleeping dog. The lights of cars driving up and down the dozen streets traced a map of the town, and the still lights of the banana boats, the private yachts and fishing boats marked the depths of the dark waters of the Port. Channel markers at the ends of Navy Island flashed like sudden insights, their locations forgotten as soon as the flash had passed, only to appear again seconds later seen as if for the first time. It was a warm, balmy evening, the smell of woodsmoke and cassia blossoms mingling with the breeze off the sea, while from the road far below me came the occasional honk of a car horn, from the darkness of the bush behind the cabin a transistor radio blatting reggae, the cry of a baby, a woman calling after her oldest son to come carry water as he scrambled down the rocky pathway to the road and the nightlife of the Port, bars and whorehouses and smoky backroom gambling dens or an interlude in someone's packed dirt yard squatting on the ground in darkness and passing a ganja spliff back and forth.

Looking down at the Port, I naturally thought again of Errol Flynn, for he had kept his boat anchored in that darkness and, I had learned that afternoon from Holmes, at one time had owned all of Navy Island, had won it in a poker game at the Princess, a bar and whorehouse on the waterfront. So I asked Smith if he had known Errol Flynn during the forties and fifties, when the man had made Port Antonio his primary place of residence. Talking with Smith was not like talking with Terron, because Smith translated himself for me whereas Terron would not, or could not. Terron spoke in images—not parables, allegories, symbols, or metaphors, but images—and translation destroyed his meaning. Smith, however, permitted different rules for the game, which of course meant that he communicated a different kind of information. Terron used language the way the old Maroons did, so that abstractions came across with the power of physical attacks, violently, irresistibly; Smith was better able to provide data. He was a type of Western man that Terron and the old Maroons and Rastafarians were not. In my fatigued condition, I was glad for the difference and for that reason risked a conversation concerning Errol Flynn.

Yes, he had known him, not personally, of course, only a few black people knew Flynn personally, those who worked for him out at his ranch or on his boat, and many women, though one may not want to call that knowing him personally. Errol Flynn was a bad man, Smith rasped, pouring himself an inch of rum, bringing mine back up to the same level. A bad man. Not like most men, though, who are bad because they have suffered or have something wrong with their heads. Errol Flynn was bad when he had no reason for it. Men cheat and steal and sleep with other men's wives, and they mistreat children and sometimes they kill a man, and yet it's always somehow understandable. There's always an explanation. It doesn't make them into good men, of course, but it explains why they were bad. With Flynn, though, it was different. There was never an explanation for why he did those things. He wasn't even crazy.

He started telling me how Flynn had come to own Navy Island and what he did over there afterward, how people would stand on the docks in the Port at night and

gaze in horror across the half mile of water to the flickering firelight and dancing bodies on the beach facing
them. As he told this a slow smile spread over his broad
face, almost as if he admired Flynn, so I asked him
about DeVries and the death of his wife, did Smith know
that particular story, insofar as it concerned Flynn? Oh
sure, sure, everyone knew that one, but it wasn't too
interesting. What interested Smith were the special kinds
of debaucherie that went on at Navy Island after Flynn
had won the island in a poker game at the Princess.
Everyone used to watch from the docks, he repeated,
and once in a while kids, boys, would sneak into the
water and swim across, but no one ever saw them again,
except when a few weeks later their bodies would show
up tangled in one of the channel markers of caught on
the rocks at the point near Titchfield. The official report
always said they had drowned trying to swim over to
Navy Island, which was acceptable, Smith said soberly,
because the current is strong in places, especially when
the tide's moving. Navy Island is owned now by big
guys from Miami and Las Vegas, he told me. Flynn sold
it to them before he died.

I didn't believe him. I wanted to hear about Errol
Flynn and Dr. Menotti and his son Dario and DeVries
the butcher and his dead wife Waila. Did that happen
the way Terron said it did? I asked him, and told him
quickly what I understood Terron to have told me.

No, of course not, he said, laughing. A lot of people in
Port Antonio believed that story because for most of
them a Doctor was an obeah man. These Jamaicans are
backward people, he explained, pouring another inch of
rum into our glasses, and it's much easier for them to
explain events by pointing to magic, voodoo, and obeah
than by pointing to the facts. The facts in this case were
that DeVries killed his wife and then was seen trying to
dispose of the body, so when he lied and told the police
that she had gone to Kingston to visit relatives, they
arrested him. The witness, a man who worked for Flynn,
saw DeVries early one morning out at Dolphin's Bay,

saw his wagon and old horse, which were well known, by the road and then saw DeVries out on the cliff hacking at something with his machete. This all came out at the trial, and there was nothing DeVries could say to defend himself. Flynn and Dr. Menotti and his son had nothing to do with the case, except that the witness happened to work for Flynn and that was why he was out on the road past Dolphin's Bay so early in the morning. And except that Dr. Menotti happened to own the land on both sides of the road at Dolphin's Bay.

Beyond that Smith wasn't even faintly interested in the Doctor and his son, and the only thing about Errol Flynn that interested him was what he used to do out there on the beach at Navy Island. But I could see that he was interested in the DeVries case itself, because he had known DeVries back then, he told me, had known him since childhood—they were both about the same age—and he had always been a bad man, wild, violent, and everyone had been saying for years that someday he would kill someone. Then, for some unknown reason, Smith was telling me about the hurricane of 1938. In those days no one knew when a hurricane was coming until a few hours before it actually hit, when suddenly the rain would slow and stop and the air would get heavy. Birds would fly inland in flocks, and the sea would turn silver and smooth as a fish's belly. But the hurricane of 1938 hit Port Antonio in the evening, so that the only warning they had was the sudden cessation of the rain that had been falling relentlessly for three days and nights, a warning that most people misread entirely, believing that all it signalled was the welcome passing of the storm. People opened their stores, threw up their windows, went out for walks in the street, and had conversations on corners for a change instead of inside their houses and cabins.

Smith was a young man then, unmarried, and he had gone to a dance at the Marblehead Pavilion, where now there is a hilltop hotel with a famous view of the mountains and the sea. In those days it was a dance hall, and

it was customary on a Saturday night for young single
men and women to meet there and dance and walk home
together in pairs. At the dance Smith met for the first
time the woman he would marry, a woman slightly older
than he who had two young daughters. Their father had
gone to the States to work in the orchards and had
jumped contract and hadn't returned. The woman was a
nurse, working for a doctor in Port Antonio, and she
was lonely and she liked him, and he fell in love with
her, and after they had danced for a couple of hours
they had started the walk back down the hill to town,
when the hurricane struck. The wind started to blow, in
gusts at first, then steadily and building, and the rain
started falling, first in billowing sheets and then, driven
by the wind, rushing straight into their faces, as if being
shot at them by a weapon. Heads down, they ran, the
young man and woman, down the long, steep, hillside
road to town, and then down the street toward the
woman's house, where her sister was staying with her
two daughters.

Smith spent the next three days at the woman's house,
a three-room cabin located on one of the narrow alleys
that cut back into the bush from the Port. He spent his
time comforting the woman and her sister and children,
nailing back boards and sheets of galvanized metal as
the hurricane wrenched them loose, telling stories with
them, singing songs, all of them warm and secure together for three days and nights while the hurricane
battered the Port, the whole island, eventually the entire
Caribbean and Gulf Coast. Until at last it moved away
and slowly chewed a path north and east along the
Atlantic.

The sky brightened into a silvery, satiny canopy, and
the rain stopped. Birds returned from the hills behind
the Port and hungrily headed out to sea. Dogs were barking, babies crying, engines starting up. The woman cooked
Smith a large breakfast and sent him on his way, a
happy man. Strolling down the street, whistling, nodding
hello, and chatting with everyone he passed, he made

his way toward his mother's house, which was situated, as it happened, a few buildings down from where De Vries lived and kept his butcher shop. As he approached DeVries' building, he first had to pass a small walled-in garden that the butcher had planted and tended, a vegetable garden that gave enough produce for his family with a little left over to sell to the higglers. Smith passed the wall, a flimsy structure made of scrap lumber and cast-off sheets of roofing tin, and heard a sound—Whap! —like the sound of someone beating a carpet. That seemed strange to him, beating a carpet right after a hurricane. Then he heard a man's voice, cold and harsh, You *bitch!* Again the hard slapping sound, and again the curse, You *bitch!*

Smith stopped, his whistle had died, and he felt sorry for DeVries' wife. It was a glorious morning, people were alive, the hurricane had passed over and had left them all among the living. But on a glorious morning a man's wife was being beaten, Smith thought sadly. A shame. A damned shame. Again the crack of a hand against flesh, and again the curse. Smith cringed and walked slowly on, passing the ramshackle wall and nearing the house itself. He peered into the house as he walked by an open window and saw a woman inside, a woman he knew. It was DeVries' wife. She was a pretty young woman, Smith told me, slender and brown. She was cooking ackee and salt fish—he remembered the smell—and she smiled at him. He smiled back, tipped his hat—he had a brown porkpie hat then; he wished he had it now—and quickly walked away, thinking about DeVries, trying to understand what kind of man would beat his girl friend with his wife not twenty feet away.

I got up from the table and discovered that the rum had been working on my body without my knowing it, for I had difficulty gaining my balance and nearly fell forward onto the table. Feeling like a tower about to topple, I stepped carefully outside and walked a way into the bushes, where, my feet spread, I stood and urinated, and while the water noisily splashed from my

body, watched the town and port below, the half mile of
black water between the docks and island that Errol
Flynn had owned, and the flashing channel markers
where the mangled bodies of curious boys had been
found. On my right and about three miles away at the
same altitude as the knob where I was standing were the
lights of the hilltop hotel which in 1938 had been the
dance hall where Smith had met his wife.

Smith was right—it was difficult to understand what
kind of man could beat his girl friend when his wife was
barely twenty feet away. That was the kind of man who
could kill his wife, however. And a satisfactory way of
explaining *why* he killed her, Smith had reasoned, was
simply to describe him as the kind of man who would
beat his girl friend in the garden while his wife was
cooking breakfast next door. One didn't need a motive
to explain violence; there are none. One needed a psychology. And for Smith, and now for me too, DeVries'
psychology was available, whereas the Doctor's and his
son's and Flynn's were not.

I buttoned up and started unsteadily back toward the
house, when suddenly I realized that, yes, the psycholo-
gies of the white men might well be a mystery for Smith,
but not for me. I understood them, just as Smith understood DeVries. It was DeVries who had been the mystery for me, in Terron's story as much as in Smith's—a
man who would peddle his own wife to another man and
who, when it turned out that the client had slain her,
would take her body and destroy it and toss the remains
into the sea, a man who, when accused of killing her
himself, would double in on himself and go silent, a man
who would finally let himself be executed for the crime.
That business of Menotti as obeah man, of course, I
discounted altogether. After all, I understood the white
men. I was one myself.

3

MY WORK AMONG THE MAROONS WAS SOON COMPLETED, and again I had to return to the States to resume my usual activities. I turned in the by then nearly useless yellow Toyota at the Montego Bay airport, gravely said good-bye to Terron and his brother Holmes, who had decided to travel with us from Port Antonio to Montego Bay, and moved regretfully into the line of returning American tourists, all of them sunburnt, straw-hatted, and grinning. I had no sunburn to show for my month in the tropics, no straw hat decorated with an impossibly contorted limbo dancer, and no anticipating grin for what the girls in the office would say on Monday when I strolled, luxuriously colored, into work.

Instead, my mind was jammed with images that in their darkness and conflict with one another made me uncomfortable—images of Errol Flynn as Terron saw him—Captain Blood, obeah man, a proud, laughing prince of darkness—and images of Errol Flynn as Smith saw him—an elegant mafioso don, a wealthy and famous land baron, a possible CIA agent—and images of Errol Flynn as I saw him—a sybaritic debauchee, an aging and decadent movie star. But it was the conflict between the images, rather than their number, that troubled me, for while I saw the man mainly in psychological terms, Smith saw him in social terms, and Terron saw him in mythic terms. This raised in me an irritated grasping after certainty, an insecurity that was distinctly unsettling.

One couldn't resolve the conflict simply by saying that Flynn was all these things at once, that an image, like a text, functioned on all three levels simultaneously and equally. One wished instead to establish a priority among them, a hierarchy, and for a long time now in his investigations one had organized his perceptions under the assumption that the psychological led to the social and historical, which in turn led to the mythic. This was the assumption of the age, the convention of rational analysis, that one had been trained to trust. Simply put, one could not know Errol Flynn as mafioso don until one had come to understand him as debauchee, and one could not know him as Captain Blood until one had probed his role as land baron. Cause and effect. It was presumed that his psychology caused his social identity which then caused his mythic function. Each stage was impossible without the previous stage as underpinning. Certainly Flynn could be perceived separately at any one of these three levels by different individuals who by their conditioning and circumstance were more or less better equipped to perceive him at one level than at another, and it did not depress one that Terron, Smith and oneself happened to perceive Flynn at different levels. What depressed was that, for Smith and Terron, the social and mythic levels, respectively, seemed sufficient, as if they were self-determined. For Smith and Terron, there was no irritated grasping after certainty. The perception alone was both adequate and certain. They had peered out from the house of their own perceptual apparatuses, and they had each seen an image, Errol Flynn, and for them the view had the clarity and certitude of a vision. For me, however, from my house the view caused anxiety, mistrust, depression.

But I saw no necessity for that anxiety, mistrust and depression. They were not expressions of the nature of the world; they were expressions of the nature of my training. I determined to neutralize the effects of my training somewhat. As soon as I had put my affairs in the States into an order that would permit me to be absent from them for a long period of time, I would return to Jamaica. I would come back and live there for at least a full year, and my purpose this time would be to establish, in place of a point of view, a vision. And I knew, as I boarded the plane for New York, that to do so I first might have to destroy my point of view, all my points of view.

A GRANT FROM A LARGE PRIVATE FOUNDATION AFFORDED me the luxury of returning to Jamaica that September. Once again I took up residence in the house on the hillside in Anchovy and proceeded to throw myself into researching the Maroons. I had already familiarized myself with their history, through a set of written documents, all lodged in the Library of Congress in Washington, D.C., and the West Indies Institute in Kingston. What I was after now, what I thought I was after, was an understanding of how the Maroons today experienced their world. At this time of my life I, like most Americans, believed more in the essential sameness among people than in their difference. I thought I could learn to know what it was like to be a Maroon. I could not then see any conflict between that belief and my ambition to replace a point of view with a vision.

Shortly after my arrival in Anchovy, Terron appeared, literally as if by magic, strolling delicately from the dense undergrowth and ledge one dark night, peering over the wall of the terrace and with his bassoon of a voice singing, "Yass, Rasta!" I hadn't told him when I would be arriving or where I would be staying; I had merely written him in the early summer to say that I would be returning to Jamaica sometime in September and that I hoped he would once again "move with me in the country," which was how he described his activity apropos my activity. So here he was, ready to move with me in the country again, after having come forty-five miles across nearly impassable Cockpit Country, jungle-covered limestone pits and craters that from the air resemble nothing so much as the surface of the moon. There were a few narrow roads curling around the edges of the region, along which great, lumbering, top-heavy buses carried passengers and market goods back and forth between Montego Bay and the interior villages. But travel to and from the interior, for the impoverished Maroons especially, was expensive, difficult and never casual. Terron's sudden appearance, therefore, was all the more surprising to me. He could not have known I would be here in this same house on the hill, sitting out on my terrace smoking a Royal Jamaican cigar and watching the sky over the Caribbean shift from blue to rose to purple and finally, as clouds streamed in from the northwest and blocked out the stars and moon, to black. I asked him how he had known I would be here, and he smiled and in rapid country patois said something about a dream, and I concluded that he probably spent a lot more time testing the prophetic powers of his dreams than I did.

I won't go into the details now of how I spent the next six months because my purpose here is to describe the encounter between Errol Flynn and DeVries, an almost forgotten murder case that, by my attempts to get straight what really happened, led me into understandings I did not expect or particularly desire. Let the six months pass, then, and assume certain changes in the narrator. Assume an increased ability to understand and speak Jamaican patois, an increased tolerance for the crisp fire of white rum, a growing respect for the difficulties of understanding what it was like to be a person from a different culture, race, landscape, economy and language, even as I was daily growing more familiar with the intricacies of that culture, race, landscape, economy and language. I learned the names of the trees and the flowers and the foods that surrounded me, learned how to play dominoes as ferociously as a Jamaican, and even learned how to talk with Jamaican women sufficiently for them to forget for whole long moments the tremendous advantage to their economic position I represented, so that they would now and then briefly cease trying to tell me only what they thought I wanted to hear. This does not mean that I then understood what they said to me.

At the end of March I went alone to Port Antonio, one hundred miles away at the opposite end of the island. Terron stayed in Nyamkopong to deliver his fifth child, but I had planned to make this trek alone anyhow. I had bought a car, a used Mazda van, in September on my arrival, and by this time had coaxed, pushed, and jammed some ten thousand miles of backcountry crushed limestone road onto it and had given up my earlier capitalist fantasy of selling the car when I left the island for the same four thousand dollars I had paid for it.

I parked the blue van in front of the Hotel de Montvin at George and Musgrave Streets on Titchfield Hill, a high-rising neck of land that swung around the Port on the western end of town where there were a dozen narrow streets and weather-beaten, unpainted, old houses from the last century, the remains of a hotel that seemed to have been partially constructed and then deserted. The de Montvin was like the houses, dilapidated, but fallen from a considerable height, so that enough remained from its original tropical opulence and excess and the colonial love of detail to make it still comfortable and interesting to the eye. I was given the key to room number thirteen by a rotund, bald, brown-skinned man at the desk and was directed to a small but airy and clean room at the back on the second floor.

The hotel had the feel of a rooming house. The guests I saw seemed to be residents, not tourists—a white man, who turned out to be Scottish, in his sixties and crippled so that he moved in tiny steps with the aid of two canes, his newspaper in a tight roll stuffed between his arm and tense, bent body, a pair of thick-faced black men in short-sleeved, double-knit tropical suits, apparently salesmen from Kingston; and an elderly woman, very black, with her hair wrapped in a lavender gauze scarf. Everyone in the hotel—the fat desk clerk, the chambermaids, the long-armed youth setting the tables in the dining room, and the guests—seemed to be locked inside his own thoughts, totally uninterested in what was going on around him, even the fact that a white man, obviously a foreigner, was registering at the desk. This pleased me. It was as if I were watching a meticulously detailed movie in which I was a minor character, a movie set in a Caribbean country in the 1930's designed to demonstrate a socialist view of history by killing off all the characters one by one until only the innocent working-class young are left alive. I knew that I would be among the last to go, not because I was most nearly innocent but because I was most representative of capitalist evil. To kill me off early would destroy any possibilities for dramatic action, and even ideology must allow for drama.

At the hotel bar, a small anteroom off the dining room, I drank a Dragon stout and asked the barmaid, a lanky girl with a lovely wide gap between her two front teeth, how to get to the famous Blue Hole. I noticed, behind me and almost out of sight, that the desk clerk (who now seemed to be a manager, for I saw that he was wearing a necktie) was attempting to watch me without my noticing it. When I had registered, in the space marked "Occupation" I had written "writer," and, though I was obviously American, I had put down my Jamaica address. This may have confused him, aroused his suspicions slightly. To be a "writer" in an anxious, politically intense society is to be under suspicion, and to contradict nationality with place of residence is worse. From now on, I decided, I would put "teacher" for my occupation, and I would only provide my U.S. address. Better to be a tourist and allowed to settle into a trusted generality than to make myself unique. I wanted information; I wanted to see, to make a vision for myself; I did not want to become someone else's

information, to be seen, to be inside a vision. So I would
lie. Let the truth take care of itself, I decided. It's done
all right on its own so far.

I PARKED MY CAR IN THE RUTTED LOT NEXT TO THE WHARF,
facing Navy Island, the United Fruit pier on my left, and
walked carefully into the clubhouse of the Eastern Jamaica Anglers Association, which passes for the Port
Antonio yacht club. The bar was open to the water on
three sides, so that boatsmen could tie up on the low
dock and step directly into the clubhouse for a drink.
There were three or four small, unkempt sailing vessels
and a noticeable absence of customers at the bar, but it
was still early—not quite ten in the morning. This kind of
sailor likes to sleep late, I thought.

The bartender, a swollen black man in his fifties with
purplish lips and rings around his eyes like a racoon's
was slinging beer into the lockers below the bar when I
sat down and ordered a cold Red Stripe. He yanked it
open, set it in front of me, and went back to stocking his
lockers. Where did Flynn used to dock his boat? I asked
him.

Flynn? Flynn? What the hell was this guy talking
about? Ah, Errol Flynn, the movie star. Right out there,
he pointed. In the stream, actually in an eddy in the
stream between Navy Island and the mainland just below Titchfield Hill. He liked to keep his boat a little
ways off the Jamaica Reef Hotel that used to be there on
the cliff, where Titchfield Hill juts out against the sky
and then drops several hundred feet to a sudden beach.
That was the concrete wreckage, the pilings and empty
pool I had seen this morning before I checked in at the
de Montvin.

The Jamaica Reef, eh?

Well, actually, when Flynn was alive it was the old
Titchfield, owned by a friend of Flynn's, Captain Ausley,
now manages Navy Island.

Navy Island? The whole island?

Well, actually it's called the Windjammer Hotel, still under construction. You can't get out there, though.

Why not? I asked him.

They're not ready yet.

On my way back through town to the wreckage of the Jamaica Reef Hotel, I turned left at the square and passed the Delmar Theater and observed that a karate film made in Hong Kong and starring Bruce Lee was the current feature. This seemed significant to me—but practically everything seemed significant to me then. That was how I wanted it. I was losing momentum in my quest, and I was consequently falling backward into myself, so that the only way I could continue to justify my continuing the quest was to attribute significance to everything that passed before me. I was becoming unhappy.

The Jamaica Reef was no more than a carcass now. This morning I had thought it was a project that hadn't been completed. Now I saw that it was the picked-over remains of what had once been a lavish and elaborate installation. Holes in the ground, like foundations for bunkers, were empty swimming pools littered with broken beer bottles and flakes of aqua paint piled like dead leaves. Columns that had looked grecian turned out to be the trunks of concrete palm trees supporting long-gone thatched roofs above terraces that had overlooked the stream flowing between the Port and the open sea. Across the stream, no more than a quarter of a mile away, was Navy Island. And halfway across were three red markers, where Smith had said they found the bodies of the boys who had tried to swim over, or maybe the boys had been caught trying to swim back with their precious knowledge to the safety of the mainland. Who knew? Who, besides their families, cared any longer? Between the markers and the narrow strip of sandy beach below the hotel the water was slower, and here Errol Flynn must have anchored his boat, coming over by launch in the evenings to drink and eat with his friend Captain Ausley at the hotel.

The story about DeVries was beginning to look like just that, a story. Under the placid intensity of the late morning sun, surrounded by the remains of a hotel that had burned down years ago, I stood on the beach staring out at the rippling current that ran between Titchfield Hill and Navy Island where a new hotel complex was erupting from the jungle, and slowly the several stories of Errol Flynn and Dr. Menotti and his son and the murder of the wife of the butcher DeVries faded into local gossip and superstition, a shapeless batch of unrelated details. In place of all those details a new set was appearing to me, bringing with it a new story, the tale of an idle American trying to make his ordinary life seem more mysterious and interesting to himself.

I was disappointed in what was appearing to me to be true, and I was disappointed in myself, for it meant that I was disappointed in reality. I walked sullenly to the edge of the sand, took off my shoes and rolled up my trousers, and slogged a few yards into the water, and I let the depression come over me.

LATER, DECIDING TO GO OUT TO THE BLUE HOLE ANYHOW, I scrambled back to the road and got into my car. The Blue Hole was where Terron had been heading in his canoe when he saw the leg from the body of DeVries' wife, and it was where they had discovered the second leg. And it was a tourist attraction, I reminded myself, and I was a tourist. So I drove the half dozen miles along the coast road, past sprawling, slumbering estates surrounded by palms and carefully tended lawns and hibiscus and poinsettia beds, following hand-lettered signs and arrows, until I pulled left off the main road and passed into a large, grottolike opening in the cliffs, a lagoon with a narrow opening to the sea where there was a beach with a half dozen dugout fishing canoes drawn up on the sand and, between the beach and the lagoon, a bamboo-walled and thatch-roofed restaurant. Parking my van in the shade of a cashew tree, I strolled into the restaurant, which was deserted, except for three

young men in white waiters' coats talking at one of the
tables.

None of the waiters had ever heard of DeVries. But
after I had ordered a plate of curried goat and rice and
we had chatted in a casual way about the lagoon, one of
the waiters yelled for the cook, who turned out to be a
man in his fifties, dark-faced and scowling, short and
slightly bent. He came out of the kitchen wiping his
hands on a spotted apron, disliking the waiters, who
were boys to him, fresh kids who teased him about his
relations, or lack of them, with women. He'll know that
man DeVries, the waiters assured me, and he did, happy
for the chance to show these fresh kids that age has its
uses.

DeVries was wicked. That's what the cook insisted. A
wicked man. And no, Errol Flynn had no involvement
with the case. There was a Dr. Menotti involved, but
only because he owned the property where DeVries had
tried to dispose of the body, which was not in pieces,
but merely headless, and DeVries had got caught trying
to stuff the body down a hole that dropped through the
limestone ledge at Dolphin's Bay to the sea below. The
waves slammed against the cliffs below and carved huge
caverns there, and along the top one could now and then
find holes that dropped twenty or thirty feet through the
ledge all the way to the cavern below. DeVries had been
trying to drop his wife's body down one of these holes
one morning, so that it would get swept into the sea with
no chance of its turning up on a sandy beach someday.
It would have worked too, the cook assured me, if he
hadn't been seen by a man from town who was on his
way to work at Flynn's estate. So Errol Flynn *was*
involved! I declared. Yes, one could say that, the cook
supposed. But the Doctor was also involved slightly because at that time he owned all the land along Dolphin's
Bay, and for a long time people thought that he had
killed the woman for DeVries, because he was a Doctor,
you see, and they can do that. Do what? Kill people.

That's what people say, he meant. That's what people in those days believed.

The waiters had stopped stepping with the reggae on the radio and had suddenly become serious. They were watching me. I quickly told them I wasn't so much interested in DeVries and the Doctor as in Errol Flynn, and, as if relieved, they all started talking rapidly in patois, pointing and gesturing and moving with the music again, that pretty dance with the upper body swaying and the feet making tiny shuffling steps forward and backward. They were telling me about Mrs. Flynn, the widow, and the Flynn estate, a few miles east from here.

I walked to the edge of the lagoon, where there was a dock and a glass-bottomed boat tied to it. One of the waiters offered to take me out in the boat so I could look at the coral and schools of fish. Shaking my head no, I asked him how far down you could see from a boat. Maybe thirty feet. And how deep is the lagoon? One hundred eighty feet. And what's the bottom like? Muddy. What's down there? Stolen cars, he said, and all three waiters and the cook laughed and slapped hands and kept on stepping to the reggae, even the cook now, dancing back into the kitchen, pleased with himself.

A PROFESSIONALLY PAINTED SIGN ON A POST SET IN A FIELD beside the road seven miles from Port Antonio, two miles beyond the Blue Hole:

ERROL FLYNN ESTATE
MEMBER
JAMAICA RED POLL BREEDERS SOCIETY
FOUNDED 1952

Clumps of cattle the color of dried blood spotted the rolling, pale green fields of guinea grass for the next mile or so on both sides of the road, and then, at Comfort—a settlement with a half dozen stucco cabins and police station—I saw on the right another, smaller sign: CASTLE COMFORT ERROL FLYNN ESTATES. The land drifted up to a ridge, and at the top of the ridge, facing the sea, sprawled a low glass-and-stone ranch house and several large outbuildings. Behind the ridge loomed the blue, quick-sloping mountains. The sky had clouded over, and the air seemed heavily expectant, still, humid, as if I were suddenly located at the center of a storm.

Turning off the main road I drove my van along a rutted lane lined on both sides by a carefully made, head-high stone wall, what Terron called "slavery walls," not because they had been used to pen slaves but because they had been built by slaves. In his mind, anything constructed by slaves served as effectively as manacles to bind them to slavery. Barns, churches, houses, office buildings, counting houses, docks, and walls, it didn't matter what the stated purpose; to Terron they essentially served to bind the Africans, and that was why they existed. Their first cause was enslavement.

At the top of the ridge I turned into a smooth parking area next to the house, which would have looked right in southern California, and parked my car. I had no idea what I would say to anyone who answered the door—a maid, I assumed. Mrs. Errol Flynn herself would not answer the door for a stranger arriving in a battered, old, blue van. I supposed I would ask to see Mrs. Flynn. Simple. But then what would I say to the widow Flynn? That I wanted to ask her some questions about a murder case she may never have heard of before? Was Errol capable of a ritual killing? Did he dabble in obeah? What about Dr. Menotti? Would you say that your late husband was pathological, or would you simply call him decadent, or how about evil, wicked? Was he sybaritic? Was he real? I wanted to be like that old Maroon chieftain, I wanted to tell her a story with questions.

Suddenly a pair of enormous German shepherds came racing around the far corner of the house, their mouths roaring at me, hurling their beefy bodies against the tin sides of my van. Quickly I cranked the windows up and stared out at the beasts as they circled the van and now and then walloped it with their huge heads. For several minutes I waited, expecting the maid to appear from around the same corner, to calm the dogs and send them away. But no maid appeared, and I grew more and more uncomfortable inside the closed, sweltering van. All right, then. Goodbye, Widow Flynn. Now you will not have the chance to hear my story. Instead, you and your dogs have become details in the story I will tell to someone else.

I drove back down the lane and turned onto the road headed back toward Port Antonio. Still sweating, I pulled over at the first shop I saw, a small tavern open to the road and surrounded by the Flynn property. Across the road hundreds of pale green acres bellied down to the sea. I bought a cold Red Stripe from the large, smooth-faced woman behind the bar and guzzled it noisily. She smiled at me and told me I was hot, and soon we were talking about Mrs. Flynn.

She runs this whole place alone?

So she says, the woman told me, emphasizing the *says*. The woman didn't like Mrs. Flynn, but she liked her daughter Arnella, a "hippie girl," which probably meant that she had long, straight hair and went barefoot most of the time. She sunbathes down at Boston Beach, the woman informed me, suggesting with a helpful wink that I might catch her there now if I hurried.

Ah, I said, and remembered that Boston Beach was where Terron had said the head of DeVries' wife had come tumbling in on the morning surf.

I stood at the bar and stared out at the sea, drank my beer, and wondered what I was looking for. The truth? I knew how to find the legal, official truth of what had happened to DeVries' wife. That was easy. The mayor of Port Antonio was an old friend of Evan Smith, and the previous April Smith had been proud enough of that fact to want me to meet the man. That would have given me quick access to the records kept at the large, garishly red City Hall. And I could obtain newspaper accounts from the *Daily Gleaner* files in Kingston. Then I would own the official truth. But I already knew what that would give me—a story about some small-town butcher who'd slain his wife and been seen trying to dispose of the body and been convicted and then hung for his crime. I wanted more, though. That story, the official one, only frustrated me.

The thought swept through me, the thought of my likely eventual frustration, and at the same instant it began to rain, as if to wash away the webs of ambition that had kept me from satisfying myself up to now, and, resigned, I settled down to watch and listen. Gray sheets of rain moved up the sloped fields from the sea and crashed against the tin roof of the shop, drumming wildly, making it impossible for me and the woman to talk any further, so we just smiled at each other, while she opened a bottle of Red Stripe for herself and, at my signal, another for me. I placed my arm on the counter and peered out at the torrent, while she stroked my arm slowly and evenly. I put down my bottle of beer and held her hand for a long time and, when the rain began to lighten, I said good-bye and ducked out.

The rain was still falling when I reached Port Antonio. As I drove through puddles toward the hotel, I saw Evan Smith hurrying along Main Street between the higglers market on Musgrave Square and the public works department, as if he were late for work. He waved when he saw my car, got in next to me when I stopped, and agreed eagerly to sit out the rainstorm and renew our friendship in the Princess, a combination bar and whorehouse that at that time of day would be pleasantly quiet. Smith hated rain, he explained, saying that he was like a cat. I remembered his story about the night he met his wife and how he spent his first three days and nights with her, and I wondered if there was a link, other than the one in my mind.

The Princess was a light, airy barroom with a dozen small tables, swinging doors that opened directly onto the street and, next to the bar, swinging doors that led back to the cribs where the whores worked. An old, bent woman was tending bar and between serving us and washing down the tables kept shouting at a pair of skinny kids who were supposed to be helping her but persisted in studying the juke box selections. After a few moments of the woman's shouting, I got up and put some coins into the box and told the boys to play some music and go help the old lady.

Smith told me that since he last saw me he'd learned that Errol Flynn didn't win Navy Island in a poker game; he bought it for three thousand pounds from a friend of his who was an attorney handling the estate of a rich widow from the States. And after a few years he sold half the island for thirty-three thousand pounds, Smith said with evident admiration. As far as he knew, Mrs. Flynn had continued to own the other half, until recently, when, he had heard, she had become a partner with the people who for the last ten years had been building the Windjammer Hotel and villas out there. It was the property at Comfort that Flynn had won in a card game, Smith informed me, a game played right here at the Princess. He'd won sixteen hundred pounds that night, and the man he won it from had no money and had to sign over the deed to a thousand acres to pay off his losses. That's how the old Englishmen used to do it, Smith said with wonder in his face and voice, gambling away estates and slaves and horses and women, as if they meant nothing to them.

I asked him about Menotti again, if the Doctor still lived in the area.

No, of course not, Smith said. He left Port Antonio and the island right after DeVries was convicted, didn't even wait around for him to get hung, because of the scandal. The scandal? What scandal? Oh, you know, all that superstition and rumor.

That evening, after dinner at the hotel, I drove out to the western end of town where the United Fruit pier and warehouses were located and watched the loading of a banana boat, the *Northern Isle,* a rusting, wheezing, dripping freighter bound for Liverpool. Work gangs strung along broad tables were packing bunches of green bananas into cartons while a counter with a bell in his lap tallied the cartons from his high stool. Conical lights hung down from the high, tin roof, and yellow forklift trucks zipped around the wide space of the dock snatching up pallets of the stacked cartons of bananas, stashing them into the refrigerated hold of the ship. Up high, along the deck, leaning over the rail and watching the activity below, was a small group of white sailors and an officer or two, here and there a male passenger in shorts and T-shirt, all of them looking passively at the scene below as if they were watching a movie. A character in the movie, I strolled forward from the counting table and, standing a few feet from the side of the ship, stared up at the white men—my brothers. For a second our eyes met, and I felt myself about to step out of the movie and join the viewers, when suddenly a man walked out of the darkness on my right and stood beside me. It was Holmes, Terron's younger brother. He had seen my car parked outside and had come onto the pier to find me.

His big horse face grinned handsomely, and we shook hands. Unlike his brother, Holmes was tall and shyly quiet, spoke slowly and precisely in terms that he felt I would be comfortable with, terms of measure, of exact quantity, terms that defined by setting limits. I knew that he spoke this way out of a desire not only to make himself understood, but also to make me comfortable, for I had heard him talking with his brother and friends, and with them he flew through limits and spoke always in grand Rastafarian metaphor. Like his brother, he was a Rastafarian and wore the locks and beard. In certain ways, however, he was more political and orthodox than Terron, who, even in the context of Rastafarian alienation from the world of Babylon, remained poetically alone, as if he were seeing and saying everything he saw and said for the first time in his or anyone else's life, as if he personally had discovered the Rastafarian perspective.

We left the pier and got into my car and drove slowly down the street, the prostitutes hissing good-naturedly at us as we passed. Once again, I was asking questions about Errol Flynn and DeVries and Dr. Menotti and his son. Holmes' version of the story was the same as his brother's. Evan Smith, he told me, was frightened of obeah because he was an old man and a Christian, and that was why he didn't think Flynn and Menotti were guilty. He didn't want to make himself vulnerable to Menotti's power or Flynn's who, even though the one was out of the country and the other dead, could still make Smith suffer.

We stopped at the Princess, which was crowded with whores and local workingmen and loafers. Holmes indicated to the old lady I had seen that afternoon with Smith that we were only interested in drinking, and we took a table in a corner and ordered beers. What should I do with this story? I asked Holmes. You should go out to Navy Island, he answered, and talk to Captain Ausley. And you should see Mrs. Flynn, if you can. And you should talk to the man who saw DeVries that morning out at Dolphin's Bay chopping up his wife's body, and you should go out there yourself and see the hole where he tried to drop her into the sea.

And you should talk to this woman! he said, turning suddenly in his chair and grabbing the hand of a chunky young whore standing at the bar not far from our table. He pulled her over to the table and said that this was Dorothy. She grinned broadly and punched Holmes on the arm, and they wrestled for a few moments, grabbing each other's arms and shoulders and jamming their faces into each other's necks. Then he pulled her into his lap and told her my name and said that I was the brother of his brother.

She was a young woman, probably not more than twenty, large-breasted and dark-skinned, wearing tight jeans and a T-shirt decorated with a sequined palm tree that undulated across her breasts. She wore her hair cropped close to the skull, had large, expressive, joking eyes, thick, unpainted lips and a flat, broad nose with large nostrils that flared like wings. Her shoulders and arms were as broad and thick as Holmes', and every few seconds she would whack him on the thigh or chest.

The evening wore on. I grew tired, bored and slightly drunk. Holmes and Dorothy talked more and more exclusively to each other and in patois uttered so rapidly that I could no longer follow what they were saying. Once in a while one of the women would come over to our table, Holmes would look at me to see if I was interested, and as soon as he saw that I wasn't, he'd say so to the woman and she'd leave for another table. I was grateful for his willingness and ability to play this intermediary's role, because, though I had moved very close to his world, had come right up to the line where his world and mine met, I still had not stepped off the landing there and onto dry land. I remembered the white faces of the sailors staring down from the deck of the *Northern Isle,* how familiar they had seemed to me, and how easy it had been for me to start sliding upward into their eyes. Errol Flynn, you may have been a madman, I thought, but you knew this line well. There must have been a night here in Port Antonio when you too stepped over it, when you walked off the pier between the sea and the shore, strolled down these shadowy streets, and ceased being who you were. What did you become then? I wondered.

4

HOLMES MET ME AT THE HOTEL IN THE MORNING. I WAS still sitting in the crowded dining room, crowded not with diners but with high sideboards jammed with cut-glass vases, goblets, sets of hand-painted dinnerware, glass animals, paperweights, statuettes, and ornamental bric-a-brac that must have come from a half dozen different little old Victorian ladies' lifetime collections. On the walls of the room were large, framed, rotogravure portraits of Martin Luther King, John Fitzgerald Kennedy, Queen Elizabeth II, and the Jamaican Prime Minister Michael Manley, with smaller, framed photographs of the manager's family, all of them full-faced, chubby, black adults and children dressed in their best clothes and posed carefully in front of a large car on a street in one of the boroughs of New York City. The manager was at his post by the door, reading the *Daily Gleaner* and keeping a close watch on the house keys dangling from a board next to his desk. I handed him the key to number thirteen, and Holmes and I strode out the door to my car.

Captain Ausley, Holmes explained to me as we drove down the Main Street toward the landing next to the public works department, was a friend of his. Otherwise we'd never be able to get over to the island. Back when they had first started building the Windjammer, Ausley had trained Holmes and several other local boys in basic mechanical and construction skills and, once trained, they had been employed for several years on the island—a chance both to work and to learn a skill they could use elsewhere. An opportunity for Ausley, too, I thought: cheap labor can be made skilled and still kept cheap if you train it yourself.

At the narrow plank dock, Holmes and I sat and smoked a spliff and waited for the regular morning launch to come over from Navy Island. Ausley made the trip over every morning to get mail and do some business in town, Holmes explained. In a short while we heard the launch start up, and soon we could see it crossing the quarter mile of water toward the mainland. It was a sixteen-foot, open boat with a banging old inboard motor and a blue-and-white-striped canvas tarpaulin stretched overhead for shade. A small-faced, shiftless and barefoot black youth ran the motor with one hand and held the tiller with the other. Standing like George Washington in the bow all the way across from the island was the man I assumed was Captain Ausley, the friend of Errol Flynn. He was a thickset man in his mid fifties, also barefoot and shirtless, with a sandy gray crewcut. Holmes whispered that he never wore a shirt, just like a Jamaican. But look at how red his skin is, I said. The man looks like he took his shirt off for the first time a few hours ago and got himself badly sunburnt. He always looked that way, Homes said. Red. When the launch drew near, I saw that Ausley's scarlet chest was covered with a pelt of perfectly straight gray hairs, like an animal's, each one laid softly down against the next and all of them about a single inch long. And I saw that he had a woman with him; she was slender, wearing a sleeveless yellow dress and string sandals, legs carefully crossed at the ankles. She was in her early thirties, but looked tired and cross. She was the kind of woman whose looks had been responsible for whatever career success she had met and whose career, therefore, had reached its zenith about three years ago.

The Captain jumped from the bow of the launch before it touched the dock and, ignoring the woman, walked briskly toward the parking lot, passing Holmes and me as if we were a turnstile. Holmes hailed him, and he wheeled around, squinted, recognized the tall black man and proceeded to scrutinize me. Walking slowly over to him, Holmes entered into hushed conversation with the red-skinned man, who continued to regard me with suspicion. Ausley shook his head negatively several times, but Holmes kept on talking.

Finally the beefy white man gestured with his hand for me to step forward. You some kind of reporter? he wanted to know. Absolutely not, I assured him. I'm more of a scholar, a teacher, I said, smiling, and then I told him I was interested in the island for scholarly and historical purposes, hoping as I burbled on that I wasn't contradicting anything Holmes might have told him.

We're very security conscious, Ausley said. If you let everyone onto an island, pretty soon it isn't an island anymore, he aphorized. Then he was talking only to Holmes, ignoring me as he had ignored the woman, telling Holmes we could ride out on the launch now and get off the island when the launch returned to shore in an hour to pick him up.

THERE SEEMED TO BE A CRIME THAT I WAS INVESTIGATING, and somehow my visit to Navy Island was part of the investigation. But I didn't know what I was looking for. As we crossed the smooth water of the Port, I grew quickly excited by the mystery. There was a crime, yes, but what was it? This world was corrupt at the center, I knew that, and a primeval crime had determined that corruption, a crime known to everyone, white or black, Jamaican or foreigner. Despite the almost transcendent beauty of the place—the mountains, the sea, the lush green vegetation, the glossy-skinned, passionate people— the world here was tipped off to one side, canted, wobbly, precarious, and everything here was tainted somehow. It was as if there existed an explanation for its precarious, tilted state that was known but never acknowledged, as if the purpose for this abundant, splendid beauty were solely to hide some shameful secret. Flynn was a part of the secret, and Dr. Menotti and his son, and so were DeVries and his wife. Mrs. Flynn and her German shepherds, and the operation of Navy Island, too, were parts of the secret. Old Evan Smith was one of the willing keepers of the secret. Holmes and Terron Musgrave, the Rastafarian brethren, they all knew the secret but couldn't communicate it to me. The Maroons knew the secret too.

Unable to translate it, I would have to perceive the secret on my own. I had been innocent, but now that I had begun to sense the impossibility of innocence in this world, I was fast losing it. One didn't have to participate in the crime in order to lose one's innocence; one merely had to acknowledge its existence. Innocence, I suddenly realized, is a point of view. Perhaps the only way to break the limits of a point of view, then, was to lose one's innocence. And wasn't that what I had come back here to accomplish, to break down the limits of a particular point of view?

Now the details began to flow more rapidly into my ken. Navy Island did indeed seem nothing more or less than a laundromat for Mafia money. Everywhere there was evidence of enormous expenditures of American cash, with no evidence of any organized attempt to obtain a return flow. This was no business; it was a safe-deposit box. Half a dozen thatched roof, two-bedroom cottages filled with modern appliances and furniture had been completed and were meticulously maintained, but unrented. A cocktail bar and restaurant building cantilevered over the water facing the Port was designed to accommodate a small number of people in an outsized amount of carpeted and paneled space. There were several isolated beaches, carefully maintained paths and gardens and a roadway that circled the island and threaded the scattered cottages together. A large Quonset hut near the dock was filled with machinery, a diesel generator, golf carts in various states of repair, and a half dozen shirtless mechanics and laborers. The golf carts apparently were used to transport the "guests" from their cottages to the restaurant, which seemed to have several conference rooms above the cocktail lounge and dining areas. And all over the island were structures left half finished or foundations with no further work done, pathways cleared once but not maintained or paved afterward, piers and breakwaters begun but not completed.

I sat in the shade of the Quonset hut on top of an oil drum and asked questions of an intelligent-looking youth who was pulling the engine of a golf cart, and I learned that the architect had been deported from the island because his work permit had expired, that the whole resort was owned by a man named Casey—an American from Miami who showed up every few months for a week or two with a new girl friend each time and with other businessmen and their girl friends. He also told me that, besides Casey, Mrs. Flynn was one of the owners, which he said was required by law, Jamaican law. And the reason they had stopped construction on everything, the boy told me, was because the architect had left the island. Oh, I said.

As Holmes and I were about to step back into the launch for the return to the mainland, four burly policemen from Port Antonio in a sleek, white police boat came skidding up to the dock, got jovially out of the boat, and started walking up the path toward a forest of coconut palms. They were thirsty, Holmes explained, as the group joked and jostled its way along the path, quite at home here and confident that they could take their pleasure here, cut and drink from a dozen coconuts, urinate on the grass, tease and intimidate the workmen in the Quonset hut, and return to their powerful boat, which they had left tied at the dock with its motor still running, gulping gasoline patiently, and roar off, laughing, making plans for the weekend. They were all wearing blue coveralls and colorful knit tams on their close-cut heads—dark, muscular, well-fed men who passed me and Holmes by in precisely the same manner that Ausley had passed us earlier when he had landed at the mainland.

As we sat down in the launch and started back toward the Port, Holmes leaned over and told me that about six months ago Mrs. Flynn had used the police to kick a dozen families off her land—squatters—homeless, desperate families who had decided to build shanties on fallow land that had been won in a card game in a whorehouse. A number of the squatters had been shot up, Holmes said, but no one was killed.

The kid running the launch for Ausley was named Rocco, and on the way back Holmes unexpectedly revealed that Rocco was the son of the man who had been the witness to DeVries' attempt to dispose of his wife's body. Rocco smiled at me when he heard his name mentioned and nodded hello, acknowledging for the first time that we were aboard. Holmes handed him the butt end of the spliff we had been sharing, and the youth finished it off, flicking the remains into the water as we pulled up at the dock, where Ausley was waiting for his ride back to his island.

DEVRIES HAD NOT OWNED A HORSE OR A PAIR OF HORSES. HE had owned two old mules, a brown and a gray, named Deke and Mitchell. A man named Jack told me this in the Princess in the early afternoon light. And, according to Jack—who was small, evil-smelling, alcoholic, a man in his late fifties who wore cast-off elegant clothing, evidently the remnants of the wardrobe of someone he had once worked for—DeVries had been a generally silent, grim man who talked more to his mules than to any man.

The witness to DeVries' crime was named Rocco, like the son, Jack said, and yes, it was true that Rocco had seen DeVries out at Dolphin's Bay trying to shove the body into a hole that opened into the sea below. DeVries had cut off the head of the corpse and had tried to stuff the body down a hole that a few feet down got too small for the body to pass through, and as a result the legs were sticking up in the air and DeVries was shoving at them when Rocco happened to pass along the road on his way to Errol Flynn's ranch where he worked. DeVries saw Rocco and went after him with his machete, Jack said, but Rocco was young then and could run fast, so he got away. The reason the body was cut into pieces, Jack said, was because that was the only way they could remove it from the hole after DeVries had jammed it in there. Then they put the pieces, except for the head, which was never recovered, into a box and stored them in the freezer out at Frenchman's Cove, which is owned by Mrs. Flynn, Jack said. The police went directly to DeVries, of course, because of what Rocco had told them, and asked him where his wife was. They knew the body belonged either to his wife or his girl friend, but without the head and with the limbs all hacked off, they couldn't tell which woman it was. DeVries lied and said his wife was in Kingston and, a few weeks later when they went back to see if she had returned, she hadn't, and that's when DeVries went dumb. He never said another word. Because of the Doctor, Jack said. Errol Flynn's friend, Dr. Menotti. He owned all the land at Dolphin's Bay where DeVries was seen trying to stuff his wife's body into the hole. His house was located on the other side of the road from the bay, a large house that he had set up as a hospital but that he never used as a hospital. What did he use it for? I asked.

Abortions. Mostly white American girls. A few English and Canadian girls, though. He did a lot of experiments there too, Jack added.

What kind?

Obeah.

On my way out to the Flynn estate for the second time, I saw Evan Smith walking along Main Street again, as rapidly and urgently as he had been walking before, but this time there was no rain for him to avoid, so I concluded that the rush must be his manner and that he was a more anxious man than I had first thought. He let me drive him to his destination, the Town Hall, where he seemed to have no other business than to turn around and head rapidly down the street again.

Men named Krucknik and Crandall, Smith told me, owned Navy Island after Errol Flynn, and then Krucknik died in a plane crash in Miami and Crandall inherited his half. Later he was joined by a Mr. Illa from California, who still shows up out there once or twice a year for a few days. A man named Rex Rand, Smith said, owned the Titchfield Hotel property, and Captain Ausley, who now manages the Navy Island property, used to manage it for him. Mr. Rand, as Smith carefully called him, wanted to build the Titchfield back up again after it burned, but he, too, got killed in a plane crash in Miami. Mr. Rand had also been one of the owners of the Biscayne Bay Hotel in Miami and a close friend of Richard Nixon. But Smith had never heard of anyone named Casey.

AT THE ERROL FLYNN ESTATE, CASTLE COMFORT, I WAS met again by the brace of German shepherds, and this time a maid—a white woman, surprisingly—in a uniform came along behind the beasts. She was an old woman, but tough and crisp, and when I asked to see Mrs. Flynn and was compelled to confess that I had no appointment, she told me that Mrs. Flynn was not at home. She asked where Mrs. Flynn could reach me, and automatically I gave her the name and telephone number of the de Montvin Hotel, when it suddenly occurred to me that I might be making a dangerous mistake. I could no longer stroll through these lives, like some kind of idiot tourist, without protecting myself. This was a world where evil powers—obeah, Mafia, corrupt cops sucking complacently on someone else's coconuts, ritual death, kangaroo courts, decadence, and immense, exploitive wealth—all worked comfortably side by side like pickers in a vineyard. To be white was not necessarily to be evil, but to be white and then to come to know Errol Flynn in Jamaica was to lose one's innocence. And once that happened, only a fool would not begin to protect himself.

No, no, that's not right, the business about the de Montvin, I stammered to the maid. I'll be somewhere else tonight, with a friend, and I'm leaving Port Antonio for Montego Bay in the morning, heading back to the States.

She nodded. I said that I would telephone Mrs. Flynn later, kicked my van into gear and headed down the hill to the road and swiftly back to the Port, bouncing past the slavery walls, past the remains of the old sugar plantation that Flynn's ranch had replaced, past the mill wheel, the cut-stone sheds and barns, and the huge open cistern, like a crater, with the ridge and the mountains lofting darkly on one side of the road and the turquoise sea and meadows on the other.

AT THE PRINCESS I MET HOLMES, WHO WAS SITTING WITH
Dorothy at the bar. He had been looking for me, he
said, because he thought before I left town I ought to
talk with Rocco, the witness. The bar was filled with a
cool, light green light, the same clean color as the fields
of guinea grass at Castle Comfort. I nodded agreement,
and we left the Princess, walking past my van on the
street and turning left after a block, then quickly through
back yards and pathways that cut behind cabins and
sheds, under laundry lines, over board fences, until we
were deep within a jungle of tin-and-old-board shanties,
wrecked cars, refrigerators, washing machine tubs, pigs
rooting in the packed dirt, goats meditating on an orange
peel, slender, hairless dogs barking feebly and scratching at their mangy backs, and children, dozens of children, naked and near naked, scattering like clouds of
gnats as we walked purposefully through them and moved
gradually uphill from the Port, until finally we were over
the first ridge and were out of sight of the sea, in a clot
of cabins and blood-red mudded ground scraped clean of
anything that could be burned or eaten by man or beast.

We stopped before a closed-up cabin with one small
window, and Holmes shouted for Rocco. After a few
moments, a man appeared at the door, a man who at
first seemed to be very old but soon came to look
not much more than fifty. He was brittle and stooped,

somber and frightened, dressed in rags the color of ash and tobacco.

He knew Holmes, smiled quickly, then stepped out to the yard, where Holmes introduced me and told Rocco that I wanted to hear his story about how he came to be a witness against DeVries. The man looked first at me and then at Holmes with deep, gray-faced suspicion, until Holmes squatted down and started rolling a large cigar-sized ganja spliff, fussing with the brown paper cone, tightening it and twisting the end precisely, then lighting it, bathing his head in the fragrant, silver smoke. Rocco and I squatted down next to him, and Holmes passed the cigar to Rocco. We smoked in silence for a few moments, with the sounds of children playing, dogs barking, a woman yelling shrilly in the distance. Then Rocco began to speak, in a rapid country patois, with a high, thin voice, more like an Oriental's than an African's.

He had been a young man when DeVries killed his wife, he said.

So DeVries actually did kill his wife, then? No, no, of course not. Errol Flynn and Dr. Menotti and his son killed her. But first they had tried to kill him, Rocco himself. He explained that his job at the Flynn ranch took him out there early every morning, before sunrise, and about three months before DeVries' wife was killed, he had been walking along the road on his way to work, and as he passed in front of Dr. Menotti's hospital on Dolphin Bay, he had noticed the outlines of several figures and the flashes of lanterns at the edge of the cliffs overlooking the water. Then he saw DeVries' meat wagon and his two mules, Deke and Mitchell, standing a few yards off the road. He knew DeVries well, had even worked for him for a few years when he was a boy learning how to take care of livestock, so he stepped off the road and started walking toward the figures with the lights, to see what DeVries was up to out here this early.

Maybe he needed some help, he thought as he walked through the brush and rough rock toward the edge of the cliff in the darkness, when suddenly he realized the lights were approaching him, three of them, and they had separated so that one light approached him from the front and the others approached him from the sides. He stopped, then called out DeVries' name. No answer. But the lights kept coming steadily on. Rocco took a step backwards and called again. Still no answer. He could see that the three lights were being carried by three men, two of them white and one black, and then he saw that one of the white men was Errol Flynn and the other was Dr. Menotti, and the black man was DeVries, who was carrying his machete.

They were about twenty feet away when he turned and ran, darting back through the brush and rock toward the road, with the three men noisily behind him. He heard Errol Flynn call out, Rocco, wait! We only want to talk to you! But he knew they wanted to kill him and so he ran, terrified, past the mules and wagon to the road and down the road toward the Port, three miles away.

He got safely back to his mother's house, he said, this house here before us, he explained, pointing back at the cabin he had emerged from moments before, and he never went back to the Flynn ranch or to Dolphin's Bay, except of course when the police took him out there to the cliffs so he could show them where he saw DeVries hacking at his wife's body trying to get it through the hole to the sea.

But if you never went out there again, I said, how did you see DeVries hacking up his wife's body there?

Rocco looked at me as if I were stupid. How could a white man be so stupid? his expression seemed to ask. So he patiently explained that after DeVries had been arrested, he was sitting in his house one day, still afraid to leave even to go down to the Port for a drink or to see his friends, when he heard someone in heavy shoes coming up to the door, and before he had a chance to see who it was, two large black men in suits and ties walked into the house. They were policemen, detectives, from Kingston, and they took him from the house, down the ridge to the Main Street where they had parked their car, a large black Land Rover, and they drove him out to Dolphin's Bay. And that was the first time, he said, that he saw what you call a tape recorder, a big one in the back seat, between him and one of the policemen. They stopped the car and sat there for a while, asking Rocco questions about what he had seen that morning when he had run away. Nothing, nothing, he kept saying. Just DeVries' mules and wagon, that's all. Then the policeman sitting in the back drew out his revolver and placed the tip of the barrel into Rocco's ear and pressed his head hard against the side of the car. You saw DeVries out there, didn't you? the man in the front seat said. Yes. And you saw him chopping at something over near the edge, didn't you? Yes. And you got scared and ran home, didn't you? Yes. Now, the driver said, as the other one withdrew the barrel of his revolver, now you are going to tell your story from the beginning, how you came out here on your way to work at the Errol Flynn ranch and how you saw DeVries' wagon and horses and then saw DeVries himself. Because we're going to hang DeVries, and then you won't have to be afraid anymore.

AFTER I'D LEFT HOLMES OFF AT THE PRINCESS, I DROVE back to the hotel. It was late in the afternoon, and I was exhausted, sweaty, my mind churning. As I walked up to the desk for my room key and passed the manager, who was stretched out on a chaise longue in the lobby with a newspaper spread across his large belly, he cocked one eye open and asked me if I had enjoyed my visit to Navy Island this morning.

What?

Navy Island. Did you and your friend enjoy your visit?

Yes, yes, certainly, I stammered, wondering how he had learned that I had been out there. I asked him if there had been any telephone messages for me.

No, he said, slumping back down beneath his newspaper. Nothing at all.

After showering and changing my clothes, I rested on my narrow bed for an hour, running the links between people through my mind—Mrs. Flynn and Captain Ausley, Errol Flynn and the Miami Mafia, the CIA and the Miami Mafia, Errol Flynn and Menotti's abortion clinic, the abortion clinic and the Kingston police force, Rocco and DeVries, Flynn and DeVries, Mrs. Flynn and the Frenchman's Cove Hotel, Mrs. Flynn and the manager of the de Montvin Hotel, the manager of the de Montvin and Captain Ausley's Windjammer, Errol Flynn and the Princess, Errol Flynn and the Titchfield Hill Hotel—until my links led back to the beginning and new linkups appeared. Everything was significant, everything was tied to everything else.

This was true magic, I thought, this was obeah. The distance between the world of the wealthy and the world of the poor was so great that he who had wealth was truly a magician, was outside the powers that controlled the lives of ordinary men and women. But it wasn't that distance alone, I decided. It also had to do with knowledge. Wealth and knowledge went together, like Errol Flynn and Dr. Menotti, and the power they created together was frightening to those of us who had no access to it. We could be victimized by it instantly and with no appeal. It was satanic, stolen fire, a Faustian exploitation of a corrupted racial and economic history. Was evil.

TO AVOID MAKING ANY NEW LINKS, I DECIDED TO EAT DINNER at the Bonnie View Hotel, the place at the top of Naylor's Hill where Evan Smith had met his wife the night the 1938 hurricane struck. A narrow, unlit, winding road that switchbacked up the knob ended in the hotel parking lot. The hotel itself was a flat-roofed, two-story structure that spread formlessly over the top of the hill in terraces, dining room, lounge, and living units in various combinations.

Out on the main terrace a fat Chinese woman was complaining to a black man in a bartender's uniform about the lack of tourists and the difficulties of meeting her payroll. I took a seat by the railing and looked out at the Port below, the same view as from Smith's house but from the east instead of from the west. The waiter brought me a drink, called me Doc, which I thought strange, and went back to his conversation with the Chinese woman, who had been joined by a slender young black woman in a waitress' uniform. She wore glasses and looked more like a middle-class college girl from Kingston than a waitress in a Port Antonio hotel.

Half turning in my chair, I peered through the large window into the dining room beyond and immediately saw that it was empty, except for one table, where sat Captain Ausley, in a white shirt now, and his glassy-eyed girl friend, and a handsome, well-dressed white woman, middle-aged, blond, coldly pale. Mrs. Errol Flynn, I decided.

Swiftly finishing my drink, I signaled for the waiter, who came smiling over. Another one, Doc?

No thanks, I just remembered an appointment, I said, paying him quickly.

You don't have time to drop that girl off downtown, do you? he asked politely. I couldn't say no, and left, with the waitress in tow.

Halfway down the hill, she broke the silence and asked if it was true that I was a doctor. She was studying to be a nurse, she added quickly, in Kingston, but she worked at the hotel during holiday. Her father was a Baptist minister in town, she said. I asked her why she thought I was a doctor. The waiter had told her my name was Dr. Ajax, she said, and that I was from the States.

He was only kidding you, I said somberly, and followed her directions to a well-kept old house on Titchfield Hill, a few blocks from my hotel.

She slid out of the car and, closing the door, said through the open window, in patois—as if it were safer that way—that I should come and see her when I got some time and didn't have any appointments to rush off to.

Thanks, I said, but I'm leaving in the morning for Montego Bay.

Well, another time then, she answered, and strolled into the house.

It was late evening now, around ten, palm trees pronging the moonlit sky and silvered hills, the whores of Port Antonio hissing and kissing from the sidewalks as I cruised past, drifting in my thoughts and fears. A clutch of lights out in the port signified the sleepy, lazy presence of sailing yachts from the States. New arrivals. What kind of brother Americans were aboard those boats? I wondered, as I drew my car over to the curb in front of the Princess. Rock singers, I speculated, and their girl friends and producers. A vice president in charge of marketing for Chemgro Corporation, his bored, alcoholic wife and their eldest female child. A well-known sculptor and his girl friend, twenty-five years younger than he. The dean of academic affairs at a large midwestern university, in company with the managing editor of a fashion magazine, two middle-aged men conducting a secret love affair as if negotiating for a job in each other's industry.

Inside the Princess I met a blue smoky haze cut by the blat of the juke box, the laughter of the whores, and an old drunk screaming curses at the Prime Minister's photograph over the bar. The smell of cheap perfume and curried goat and white rum mixed together in a sweet, warm, seductive blend. Over at the bar Dorothy stood nursing a beer with penurious care, wearing a denim cap cocked over one eye, a black T-shirt, tight Levis, white, wedge-heeled shoes with ankle straps, jangling metal and colored plastic bracelets on her wrist: a thick, muscular, satiny black woman with a broad, good-natured, intelligent smile as she saw me come through the door. I could see why Holmes was so fond of her. Her humor and intelligence combined with her profession, and she came out looking almost wise, the possessor of an ancient wisdom, not necessarily a woman's alone. She knew how lovely we are and how utterly insignificant. It made her a skillful gossip, a tender lover probably, a joker, and a hard person to lie to.

I sat down next to her at the bar, and she seemed glad to see me and asked about Holmes. But I'm looking for him too, that's why I came in, I said quickly, too quickly, for she saw through me with ease and knew that I was merely trying to give her information concerning the degree and complex ways in which I felt myself available to her.

I bought her a drink and she switched from beer to gin and tonic, asked me for money for the juke box, played sexy, slow reggae, and dragged me off my stool to dance with her. She threw her pelvis against mine, shoved her head between my chin and shoulder, pushed her breasts against me, and we danced slowly, grinding into one another, saying nothing to one another, just cranking our tired bodies up, opening sticky gates to let the juices flow, me saying to myself, What the hell, I like this woman, it's not as if she's not a friend of mine, this is *personal,* which somehow freed me from my one last fear at this moment, that I should be confused in anyone's mind, especially in my own, with any other of the white Americans who come into the Princess to pay for a girl, a black, thick-armed, big-breasted Jamaican girl from the country.

But no business tonight at the Princess, except for mine, and mine was merely that of buying an occasional round of cheap drinks, another couple of bucks for the till, nothing for the girls. Until around midnight, when I discovered that I was hungry and remembered my flight from the Bonnie View Hotel and Captain Ausley and Mrs. Flynn. I'm hungry, I said to Dorothy. Let's go get something to eat.

She smiled and put her arms around me and stared into my face. Fish and peppers, she said. She knew where we could get the best fish and peppers in Port Antonio.

It was raining outside now, and the streets were empty. No cars blatting by, no pedestrians, no higglers, no beggars, no tourists. No old drunks stumbling in a rum haze through the garbage, no burly cops swaggering from the alleys where they seemed constantly to be urinating, like male dogs. No clever blond co-eds in convertibles looking for ganja and cocaine, no one cashing American Express travelers checks at the Bank of Nova Scotia or Barclay's. Just me and Dorothy in my blue Japanese van turning right, then left, then right again, down the alley to a closed shop, where we parked the car, stepped out and rapped on the iron grated door, until someone called from inside that they were closed. Dorothy yelled her name, and then the door was opened slowly and the grate unlatched, and an old man turned away and shuffled back into the darkness again. Dorothy and I followed him, after latching the grate and relocking the door, back into a dimly lit room filled with the smell of fish and peppers and onions cooking on bits of coal and the sweet smell of an open bottle of white rum being passed from one dark figure to another.

These were the night people, shadowy, tired figures smoking, drinking, gnawing on fish, licking fingers, talking peacefully in low, guarded voices—thieves and whores, a couple of cops with holsterless revolvers stuck into their belts, wearing street clothes, slightly drunk, and smiling easily here among their childhood friends and family; and gamblers totaling the night's take; a Chinese numbers man, fat and sleekly admiring his rings; a couple of teen-aged boys in knit tams who ran errands for the thieves and gamblers while plotting their deaths; and Dorothy, my Dorothy, who knew everyone in the dark room, was probably related to a few, a cousin or maybe she was the niece of the fat old woman behind the counter handing out the fish and peppers and onions on sheets of brown wrapping paper and then two large glasses half-filled with white rum.

We smiled at each other as our faces greased up, lips and teeth pulling the fish apart, chewing, spitting back the bones, chomping into hot peppers, sucking down the circles of onion, gulping rum, dowsing one flame with another. Dorothy introduced me to a couple of the men in the dark, crowded room, called me her friend. Brother to Holmes Musgrave's brother.

A man who knew Holmes and Terron said he'd been schoolmates with Terron and back then he'd had a stammer that was so bad his mother couldn't even send Terron to the store for rice, because he'd only be able to say, *R-r-r-r-r-rah-rah-rah* . . ., and then would give up and run back home empty-handed. We all used to call him Stammer, the man told me. But I guess the dreadlocks unlocked his tongue, he said, smiling, gold teeth shining glossily in the kerosene lamplight. He was a fat half-Chinese man with a flicker of a mustache and thick, dry lips that he wet constantly with his pink tongue. His chubby brown hands, laden with rings, he kept carefully exposed on the counter, as if he were a gambler with a reputation for cheating at cards.

A second man moved in beside me, one of the cops, a large, muscular man with a white knit tam tightly pulled over his bullet-shaped head. He was very dark, the color of a grand piano, and thick bodied, and his face was watery-eyed and expressionless. His gun in his belt was between us, and I stared down at it, as if it were a snake whose gaze had caught and held me helplessly in my spot. The cop looked over at my empty glass and with a short gesture to the woman behind the counter had it refilled, then closed his eyes and sleepily nodded acceptance of my thanks.

The fat man with the rings went on talking in his thin, relaxed voice, asking me if I played dominoes and could I play like a Jamaican, and if so would I care to sit and play a seven. He'd find me a partner, maybe even Dorothy, he suggested, with a broad golden smile, who ought to be able to control anyone in the place. She once nilled me, he said. Seven-nil. Only woman who ever nilled me, he added with a light nostalgic grimace that made me believe the information but question his reason for offering it. The cop next to me, named Larry, would be his partner. I nodded hello to Larry.

Dorothy had come up behind me, and now she reached around and locked her hands together against my belly and squeezed while she nuzzled her face against the back of my neck.

No, I don't think I'll play any dominoes tonight, I said to the fat man, but thanks anyhow.

I turned away from the counter, said good night to everyone in the room and, holding Dorothy's hand, stepped outside to the hallway where we waited by the locked door for the old man to come and let us out.

Where do you want to go now? Dorothy asked me.

We can go to my room. Fine, she said, smiling contentedly.

The dark rain was still slopping heavily onto the streets, thickly drumming against the top of my blue van, as we headed back through Port Antonio, talking rapidly, cheerfully, the two of us astonished that we could exchange views, as Terron would have called it, when here she was talking in Jamaican patois while I flapped along in my New English dialect, like a Sicilian and a Florentine, discovering that we were repelled and attracted by the same things, excited by the contact, the momentary tangency, two planets suddenly sharing an orbit and a sun, when all along we had thought we were in separate, even if identical, galaxies.

At the hotel I parked the car and the two of us ran beneath the rain for the lobby, which was deserted. I plucked my key from the board above the desk, and we strolled, joking, arm in arm, up the stairs, back down the narrow unlit hallways to my small room with the single bed.

EVENTUALLY WE SLEPT, WRAPPED IN THE NARROW BED IN ONE another's bodies like animals in an underground den, the big bulky country woman with nostrils that stared straight at me and lips as thick as fingers and skin as black as shoes, with the flat-muscled middle-aging man from the cities of Europe and America, wedge-faced and pencil-lipped, with skin the color of rattan.

In the morning we made love again for a while, and afterward, lying in the slats of clean, bright light that fell into the room from the shuttered window, she asked me if I would be her pimp. Then she showed me her knife, a six-inch switchblade with a white bone handle, and told me she would kill any woman who tried to take me from her.

I could only think of cheap jokes and teasing one-liners for an answer. I bet you say that to all the boys. But she seemed serious. And then I knew, because she was desperate in ways I could never be desperate and a survivor of hardships I would never have survived, that she was serious, so I tried to describe myself to her.

She listened with thoughtful care, and the distance between us quickly grew, and soon she was joking again, complaining of hunger, punching me on the shoulder to get me out of bed, then yanking me back to her, as if I were some kind of large but easily handled rag doll. You look like Robert Redford, she said to me.

I bet you say that to all the white men, I answered, and we both laughed, got out of bed, dressed, and headed out for breakfast.

The Princess, empty of customers, was bathed in morning sunshine, and quiet, except for the noises from the street, bicycle bells, greetings, and battered old cars rattling by. The old woman was washing the floor behind the bar when we came in and took a table next to an open window that looked out on a cluttered yard next door. On the far side of the yard two men and a boy were hanging the carcass of a black, just-killed ramgoat from a tree branch.

Ackee and salt fish and coffee was what the woman could offer us. She went back to the kitchen to dish it out, while we turned in our seats and idly watched the butchering of the goat. One of the men, grizzled and gray-haired, expertly removed the head and testicles and set them in a tub on the ground. Returning to the carcass, he split and gutted it, removed the feet, and carefully stripped off the skin, until the goat had been converted into a long sinewy, muscular piece of meat, which the man proceeded to dismember at the joints with his machete. As each limb was lopped off, the second man and the boy carted it away to a bench or table somewhere just out of sight behind the building, until all that hung from the tree was the trunk, which the man untied and lugged back to the bench. Soon we could hear the whacking sound of the machete against the bones, breaking the meat away, delivering up the marrow.

Our breakfast came, and we ate in silence. She asked me if I was going to leave today, and I said yes and offered to drop her wherever she wanted.

That was agreeable, I could take her home, she said, where her sons were waiting. It wasn't far, just a few miles out of town toward Montego Bay.

We drove out along the port, past the knob where Holmes and Evan Smith lived, and wound along the coast for a few miles, until she instructed me to turn left, and we bumped along a narrow, marl-paved lane for a few hundred yards and stopped in front of a cabin made of cast-off lumber, old doors and stained corrugated iron. Two small, bare-bellied boys wearing pee-smeared underpants peered out from the darkness of the cabin into the glaring sunlight, where we sat inside my car.

Dorothy waved to her sons, who each flicked a wave back but held tightly to the doorjamb with the other hand. You got a pencil and piece of paper? she suddenly asked me. I tore a sheet from my notebook and handed it and a pen to her. Hunched over the paper, she started to write and for several minutes scratched away intensely, while I studied the boys in the doorway and they studied me.

Finally, she handed back my pen, and folding the paper carefully several times, pressed it into the palm of my hand. I looked down at the square and then at her.

Read it, she ordered, so I unfolded the paper and read

the large, childish letters. I DON'T WANT YOU TO PAY ME NO MONEY. BUT I BROKE. WILL YOU GIVE SOME MONEY. I LOVE YOU.

I gave her twenty dollars, two tens folded twice, the same way her note had been folded, and pressed them into the palm of her hand, as her note had been pressed into mine. Then I kissed her, and said good-bye. She leaped from the car and ran powerfully across the cluttered dirt yard to the boys and grabbed them both up in the air, one in each glossy arm, turned and yelled good-bye to me. I backed my car slowly out to the main road, turned left, and headed back toward Port Antonio. I had one last stop to make before I left the town.

I PARKED THE BLUE VAN ON THE SEASIDE OF THE ROAD, facing east, with Dolphin's Bay on my left, the large, rambling, white house that once had belonged to Dr. Menotti on my right. An estate, not a home, with an acre of lawn and meticulously tended flower beds, rows of crotons and poinsettias, thriving clutches of coconut palms and fruit trees planted in cosmetic relations to the buildings— the place signified control, order, awesome confidence and calm, and, of course, great wealth. On the other side of the road, between my car and the open sea, a tangled, rock-strewn field lurched awkwardly for about two hundred yards to a cliff, where, a hundred feet below, the sea plowed beneath the ledge, crashing itself against unseen cavern walls. The day was overcast now, the early morning sun gone and with it the glaring tropical light. Though the air was warm and the offshore breeze bumping across the field before me slight, as I walked through the macca bushes and Jerusalem thorns, stepping around large, pale, limestone boulders and outcroppings, I felt cold, withdrawn to some place deep inside the center of my body.

At the edge, I peered down and watched the water rush beneath me into darkness and heard it shatter against the rocks, saw it surge back again, swirl and return with renewed force, leaving behind dark eddies and whirlpools that drifted in patterns that, though random-seeming, indicated currents running shoreward toward the Port in the west and towad Frenchman's Cove, the Blue Hole, and Boston Bay in the east. A body or parts of a body thrown from this place could easily end up at any one of those beaches, to be discovered one morning turning over and over in the surf. No one who knew this place and the currents would dispose of a body this way, I thought, as I turned and walked back across the roof of the huge cavern below, staring at the ground a few feet in front of me for the opening, like a chimney, that was supposed to be there.

After a half hour of prowling through the tangle of thorny bushes and low green cacti and pocked limestone rocks, I finally saw it, a hole in the ground large enough to swallow a human body. Standing at the edge, my toes curled over the lip of the hole, I peered down. At first I saw only darkness, as if the hole went straight to the center of the earth where there was nothing but heat and the groans and cries of the damned, and I wanted Errol Flynn to be down there, looking helplessly up at me, my head and body outlined blackly in relief against the silvery gray sky.

Cupping my hands around my eyes to block out the daylight, I brought my face closer to the hole, until I could see into the darkness and could hear the sea thrash itself against the walls of the cave below. About four or five feet down, the hole jaggedly narrowed to the size of a human head and became too small for a woman's body to squeeze through. Then it opened and widened again, until there was a quick drop to the water, which carried flashes of light from the mouth of the cave on its back and moved rapidly back and forth like a huge slick-bodied beast trapped and insane in a stone cage.

I stood up and turned away. Hurriedly I picked my way back across the field to the road and got into my car. The wind was offshore now, and the sky had darkened, and I knew that in a few moments it would be raining. I started the car, turned it around in a sandy clearing a short way down the road, and headed home.

Nyamkopong

Only he who has made his dialectical peace with
the world can grasp the concrete.

WALTER BENJAMIN

1

THE FIRST TIME I VISITED THE COUNTRY OF JAMAICA WAS IN mid-December 1975, and I stayed until February 1976. Though I knew little about the island and the people who lived there, I had read two or three travel books on the subject, and I had visited other Caribbean islands in the past—Saba and St. Maarten's in the Dutch Antilles and the several U.S. Virgins. But always as a tourist and never for longer than two fun-filled weeks. In the fall of 1975, however, it became apparent that I was going to be freed of my teaching obligations for an unusually lengthy midwinter break, so I determined to spend that time and regularly forwarded bi-weekly paychecks where I would not have to wage a day-to-day battle against the cold, snow and ice of another New England winter. I would go to some Caribbean island, any Caribbean island, and rent a house on a breezy hill overlooking the sea, staff it with a polite, scrupulously clean, black-skinned housekeeper and cook, smoke cigars I couldn't afford to pay the import duties on, drink frosty rum drinks in the cool of the evening, and maybe take a swim in the pool every morning before I began my regular three or four hours' work on the novel I had been writing for the last three years. I might even be able to rent a terraced flower garden with a fussy but cheerful gardener to tend it.

What I especially liked, however, was the idea of

living in a pastel-colored, stucco-walled house up on a hill and away from the tourists, those loud, sunburnt, overweight Americans and Canadians, their whining children, their nervous shopping for souvenirs, their constant computations of the rate of exchange. This time, I told my wife and children, we will not be tourists. This time we will not even have to *see* any tourists! We will see only the *natives!* They will be black, of course, and mostly slender, smiling, and poor—but when they learn that we are not tourists, they will be honest, and they will like us, because even though we are rich and white, we are honest and we like them.

I phoned an old friend from college, a white man who had been raised in Jamaica and whose parents still lived there. My friend, whose name was Upton West, was a photographer who had recently become a successful producer and director of feature-length documentary films and books with subjects like autoracing, body building, integration in the South. He lived in New York City and New Hampshire, and when he was in New Hampshire I occasionally saw him for dinner, when we would eat fresh vegetables from his garden and thick slices of beef cut from black Angus cattle raised on his own land. Later, over brandy and cigars in the library, we would talk about our days at Chapel Hill, famous people he now knew, the future of the New Left, and sometimes the beauty and mysterious complexity of Jamaica.

Upton loved Jamaica and returned there often to visit his parents and their friends. Two years ago he had taken a whole month away from the production of his film on body builders to travel alone over the entire island, snapping thousands of photographs that he had vague plans for bringing together someday in a large paperback book. You would love Jamiaca, he often told me. There's a beauty and a mysterious complexity to the island that are unmatched anywhere in the world.

I was sure that Upton knew what he was talking about, because he had traveled to most of the beautiful and mysteriously complicated places in the world. If you ever decide to go down, he told me, let me know and I'll have my mother find you a house. She dabbles in real estate. She trains the help in her own house. Upton's father was a retired British army captain who dabbled in insurance in Montego Bay. Upton always referred to his father as the Captain. His mother he called Mother. She was an American out of a well-connected family from Cambridge, Massachusetts, and her marriage to the Captain had been celebrated in the society pages on three different continents. Upton thought that was amusing and once had shown me the clippings.

Over the phone I asked him if he thought his mother could find a house for me to rent for two months, a house close enough to the sea and a city like Montego Bay that I would be able to obtain the usual amenities, yet far enough into the country that I would not have to cope with the tourist business. Three bedrooms, a pool, if possible (for the kids, I explained), and a housekeeper who would be able to take care of some of the cooking. It doesn't have to be anything luxurious, I assured him. We're quite willing to accommodate ourselves to a few inconveniences. It was to be a working trip for me and an escape from the New Hampshire winter for my family.

Eager to share his beloved Jamaica with an old friend, Upton immediately contacted his mother and in two weeks I was corresponding with a man named Preston Church, an electrical contractor in Montego Bay who owned two houses in the small town of Anchovy twelve miles outside of Montego Bay. He lived in one house himself; his son and his son's family had lived in the other before their departure for Canada. I did not then understand or attribute any meaning to this departure for Canada, because I did not then understand or attribute any meaning to the flight of capital and capitalists from a country whose government had determined to eliminate, even by gradual and democratic procedures, capital and capitalists. Nor did I understand or attribute meaning to the flight of white people from a black coun-

try that had always been black but had only recently
come to be governed by people who were black.

The son of Preston Church, I learned from Upton, had
been a schoolmate of Upton's and for ten years had
helped his father run the contracting business in Montego Bay. They had done exceptionally well during that
period, because from 1965 to 1975 there had been a
building boom along the north coast of Jamaica, as increasing numbers of Americans and Canadians decided to
invest capital in the construction of three- and four-
bedroom villas that could be rented to other Americans
and Canadians. Now, however, as Upton explained it,
there had come a leveling off, and probably young Church
could do better for himself in Canada. Therefore, when
the elder Mr. Church wrote and told me that he would
be willing to cut the cost of renting his son's house
practically in half if I would be willing to pay with a
personal check made out to his son and mailed from my
American address to his son's Canadian address, I saw
nothing wrong or particularly unusual about the arrange-
ment. Naturally, his cutting the rent in half was something of an aid to my not seeing anything wrong or
unusual. I merely felt lucky. It's amazing, I thought,
how lucky I am.

It was the wife of Preston Church, Abbie, who met us
at the airport in Montego Bay. She was an extremely
short woman with a blocky body and the tiniest feet I
had ever seen on an adult. She chain-smoked Craven
A's and talked rapidly, unsmilingly, and walked ahead
of everyone on her tiny feet first to the car rental desk,
where I rented a red Toyota sedan, and then to her dark
gray Mercedes, where her driver waited.

The house, when we finally saw it, was even more
appropriate than I had hoped—four bedrooms, if you
counted the maid's quarters, high ceilings and sliding
glass doors opening onto patios and terraces that looked
down two thousand feet of hillside jungle to the sea.
And a pool, too, with lights for night swimming. There

were lights and switches all over the house and grounds, and it took an hour for Abbie to show me which switches operated which lights. I could flick a switch over a kitchen counter and flood the side yard with light from a cotton tree; a switch next to the bed in the master bedroom turned scary nighttime into comforting midday all over the grounds; a bank of switches on the patio threw the narrow, winding, private road out into the open for several hundred yards back down the hill toward the main road, halfway to the village center; and hidden in the leaves of the crotons and macca bushes and forty feet up in the breadfruit trees scattered through the terraced gardens in front of the house, blue- and red-lensed floodlights had been secreted, so that a flick of the switch on the living-room wall next to the glass doors would turn the place into something that resembled a cocktail lounge in a Florida suburb. Abbie was naturally quite proud of this system; apparently there was one to match it for the house she and her husband lived in, which, as it turned out, was only two hundred yards away, our only neighbor up here on this hill, for, as it further turned out, the entire hill was owned by Church.

When Abbie had finished showing the place to us and explaining how all its machinery worked and had introduced us to Caroline, the young woman who would be our housekeeper, a small, smiling woman whose starched uniform was so white and whose skin was so black that I did not see her, she wheeled on her tiny feet and trotted her box-shaped body back to her Mercedes where her driver, a man whose face was also so dark that I did not see him, sat reading the *Daily Gleaner*. Then she turned and said with sudden gentleness that my first name was the same as her son's and that my two children, though younger than his, numbered the same as her son's. How old are you? she asked me. I told her my age, thirty-five, and she sighed, then stuck her cigarette into her mouth and jerked herself into the front seat next to the driver. As she closed the door, she spat, It's all that goddamned Michael Manley's fault! Then she drove off, leaving me and my family in our house in the tropics.

ONE SUNDAY MORNING ABOUT TWO WEEKS LATER, BY WHICH time my family and I had more or less accommodated ourselves to our new environment—insofar as that environment went no further than the luxurious and, as I had by then discovered, walled-in compound owned by the Churches—my friend Upton and his father the Captain drove up in a dark blue Land Rover. During a pleasant breakfast on the terrace, while the Captain jovially complimented my wife on the quality of her coffee, Upton told me about the Maroons. It was the first time I had heard the word.

Upton had an interesting and engaging way of speaking: his accent was not quite British, not quite Proper Bostonian, not quite white Jamaican, but a unique amalgam of the three, which he uttered in a nasal monotone that made him sound as if he were reading aloud, an effect heightened by his habit of speaking not only in complete sentences but in whole paragraphs as well. The Maroons, he said, are a beautiful and mysteriously complex people with a noble and violent history. Direct descendants of the Ashanti, who were the most ferocious and independent of the Africans brought over to Jamaica in the sixteenth and seventeenth centuries, they escaped in large numbers into the unsettled and inaccessible bush and quickly banded together. For the next hundred years or so they fought a guerrilla war against the British, until finally the British had to settle with them by granting them relative independence and several large sections of land back in the Cockpit Country here in the west and up in the Blue Mountains in the east. Since then they've lived in relative isolation, with many of the old African ways preserved, in small villages that are governed by self-elected officials. They're not unlike, Upton said as he refilled his cup, certain American Indian tribes.

Remarkable people, the Captain added. The Captain's way of speaking was opposite to his son's: he never spoke in sentences. Expletives, fragments, bits and pieces. Honest too, he said. Not like your typical Jamaican at all. The Ashanti in them. Makes them proud. Quite a remarkable people. Fierce still, even today. Who . . .? he asked his son. What . . .? His name, the chief up there in Nyamkopong?

Phelps was his name, I believe, Upton said. Colonel Martin Luther Phelps was what he called himself. Upton had visited Nyamkopong two years ago during his tour of the island, and he had photographed the chief and a man Upton said was his Secretary of State. There was a book I should read, a brief history of the Maroons published and sold by the Sangster Bookstore chain. Then, Upton instructed me, I should drive up to Nyamkopong one day and meet Colonel Phelps. Upton said I should use his name as an introduction. Just tell him you're a friend of mine, he said, getting up to leave.

Quite, the Captain added. Everyone on the island. Upton meets them all. Sooner or later.

Then politely, even graciously, the two men made their way along the crushed stone pathway to their Land Rover. Upton was returning to Manhattan that afternoon; he was scheduled for tomorrow's Today show. The Captain had to get back to Montego Bay and start preparing his annual first of January breakfast for a group of black Jamaican men he called "my old boys," veterans of the Great War. Bit of a ritual, the Captain explained. Means quite a lot to the old boys. Biscuits, ham, eggs, lots of coffee. Fewer and fewer of them every year, though, he said, as he climbed into the Rover.

From the driver's seat Upton called out to me. Get up to Nyamkopong on January sixth, if possible, he advised. That's a day of celebration up there, the main Maroon holiday. It ought to be fantastic, from what I've heard. In fact, one of these Januarys I'm coming down precisely for the purpose of photographing that event.

Maybe I'll film it with a small crew for television. It's the sort of thing that goes over beautifully on PBS.

I assured him that I'd do exactly as he had advised. I'd buy the little history of the Maroons, and I'd drive up there on January sixth, and I'd certainly look up Colonel Phelps. Give the old boy my regards, Upton said, waving good-bye. I waved back.

THE FIGHTING MAROONS, BY A MAN NAMED CAREY ROBINson, is a slender, unpretentious, and skillfully written history of the Maroons, popular among foreigners in Jamaica and sold, therefore, at the several stationers and bookstores in Montego Bay and even at some of the fancy hotel shops along Gloucester Avenue near the beach club at Doctor's Cave. It describes, with surprise and admiration, a courageous and intelligent people, slaves who chose the wilderness over slavery and who managed to survive that choice. The book was written, I deduced, by a white Jamaican for an audience of white readers who wished to know more about the beautiful and mysteriously complex land of Jamaica. It was not written for the reader who wished to know more about the ugly and bewildering history of the enslavement of black Africans in the New World. And it surely was not written for the reader who felt morally compelled to attempt to imagine how it was to face the choice the Maroons faced: whether to be a dumb domesticated animal—livestock—or to live the life of a feral pig— livestock gone wild.

For that is where the word *maroon* originated, I learned as I read Mr. Robinson's little book. It derives from the Spanish *cimarrón* which was a term generally used in the New World to refer to feral cattle, but in particular and in Jamaica to pigs that had taken to the woods and gone wild (again). A beast wasn't a *cimarrón* merely because it had successfully escaped into the swiftly rising hills and wooded, pathless mountains behind the plantations along the coastal plain; it became a *cimarrón* and, in the case of human beings, a Maroon, only when it had managed to survive there and breed with others like it and provide food and shelter for itself generation after generation.

The morning that Upton West was being interviewed in New York on the *Today* show, I drove down to the village of Anchovy from Church's hill and then down the winding seven-mile-long incline to Montego Bay and purchased there a copy of the book he had recommended. I read it that afternoon and that night determined to take Upton's sugtestion that I visit Nyamkopong, the nearest of the four remaining Maroon enclaves in Jamaica. I would go there the following morning, the third of January, alone, and, if it seemed "safe," I would bring my family back with me on the sixth for the festival that Upton had mentioned over breakfast.

My anxiety over the safety of such a venture was not based on anything that I or members of my family had experienced in the several weeks we had been in the island. Rather, it was the result of a hundred conversations I had by then had with white Jamaicans, with Upton West's parents, with the Churches, with Mr. and Mrs. Hilliard Beard, a retired American publisher and his wife who lived on the side of the hill adjacent to the Church property, and with a half dozen or so of the similarly white, retired and semiretired residents and visitors these people had introduced me to. Upton's mother would telephone and invite me to come by their home in Reading for lunch or for drinks that evening, and, because of my friendship with Upton, my idleness and what I thought was my genuine curiosity about this class of human beings, I would accept. When traveling, one condescends to spend a considerable amount of time with people one would find excuses to avoid when at home. Or at least one believes he is condescending. As did I, when I would graciously accept their invitations and later when I would attempt to interest and charm these people and their always white, well-dressed guests—doctors, lawyers, realtors and developers and, occasionally, because I was known to be somehow "in the arts," clothing designers with boutiques in Montego Bay, Palm Beach, and Fifth Avenue, or a London librettist or the brother of the president of a large midwestern university.

At these gatherings the conversation seemed to turn obsessively to the subject of imminent racial war. A number of newspaper and magazine articles had recently appeared in the United States and England suggesting that racial war was a likely if not a necessary consequence of the Jamaican prime minister's economic policies, and there had in fact been a recent rash of ghetto fires and street shootings in Kingston, events that from the distance of calm, affluent Montego Bay looked clearly political and, therefore, racial. So far, however, no rich or white people had been killed or even shot at. Still, the imagery was there, fire, and wild-eyed, ganja-smoking black people with guns and machetes and raised fists, and a charismatic, self-proclaimed "socialist" leader who was frighteningly popular with the illiterate masses. And the history was there too, three hundred years of relentless racial oppression and economic exploitation. Also, it was a fact that these white people, with their fashion designer gowns and jackets, their cut-crystal cocktail glasses, their parquet floors and real estate holdings, had a lot to lose. Many of them had children in private schools and colleges in New England. Many of them owned lovely, walled-in estates along the coast and in the hills around Montego Bay. Many of them owned several twenty thousand dollar automobiles, jewelry, antiques, boats, Belgian hunting rifles for dove-shooting expeditions in Nicaragua. Most of them had fleets of servants. And all of them, without exception, said that they loved Jamaica.

For these reasons they feared economic collapse and racial war as if the two events were one and the same. If the balance of payments looked bleakly out of balance, they would purchase a second vicious Doberman pinscher to patrol the yard. And if a crazy black man on the street was rude to them one morning on the way to the office, they would smuggle another thousand dollars to Miami that afternoon. Thus racial terror was explained in economic terms, and dissatisfaction with economic policy and conditions was expressed in strictly racist terms, so that it was not shocking, once it had occurred, for me to find myself listening to an elegantly dressed and manicured physician my own age recommend forced sterilization as a solution to the problem of "overpopulation." It was, of course, the poor who were too numerous and whose uncontrolled breeding with each other made them only more numerous. And since with rare exceptions in Jamaica for three centuries the rule had been, simply and purely, as one's skin color darkens so does one's poverty approach inescapability, then the calm, good-looking physician before me was not only recommending forced sterilization, a kind of murder, but the forced sterilization of poor black people, a kind of genocide.

This was madness I had never seen before. And it frightened me. How *could* the island be safe for people like me and my family if people like this man had been running it for hundreds of years? So in that way I began to share in their fear of imminent racial warfare, and I too began to anticipate signs of its coming by how black strangers treated me on the streets of Montego Bay, in the marketplace, in the tavern at Anchovy, even in my own kitchen when I chatted with Caroline, the young woman I had hired as a housekeeper.

THE MORNING I WENT TO NYAMKOPONG FOR THE FIRST TIME I sat out on the patio and ate my breakfast of chilled mango, coffee and boiled eggs and talked with Caroline. She stood in the doorway to the dining room, one hand lightly touching the doorframe, one foot slowly scratching one of her muscular calves, and gave to the content of our conversation barely half her attention, or so it seemed to me, the rest of her attention scrupulously watching out for disaster. Before me a gold-tinted mist drifted up the blue-green, slowly ascending valley to where, a half mile west of the house, a pair of long ridges came together. To the east was the turquoise sea, and looking south I could see the curve of Montego Bay and the tan and white cluster of cubes that made up the city. A pale blue Scandinavian cruise ship had docked at Freeport where, presumably, tourists from Stockholm were already lining up to buy duty-free Japanese wristwatches and English china. Behind me the hill shouldered a few hundred feet further up to protect the Churches' other house, more exposed to the sea and breeze than the one they had rented to me, their son's home, the house built by the man my age, with my first name too, who was now in Toronto depositing the checks I had mailed him from my home in New Hampshire. I now understood why I had been asked to pay him in that careful a way, why the rent for this estate had been so absurdly low, why I felt one kind of guilt for having accepted the bargain offered by the Churches and a wholly different kind of guilt for having accepted the bargain offered by Caroline the housekeeper, whose time and labor cost only fifty cents an hour. Fifty cents an hour! I had exclaimed to my wife. Imagine that! Her husband's out of work, and she has five children. How do they *do* it? I had asked, as if it were a trick performed by a carnival magician. That has been in the beginning, of course, for now, after two weeks of consorting with people who were complaining fearfully of having to get along on a hundred thousand American dollars a year in a country whose rate of exchange worked in their favor, I no longer thought of Caroline's survival as a magician's trick. I was beginning to see that it had something to do with character. Insights like this were only glimpses, however, glimmers that only now and then filtered through the fog of my greedy ignorance.

I asked Caroline about the Maroons. Had she ever heard of them?

Oh yes, sir, she had heard of them all right. "Dem ol' Africans," she called them, smiling.

What are they like? Is it all right to drive up there to Nyamkopong and visit them? I asked.

Don't know, she shrugged, slowly scratching her calf with the toe of her other foot. You planning to go up there? she asked.

When I told her that I certainly was, and also that I planned to go up alone, her eyes widened in what looked like amazement and admiration. Then, saying nothing more, she turned and went back to the kitchen to prepare breakfast for the rest of my family.

I drained my coffee cup, grabbed my camera from the mahogany sideboard in the living room, and went out to the car. Inside, with the window glass and windshield silvered over by a skin of dew, I suddenly felt cut off, as isolated as a dream in a stranger's sleep. The unreality of the last two weeks and my compulsion to sort out the truth by thinking about it, by reasoning and by applying to other people's terrified descriptions of their world my own understanding of history, had driven me deeper and deeper into my head. Jamaica, which in the beginning may have been for me no more than an image off a travel poster, was now becoming an idea. What made it painful was that it was an idea I did not fully believe corresponded to any reality outside the books I had read, books that were not about Jamaica but were instead about abstractions like history and race and economics.

And the book I had read about the Maroons—what was that really about, I asked myself, but the historical, racial and economic superiority of the people the Maroons had fought against? And if I believed that particular idea was true, then the reason I was driving into the backcountry to see these people for myself was a tourist's reason—merely to wonder at their quaint peculiarities. But if I did not believe that idea was true, in heading off to where no one had invited me, I was going as a social scientist, to collect evidence that would support my own idea about history, race and economics. Is that all I can do with this place, these people? I asked myself. Is it only possible for me to *think* about them? Why can't I simply *see* them, talk to them, engage myself with them the same as I do with my neighbors in New Hampshire? The people I dealt with here were essentially the same as the people I dealt with at home—carpenters, farmers, upholsterers, and now and then a professionally trained person, a doctor or lawyer or schoolteacher, and once in a while a rich man or woman. At home, though, my neighbors were people, concrete people as real as I; here they remained abstractions, and only I was real. It made me feel very lonely. Part of the problem was race, of course. But it was larger, or at least much more complex than anything I'd yet imagined. I believed that I was just as cut off from the white people I had met as I was from the black, just as separated from the middle-class American and Canadian tourists as from the decadent Jamaican neocolonials, just as alien to my old friend Upton West as to the black woman who served me coffee on the patio. It was as if I had slipped into an episode of *Pilgrim's Progress* and everyone I met there and every place I went to had a strictly allegorical function and no real life of its own—except for me, who, alone among the characters, was also the reader of this book.

IT WAS STILL EARLY, ABOUT EIGHT O' CLOCK, WHEN I LEFT the compound. That was how I referred to it now, the compound, because of the cut stone walls, the elaborate lighting system all over the grounds, and the location of the two houses up here on the hill facing the sea and valley, our well-protected backs to the village and villagers of Anchovy. The Vikings had build compounds like this when they conquered Ireland and Scotland: walls to hold off the peasants behind them, and terraces and towers facing the sea, where the next set of raiders would come from, pillaging seafarers like themselves who would come to displace them, as the British had displaced the Spanish here in Jamaica, and then the British had been displaced by the Americans and Canadians, and now, if you believed the Wests and the

Churches and their friends, the North Americans were being displaced by the Cubans or possibly the Russians.

Down the hill I drove, following the steep, narrow lane to the village, goats scattering before my car and scrambling nimbly up the rough limestone hillside to stop and stare back at me with dull irritation, scrawny chickens fluttering for the gutters as I passed the dozen or so small cinderblock houses at the base of the hill where the lane crossed the railroad track and turned onto the main road that connected the interior and the southwest coastal towns of Black River and Savanna-la-Mar to Montego Bay. Strings of children in uniforms—boys in khaki shirts and pants, girls in brightly colored jumpers and white blouses—were walking to school, while cars and huge smoke-belching buses top-heavy with sacks of yams, breadfruit, and greens whizzed past, horns blasting at the curves and quick bends in the road to force the children into the gutters as the vehicles flashed by. Shopkeepers were opening their shuttered taverns and small, dark grocery stores to the traffic, selling "box milk" and sweets and ten-packs of Craven A's to the kids and people on their way to work, those few in town who had jobs, because at this time in these country towns over half the employable adults were without jobs. And because the public schools were operated after the British model, which meant that parents had to pay for uniforms for their children and for their books, pencils and lunches as well, most of the children were not able to go to school for longer than a few years, when the uniform would get passed down to the next youngest child and the older one would go to sit on a wall in the shade of a breadfruit tree with the other children and talk all day and dream and grow slowly and bleakly and barely literate into adulthood.

Turning left at the main road in Anchovy, I drove south, inland, across the relatively flat grassland plateau to Montpelier, still in the familiar parish of St. James. Sleek red poll and hump-backed white Brahman cattle grazed sleepily in the pale green guinea grass, while behind them, in the shade of cottonwood trees or at the top of a rise facing the meadows, glowered the great houses and barns, one after the other restored in the last thirty or forty years with the energy and cash that depends on a capitalist government's attempts to foster an industry by means of subsidy and tax benefits. These fat cats whine about what they call socialism and creeping communism, I grumped, and the country remains only a little less "socialized" than Canada.

From what I could see, the Prime Minister of Jamaica, in almost any industrialized country of Europe or North America, would have found himself only slightly to the right of the center and probably, instead of calling himself a socialist, would have said he was a Christian Democrat. In the peculiar contest of Jamaica, however, Michael Manley, because he was attempting to institute a public education system and a realistically graduated income tax and something like an economy designed to feed, clothe and house the majority of the people who lived in Jamaica, was indeed a socialist. What had happened in modern Jamaica was that the old British colonials had been replaced by a breed of home-grown parasites, neocolonials who, rather than endure the presence of a black entrepreneurial middle class, a class whose existence would had to have been deliberately created by means of decent public education and health care systems, instead had permitted the entrepreneurial functions and rewards to fall into the hands of other groups of people—mainly East Indian and Chinese immigrants, people who had not sufficient identification with the land of Jamaica, people whose history lay elsewhere and who, therefore, were extremely unlikely to need to replace the white Jamaicans who sat at the top of the pyramid. The Indians and the Chinese moved horizontally; the blacks could not be counted on to be satisfied with that. No, if Jamaica in the next decade were indeed to collapse into famine and chaos, as the Wests and Churches kept insisting it would, to be followed, as they assured me, with a "Communist takeover," it would not be because of Manley's policies; it would happen because the country had already died, sucked of its life-blood for tens of generations until, a generation ago, there was nothing left for it but a series of last agonies.

At Montpelier, little more than an ESSO station, railway shipping station, post office and police station for the farmers and grain producers of the area, I forked to the left, and slowly the land started to lift toward hills shaped like bright green bowlers, strange hills that seemed to have been taken from a child's drawing. Scrawny blond dogs loped alongside the road and ignored my car as I passed. Kids smiled, waved and called, "White head!" and adults gazed blankly after. Bickersteth, Seven Rivers, and alongside the Great River, Cambridge, Bruce Hall, and Catadupa, where I stopped at a roadside shop for a Dragon stout and confirmation that I was on the right road.

Oh yes, man, you're on the road to Maggotty, the barman assured me as he cracked open a warm dark Dragon and set the bottle in front of me. I loved these combination bars and grocery stores the Jamaicans called shops. Usually one side of the room was given over to the sale of tinned food, soaps, boxed milk, and cheese from New Zealand in circular tins the size of paint buckets, rice, flour and sugar weighed out and wrapped in brown paper, and sometimes fresh meat from a pig or goat slaughtered that morning in the back yard, as often as not with the head of the beast grinning from the counter while flies danced joyously in the air around it. On the other side of the room, beyond a screen plastered with cigarette and beer ads, was the bar, a counter ten or twelve feet long, no stools or tables with chairs, nothing to accommodate anyone who did not wish to stand against the counter and drink.

In one corner there was inevitably a juke box that played three songs for a nickel—the ever-present reggae, of course, but also a dozen or more records by people like Al Green, Otis Redding and Aretha Franklin. Jamaican taste in music, and I mean the taste of the

average working-class Jamaican in the back country,
was perfect taste to me—impeccable and serious, knowledgeable and refined. Sometimes a whole culture has
perfect taste, as in New Orleans three-fourths of a century ago or, regarding architecture, in New England two
and three centuries ago, so that a wholly ordinary person, even children, can make aesthetic distinctions usually thought to be the exclusive prerogative of only the
most elaborately educated members of the society. It
seemed to me, regarding music, that Jamaican culture
was wise in this way, and for that reason a barely
literate or even illiterate workingman, toothless, barefoot, alcoholic, a man who believed that Queens Elizabeth I and II were the same person and thought Jack
Kennedy and Jimmy Carter were brothers who had separately employed Martin Luther King on their farms, a
bizarre man to someone like me, such a man when it
came to music had flawless perfect taste. He could instantly distinguish the phony from the authentic, the
derivative from the original, the merely sentimental from
the genuinely romantic. And he would be a scholar in
this field, would know precisely by what routes and
through the work of which musicians calypso had got
bebop from black nightclubs in Florida and become ska,
how ska got rock and soul from London, Liverpool,
New York and Detroit and had become reggae, reaching
its literary and self-conscious phase, was now reinvesti-
gating African roots while at the same time getting itself
electrified in Nashville and Los Angeles. This old cane
cutter, scratching the welts on his forearm with the back
edge of his machete, would know the effect of poverty
on the sound of reggae, how cheap guitars imitating the
tinny thin sounds of the Beatles on Japanese transistor
radios and plastic stereos from a Woolworth's in the
Bronx had stripped sixties rock of its baroque density of
detail to produce a high, thin clarity not heard in Western popular music since the 1920s.

I left the shop, turned my car onto a one-lane road,
headed southeast into the hills. I was in Cockpit Coun-

try now, the roads unpaved and curling along the edges of ocular pits, huge pocks, with strangely shaped hills extruding from the earth like weathered stumps rounded at the tops. The sides of the hills, almost vertical, were covered by a dense, impenetrable skin of macca bushes and short, twisted trees, now and then the bone white ground showing through where a slide, like a gash, had occurred after heavy rain. Because the cockpits themselves, deep adjacent craters ridged by their linked edges, were the result of slow underground erosion of the essentially limestone surface, a process directly opposite the familiar process of uplift, the land forms seemed bizarre and even wrong to me, an unnatural landscape. Valleys aren't supposed to be created by the land's dropping; they're created by rivers or when the adjacent land rises. Though topology expresses its own geologic past and can be read as a text, this text was backward to me. I had always understood craters as the result of eruption or penetration, valleys as the product of uplifting, of emerging, standing slabs of earth—all male processes, somehow. Here, though, the land forms were the expression of female forces. The power of this geology was the power, by yielding, to create space, not by coming forward, to penetrate space. It was the difference between tai chi and karate. It was the difference between a Druidic stone circle and a ziggurat, between Stonehenge and Sumer. And for me to perceive it as "natural" required an enormous shift in what had seemed natural up to now, natural and therefore inevitable. The tourist in me took another step backward, and the traveler came forward one.

On the map where the three parishes of St. James, Trelawny and St. Elizabeth came together a large area is marked "Cockpit Country." It's an area of about four hundred square miles, and there are no roads or settlements marked on it. The roads crawl like vines around the edges, sometimes sending a single tendril into the area for a few miles before it disappears, as if that blank space on the map had swallowed it. At Mocho, Niagara, and Elderslie, I was traveling along the edge of this Cockpit Country, passing through tiny settlements of a few dozen cabins perched over dark red ground, a patch of yams and an ackee or breadfruit tree in back, the chassis of a wrecked car in front, with five or six small, half-naked children playing by the road, waving and calling out to me as I drove by. "Whitey!" and "White head!" they cried, and sometimes just "White!" I tried always to smile and wave back, but the road was getting rougher with each mile and more twisted as it switch-backed up and then quickly down the sides of the hills and along the rims of the cockpits, and I was forced to hold grimly to the wheel with both hands and keep my gaze fixed in front of me.

From the map, and from Carey Robinson's little book, which had traced the course of the two Maroon wars in admirable detail, with charts and elaborate descriptions of British troop movements and Maroon guerrilla ambushes, I knew that I was now in Maroon country and that many of the people I was seeing were the descendants of those wild Ashanti warriors. According to Carey Robinson and also to my friend Upton West, these people were supposed to look different from the ordinary Jamaica countryman—taller, straighter, more muscular, and with a slight reddish tint to their skin.

Though I wanted it to be true and did attempt to see that difference, I could not see it. In fact, if anything, the people I was passing as they walked along the road with bunches of green bananas on their heads or carted water in cube-shaped tins or simply stood by the road, watching me, seemed stockier than the people of Montego Bay, and darker. The red was in the soil, rich in bauxite, a deep red soil the color of dried blood that in this dry season made a reddish dust that settled over everything. The huts and cabins, the vegetation, the road, animals and people all seemed to be on the other side of a red-tinted lens, so that only when I looked up at the sharply blue sky could I be sure that the redness over everything was not the expression of my own eye.

This was the region, during the first Maroon war, that Cudjoe had held for forty years against a half dozen British commanders, one after another falling victim to disease, heat and insects, the tangled unmapped country, these endless cockpits riddled with caves and narrow passageways known only to the Maroons, and the brilliance and courage of Cudjoe and the several separate bands of Maroons he had united under him. From the accounts of the period, British accounts, Cudjoe was not so much brilliant as wily, not so much courageous as stubborn, and not so much a leader as ruthless. But, looking back to the early 1700s and imagining the difficulty of conducting a successful forty-year military campaign against the mighty British army on a tiny island in the Caribbean, with no allies and nothing but three or four rag-tag, quarrelsome groups of ex-slaves who variously spoke versions of several African and at least two European languages, with no weapons except what they made or could steal in raids on the coastal plantations or took from the bodies of the soldiers they killed, and no food except what they could grow in hiding in the cockpits, an army that had no bases and had to move with its women, children and old people or leave them to the British and re-enslavement or worse —imagining that difficulty, one has to believe that a merely wily, stubborn and ruthless man could not have succeeded for six months. If the British hadn't killed him by then, his own people would have.

By now, when I passed a house or a small, hand-cultivated field, the people would stop what they were doing and stare at me with hard faces. Children no longer smiled and waved at me or called out the color of my skin to me; instead they got behind the nearest adult and peeked around pant leg or cotton skirt. Every few hundred yards my Toyota slammed the oil pan or banged the muffler against the craggy limestone road, and I winced, suddenly picturing my isolation if the car broke down here. I could handle a flat tire, but that was about all. The men and women whose country I was passing through did not look friendly or helpful. I didn't dare stop and ask for directions, something, like most men, I was reluctant to do anyhow, anywhere, but here my old barely conscious reasons for driving on regardless of not being sure where I was—fear of losing face (real men are supposed to have a good sense of direction; only sissies get lost), fear of being misled, and a simple unwillingness to delay my forward motion, gambling that as long as I was still moving away from where I had started I was somehow moving closer to my destination—these fears were suddenly given a strange new cast that originated, I knew, in my fear of black people. And even more complex than that, my fear especially of people whose ancestors had fought generations of a just war against my ancestors. Will Americans traveling in Vietnam two hundred years from now feel as I do today? I wondered, as I struggled to separate the several braided strands of my fear, the purely racist strand from the political one, the narrowly economic from the broadly historical. Will a middle-aged American traveler in the twenty-second century, lost in the Montagnard highlands, look at the grim face of a man in a rice paddy next to the road, and suddenly picturing the maddened faces of both their ancestors, drive quickly on, preferring to remain lost a little longer?

My map was out of directions altogether, and when I came to forks in the road I took the one that looked the more traveled—right, then left, then right again. There was no logic to my turns; I had no sense of drawing gradually nearer to a settlement. Now and then I saw a cabin, thatched roof and daub-and-wattle walls, a small shed build from old odd-shaped boards a few yards in back that, I knew from the smoke trickling out the hole in the roof, was a kitchen. Sometimes a woman's sweating face stared expressionless out a window as, taking great care on the rutted track so as not to smash my rented car, I passed slowly by.

At last I began to see small groups of houses, two and three at a time, alongside the road. Behind them, where the ground fell away from the ridge and became the steep side of a cockpit, I saw short, terraced fields tended by men and boys and sometimes women. In the distance, far from any house, more land was similarly cultivated. There was some cane, but mostly I could make out yam plants on poles and corn stalks spaced in what seemed to me erratic relations to one another. No neat rows or files, no geometric patterns—spirals, rather, and splotches, blotches and patches, one crop mixed indiscriminately with another, kalaloo and onions sprawling at the feet of pole beans and yam plants, corn stalks planted like bystanders around a cabbage patch.

Then I was in the village of Nyamkopong itself. Or at least I hoped it was Nyamkopong. Along the curling length of a high ridge that linked a dozen craters were scattered fifty or sixty small houses facing both sides of a central lane, with several narrower, grassy branches off to either side, houses at the end, a small masonry building that was an unfinished church, another, finished, painted white. I passed three or four shops open to the street and, at the far end of town where the ground lifted and flattened into a kind of parade ground, a new masonry schoolhouse and a bare playing field in front of it. Then the cockpits again, with cabins in the distance and the road quickly becoming a footpath.

I turned my car around at the schoolyard and drove slowly back to the center of the village where two shops on either side of the street faced each other. A half dozen people, old people, stood in the shade and watched me. I stopped, and realized that I didn't want to ask if this was Nyamkopong, not because I was afraid that it wasn't but because I was reasonably sure that it was and thus the old woman staring at me with her set face would be able to snarl, Of course this is Nyamkopong, you idiot! So instead I took a chance and politely requested the group to direct me to the head man. With no sign to go on, I was relying not on the evidence of my senses but on a connection between my intuition and my reason to determine where I was now located. I felt as though I had just dived headfirst down a well.

A young man, short and wearing a red, yellow and green knit wool tam and beige sweater, a bearded man and, as I could see from the bulbous shape of his tam, wearing Rastafarian dreadlocks, emerged from the mauve darkness of the shop on my left and pointed grandly down the street ahead of me. The Colonel lives there, he informed me in a large voice, and he called me his brother.

The old people, men and women, said nothing and stared darkly after me as, greatly relieved, suddenly exhausted, I drove slowly away. This is not a brave thing to be doing, I thought. Why, then, am I so afraid? I would have liked to have been like Gauguin in Tahiti, all awash with open-eyed enthusiasm for the newly revealed alternative to bourgeois France, or Forster in India, skeptical, shrewdly compassionate, confident that what one did not know at the moment was really not worth knowing at the moment, or Dinesen in Africa, tender and secure in the tower of her absent self. But I could be none of these people, and as a result I saw very little at that time of where I was and what people I was among.

Oh, certainly I saw the way the light at midday glared off the palm fronds, baked the dirt yards dry and turned the tin roofs of the buildings to griddles, and I saw how the people wore sweaters and caps and complained that it was winter while I sweltered in my Dacron-and-cotton, short-sleeved shirt. I saw how the Colonel's pink, four-room, cinderblock house was the largest and best kept in the village, saw his department store furniture and dishes, saw the plump, well-fed faces of his children; and when one of those children ran for him in the fields and brought back to the house a scrawny, rabbit-faced, brown man wearing tattered clothes and dirt-caked rubber boots, I saw that the Colonel, despite his office and its emoluments, in a country that accepted bribery as the sole legitimate access to those in power, was still a poor man. I heard his mannered Jamaican English, his careful avoidance of patois, his ingratiating queries about me. And I heard his sharp, sudden command to his sour-faced wife in the back room to bring us a bottle of rum and then his polite request that I sign his guest book and write my home address next to my signature just below the name and address of the Canadian professor who had preceded me by about six weeks.

I saw and heard it all, and yet, throughout, it seemed that I saw and heard nothing, because at every moment I was aware of these people being black-skinned. Yes, consciously I could and did methodically and sensitively add to that awareness my new information about them—that they were Maroons, that they lived on what amounted to a government reservation and that they owned their land more or less communally, that they were among the best farmers in Jamaica, that they were proud of their Maroon past even if only partially aware of it, and that, however they saw and heard me, they did not see and hear me the way a black American would. Even so, I could not stop viewing them as if I were seated, not on a stoop in the Jamaican bush, but in Detroit or Roxbury or Watts. And that is why I was afraid, afraid the way only a white American can be afraid and the way Gauguin and Forster and Dinesen were never afraid. They may not have known precisely where they were when they found themselves in Tahiti, India or Africa, but they knew they were not in Paris, Cambridge or Copenhagen. And that, at least, let them see more clearly than I could now where they had traveled to and whom they were moving among. A white American, I was blind, and lost.

COLONEL MARTIN LUTHER PHELPS, WHOSE NAME I REalized after a few moments was in honor of the Reformer, not the American, drank off his rum with me, obviously glad for the break in his workday. I didn't dislike the Colonel, but he kept moving and talking like a barber or tailor, a nervous shopkeeper who continually referred to the sloth and bad habits of his neighbors so that no one, least of all I, would confuse him with his neighbors. He smiled and spoke enthusiastically of the village's upcoming celebration of the heroic Cudjoe's birthday, inviting me to join them and to bring my family, for, as he stated over and over, the Maroon people wanted the world to know of them. And all the while he nervously took care to straighten and thereby indicate the pictures that hung on the wall behind him of his children in the States, the glasses, ashtray and bottle of rum on the table before us, the plastic doilies on the sideboard and tables at the ends of the sofa, even getting up quickly in the middle of a sentence to close a door off the tiny living room so that I could not see the clutter in the room beyond and the members of his family seated on the double bed where together—mother, daughter, and two small sons—they listened intently not to our lofty conversation but to the slabs of emotion and fantasy coming from a radio soap opera taped in a London studio and broadcast daily from Kingston—old stories about working-class girls from the provinces being corrupted by upper-class male executives in the cities, characters played by white English actors whose accent, though it made their characterizations into comic-book figures for me, seemed to make them wholly believable to the people in the next room.

After a while of pleasantries, I started to find the Colonel irritating, mainly because I saw how much his manner was the type that pleased people I now disliked— people like the Wests and the Churches—so I rose from the blue plastic-covered sofa and said that I would leave now. He stood also, and as he reached to shake my hand and urge me once again to return on January sixth for the celebration, he suddenly extended his reach into my private space and plucked something tiny and unfelt from my throat. Rubbing his thumb and forefinger together, he warned me to be careful of the ticks out here in the bush.

Yes, I said, thank you, thank you. I asked him to say goodbye for me to his wife and family, and quickly headed back to the safety, as I suddenly thought of it, of my car. There seemed to be no perspective I could hold consistently enough to trust. I declared to the Colonel as I left his house and crossed the packed dirt in front that I would definitely return on Tuesday the sixth. He smiled appreciatively. And I'll bring my family! I shouted, touching my throat where the tick had been.

Unlocking the car door, I ducked into the vehicle as if it were a hut and swiftly cranked the window down, opening it to fresh, cooling air and the broad, bearded face of the Rastafarian who had directed me to the Colonel's house. He didn't look as young now as he had at the shop; he seemed to be in his mid-thirties. His dark brown eyes were wet like a horse's and though his face was crossed with a huge smile, it was lined with worry and puzzling thoughts. A *serious* man, I decided. His nose was shaped like a shoe horn, broad and smooth, and he had huge teeth. Once again, he called me brother, gave me an old sixties black-power handshake, and told me that now I should see the rest of the village of Nyamkopong, home of the Cockpit Maroons, whom he called his "ascendants."

I got out of the car, closed the window and locked the door again, which seemed to meet with approval from my friend, and followed the man down the road. What is there to see here? I asked him, a tourist again, needing someone to tell me what to "see," as if I could not see on my own.

The boneyard, he answered, and then unexpectedly moved close to me, too close, and began to chat, a sudden master of chat, it seemed, for nothing he told me was of consequence; regardless, he held my attention, forced me to concentrate on trivia as if it were of the most crucial importance to me. Over there was where the mother of the schoolteacher lived. Her father had been the Colonel before Martin Luther Phelps. And there was where the Chinaman would set up his diesel generator and speakers for the music on Tuesday. Down the road a friend of his, a man named Rubber, was setting up his generator and sound system. There was lots of money to be made on January sixth, he told me, because the Maroons came from all over the island to celebrate their victory over the slavemasters. And over there was the house owned by a woman who had two boys by him. A good woman, he told me, but not heavy enough for him. Heavy? I asked. Yes, too thin. "Maugre," he called it.

His name was Terron Musgrave, and I decided, while we stood and peered down at the late nineteenth-century graves in the high grass behind a small whitewashed Presbyterian church, that Terron was a hustler. I would make the same decision many times over again before I left Jamaica for the last time. It happened whenever I did not understand him.

What I couldn't understand now was why he was guiding me through these very conventional and, to me, boring aspects of Nyamkopong: here the nineteenth-century Protestant church; there the home of the school-teacher's mother; there the school itself, a gift from the government of Canada, it turned out; and over there the Chinaman's stereo system. A native New Englander, I had looked at thousands of Protestant churches and graveyards a hundred years older than this one; and I had seen too many cinderblock schoolhouses built in the 1960s in the small towns of America; and as for the Chinaman's outdoor stereo system, it reminded me of what my students at New England College liked to set up on the quad in early May.

My tour seemed to be coming to a close. We had looped through the town and were approaching the Colonel's house and my car from the other side, so I asked Terron if I could buy him a beer and pay him something for his trouble. Declining the beer by smiling graciously and explaining how he had long ago withdrawn from "the alcohol world" because of having come "to know I," an expression I did not then know how to translate, he nevertheless agreed to accept whatever I wished to offer him as payment. But first, he said, he wanted me to meet his father.

Suddenly I trusted him again and felt ashamed for having thought him only a charming country hustler. Of course! His father! What a natural and simple impulse, to want to introduce me to his father, I thought, as if my visit were a prized possession that he would want to share with his people.

He began to walk faster, passed my car and the Colonel's house, and turned down a grassy lane toward a blue stucco house at the end where a dust-covered pig and some scrawny white chickens scavenged in the yard in front. Over the door in rough hand-painted letters were the words "Trelawny Town" and the dates 1738—1739, which I knew was the date, new style and old, that had ended the First Maroon War, the one that had closed off the hundred years of guerrilla warfare that had begun when the British took the island away from the Spanish.

As we neared the house, it must have become clear to Terron that I was under the impression that he was taking me to meet his genetic father, his "real" father, as they say. No, no, this was his *spiritual* father, he corrected me, a man of much culture who knew all the history of the Maroon peoples and who besides all the knowledge had in his care the Maroon Treaty, for he was the Secretary of State for the Maroon peoples, and besides, Terron said with obvious scorn, this man was much heavier than the Colonel.

Heavier? I asked, spreading my hands to indicate girth.

Yes, a wise man. Much culture, lots of culture in the upstairs.

Ah, yes, of course, I said, stumbling behind him over the rough ground.

When I drew up in front of the house, I realized that it was like a Hollywood set. The blue stucco front of the house, with two bay windows and a wide door between, was barely one room deep and was attached to an old and larger daub-and-wattle cabin behind it, while off to one side was the typical kitchen shed, blackened and scorched like an old kettle, from generations of cookfires. While the Colonel's house had been in fact and not just appearance a four-room stuccoed cinderblock house, a bungalow, not a cabin, this one was a bungalow only if looked at from a certain angle and distance.

A scrawny, spotted dog with an intelligent face stood at the top of the front steps and barked rapidly at us. Scattered over the bare ground around the house were rusted-out buckets, old, emptied rum bottles, flattened toothpaste tubes, the pink arms of a baby doll, a worn-out tire, the spirochetelike peelings of a half dozen breakfast oranges: all the evidence of the usual busy and distracted Jamaican family life. I could see smoke wallowing from the kitchen shed and could smell pork cooking. Somewhere in the back of the house a tinny transistor radio was rapping out reggae and Kingston disc jockey fast-talk.

We stood at the bottom of the steps, and the spotted dog at the top kept barking, while behind us the pig rooted and the chickens scratched in the dirt. The direct sun was very hot. Sweat blossomed under my arms and drifted down my trunk. Off to the sides of the house, where the ground tipped and fell away to cockpits, banana trees clustered with a tall breadfruit tree and a pair of ackee trees just past blooming and, further down, in the usual random-seeming patches, yam plants and a few stalks of puny corn. Several yards beyond, at the beginning of the impossibly tangled bush, was a battered two-door privy that looked as if it were about to topple into the cockpit.

I looked up and saw that an old man had come out of the house and was trying to quiet the dog by patting the air above the dog's head, which seemed to work, for the dog quickly ceased yapping and slinked back inside. Then the old man smiled at us. He wore a porkpie felt hat carefully squared on his head and horn-rimmed glasses, a plaid flannel shirt and baggy gabardine trousers held up with braces.

Come in, come in out of the sun, he said and waved

us inside. He moved slowly, carefully, as if with a certain discomfort, but he stood extremely straight, his head as erect as a young man's. When I had climbed the five steps to the doorway, I saw his eyes for the first time—pale blue, like agates, except that the blue outer ring of the pupil held a brown center ring around the iris, like a pair of concentric blue and brown rings around a black planet.

Terron introduced me by my first name, and the old man removed his hat with his right hand, shook mine firmly, twice, with his left, and said his name. Mann, Wendell O. Mann, he pronounced, and then, like an English gentleman, "Delighted," with a pleasant nod of his head. Replacing his hat on his head, his close-cropped hair black except for a white streak running from front to back, he bade us follow him inside where it was cooler. His skin was as dark as any Jamaican's but for some reason I could see this man despite the darkness, as if my eyes were at last growing accustomed to the absence of white skins and had dilated sufficiently to bring in details of texture and form, so that I could see his high, almost oriental cheekbones, his crisp mouth and lips, the delicately woven net of lines covering his forehead, the veins that disappeared above his temples into his hair.

We followed him—Terron, the master of chat, silent for the first time since he had appeared at my car window—through the door into the hallway beyond, where there was a long, narrow table in the center, a closed door leading off the hall at either side, and a third closed door at the back. The table was bare, the walls, painted pale blue, were bare, and the room, if it was a room, was chairless.

Mr. Mann bellowed in rapid-fire patois toward the closed door at the back, and I lost him completely, only to understand when, a few seconds later, the door opened and a ten- or twelve-year-old, shirtless, barefoot boy appeared carrying a wooden kitchen chair, followed by a second boy and chair, and then a third. They placed Mr.

Mann's chair on one side of the long table, stuck mine and Terron's on the other, and then took up squatting positions on the stoop just outside.

Sit down, sit down, he said, and we did, while he barked again at the boys and sent one of them scurrying off. We waited in silence until momentarily the boy reappeared with a packet of Craven A's and a sardine tin ashtray. The old man tapped a cigarette out, offered one to me, then to Terron, and the three of us lit up, inhaling deeply and smiling with pleasure. Then he began, in careful English, to ask me questions.

They were polite but effective questions, framed as statements but demanding answers that provided concrete information. You are Canadian?

No, I'm American.

Ah, and from New York?

No, New England.

A pause. New England, he slowly repeated, as if I had lied.

Actually, I'm from New Hampshire . . . near Boston, Massachusetts.

Ah, yes, he said. Boston. And near Boston you are a businessman?

No, no, not that. I'm a college teacher, I rushed to correct him, as if it were a far better thing to be a college teacher near Boston than a businessman.

He raised his eyebrows; he had heard my rush and what it implied, and now I had heard too.

And you are here in Jamaica on a holiday? he went on, smiling.

No, not exactly. I told him that I had rented a house for two months in the town of Anchovy in the parish of St. James and was living there until mid-February when I had to return to my teaching. But as I said it, I knew I had evaded his question.

And you spend your time in your house in Anchovy, resting and learning about the people of Jamaica?

Yes, I confessed. And I have my family with me, my wife and children, I weakly added.

You are an educated man, he declared, who is trying to learn about the Jamaican people, and now you have come to Nyamkopong to learn about the Maroon people?

Stammering, I first said yes, then no, I didn't think I should be called an educated man, but yes, I was trying to learn about the Jamaican and now the Maroon people.

Terron had remained silent throughout, listening and smoking his cigarette with satisfied concentration. But it was somehow as if he already knew what my answers to Mr. Mann's questions would be and was unfamiliar only with the questions themselves, because he watched the old man when he spoke to me and turned back to his cigarette when I spoke. The three boys, however, still squatting in the doorway, watched me and not the old man, their faces expressionless, not curious, frightened, or bored, merely attentive. Everyone in the room seemed to have a kind attention that I did not have and, further, that was wholly foreign to me. I couldn't even imagine how to simulate it. I felt scattered, my own attention ricocheting around the room and across time, from this present moment back to my life in New Hampshire, to my life of "resting" in Anchovy, to my timid drive up here this morning, to my conversation with Colonel Phelps barely an hour ago, bouncing from the clear and intense face of the man in front of me over to Carey Robinson's little book, to the engraving reproduced there of Cudjoe, an ugly, frog-faced, broad-shouldered man with a hunchback delivering his short sword to a tall and gallant British military officer, then leaping again, to Captain West and his son Upton, who was my friend, and then to my friend's mother, who dabbled in real estate and servants, and the Churches, whose son had fled with his wife and children to Canada, where the cold air, his father had told me, made his nose bleed.

The Maroon people, Mr. Mann said in his rapid, gravelly voice, are the heart of Jamaica, and the British are the head. But I am glad that you are American because I love the American people, especially Mr. Kissinger, who as you know is also Secretary as I am the Secretary.

Some day before you return to your home near Boston, I will give you a message to take to my brother Secretary Mr. Kissinger. He paused then and lapsed into quiet diminishing yes, yes, yeses.

We smiled across the table at each other. It grew silent. Then it occurred to me, and I turned to Terron, who was listening to his cigarette, and asked him if I could send one of the boys to the shop on the street for some rum.

Yes, Poppa loves his waters, Terron said without a smile, and he called one of the boys over, a kid about twelve who had been eyeing the pack of Craven A's, waiting, I knew, for us to empty it so he could grab the foil liner and strip it of the white tissue backing that made such an excellent wrapper for rolling pen-sized ganga cigars. I passed the boy a couple of dollars and asked him to bring us some rum, and Mr. Mann, perking up, swiftly followed by ordering one of the remaining two boys to bring us some glasses and water. Nothing for the Rastaman! he shouted, and Terron laughed and chanted, Alcohol world, alcohol world! I-man no deal with no alcohol world!

Some talk about white rum followed, its power to heal and to make ill. Wisdom is not for the weak-minded, Mr. Mann warned, and said that except for the Rasta brethren, who refuse alcohol because of their preference for the herb and their knowledge of the bad effects of mixing two types of wisdom, he didn't trust a man who would not drink white rum, even though he well knew that most white men would not drink it. You have to choose your wisdom, he pronounced. Just like Gary Cooper said, you have to choose your poison. Water and oil won't mix, so taken together they're good for nothing, can't drink it and can't use it to run your machine. One or the other, rum or the herb. Only boys and fools try to use both, except for the weak-minded who happen to know themselves, and they use neither one.

By now the boy had returned with the rum. Our Lord and Savior Jesus Christ instructed us, Mr. Mann said, pouring the rum first into my glass and then his, that he that hath an ear, let him hear what the Spirit saith! Which is why we call this thing spirits, he explained, as he raised his glass and emptied it, following with a nip from his water glass.

I knew to reverse his procedure and nip at my rum and practically empty the water, then placed my hand over the top of my rum glass while he refilled his own.

Turning in his chair and peering intently at the ceiling as if for inspiration from above, Mr. Mann suddenly blurted, Veni vidi vici! I came, I saw, I conquered. And so uttered the great Queen Elizabeth when she last visited the country of Jamaica as it was about to commence the celebration of its independence from the mother country of Great Britain, thanks to the wonderful work of those national heroes, Sir Alexander Bustamente, Honorable Norman Manley, the father of the Prime Minister Michael, Marcus Garvey, who commanded the prison walls in Spanishtown to come down and they obeyed, and Nonny, the greatest of all Maroon scientists who slew the British soldiers by firing bullets at them from her cunt. You have heard that story? he asked me.

No, no, I said. All I knew about the Maroons I had learned from Carey Robinson.

Well, briefly, the great Queen Elizabeth heard about this beautiful land of trees and running waters from Sir Francis Drake, who was an expert sailor, even better than Christopher Columbus, who had come over here in his sailing ship at the same time but hadn't been able to control his men, so they mutinied on him and left the poor man for dead on the beach near Ocho Rios, what's now called Discovery Bay. Sir Francis Drake came along, on his way back from conquering India, and heard pathetic cries for help, so he told his men, Wait! I hear someone crying for help! So they pulled in their sails and went ashore at Discovery Bay and found the poor, skinny man Columbus, all filthy and with his beard long and matted, and they saved him just as the Arawak Indians were sneaking up to kill him for what the Span-

ish had done to the Indian people on the island of Jamaica, which was to make them slaves and work in the
gold mines and kill them until they all ran away to live in
the bush and teach the Africans there how to live in the
cockpits. The Africans were there because they had
learned over in Africa how the Indians were being treated
by the Spanish, and so they sent the warrior queen and
scientist Nonny and three hundred of the best Ashanti
fighting men across the ocean to aid them in their strug-
gle against the Spanish. But this was the same time as
the English people were starting to make slaves of the
Africans and bring them here to work on the plantations,
and when these Africans in slavery heard about Nonny
and the free Ashanti warriors up in the cockpits with the
Arawak Indians, they started sneaking away from their
masters to join them, until pretty soon there was a
whole army of them up here and in the mountains in the
east, all men, too, except for Nonny who was their chief
and their main scientist. This is why Columbus' men had
mutinied and why the great Christopher Columbus himself was so frightened as he stood alone there on the
beach, crying out pitifully for help. Sir Francis Drake
was Queen Elizabeth's chief sea captain before Sir Winston Churchill took command against the Germans and
their Kaiser and after Julius Caesar was the chief of all
the fighting forces of the Empire, and he had lots of
business waiting for him back in England because he
had been over there in India for so long, it was a big job,
conquering India, so he didn't stay in Jamaica long enough
to learn of the Maroons or how the Spanish were treating the Arawaks in those days, he didn't even know that
the British themselves had started to capture Africans
and bring them over to force them to work the sugar
plantations and be slaves. He just picked up Columbus
from the beach at Discovery Bay, who only had one
friend by then, his servant Friday, an African who had
remained loyal to Columbus when the rest of his men
had mutinied, and Sir Francis Drake carried the two
men back to Spain where he dropped them off and sailed

home to England to report to his queen, the great Queen
Elizabeth. Now Christopher Columbus and his assistant
Friday, who couldn't speak English anyhow, although
Columbus could speak it fine because he was an educated man, never mentioned to Sir Francis what had
been going on in the island of Jamaica between the
Arawaks and the Maroons in the war against the Spanish or even about how the English plantation owners
were capturing people in Africa and forcing them to
work themselves to death in the sugar fields. No, he just
said that he was an explorer and his troops and sailors
had mutinied on him and had gone to America because
they had heard about the gold strike in California. That's
why Queen Elizabeth didn't know about the slavery
business. But Sir Francis did tell her how beautiful the
island of Jamaica was, and so she claimed it for part of
the British Empire and promised some day to come and
visit us over here. Sir Francis promised to bring her
over on his own ship, the *Golden Hind*, but he died
before he had a chance, and then Sir Winston Churchill
was too busy with fighting the Germans and Kaiser
Wilhelm to do it, so she had to wait until nineteen and
sixty-two before she could come over and see this place.
She had been pretty busy herself because of her fights
with Mary, the Queen of the Scots, and Queen Victoria,
who wanted to be queen of the whole British Empire,
and they had to be put down and beheaded first, but as
soon as she had things under control back in England
Queen Elizabeth came over, and when she found out
what had gone on here on the island of Jamaica, she
understood why Jamaica had decided to be independent
of the English and elect our own Sir Alexander Bustamente as Prime Minister so there could never be slavery
again on the island of Jamaica. There was a great celebration for her, as it was her birthday jubilee, and a
whole group of us Maroons went down to Kingston and
did the Maroon dances for her, which surprised her and
made her think she was in Africa instead of Jamaica,
until Sir Alexander Bustamente took her aside and told

her our history, just as today I am telling it to you. And then she understood and was glad that the island of Jamaica had decided to be independent, and she was proud of the way the Maroons had fought her own British soldiers all those years in the cockpits and she decided then and there to make Nonny into a national hero along with Marcus Garvey and Sir Alexander Bustamente and Honorable Norman Manley, the father of the present Prime Minister. That's when she said it! Mr. Mann proudly exclaimed.

Said what?

Veni vidi vici! I came, I saw, and I conquered! And a great cheer went up and down the whole island of Jamaica, and men threw their hats into the air, and women held up their babies for the Queen to look upon. Oh, it was a great day for us Maroons!

The pint bottle of white rum was emptied and all our cigarettes had been smoked, mine as well as Mr. Mann's. Without my knowing, the boys had scuttled in from the stoop and had pilfered both boxes for the papers inside and now were seated on the bottom step outside passing a pair of huge joints between them. At some point in Mr. Mann's narrative, Terron too had left his seat to go out and sit on the stoop, where he was puffing on a spliff rolled in brown bag paper, a cigar-long cone of perfumy ganja that, when the old man had lapsed into reflective silence, he extended to me.

No thanks, I said. One kind of wisdom at a time. Then I got up and, after thanking Mr. Mann and assuring him that I would return with my family for the celebration on the coming Tuesday, I took my leave, walking slowly, carefully, struggling to clear my head before I reached my car and had to drive the long, dangerous road back to Anchovy.

CAPTAIN WEST REACHED OUT HIS LONG ARM AND, WHILE HE pumped my hand, peered over my shoulder into the darkness beyond. He was holding a gin and tonic and wore cherry red trousers and white buck shoes, a pink, short-sleeved shirt with a dark blue and white polka dot ascot at his soft throat. Preoccupied, or distracted, I couldn't tell which, he hurried me into the living room, while he remained behind, still scanning the yard where I had parked my car next to a brown Mercedes sedan.

Mrs. West, her wide face florid and sour at once, sat me on the sofa next to her and demanded to know what I would drink. One of the servants, presumably one that she trained in her own house, as the brochure had it, a young man wearing black trousers, white shirt, dark gray bow tie and cummerbund, came forward for instructions.

White rum, I said.

Mrs. West looked across at me as if I had asked for LSD, and the servant, apparently puzzled, looked as if I had just named a drink he had never heard of before. It was bad form, I knew. But I persisted. No ice, I said, and half water.

Expressionless again, the man nodded and withdrew.

It was a small dinner party, and I had agreed to come, despite my promises to myself never to visit the Wests again. But I was still unable to give up my belief that I could remain outside the two worlds I had discovered in Jamaica—the world inhabited by the Churches and the Wests, and the world I believed was inhabited both by the Maroons and also by the half dozen black Jamaican men who lived in the town of Anchovy and with whom I had lately been drinking and from whom I was then learning to play dominoes in the back room of Barrett's shop. I had learned by then that, with regard to the second world, I had no choice but to remain outside, an observer with clouded vision at best. With regard to the first world, however, I believed that the simple exercise of my will was sufficient to guarantee my remaining outside. Yes, I told myself, I am white, and I do understand and speak their language, but, after all, I was raised by working people, tenement dwellers, people who for countless generations had worked with their hands and backs. Surely that counted for something. Surely my class status, or rather as I saw it, my lack of class status, permitted me the luxury of remaining detached and untouchable, uncontaminated by these people—in the same way that my race and inability to speak or easily understand their language deprived me of the easy trust and intimacy of the Maroons and my new friends at the domino table at Barrett's.

I was seated next to Mrs. West and we talked at length about her son's success. I drank before dinner rather steadily, then at dinner also, swiftly becoming drunk. At some point during dinner the slender young man who had brought me my first drink (after that I had bellied up to the bar and fixed my own)—a man I had by then learned was the son of Mrs. West's "regular" maid, the sleek heavy-set woman now serving vegetables—refilled my water glass by pouring from my left side, after I had emptied it and set it there myself, precisely between me and the young man's employer-trainer. Mrs. West, her chunky body wrapped in a bolt of sumptuously colored African cloth, realized what the man was doing, glared at him ferociously, then cracked him sharply across the hand with the flat of her butter knife, causing him to drop the pitcher of water to the floor.

You idiot! the woman shrieked. He had ducked to the floor to retrieve the pitcher, which luckily had been nearly empty anyhow and hadn't spilled more than a few ounces onto the waxed parquet. From the *right!* Serve from the *right,* you idiot!

I looked down at the man's woolly head at my side, then across at the horrified face of his mother, who had stopped serving the vegetables and held the ladle of snow peas and almonds in midair. The Captain was still looking nervously toward the windows and had heard nothing. There were three other people at the table, an elderly couple from Beverly Hills, where the man had been an extremely successful film producer for several decades, and a middle-aged Fifth Avenue socialite whose second husband, a Greek shipowner, had recently died. They had been talking together about radios and had gone silent for a second at Mrs. West's outburst. Then, as if the interruption had been no more than a phone call for someone else, the three had gone on chattering about radios.

I got one for my birthday, the baldheaded film producer said in a whining voice, and honest to God, the thing gets every station in the world, but I haven't the foggiest idea of how to make it work. I can't even get Burbank on it! he happily exclaimed, and his wife and the widow laughed to see such a smart man made a fool by a mere machine.

By now the young man had retrieved the water pitcher. Mrs. West waved him away without looking at him, and he disappeared silently into the kitchen, while his mother went on serving snow peas. I slumped in my chair and felt myself collapsing inside.

Excuse me, I said to Mrs. West. But I think I'll have to leave. I'm not feeling well.

Of course she understood. The perfect hostess dealing with the imperfect guest. The silly young American, he should have left the white rum alone. Typical male show-off. He sees the blacks drinking the stuff like water and decides he's man enough to do the same. Of course he's ill. Those people have stomachs like iron. But he's sweet. And polite. Good of him to remove himself before he starts acting up and makes a fool of himself in front of the important guests from Beverly Hills and Manhattan.

The Captain saw me to the door. Plucking a five-cell flashlight from a shelf near the door, he walked me outside, down the steps to the driveway where I'd parked my car. He kept flashing his beam across the moist lawn at shrubs and trees as he walked along beside me.

What are you looking for, Captain? I finally asked him.

Teefs! he barked.

Teefs?

Thieves. Dem teef yeh, he said, imitating patois. They're all about the grounds. Thanks to our friend, Mr. Manley! he said, his voice rising with rage. All there for the taking now. There's your social equality for you.

Right? Promise them the moon, then tell 'em you can't deliver because the other fellow's got it. So what happens. Looting! Rape! Murder! Economic collapse!

He opened my car door for me and, patting me gently on the shoulder, wished me good night and hoped I felt better by morning. I thanked him, and as he warily picked his way back to the house, I drove rapidly, recklessly, up the long hill toward Anchovy and the compound, home.

The road spiraled upward in the darkness, gigantic cottonwood trees blocking out the stars and moonlight, away from the enclave of sprawling white-washed houses with swimming pools and high fences and Doberman pinschers padding silently across the dew-wet lawns. This was Reading, not a village as much as a white settlement with a sea view, proximity to the shops and businesses of Montego Bay, and neighbors you could trust because they were like you and struggled alongside you to protect the same interests. Atop the hill—Seven Mile, it was called—was Anchovy, a true Jamaican country town where the Churches and I and my family were part of a distinct minority and the compound on the ridge above the town an anomaly, where the four or five thousand Jamaicans who lived in the town were black and mostly poor subsistence farmers, domestics in the houses of Reading, clerks, laborers and cops in Montego Bay, shopkeepers and tradesmen in Anchovy itself, or unemployed. Half the men in town were in this last category, and one-fourth of the families in town had no one, man, woman or child, who was employed. They kept a goat or two for meat, a half dozen chickens, sometimes a pig in the bushes behind their cabins, grew yams and a little corn in the corners of their yards, and spent endless days and nights waiting for things to change, drinking and talking in shops like Barrett's till after midnight, smoking ganja on the back steps, playing dominoes, listening and dancing in place to reggae from someone's radio turned up loud and placed next to an open window on the street. Sometimes a car full of thick-bodied black men and their skinny women would drive through on their way from Savanna-la-Mar to Montego Bay for the weekend, and they would stop at Barrett's for a cold Heineken and some of Barrett's famous jerked pork, and the locals would gawk at the new blue Mustang outside and then would come timidly inside to look at the strangers' clothes and the rings on their fingers. Sometimes a pair of tourists in a rented Japanese car would come through town, lost or just exploring the back roads, and hot, curious or confused, would stop at Barrett's or one of the two other shops in town for a cold beer and directions. And sometimes I found myself there, sipping on a glass of white rum, chatting with Barrett or his barmaid Yvonne or one of the regulars, when one of these couples, usually a young American man and woman in Bermuda shorts, came in, sunburnt, blond, drip-dry people with open faces and pockets full of credit cards. I would turn away from them, study my drink as if it held my future, and listen to the Jamaicans in the place ask them where in the States they were from, how long were they going to be in the country, and how did they like Jamaica so far?

When at last I arrived home, that night of the debacle at the Wests', I parked my car, walked quickly past my house and along the narrow path, down from terrace to terrace, until I came to the far end of the compound. Behind and above me the house cantilevered into the tops of the fruit trees and the mahoe that surrounded me here, down at the edge of the bush, where Church's elaborate outdoor lighting system barely reached me. There was an old, rarely used iron gate in the cut stone wall down here, beyond it the torn remnants of a paved road that Mrs. Church had told me the hurricane of 1967 had destroyed. Before the hurricane, she had said, you could drive down the backside of the hill all the way to Reading and Montego Bay without having to go through Anchovy.

Pushing the gate slowly open, I slipped through and started walking, picking my way with care over the chunks of old asphalt and marl and around the potholes that like miniature cockpits made the road impassable except for a donkey or a man walking. Here and there moonlight fell in wedges on the road and showed me my way as the road turned and twisted along to the top of the ridge and away from the Church compound before starting the descent to Reading and the Bay. Sweating now, I was walking uphill, fast, pushing my feet out in front of me recklessly, in a kind of tantrum, angry at the Wests, that awful woman shrieking and hitting a grown man for pouring water from the wrong side, and angry at the Captain for his mad terror, his visions of machete-wielding, brain-washed, Communist guerrillas come to rape his woman, pillage and burn his property, and perform obscenities on his old white body, and angry at the tourists whose prosperity and innocence protected them from knowing the reasons behind the obsequious questions and politeness of the "natives," and angry at the full-bellied black Jamaicans who ran the country, the corrupt bureaucrats and cops and petty officials who never took off their sunglasses, and angry too at the British-educated Jamaican intellectuals, white and black alike, who condescended to their own history . . . and then there was this new anger, anger at myself, a cold fury at the dreamy American who dealt with outrage by feigning illness, by politely excusing himself from its presence, who persisted in dealing in easy categories with the people he was living among, who saw Maroons, saw working-class Jamaican countrymen, saw shopkeepers, saw white autocrats, plutocrats and neocolonials, saw tourists and speculators, intellectuals and smugglers, saw petty thieves and obeah men, saw farmers and preachers, woodcarvers and prostitutes, saw Rastafarians and Christians and pagans, saw all those classes of people, and could see no further. The dreamy American had found himself, for the first time in his life, truly alone.

Prior to this, solitude had been abstract and something to admire, had even been a source of pride and something of a lived metaphor for certain of his philosophic beliefs. Oh to be sure, it had always been a painful thing, solitude, but in the past he had admired his pain. Now, for the first time, he was ashamed of it. It seemed a condition that, by his fear and his weakness, he had imposed on himself. Honest enough to admit his fear of the blacks, intelligent and sensitive enough to know that he could not know what it was like to be someone he feared, he was also too weak-willed not to curry the approval of people he loathed but did not fear. Up to now, he had avoided taking the moral position of love and hate; he had merely approved or disapproved, like some kind of judge sitting in comfortable isolation from the doings of men and women on earth. He had merely approved of the poor blacks, the Maroons, and the shop-keepers and small farmers of Anchovy; and he had merely disapproved of the whites, the wealthy plutocrats of Reading, the black functionaries, the innocent acquisitive tourists; and this was what had brought him to feel such a profound anger at his isolation.

Then, stepping over the crest of the ridge, where the bush seemed to fall away, I who was that man saw before me in the wash of moonlight, a boarded-up stuccoed house, deserted and fast becoming a ruin. It resembled my own house across the valley two miles away, with terraces and patios, an orange tile roof, paths and stony flower gardens, except that the jungle was taking it over. Vines and creepers clung to the walls and probed gutters, crevices and holes, splitting the doorframes and window cornices from the walls. Chunks of marl and limestone, worked loose and washed by several years' rain, had collected in heaps on the driveway and along the garden paths. A light breeze blew up from the sea, unimpeded all the way from Montego Bay below, seven or eight miles across jungle and tumbling hills and cliffs.

Slowly I made my way around the side of the house to the terrace that faced the sea, where there was an open, confident view of the glistening black Caribbean and, hugged by the hooked arm of land on the west, the clutch of lights that was Montego Bay. Off to my left on the same ridge perched the Church compound; around to my right the ridge drifted downhill to the broad coastal plain behind the bay; behind me, a few miles through the hummocky jungle, were the village of Anchovy and the narrow road that led one way down Seven Mile to Reading and the other inland across the Cockpit to Nyamkopong. Stepping across the broken terrace on the sea side of the deserted house—its owners with their cash and valuables doubtless in Canada or Miami, like the owners of my house—I walked to the edge, where a retaining wall dropped ten or twelve feet to the jungle below. And, thinking carefully, I decided to despise the Wests and the Churches and all the people who resembled them, and to love a people I might never understand and definitely would never become. Then I left the house, ruined and overlooking the sea, and walked quickly back in the darkness through the jungle to my own house, where my family silently turned in their beds and dreamed dreams of each other and me in our home in New Hampshire.

TUESDAY, JANUARY SIXTH, WAS A HOT, SUNSHINY DAY, AFTER several days of cool rain, and the dirt yards at Nyamkopong, the playing field outside the school, and the roads and pathways were drying out when I arrived with my family. Hundreds of cars, mostly battered and patched ten-year-old American sedans driven up from Kingston, lined both sides of the road from the Colonel's house all the way through town to the school, where on the field a wooden pole and rope merry-go-round had been constructed. A primitive machine that could, with little alteration, be used to grind wheat, it was powered by four muscular young men who, running in a circle around a vertical center shaft, pushed on the four arms of a pair of waist-high axes that had been lashed to it. The center shaft, its base in a socket dug into the ground, was topped with four longer axes from which four rope swings had been suspended. Babies and small children paid ten cents each to be swung for thirty or forty revolutions by this man-powered machine, the faces of the children alternately wide-eyed in delight and grim with fear of the height and speed of the spin.

It was midmorning when we arrived, and the town was a continuous throng of people and noise, food, rum, and the smell of burning ganja, reggae blasting from the Chinaman's sound system and the installation belonging to Terron's friend Rubber, next to which Terron himself had set up a stall to sell Ital food—Rastafarian cuisine of unsalted vegetables puréed in minced coconut and boiled rice from Guyana. At the stall a dozen or more dread-locked brethren had gathered to eat from bowls made from gourds. Behind the board counter the master of chat held court and reasoned with his religious brethren, while next to him his tall friend Rubber, stoned and sweet-faced, dropped one 45 after another onto the turn-table, the bass of his huge rented amplifier, rented from an East Indian grain dealer in Maggotty who'd invested some of his extra capital in high fidelity equipment to rent to other would-be capitalists like Rubber, turned up so loud it rattled one's rib cage when one passed the high bank of huge speakers. Rubber had placed the speakers strategically, or so he apparently thought, at the entrance to a dirt dance floor fenced in by sheets of cast-off roofing tin. His plan had been to charge admission for the use of the dance floor, but so far only six or eight teen-aged boys, probably friends of Rubber's and probably let in for nothing, were inside the fence, bopping and hopping alone to the music in corners of the yard, their faces lost behind the brilliant pressure of the music, their bodies swarming with the relentless beat, a beat that worked just as effectively on those who stood outside on the road and watched the crowd—teen-aged boys and girls looking for each other, card sharks and shell game con men, their game boards strapped to their shoulders and waists, looking through the crowd for players, mothers looking for their children, cool-eyed Rastas peering through the haze of their mysticism for "argument" and a spliff, fat daughters and sons up from

Kingston in their new clothes looking out for someone they knew in the old days who would admire and envy them, old men rum-drunk and full of quarrelsome talk sifting the crowd for alliances and opponents, a hip Levi-clad crew of technicians and cameramen from the public TV station in Kingston looking through eyes borrowed from New York and London for footage of Jamaicans to show to other Jamaicans, the ones still in Kingston and Montego Bay who happened to own TV sets, brown, East Indian, Chinese and white Jamaicans, mostly, some of whom were here in Nyamkopong today, dressed like their counterparts in Miami, short-sleeved, sun-glassed, curious, slightly embarrassed by the sweaty fervor of the crowd, its drunkenness, the motley colors and petty crime that seemed to thrive here as nowhere else, middle-class Jamaicans simultaneously pleased by and proud of the peculiarly Jamaican character of the crowd but hoping also to be regarded as separate and distinct from the crowd, so that, as they passed Terron's stall, for example, the men would point out the knot of brethren gathered there and would explain to their neat wives the peculiarity of the salt-free, porkless, often meatless diet, and the Rastafarians' awe of the coconut, which the brethren called dreadnut, as if strolling through a museum and explaining to their wives the meaning of the more esoteric pieces of sculpture.

But a museum was the last thing it resembled, this celebration of the birthday of Cudjoe the great Maroon chieftain. It was more like a medieval country fair than anything else, a midwinter rite designed to push the circle of time around again, like the rickety but effective merry-go-round up in the schoolyard, a device thousands of years old, man-made for the relief of man from the pressure of gravity and the brevity of childhood, a circle opposed to the straight, unbroken line of time.

It was a day of circles and spinning. Nobody could have been convinced to line up: people gathered in knots and clots and moved in spirals and wheels, dancing in Rubber's and the Chinaman's yards to the amplified reggae, boys and girls wheeling around each other in orbits that intersected and then interlocked with other orbits; and over at the schoolyard children played ancient circle games and chanted rhymes from seventeenth-century England and timeless Africa; and in the shops quartets of men faced each other across squares and slammed ivory dominoes onto the board between them while bystanders and kibitzers hovered behind and drank rum and made side bets; and beyond the schoolyard downhill a way and into the bush where there was a clearing around a tall cotton tree, a hundred or more of the villagers danced the old Maroon dances to the beating of the square goatskin gombay drums, a huge, thickening circle of human beings, their arms locked around one another, their feet and bodies moving up and down, backward and forward, in a rugged, mesmerizing version of the more stylized, individualistic dancers to the reggae up on the street.

At one point, after I had come to rest near the dancers at the cotton tree, I saw old Mr. Mann coming down the path from the schoolyard. He was dressed in a dark suit and broad, flowery necktie, his fedora squarely on his head, and under his arm he carried a thick ledger book. Walking carefully, picking his way over the rocky path and greeting everyone near him, he passed quickly into the crowd of dancers and then suddenly reappeared at the center, bobbing and moving in energetic, perfect time to the drums. Though I stood a way outside the circle of dancers, the old man spotted me and smiled broadly, causing many of the dancers to follow his gaze, some to scowl when they saw me, some to join him in his smile and then to turn intently back to the center of the circle.

My children were taking their turns at the merry-go-round up at the schoolyard, while their mother and aunt watched over and photographed them. Earlier, Terron had waved us into the circle of his brethren at the food stall and had passed spliffs around and then bowls of Ital kalaloo and rice, chanting Rastafarian neologism and apocryphal biblical verses into our astonished faces, whirling us faster and faster with the blend of sound, until we had spun away, waving promises of quick return. And now, as I gradually found myself being pulled into the huge, slowly rotating crowd of dancers by the cotton tree, I recalled Mr. Mann's story of Columbus and Sir Francis Drake and the two Elizabeths who were actually one, the Africans who were both slave and warrior, and I realized that I had misunderstood him completely: I had thought he was making history up. It hadn't occurred to me that he had been telling the truth.

And soon I was dancing too, for an old woman on one side of me and a fat man on the other had each slung an arm around me, and my arms had slipped around them, so that I too was facing the center where Mr. Mann danced, still clutching his ledger book, his hat still squarely on his head; but he was sweating now, we were all sweating, some with broad grins on their faces, some darkly scowling, some grimacing in deep passion, as here and there one of the dancers would shudder and fall, eyes rolled back, body rigid and trembling on the ground, while the people next to the fallen dancer would back away a few steps and keep on moving, with the drums filling our heads and chests, slowly banging our hearts around into time, the blood pumping in the same time past our ears and back down through our throats, sweeping through our bodies in swift circles of time, until it seemed there could be no end to this day, this hour, this second of awareness of the tree towering overhead, the sky spinning above the branches of the tree, the crowd moving like a spiral nebula toward a still center, where a smiling old man with a book in his hands nodded and danced in place, watching us watch him, as if the whole thing were his gift to us and his whole pleasure were the pleasure we took from him.

2

By the time I left Jamaica in mid-February, Terron Musgrave, the master of chat, had become my friend, and Mr. Mann had by then seemed to agree to become my teacher, though it was not yet clear to me who had elected him or what it was he had been elected to teach me. Perhaps he had merely agreed to become my friend and I had realized that for me to reciprocate, for me to become *his* friend, I would have to learn from him what I had not yet imagined. In any case, the old man now called me his son, though I still called him Mr. Mann, and when, a few days before leaving the island altogether, I left him and Nyamkopong for the last time, he told me to come back to Nyamkopong soon, alone, and stay with him in his house. You will see what you want to see, he said, with a broad smile.

Terron, who had practically taken up residence with me and my family at the Church compound in Anchovy following that January sixth, rode out to the airport with us, to wave us off, as the Jamaicans say. I'll come back in April, I promised him. Alone. And we'll travel to the other Maroon villages in the east. He agreed. I offered to pay him to accompany me, but he said he'd go with me anyhow. Paying him, he explained, was my business, not his.

My plan was to spend a week in Nyamkopong at Mr. Mann's home, and then to drive to the three other villages, Moore Town, Charles Town and Gordon Hall, in the mountains at the far end of the island. Terron was pleased with my plan, as he had never seen any of the other villages, and he knew of no one who had seen all four. He called them "the African cities."

I remember catching a glimpse of him on the "waving deck" of the terminal building as the plane taxied down the runway—he was in the middle of the crowd at the rail, a tiny man with a bulbous red, yellow and green tam on his head and a beard like Nebuchadnezzar's spreading from his cheeks and chin. Surrounded by Jamaicans and a few Americans and other whites who were waving furiously at the opaque windows of the huge jet, he stood with his thick arms folded across his chest, his refusal to wave seeming brilliant and dignified in contrast to the others' insistence on waving at what they could not see just so they themselves could be seen waving.

THE NEXT TIME I SAW HIM WAS WHEN I PASSED THROUGH customs in April, alone, returning as I had promised for three weeks of what he called "trampoosing." He was again in a crowd of excited Jamaicans and Americans and other whites waving happily at returning families and house guests, and again he was refusing to wave at what he could not see or call out to what could not hear him. When I drew near enough to touch, he gave me that old black-power handshake of his and said in his deep voice, One heart, one love, brother—a greeting I never tried to imitate without feeling foolish and vain and, therefore, after the first few attempts, gave it up. It was always that way for me with the Rastafarians. Their language was so directly an expression of their vision that, because I could not share the vision, I could never feel other than idiotic when trying to use their expressions and phrases myself. Speaking patois was different. It was the language spoken most comfortably and naturally by the people I was traveling among, and not to try to learn to speak it with them was a kind of rudeness. I don't know how my refusal to join the chant of Rasta talk was perceived by Terron and Rubber and the others I came to know and love, but I know that for me it was a simple act of respect.

Tossing my suitcase into the trunk of the rented Toyota sedan, a yellow, somewhat battered version of the car I had rented four months earlier, we quickly left the airport and wound our way out of Montego Bay, away from the exhaust fumes and harangue of the city, and were soon headed into Cockpit Country. The route from Montego Bay to Nyamkopong as far as the crossroads village of Mocho, which is in the high heart of the Cockpit, was different from the route I had regularly taken from my home in Anchovy throughout January and February. It was more dramatic and rose more swiftly from the coast, following more closely the British troop movements against the old Maroons from the docks of Montego Bay into the interior.

Once the road reached Welcome Hall, barely an hour's drive steadily uphill from the Bay, we were in the old Maroon territory, where they had fought the Second Maroon War in 1795 and 1796, the one the Maroons lost. Lost, that is, by the contingent that had waged it, the Maroons from around present-day Maroon Town in St. James. The people of Nyamkopong had refused to join their brothers in St. James, who had gone to war against the British not to escape slavery but because of flagrant violations of the treaty of 1738, and the split between the two groups, the chasm in their collective psyche, had come fully into the open then, and it had remained in the open all the way down to the present time. It was the gap between those Maroons who saw the Maroon people as a separate polity in Jamaica and those who wished to accommodate themselves with the larger, national entity by assimilating into it. It was the split between those who thought of themselves as Africans and those who thought of themselves as ex-slaves, between those who were grateful for the chance to wage war and those who were grateful for peace, between the rebels who saw their

rebellion, like their enslavement, as racially determined
and the bounty hunters who, after the treaty, eagerly
chased down the escaped slaves the British troops and
planters couldn't dig out of the bush themselves, between obeah and Christianity—and up close, it was the
split between the two old men in Nyamkopong, Mr.
Mann and Colonel Martin Luther Phelps.

That Second Maroon War had been disastrous for the
St. James Maroons. Deserted by their brethren in Nyamkopong and ignored by the Maroons in the east, they had
fallen into a hopeless quarrel with the British army and
soon had found themselves in chains aboard a ship bound
for Nova Scotia, shipped out a second time and this time
shipped, without irony, back to Africa, since in Canada
they had stubbornly refused to be treated except as prisoners of war. The white population in Nova Scotia wanted
no part of half a thousand black prisoners of war, wild
men and women and their children from the jungles of the
Caribbean, so the British gave up and dropped them off
at Sierra Leone in East Africa, where, at last, it appeared
that their persistence in believing themselves independent
of British law would not contaminate black men innocent
of that belief. It's an old British and, recalling the fate of
the Cherokee nation, American technique, and it usually
works.

After that, the Maroons still in Jamaica generally functioned as mercenaries, specialists in tracking down escaped slaves in the bush. In return, because their land
wasn't suitable for sugar cane cultivation, the British left
them alone, let them exist as if no national government in
London or Kingston controlled them, until recently, when
some of the Maroons' insistence on their immunity from
the Jamaican laws that prohibited the cultivation and sale
of ganja, a significant cash crop for the Maroons of
Nyamkopong especially, had again brought them into heated
and open conflict with outside authority. And with that
conflict had come the old split again. Colonel Phelps was a
friend of the police in nearby Maggotty, who, according to
the treaty, were forbidden to prosecute Maroons for any

crimes other than capital crimes. Whereas Mr. Mann, I learned from Terron, had spent a brief period in prison down in Spanish Town several years ago for helping load a small Cessna with seven bales of ganja. Half the Maroons believed that their relations with the government of Jamaica, since Jamaican independence as well as when it was under British rule, were defined by the treaty of 1738–1739; the other half believed strictly in power and hoped mainly to sustain their present untaxed relation to the government and were willing to do just about anything the government asked in return. Colonel Phelps represented this latter faction. Mr. Mann, who in fact had been Colonel himself when arrested for dealing in ganja, represented the former.

Perhaps not surprisingly, this split in the Maroons' history and sense of themselves had made itself known to me not in Jamaica but back in the States, at the Athenaeum in Boston where I read Dallas and Long and Edwards. Once a week I would drive down from New Hampshire to spend the day with the texts Carey Robinson had used to write his book. I read them not so much to learn what he had left out, which with regard strictly to the history of the Maroons wasn't a great deal, as to uncover the answers to questions his account and the present reality of the Maroons—insofar as I understood that reality—had raised in my mind. For instance, I wanted to know why Juan de Bolas, the first Maroon leader whose name entered the public record and therefore possibly the first Maroon leader of significance after the British had taken the island from the Spanish in 1655, had turned himself and the Maroons under his direct control over to the British and then had proceeded to help the British root out the remaining Maroons, the ones who had continued to enjoy in the mountains and the Cockpit the freedom they had won from slavery by having fought alongside Ysassi and the Spanish rear guard against the British takeover. After de Bolas and his men went over to the British, Ysassi had to flee the island for Cuba, leaving the remaining black guerrillas, those who hadn't gone over with de Bolas, to hide themselves in the mountains and Cockpit where they, and only they, could survive and even prosper. As indeed they did, not without occasionally descending to the coastal plains to plunder the now English plantations for ammunition, salt, and a few necessities and, in passing, free a few slaves too. And, of course, because they prospered up there in the trackless wilderness, like the feral hogs they had been named for and that they themselves hunted so successfully, they were able to give sanctuary to slaves who on their own had succeeded in escaping from the barbarous plantation system the British had designed for growing sugar. Their success meant to the British that they had to be exterminated.

But first they tried to talk the Maroons into coming down on their own, and to that end they advertised freedom under English law and settlement land anywhere on the island. But at that time freedom under English law meant conscription into the British armed forces for the duration of the present campaign against the remaining Maroons—this was the deal de Bolas had made for himself and two hundred of his men back in February 1660, when there were still Spanish to be fought: de Bolas, or Lubolo, his African name, had exchanged freedom under Maroon law for freedom under British law, black tribal law for white imperial law, communal property law for private property law. Juan Lubolo, however, was ambushed by the very Maroons he had agreed to lead the British against, after the threat of Ysassi's tattered remnant had been removed, and his body was hacked to pieces. Most of his two hundred followers swiftly returned to the Maroon brotherhood; the others denied they had ever been Maroons and joined the small number of "freedmen" in Montego Bay, Port Royal and Spanish Town, disappearing there quite as effectively as their brethren had disappeared into the bush.

Juan Lubolo's decision fascinated me, as did the great Cudjoe's reportedly submissive behavior, enthusiastically described by the later English historians, when in 1738–

1739 he finally agreed to peace terms with his adversary, Colonel John Guthrie. Though the treaty was quickly denounced by many of the plantation owners and politicians as an abject and humiliating surrender to the black savages, the document in effect put the Maroons under the proprietory control of the British government. Nevertheless it left them free men with their own land and laws, their own judiciary and penal code (except for capital crimes or crimes against non-Maroons), and their own elected local leaders. It was indeed a *peace* treaty, with no mention of surrender. Even so, Cudjoe had come out of his enclave and had prostrated himself before the man who had come suing for his peace, had groveled at the man's feet, and had begged for his personal forgiveness. Why did he do that? Didn't he have any idea of the magnitude of his accomplishment? Even Carey Robinson had paused over that one.

And a half century later, when the British had flagrantly violated Cudjoe's treaty by publicly flogging a pair of Maroons from St. James for stealing a pair of pigs, the outrage was felt only by the Maroons around Flagstaff and Maroon Town, then called Trelawney Town, while over in Nyamkopong they turned away and behaved themselves. The Second Maroon War had resulted from the British refusal to permit the Maroons to express their outrage, peaceably at first, then with increasing violence, divided the Cockpit Maroons in half. The half that had opposed the British, attempting thereby to enforce the treaty that gave them the rights to try and punish their own wrongdoers, were driven literally right off the map. The half that ignored British perfidy were allowed to live on as before, encouraged to act as mercenaries and bounty hunters called out regularly in times of crisis—something that occurred every time a slave made it as far as the bush—and were with equal regularity commended by the legislature for their courageous and steadfast service to the King of England. They even tracked down and slew Three-Fingered Jack, an early nineteenth-century escaped slave turned marauder in the hills behind Kingston, a man who stopped coaches on the road from Port Antonio and killed only white men, sparing women and children and all blacks, a terrorist whom the Maroons of Moore Town were proud to have tracked down and killed, so that afterward they carted his head and three-fingered right hand in a bucket of rum all the way to Spanish Town to present to the governor.

IN NEW ENGLAND, FROM FEBRUARY TO APRIL THAT YEAR, I spent a long dark afternoon every week in the Boston Athenaeum and most of my nights in my home in New Hampshire poking through the old accounts of these people, and I continually kept coming up against the division between those who complied with and seemed grateful for their "freedom" under British law and those who believed and insisted to the point of martyrdom that they were free to live only under Maroon law. From my great distance I could not see how, if they had not divided against themselves, they could have been compelled to accept violations of their treaty. It was their lack of unity, I then believed, that had made acceptance inevitable. And their apparent gratitude for British rule and old Cudjoe's abject behavior toward the man suing for peace with honor and their alacrity when called out to put down a growing slave insurrection in 1832 and, later on, the rebellion in Morant Bay and Lubolo's treachery and the tracking down of Three-Fingered Jack—that eagerness and gratitude, the pleasure they seemed to take from British pleasure, were beyond my comprehension.

I sat there in my armchair at home, surrounded by my books and pictures, Brahms on the stereo, my children sleeping peacefully upstairs in their bedrooms, the cold Yankee wind shoving against the house outside while inside a fire crackled in the fireplace and every now and then the furnace in the cellar kicked in; or in the first floor reading room of the Athenaeum on Thursday afternoons, I sat in another armchair in a bay window overlooking a seventeenth-century graveyard and the brick backsides of Georgian office buildings, with the rain dribbling down the glass outside while tea was being served inside and every once in a while a white-haired, gray-faced man in a dark blue cardigan sweater would cough lightly and apologize to the rest of us for the interruption: I sat there and read and did not understand what I was reading.

THE FAMILIAR APPROACH TO NYAMKOPONG, IF ONE WISHES to avoid risking damage to his car, is from the town of Maggotty across the broad Appleton sugar fields, then swiftly into the highlands, the humpbacked hills of the southwestern Cockpit region, from paved road to unpaved to a rutted trail that loops and climbs steadily away from the bright green flats around Maggotty, through the fistful of cabins called Whitehall, then into the Cockpit itself, dense green planes of land tipped at wild angles to the trail, lips of limestone pouting overhead and lopped off below, with careful terraces wedged into the steep slopes where a lone farmer in knee-high rubber boots shoves his spade into the red earth and prepares the ground for yams, Bermuda onions, corn, and Irish potatoes, the trail rising steadily, switchbacking away from Whitehall now, with a scattering of one-room, tin- or thatched-roof cottages alongside the trail or off a way in the bush, approachable only by meandering and nearly vertical footpaths where a broad-hipped barefoot woman with a five-gallon tin of water from the spring below balanced perfectly on her head ascends as if climbing the stone steps of a temple. Then, suddenly, we were entering the village, Terron and I, past the unfinished cinderblock church, the few dozen houses, and the clutch of shops where the people stood and stared at us, while children ran along behind the Toyota calling out my name instead of the color of my skin, until we reached the familiar blue false-front of Mr. Mann's house, where the pig still rooted in the yard and the chickens clucked and scratched by the door and the little spotted dog stood at the top of the steps and barked fiercely at our approach.

In a few seconds the old man appeared, squinting in the glare of the sun. Recognizing us, he hushed the dog and spread his arms to greet us. When he had placed wet kisses on both my cheeks, he hurried us inside the house, away from the sun. As always, he shouted at the boys to bring us some chairs, which they promptly did, and we sat down at the long table, where I presented him with a full quart of white rum and the bag of groceries I had bought in Maggotty and had carried with me from the car. From the States I had brought along a five-cell flashlight, the same type as that used by Captain West, and a bag of batteries, and these I presented to the old man.

When I asked for his wife, Devina, he hollered her name, and she quickly appeared, a scrawny brown-skinned woman who, though a shyly quiet woman, nonetheless had managed to obtain from me, every time I had come to the house during January and February, a five-dollar pledge for the Baptist church she attended. And once again, with barely a word, she presented me with a tattered yellow pledge card, which I dutifully signed and returned with a five-dollar bill. Then she swept up the bag of groceries and silently disappeared into the back of the house.

The front of the house was divided into two rooms and a central hallway, where we now sat. Mr. Mann slept in one of the rooms, and Devina, their daughter Priscilla and her baby boy, and the three other boys—Mr. Mann's grandsons by a daughter living in Kingston in a single room in Tivoli Gardens—all slept in the other. From the hallway a door led to the original daub-and-wattle structure, a chain of three tiny rooms, one leading off the other as in a railroad flat. One of Mr. Mann's sons, Jake, and his woman Greta slept in the first of the three; the second was empty because the floor had rotted away, exposing nothing but the muddy ground a few feet below where the chickens roosted at night and when it rained; in the third room Mr. Mann and his family had stashed, stacked, propped, and tossed all the items that either needed repairing or were supposed to be used for repairing those things: old doors, half sheets of corrugated iron, broken kegs, a fifty-pound bag of Portland cement that had gotten wet in the rain and had turned from powder to rock, chairs with one or more legs missing, broken picture frames, a bent bicycle wheel, a long two-by-four, a piece of chain. This part of the house was on short poles, like most of the older buildings in Nyamkopong, and was perched more or less squarely three feet or so off the rocky, tilting ground. Behind the house and a few feet from the back door was the kitchen shed where Devina was now building the fire to cook the large sea bass I had bought from a higgler in Maggotty when I had stopped to buy groceries. It was rare that one could buy relatively fresh fish this far from the coast, and the price had been high. Devina had grabbed the fish from the bag while she was still in the hallway and not yet through the door and had taken a swift approving look at it. Then, out back, she had quickly and deftly gutted, scaled and filleted it, saving the head and entrails for soup, and had set the fire in the waist-high stone firepit to blazing. There was no chimney, not even a smoke hole in the roof; smoke was allowed to drift around the cook and then gradually, unless a wind was blowing, out the open sides. Indeed, the whole affair was little more than a five-foot square, canted, tin roof on poles over a rough stone firepit with blackened pots and pans and a couple of gallon tins of water on the ground next to it.

For reasons I couldn't name at first, I had from the beginning preferred being in the back part of Mr. Mann's house or in the kitchen shed to sitting in the narrow hallway around the long table in front. Perhaps it was the cinderblock walls that put me off, their density and the way they closed us off from the light and color of the outdoors. In the back, holes in the walls let chinks of light fall erratically into the rooms, and the rough framing poles of the structure, cut and trimmed by machete a hundred years ago, somehow comforted me. Terron's

home was like this, even though he had built his barely
ten years ago, when his heavy woman had first gotten
pregnant—one room, two doors, a pair of tiny glassless
windows with drooping, leather-hinged shutters that he
drew closed at night. It was the type of building that
revealed instantly the method of its own construction
and the pleasure the act had given to the builder. Tilting,
haphazard, patched together from scraps and cast-offs,
constructed without level or square and with too few
salvaged nails, only a step or two from the size and
shape of cabins the Maroons had built for themselves up
here two hundred years ago, the building would have
bewildered and maybe offended my neighbors and the
men in my family back in New Hampshire. Nothing here
was square or, as my father liked to say, true. None of
the buildings, even though many of them were old enough
to have raised four or more generations with the same
name, looked like they could withstand a single rainy
season. Except for the cinderblock houses, of course.
My New Hampshire neighbors and my father and uncles
would have respected them, would have understood their
rational sturdiness, their geometry and physics, though
the colors, pink, orange, bright blue, would have seemed
a little loud.

Gradually, though, I had come to appreciate the pole-
frame, daub-and-wattle houses, and for better reasons
than how quaint they looked, how native. They were
cool, off the frequently wet and muddy ground, easy to
modify with a new window or door or addition on the
back, and they could be built with materials that grew or
lay in the ground right here in Nyamkopong. Cut the
mahoe or young cottonwood poles, lash them together
with sisal, gather local red mud and thatch and fill the
chinks and holes between the poles, mix up mortar from
crumbled limestone and spread a skin over the outside,
thatch the roof, and then with basic handtools split and
plane a few logs into boards for shutters and doors and,
if a pole floor is uncomfortable, for the floor. Build a
lean-to in back for the kitchen and, downhill twenty

yards away, a privy. And then carry a mattress on your head all the way from Maggotty, an old double mattress sold to you by a distant cousin for ten dollars. Pick up a stolen transistor radio from one of the teenaged boys who travel down to Montego Bay to sell ganja, and move in. Your woman will have her first baby there, and the three of you will sleep in the same bed. When she has her second baby, the four of you will sleep in the same bed. Then her third, and fourth, until finally there is no more room for you in the bed and no room in the house for a second bed, so you start sleeping elsewhere until you can scrape up the help and the few dollars necessary for building an additional room, where you'll make the four children sleep, and then your woman will have fifth baby and you and she and the new baby will sleep in the old bed in the original house. In later years, your oldest child, a woman now with her own child fathered in Kingston by a handsome eighteen-year-old boy who runs errands for a Chinese numbers man, will come home to Nyamkopong because the baby's father was shot in the head one night by the police outside a club in Trenchtown, and you will build a third room for her, her baby and the local young man who will move in with her, a strong young man who wants to go to the States and is continually scheming about how and who to bribe in Kingston so he can get on the lists and go up to Virginia and pick apples for six weeks and earn enough cash money to buy a Honda so he can get a job in Maggotty and break this terrible cycle. He doesn't want to be a subsistence farmer like you all his life and live in a tiny two- or three-room cabin with five or more kids, no electricity, no running water, no furniture except an old mattress or two, a transistor radio, and a few blackened pots, breaking his body around a spade and hoe on a half acre of red dirt growing yams and red beans and patches of corn with barely enough left over to sell for cash to buy rice so the kids won't go to sleep hungry.

The daub-and-wattle houses in the town told one story, but the cinderblock houses told another. Theirs was the

tale of the sudden but long-awaited arrival of an enormous amount of cash money, often from abroad, England, or the States, where your son has a job as a taxi
driver or your daughter is a housekeeper for a rich white
family in Scarsdale or Arlington. But sometimes the
money can't come from abroad, because your son has
five children, can't find a job and is living practically in
hiding in Roxbury on his American girl friend's welfare
check, or your daughter in London is dying of cirrhosis
of the liver, both of them promising for so many years
to send you money and never sending you more than
a five- or ten-dollar postal order at Christmas that you
have given up on them and imagine their life abroad,
new Mustang, hundred-dollar shoes, Polaroid cameras,
champagne, and long, graceful dives into the hotel swimming pool.

Grumbling about the ingratitude of children, you agree
to let the ganja boys use your land in the bush, land
painfully cleared, cut and burned over and tilled by hand
for generations, your crop visible only from the air or
after walking an old pathway through the dense bush for
an hour. So you risk it, you grow your yams and corn
and potatoes in patches where the sun gets through near
your house, one fourth of what you'd have grown on
your cleared field, and you let the ganja boys set out
their seeds, thin the shoots, nip the buds and bring their
crop to full, sun-warmed, mountain maturity by September, when they harvest it, ten- or twelve-hundred pound
bales of it, which they beg you to store for them in your
third room, unused now because your daughter and her
baby have gone down to Maggotty with her boy friend
on his new Honda where he's got himself a job cutting
cane on the Appleton estate. The ganja boys offer you a
quarter of the twelve bales, and you only have to hold it
inside your house, shuttered and nailed tight, safe from
the boys in town who otherwise would steal a few pounds
week after week to smoke and sell to tourists in Montego Bay for enough money to get drunk on and buy a
new shirt and, more importantly, safe too from the other

ganja boys in town, men, really, who have their own connections in the Bay and Kingston, who in turn have their connections in Miami and New York and thus can handle all twelve bales and make those others rich enough to buy a new Honda or maybe help their father build a new cinderblock house, and a man will surely steal for that and maybe even chop someone in the way with a machete. But by the same token, a man will risk being chopped for the chance to get that much cash money, a thousand dollars, maybe, so you agree, and you stack the bales one dark night into the tiny room, stack them to the roof, then nail the shutters and doors closed, until the ganja boys come back from Kingston with the deal made. And one night about an hour after midnight they show up at your door with a fat, one-eyed Chinaman wearing rings on all his fingers. You help carry the bales down through the cockpits to a trail near Whitehall where the Chinaman and a powerfully built black man have parked a lumber truck with a hollow load that's exactly hollow enough to secret away twelve bales of ganja. If the man is a reliable dealer, that is, one in the business for the long run, not trying it out for a stake to let him do something more ambitious, like eventually starting a restaurant and bar in Ocho Rios, then he will pay you and the ganja boys right there, the black man's flashlight on the bills as he counts them, all fifties, into your trembling hand. But if the man is only making this buy so he can work up enough cash to buy and then sell a case of handguns from the States, which in turn will give him the capital to go into the nightclub business, then the black man will turn out to have a gun, which he will use to hold you and the ganja boys back while his boss climbs into the truck and starts the engine. He'll join his boss, and they will drive away, leaving you and the ganja boys to hate each other forever.

MR. MANN INSISTED THAT I SLEEP IN HIS ROOM IN THE cinderblock part of his house, while he slept in a kind of anteroom tacked on behind it and not much larger than a closet. His own bedroom was dark and damp with a huge double bed in the center that took up nearly half the space in the room, the rest of the space cluttered with stacks of old books and heaps of clothes, plastic flowers in vases, broken plaster crucifixes, sea-shell ashtrays, souvenir pillows and plaques from Niagara Falls and Disneyworld, broken pieces of cut crystal, several portable radios and one console, tape recorders, and portable stereos, their batteries dead and silently corroding inside. The room smelled of kerosene and incense and musty books and clothes. But, proud of his chamber, the best in the house, Mr. Mann overrode my wishes to sleep elsewhere—preferably on the ground or the floor in my sleeping bag, mainly because I really did not want to take his room away from him—by convincing me with his persistence that it would insult him if I did not accept his hospitality. Reluctantly, then, I dropped my satchel and sleeping bag at the foot of the bed, and when I returned to the hallway I found that Terron had departed for his own dwelling.

For the first time since I had met him, I was alone with Mr. Mann. From the beginning, though I had not realized it until now, Terron had provided a link between us that had somehow comforted me. Even though Terron was what I had no choice, so it seemed, but to regard as a religious fanatic and lived in a manner even more foreign to me that did Mr. Mann, and though I often found myself concluding, almost against my will, that he was a slick country hustler exploiting my curious mix of American racist guilt and the hip intellectual's love of the esoteric, still and all he seemed to be able to anticipate me, to know my needs and questions and anxieties far more precisely than the old man did. In fact, it was his very ability to anticipate me and the comfort it provided that kept me coming back to the belief that he was conning me. As an old Puritan, I had to mistrust anything that gave me comfort. Mr. Mann, on the other hand, though speaking an English closer to mine than Terron's was, spoke in non sequiturs, metaphor, imagery of blood, race, and family, spoke of magic and poison, history and rite, in ways that sent me grasping irritably and anxiously after certainty. He was no Rastafarian; nothing as ideological or as consciously worked out as that theology would attract him in the slightest, and he persisted in misreading it, or so I thought. He seemed to regard it as no more than an understandable, even admirable, form of youthful rebellion against the corruption of their elders. His own theology was, to me, a bizarre mixture of evangelical Protestantism, West African polytheism and Caribbean obeah, itself an eighteenth- and nineteenth-century blend of the first two, and though I was determined, in an boringly academic way, to separate the strands and examine the conversions, he had no clear interest in helping me. He probably could not conceive of anyone even wanting to make those separations in the first place and would not have been an authentic believer if he had. Furthermore, the content of his belief, the terms, structure and relations of the parts, was itself drawn from the deepest parts of my mind as well, from my own dreams and visions, from my own longings and terrors, from the forgotten ten-thousand-year reign of my own ancestral imagination and beliefs, that of the old druids who thought stones were sacred and blood carried not disease but passions.

You will see what you want to see. I kept remembering Mr. Mann's words to me in February when I had left Nyamkopong to return to Anchovy and then the States. Terron had never said anything to me as threatening as that—he was too kind, or else too clever; I could never tell which. It never occurred to me that both could be true at once; I still thought of them as opposites. And now, once again, the old man smiled and noticing my sudden embarrassment and awkward self-consciousness at finding Terron gone and myself alone, alone in Jamaica, alone in Nyamkopong, alone in the home of Wendell O. Mann, Secretary of the Maroons of Nyamkopong, obeah man, tale teller, and historian of the remnant Maroon people in the Cockpit, he told me that I would see what I wanted to see—a promise and a rebuke, and also a description of how seeing takes place.

I WAS THE ONE WHO SUGGESTED IT, THAT WE CALL ON COLO-nel Phelps as a courtesy. Though I knew the Colonel was quite aware of my presence in the village, still I felt I should honor his office by walking over there to visit him, and since Mr. Mann was my host and, as I then thought, was also Colonel Phelps' main cabinet member and, therefore, his friend as well, it seemed appropriate that we go together.

Mr. Mann's response surprised me. He lapsed into patois and seemed to be furious, referring to himself as the Monkey Judge and Colonel Phelps as one of the monkeys. The jungle's full of monkeys claiming to be human beings, he said crossly, and so there has to be a Monkey Judge, to keep things straight.

But then, as suddenly, he calmed and put his arm around my shoulder. He would go with me, he said smiling, and I would see what was the difference between the monkey and the Monkey Judge. If he didn't go with me, I might be fooled, because monkeys are clever people and sometimes can put on a decent show of imitating human beings, especially to a human being like me, who was a stranger and who therefore did not know the ways a monkey could fool a person. You can do two things with a stranger, he said. You can teach him or you can fool him, but because he's a stranger he won't be able to know the difference. Then he laughed and slapped me on the back and shoved me out the door ahead of him into the glare of the afternoon sun.

COLONEL PHELPS WAS SEATED ON HIS PORCH AS IF EXPECTING us, and he leaped to his feet when he saw us coming down the road from Mr. Mann's end of the village. I saw him shout something over his shoulder into the house, presumably to his sour-faced wife; then he stepped away from the house and came to the side of the road to greet us. Except that he greeted only me and ignored the old man beside me.

He shook my hand fervently and welcomed me back to Nyamkopong. He recalled that he had last seen me at the January sixth celebration, though he knew I had been back up to the village numerous times afterward to visit my friends, as he called Mr. Mann and Terron and Rubber and a few others among the Rasta brethren with whom I had become friendly at that time. The way he said the word *friends,* as if in italics, revealed his attitude toward them. Gradually during those weeks in January and February I had become aware that the village, with regard to its attitude toward the Rastafarians among them, was divided into two camps—those who believed the brethren to be religious people and those who believed they were thieves. Neither category quite excluded the other, for what poor Jamaican was not religious and what poor Jamaican, under certain circumstances, was not a thief? It was merely a question of which of the two activities would be used to characterize a person. Colonel Phelps and the schoolteacher, a humorless man named Dunne, and certain of the more advantaged townspeople—advantaged frequently because their children had emigrated, had decent jobs and sent money back—regarded the Rastas as ganja-smoking thieves and general troublemakers. On the other hand, Mr. Mann, a surprisingly large number of the older mothers, and most of the children in town thought of the brethren as disciplined, meditative and, in terms of their view of the society around them, wise. That they grew and sold ganja, dealt in stolen merchandise, and even when possible stole a camera from a tourist's parked car outside Doctor's Cave in Montego Bay—how could that offend anyone living in a town where the Colonel was bribed by the police who were in turn bribed by the dealers who as often as not stole the ganja plants grown by the Rastafarians themselves?

I had heard it said a hundred times or more, usually

with a sneer, that the police were forbidden by the treaty to come onto Maroon land without the permission of the Colonel, but even so, every now and then a green Land Cruiser stuffed with beefy cops from Maggotty would suddenly appear outside someone's hut, and a dreadlocked youth or two would be dragged out, beaten and tossed into the car like sacks of yams and taken away. Later someone would come back from a week in Kingston with the rumor that the youths were in Up Park Camp, two to five years, for possession, manufacture and sale of ganja. Then once again everyone would shake his dreadlocked head and note that the treaty was supposed to forbid precisely that kind of intrusion. And it was always the Colonel who was blamed.

I agreed with their interpretation of their treaty, but I also knew how impossible it would have been for the Colonel to enforce the treaty. These occasional, highly visible, random-seeming police raids were the compromise that had been worked out all over the island between police control and local, tribal autonomy, and the young Rastas were the sacrifices that made it work. That the Colonel personally profited from the compromise was as obvious as the new pink paint job on his bungalow; that he may have worked out the only realistic solution to the conflict between outside control and ancient tradition, however, was not so obvious. Even here in Nyamkopong that tradition of local rule was too weak, the numbers of believers in its superiority to what the government in Kingston offered too few, and the country itself too small for the treaty between an agent of the English king and a band of Ashanti warriors to be more than a tattered reminder of a brave past. It was like more than a souvenir, I thought. The descendants of those old Ashantis were now Jamaican nationals, and despite their differences from the average rural Jamaican, despite their memories of the African dances, the Ananci tales, the old herbal medicines, their myths, and their food, they were now part of a modern political unity and would have to be ruled by the assumptions that made the unity a concrete reality. The degree to which Michael Manley's government succeeded in instituting a public education system, modern roads, national health care, and regular democratic elections of legislators with all the party political organizing that meant, regardless of the persistent inefficiency and corruption in these institutions, was the degree to which the Maroons' treaty became a quiet, sentimentalized symbol of early resistance to slavery and colonialism. And because the government was officially in line with that resistance, was still trying to overcome the effects of those old and evil systems, it was itself actively absorbing their symbols for its own use. For this reason, Nonny the Warrior Mother of the Maroons had been made a national hero, as had Paul Bogle, the black insurrectionist who had been hunted down by the very Maroons whose grandparents under Nonny had fought Bogle's same fight a hundred years earlier. The Maroons were being swallowed by the nation, hard edges, inconsistencies, contradictions and all, the Colonel's allowing the police to make occasional shows of force to keep the people of Nyamkopong from forgetting their proper role in society was for the Maroons a holding action, a way for them to hold onto their few remaining distinctions and privileges a little longer. They still owned their land communally and passed it on to one another, not by title but by use, which made it practically impossible for the government to tax their thousand acres of arable land; and they still enjoyed relative freedom of religion, which meant that the outlawed obeah practices and pocomania could flourish more or less openly here as nowhere else on the island, subject only to the disapproval of the orthodox Christians in town and not, as elsewhere in Jamaica, to the randomly enforced disapproval of the law.

With Mr. Mann on one side of me and Colonel Phelps on the other, the three of us in folding aluminum-and-plastic beach chairs in the shade of the front porch, the Colonel's wife silently placed a bottle of rum and three glasses and an aqua-colored plastic pitcher of water in front of us. Neither the Colonel nor his wife had spoken to Mr. Mann or acknowledged his presence in any way. It was as if I had come alone to call on the Colonel. He asked me the purpose of my visit to Nyamkopong this time, and I told him that it was to see my friend Mr. Mann here, with a nod to the old man sitting in dignified silence on my right. I was also here, I added, to come to a better understanding of how the Maroons lived and to visit the three other Maroon villages in Jamaica, Moore Town, Charles Town, and Gordon Hall. I said that I would be spending a week here in Nyamkopong with Mr. Mann and then would be traveling for another two weeks to the eastern end of the island with my good friend Terron Musgrave.

Ah yes, Terron Musgrave, the Colonel replied. The Rastaman is your friend. Then he asked me if I were a Christian.

It came too fast for me to have an answer ready so I told him the truth—I stammered, Yes, I said, then, No. Finally I gave him my history, as if that would answer the question, telling him that I'd been raised as a Presbyterian Christian but that I no longer practiced the religion.

What religion do you practice now? he asked. His wife had come out from the tiny cluttered living room behind us and now stood next to her husband, the two of them leaning intently forward to catch my answer.

I couldn't understand this. Why was my religion suddenly of such importance? I had thought the big questions had to do with economics and race. Not religion. I looked to Mr. Mann, as if for help, but he seemed not to be listening and was gazing dreamily toward the road, a light smile on his crisp mouth, his lizard-lidded eyes half closed and his gnarled hands laced together like sleeping snakes in his lap. In contrast, Colonel Phelps' hands were in fists on his knees, and his scrawny face was pushed forward toward me as if I were a long way off and he could barely make me out.

Finally, I lied. When I practice a religion, it's the Presbyterian one, I said. I go to the Presbyterian church in my home town, I added.

Ah! the Colonel exclaimed, and he relaxed back into his seat. His wife almost smiled, turned, and returned to the living room, where she took up her seat by the open window to continue auditing our conversation.

Smiling broadly now, the Colonel placed his hand on my forearm and said that perhaps on Sunday I would like to attend church with him and his family, for they too were Presbyterians and regularly attended the small, white church here in town. His wife sang in the choir, and they had an excellent, well-educated minister who lived in a large house in Whitehall and came all the way up to Nyamkopong every Sunday in his car. A new Chevrolet Impala, he added with admiration.

Today is Monday, and next Sunday I'll be leaving early, I said. But maybe sometime in the future I'll be able to hear your minister preach. Then I made my move to leave, stood, and shook the Colonel's hand, nodding good-bye to the wife's grim face on the other side of the window sill.

Perhaps, because you're a Presbyterian yourself, the Colonel said, you'd like to sign one of our pledge cards. We're trying to raise money for a new chapel bell. And he handed me one of the small yellowish cards that Mr. Mann's wife was always pushing at me.

Yes, indeed, thought I, and help the preacher pay for his Impala and big house in Whitehall. I took the card, pledged five dollars, signed it and returned it with a bill to the Colonel, who seemed extremely pleased and flashed a look at his wife, as if he'd just won a bet with her.

Mr. Mann was already at the roadside, waiting for me. Wendell! the Colonel called to him, as if buoyed by his success with me. You recall our conversation about the treaty a few months back, don't you?

I do.

The Colonel smiled at me and graciously, in a loud voice so Mr. Mann could hear, explained that their

M.P., the Honorable John Bulkley, had been up to Nyamkopong last January sixth and had requested the copy of the treaty from him so he could take it back to Kingston and have it copied down there by machine. The Secretary of State, Mr. Mann, had the treaty in his possession, although the King of England also had a copy, and Mr. Bulkley had thought a new copy ought to be made very soon, as the document was old and could be lost or destroyed.

I am the Secretary for the Maroons of Nyamkopong! Mr. Mann shouted at the Colonel. And since the time of Cudjoe the Lion the treaty has been entrusted to the Secretary for the Maroons of Nyamkopong! They will have to kill me if they want to take the treaty down to Kingston or to anywhere else! And *you*, he said to the Colonel, are a *girl* if you believe that monkey of a Labour man Bulkley is just going to copy the treaty and then return it to us! If he wants it copied, let him send a copier to my house and I'll read it out to him, word for word.

Is that the way it is? the Colonel asked, his voice shaking with anger.

That's the way it is! Then the old man took off down the road at a trot. I hurriedly thanked the Colonel for his hospitality, nodded good-bye again to the wife, and ran to catch up.

IT STRIKES ME AS ODD THAT IN THIS ACCOUNT I HAVE HAD difficulty in referring to my friend as Mann, the name most of the people of Nyamkopong used in speaking of him. Again and again, I have set myself here to refer to him as Mann, and instead I write Mr. Mann. Thinking about it, though, I realize that back in Nyamkopong, whenever I referred to Mr. Mann in conversation with someone else, Terron, Rubber or the other Rastas or the schoolteacher Dunne or even Colonel Phelps, I called him mister, even though they themselves would call him Mann. Whether it was because of my respect for him, which only increased as my familiarity increased, or because of some deep unconscious awareness of our difference and my need to preserve that difference, I can't say. Nevertheless, I did not feel comfortable calling him Mann, even to his face and at his generous insistence, nor do I here, in this private a context, feel comfortable until I have placed the word mister before his name.

The course of my week in his house went swiftly. I saw less and less of Terron each day, as he had domestic business to attend to and was planting ganja in the bush with Rubber, who, to guard the seeds and plot of ground they were using, was camped out beside the furrows, sleeping under a thatch lean-to and spending his nights, according to Terron, in meditation. Terron would not take me into the bush to see their secret garden because he said that I would be observed going there and then people would know where it was, and then, when the crop was ready to be harvested, someone would steal it.

How can someone steal your ganja if one of you is out there guarding it twenty-four hours a day? I asked.

He looked at me as if I were a child, then patiently explained how, with one stroke of his machete, a man could chop off your head, and since your friends wouldn't know who had done it, and thus would not be able to avenge your death by chopping off the head of your murderer, he would be free to take all your ganja and sell it in Montego Bay. When later he showed up with new clothes and a Honda, he could say he had got the money for shooting a man in Kingston and no one would know if he were telling the truth or not.

Why bother to guard it at all then?

The birds. Birds and snakes, he said. They love the seeds.

One night I asked Terron if he had ever killed a man. No, he said, but it was as if he were saying that he'd never owned a silk shirt. He simply hadn't had the opportunity or the need.

Terron's cousin, a Rasta named Juke, claimed to have

killed a man once. In Kingston, for fifty dollars. Another man had been in line for the murdered man's job and he had given Juke a gun and fifty dollars and Juke had shot the man in the forehead one night outside a warehouse where the man had been lured by a promise of a pound of good Maroon ganja.

What kind of job was it? I asked the slender, sweet-faced, lion-locked man.

A driver of a garbage truck, he thought, but he wasn't sure. Something like that.

Another man I asked, a Rasta named Bongo Smith, pronounced Simit, said that once when he was younger he'd killed two men. Sodomites, he called them, and they had gotten drunk and tried to rape him, so he had killed them with his knife, the same one he carried even today.

Terron grunted. Sodomites *should* be killed, he said in a low voice.

We were sitting in a group of five—Terron, Juke, Simit, a fourth Rasta, a youth named Benjie, and me—squatting or lying in darkness on the ground around a small fire outside a dilapidated shanty called the House of Dread. It was a crash pad for the itinerant and otherwise homeless Rastas in town, and the walls outside and inside were covered with red, gold and green slogans and rough drawings of lion heads and Stars of David. The slogans were an odd mixture of the political and spiritual: CIA OUT! and ALL HAIL the ZION LION! MAROONS UNDER MANNERS! and BABYLON MUST FALL! As we talked the firelight flicked yellow and orange sheets of light across their faces, a quiet, peaceful exchange of memories between young men under starlight after having shared a meal and now a smoke.

Benjie, I said to the sixteen- or seventeen-year-old boy across from me. Have you ever killed anyone? His skin was a shade lighter than the others' and his face had refused so far to grow a beard, though the locks on his head were thick and long for one so young and hung over his shoulders in ropes. He was wearing jeans and a green T-shirt two sizes too large for him with the words GANJA OIL CO. emblazoned in white across the front, the kind of shirt American teen-agers liked to buy in the tourist shops in Montego Bay and wear at home to their parties in the pine-paneled basements of their parents' suburban homes.

Slowly the boy unfolded his crossed legs, got up, and walked around the circle to me. Then he suddenly lifted his loose T-shirt and revealed the dull black handle of a .38 snub-nosed pistol stuck in his beltless pants. Grinning, genuinely happy at the thought, he said that soon, as soon as he got some bullets, he was going to kill a man.

Why? I asked.

Nobody needs to know but I-and-I, the boy said, and I-and-I know. Or perhaps he said, I-and-I knows. I couldn't tell.

Has Mr. Mann ever killed anyone? I asked the group, directing my face toward Terron, however, more than to the others.

They started to laugh. *That* one, old Mann! A dangerous scientist, that one, they said, laughing.

Has he Terron? I persisted.

Some say yes, some say no, he answered. But no one could say for sure except Mann himself, and he's too sly for that. He likes it the way it is, with some saying yes and some saying no. He may not even know himself, Terron added. It's the obi that does the killing. And Jah. If Mann started claiming he was the one who did the killing, he'd lose all his powers. Also, the police would come and put him in jail, because obeah is illegal, he reminded me. Just like ganja, he said, grinning and reaching for the spliff in Juke's drooping fingers.

THERE WERE TWO CARS IN THE TOWN OF NYAMKOPONG, a pickup truck owned by the Chinaman who operated the sound system and an old Ford van that was owned and operated as a private bus by a cousin of the Colonel's, a man in his fifties who had spent twenty years working in

England as a restaurant dishwasher, saving the money to come back and buy the used van. My rented Toyota made, for the week's duration, a third car in town, and since I did not charge anything for the ride, the car was stuffed with people whenever I drove it anywhere. I limited myself to two rides a day, to Maggotty in the morning and to the Appleton cane fields in the afternoon. Down there alongside the narrow road the Black River looped lazily through thousands of acres of flat, rich land, providing at the bends numerous swimming holes not far from the road that could be used for bathing, if only one could get there.

In the mornings, the car was jammed with women and the sick and elderly, the women to shop in Maggotty for cloth, a pair of shoes, a pan, things they couldn't grow or make or buy in one of the three small shops in Nyamkopong, and the sick and elderly to visit the doctor there. I couldn't wait for them to go through the daylong process of sitting on benches outside the doctor's office before he would examine them, and their return trip had to be made with the Colonel's cousin in the Ford van, for which they paid seventy-five cents apiece. Still, the seventy-five cents they saved by riding in with me apparently was worth the discomfort of riding with twelve or fifteen others crammed into a five-passenger sedan for fifteen miles over a potholed road in the heat. After making the trip once, my second day in Nyamkopong, to buy tobacco for Mr. Mann and tinned milk for Devina, I realized its worth and made it every day after that, regardless of my own needs.

The late-afternoon drive was usually in the company of a half dozen sweating men and a half dozen more dirtcaked boys, for the pleasure of bathing in the Black River. We would fill the car up in front of Mr. Mann's house— Terron, Juke, three or four more young men, all shirtless, sweating from a day's work on their crops or houses, the most ancient types of labor and the most ancient types of sweat and dirt—and then we would grab any of the small boys in the neighborhood we could find and fit in, and then off we'd go, chanting Rasta hymns of praise to cleanliness, water, the earth, and children, all the way down the long hills to Whitehall on to the black fertile plain outside Maggotty that was owned by the Appleton Estates, where cane for rum grew in perfect green ease and where the nearest running water flowed.

The Rastas cursed the rum cane and praised the water. We splashed and played in the river a few yards off the road, shouting at one another, teasing and making up stories of water monsters to frighten the little boys, then grabbing them and yanking them screaming into the dark, cool water, where we'd calm their fears with rough-house play, tossing them like medicine balls from one man to another, until the fathers decided to hold and lather up the beautiful bodies of their sons, and the rest of us, without sons, washed the boys who had no fathers, and then set them on the bank to shiver and dry while we washed ourselves.

In the distance the minty green plain quickly lifted to the hills around Whitehall and then lifted again to the cockpits and Nyamkopong, where the sun was setting, slashing the darkening sky with orange and lavender streaks, purpling the trees and macca bushes that covered the slopes, until it was almost dark where we stood on the bank of the river, naked, cooled, drying our bodies with scraps of cloth and making plans for the future, for the coming night or for the weekend, or for the next year, and sometimes for old age and sometimes for eternity.

The morning trips to Maggotty usually took half the day, an hour into town and an hour back to Nyamkopong, and two or more hours dropping off the weak, the sickly and the wounded at the doctor's office, a neat, white bungalow beside the road with a long porch in front that served as a waiting room, and then loading and unloading the sleek-skinned, powerfully built young mothers at the dry goods store, most of whom, unlike Terron's first woman, were too heavy, all of whom were silent all the way to town and all the way back. The sick ones and the elderly men and women chattered to each other and now and then to me, but the difficulty I had in understanding their patois usually closed off possibilities of our actually conversing with each other. The younger women, though, did not bother even to try, nor did they speak to each other in my presence, so that once I had left the others at the doctor's office, the car always filled with an embarrassing silence that made me eager to be alone and doubtless made them eager to be rid of me as well.

The ride back was not quite so difficult. We would have replaced our invalids with people trying to get up to Nyamkopong, teen-aged boys, usually, who had spent the night in or around Maggotty, riders who otherwise would have gone with the Colonel's cousin, and they and my shoppers would be able and willing to talk to one another. Also, the women would have bought a few things that the others wanted to see and discuss. And, of course, having been to town, there was news to exchange: the death of a distant relation, the birth of another, the arrest of a third.

My mornings, then, were taken up wholly with the trek to Maggotty; and an hour and a half or more of my late afternoons were spent in transit and bathing in the Black River. The rest of the day I spent at work either helping Mr. Mann at his house or Terron at his, gathering and breaking up wood for the kitchen fires, digging yams, slaughtering a goat, and so on—household chores, and a different project every day. I was about as helpful as a ten-year-old boy, maybe less so, except that I was not so easily bored and would not look so diligently for ways to escape the tedium. Because to me the work was not tedious at all. Resources were so woefully thin— tools, materials, skilled labor—that nothing more ambitious than the construction of an outhouse was attempted, and even that, after a single afternoon's work, had to be abandoned until more lumber became available.

At first I had thought, My God, these people never *finish* anything! And they won't work at anything for longer than three or four hours at a time before leaving it and going on to something else. But gradually I began to see that the absence of materials, tools, and skills demanded that they scale everything down and plan only on being able to work for the few hours available to them before they reached the end of their resources and had to give it up. Consequently the town was filled with incompleteness—half-built outhouses and roofless additions, unpainted churches, dance floors with the tin roof only partially raised, plots of ground half cleared and swiftly growing back to jungle again, bicycles half put together, motorcycles lying one wheeled on their sides behind cabins and shops, diesel generators with gears, bolts, belts, and wiring lying in piles next to the casing, stacks of cinderblocks without mortar or sand, pyramids of sand and a bag or two of mortar with no cinderblocks, a chain saw without a chain, a fence already falling down at one end before the other had been put up.

That this inability to finish anything begun did not keep them from beginning anything at all amazed me. Their persistence in starting a job that could never be completed, or, if completed, done right, was totally foreign to me, made me think of myself in comparison as spoiled and childishly sullen: if I can't get what I want exactly when I want it, then I don't want anything at all. For I knew that in similar circumstances I would fall into despair and resentment and would begin to build or repair nothing at all. Let it all rot and fall down; let the jungle take it; let the wind and rain pull it to the ground and wash it into the gully.

The difference, of course, was that they had learned something hundreds of years ago that I, the descendant of an incomparably more advantaged people, had never been forced to learn. They had learned how to survive. Survival, to me, was something one took for granted, and therefore it was more than likely that, placed in similar circumstances, I would not survive. I would become the sour, scowling man who walked with his eyes on the ground, the pessimist who went around prophesying self-fulfilling disaster and failure; I would be the

suicidal one who would want to take others down with
him. There was no room in my culture for the kind of
optimism that preserved them in theirs, and there seemed
to be no room in their culture for the kind of rigor and
thoroughness, the insistence on symmetry, that I believed preserved me in mine.

TERRON ENJOYED POINTING OUT AND NAMING THE PLANTS,
herbs, fruits and vegetables that grew in the Cockpit,
sinkle bible, nightsage and periwinkle, rose apple, hog
plum and ackee, the jeggeh bush, the jack-in-the-bush,
and the cold bush. Often we had to walk through the
cockpits along narrow, usually ridge-running paths to
get from one house to another, as there was always a
back way that only people afoot single file or a donkey
could traverse, and on these walks the master of chat
would name the things of the world that we passed—
blue mahoe trees, the physic nut tree that bleeds red if
you cut it on Good Friday, the Spanish elm, pronounced
panchalon, and the poisonous cow-itch, burnwood, burn-
eye and maiden plum. We walked out to visit a cousin
who owed Terron a few dollars and on another day
chased down an uncle who had promised tomato seeds,
an aunt who had a chicken for the pot, a friend who had
borrowed a spade. And along the way we inevitably got
stopped for a visit with one or another of Terron's or
Mr. Mann's relations, for the old man frequently joined
us when our travels weren't taking us more than a half
mile from his home. At each house we would be welcomed warmly and offered a cold drink of water or, if
the people were eating their meal, a plate of rice and
pork, which of course Terron refused because it had not
been prepared in the Rastafarian manner. And at each
home, if Mr. Mann was with us, the subject of the treaty
came up, as if it were on everyone's mind and the
people had been chatting about it just as we arrived.

The Colonel wants you to give the treaty up to him so
he can turn it over to the government, was how they put
it, and Mr. Mann would immediately deliver a jeremiad

against the Maroons who were selling out their own people. The Colonel he called a Judas, and everyone nodded in agreement. If those people want to copy the treaty, he said repeatedly, they'll have to come to my house with their pens and paper and I'll read it out to them word by word. This always seemed to leave his hosts awed. That the old man could actually do that, read the treaty out word by word, was awesome to them.

I was beginning to understand the situation better now; or I thought I did. It was the same old division, between those Maroons who for a mix of reasons would pull the community out into the larger world and those who, for a different mix of reasons, would pull it in and back to the smaller world, the practical accommodators versus the impractical purists. And, as usual, the accommodators tended to justify their actions and desires by pointing to their purity, and the purists by pointing to their practicality. Colonel Phelps' party argued that, unless the treaty were turned over to the government in the person of their Member of Parliament, the Honorable Mr. Bulkley, the Maroon people would not receive the honors and privileges from that government that were due them, for the government and the people of Jamaica would not be able to see the actual document signed "in blood" between the great Cudjoe and the King of England and therefore would not believe that such a document existed. On the other hand, Mr. Mann and his party argued that once they let go of the thing itself, the treaty, the government would destroy it and claim that it had never existed in the first place and therefore all the honors and privileges that were owed to the Maroons need not be honored or provided. The Maroons would henceforth be like every other Jamaican, controlled by the outside police, paying taxes on their land, told what to grow on their land and how much to sell it for.

Then the heart of Jamaica will cease to beat, Mr. Mann warned us. And though he had not said it, I realized now that the ledger book he carried with him whenever he left the house contained the treaty, for when, in ending these talks in the bush with his and Terron's friends and relations, he intoned that the heart of Jamaica would cease to beat, he tapped the hard, pale green cover of the ledger in precise time to his words, as if it were indeed the very heart he spoke of.

EARLY ONE MORNING, TOWARD THE END OF MY STAY, TERRON appeared at the door of Mr. Mann's room where I slept. Mr. Mann and the rest of the family were still sleeping throughout the house, and evidently Terron had been sufficiently silent in his approach and entry to the house to avoid waking Spot, the dog that barked whenever anyone, friend or foe, entered the yard.

Though he said nothing to wake me, I was immediately aware of his presence, or so it seemed, for I blinked awake from a dream of New Hampshire winter and found myself staring at Terron's horse face at the door. As always, he looked bright and cheerful, despite the fact that he, Mr. Mann, and I had stayed up till long hours after midnight "exchanging views" on the state of the universe. In addition, prior to that Mr. Mann and I had played a half dozen seven-game matches of dominoes in one of the shops up on the road, an activity that demanded from me total concentration and careful abstinence from the fiery rum that the other players consumed at the same rate as I drank off Dragons stouts. I had to play well, for I was Mr. Mann's partner, his ringer who drew the others into the game—for who could believe that Mr. Mann could win more than a single lucky seven with an American for a partner? It was a pleasure for me to play well in these fiercely competitive matches, where much more male pride was at stake than the rounds of drinks we bet, and also a responsibility: I did not want the old man's ruse to fail. And it rarely did. Every night during that week we played dominoes for two or three hours against all comers, and every night we came away cheerful winners, leaving the stung losers behind to wonder if Mr. Mann's abilities as a player had suddenly improved or if I was in fact as good as the results indicated. I doubted both conclusions. Dominoes, the way West Indians play the game, is like an Arabic form of bridge, and a superior partner who understands precisely how his weaker partner will play can often beat a pair of players who separately are more skilled than either but who do not know as precisely how the other will play in a given situation. Mr. Mann understood fully my ignorance of the finer aspects of the game and how it governed my moves better than any of our opponents knew how his partner's skill would govern his play. To all but Mr. Mann I was the unpredictable player, and I was unpredictable even to myself. Therefore, despite my pride in my play, I was usually as surprised by our victory as our opponents were dismayed by their loss.

Last night, after a particularly satisfying bout against two slick and silent middle-aged players who had come to the shop all the way from Whitehall strictly for the purpose of humbling Mr. Mann and his American friend, Terron had dropped by the shop, and the three of us had left together to sit on Mr. Mann's stoop. While Mr. Mann and I sipped on rum and Terron worked his way through three or four spliffs, we each managed to give our respective views on how and where God enters into human history. Terron cited the life and prophecies of Marcus Garvey and the transcendent reality of Emperor Haile Selassie, Mr. Mann cited Jesus, Nonny, Cudjoe, and "science." That left me at the end, as the moon drifted overhead in pieces behind scraps of silvered clouds and the palm trees clattered in the breeze, to confess that I did not believe God entered human history, that we were not worth His trouble, but that sometimes human beings managed to step outside history, to lift themselves up and out of it to another plane of reality, and as "proof" I had cited the life and prophecies of Marcus Garvey, the transcendent reality of Emperor Haile Selassie, Jesus, Nonny, Cudjoe, and "science."

Mr. Mann and I were fairly drunk by then, and Terron may even have been stoned, though I was never able to tell; his behavior altered so little and so seldom and always for reasons I couldn't identify. The three of us had headed then for our respective beds—Terron to the bed he shared with his woman and four children, me to Mr. Mann's own wide bed, which he continued to insist I use alone, and he to a narrow cot in that closet-sized section of the old house adjacent to where I slept. Somberly, he bade me good night and, walking like a church deacon through his own cluttered room, he passed through the door at the back of it that led to his temporary quarters. I blew out the kerosene lantern and crawled under the sheet. After listening for a moment or two to the old man's clumping about behind me, I heard him begin to pray, in slow, careful English. Now I lay me down to sleep, I pray the Lord my soul to keep. If I should die before I wake, I pray the Lord my soul to take. Amen. Then coughing, harumphing, and the sounds of his tossing himself into his bed. And then deep, peaceful snores.

Now, in the misty golden light of dawn, with the sound of a rooster crowing and the smell of a new wood fire starting up somewhere nearby, I was hung over and tired. Only a day or two remained of my stay in Nyamkopong, and though I was daily growing more comfortable there, less afraid of the people I was surrounded by, I was also daily growing more fatigued by the effort of discovering myself in my reactions to this foreign environment, this constant Other that made my own language in my own mouth sound foreign to me, that made the whiteness of my skin appear strange and unhealthy and that made my thoughts and ideas seem bizarrely overstructured and symmetrical. The longer I stayed here, the more aware I was of difference, which in turn kept bringing me back to me as the exotic one, the strange and, because so overly adapted to a different world, inept one, the one who could not speak clearly, the one who did not look like a human being should look, and the one who did not think in an especially useful or interesting way. And the effort of having for the first time in my life to deal ceaselessly and intimately with such a man was exhausting me.

Come out of bed, Terron whispered to me, and he left the door and went out to wait for me on the stoop. Dressing quickly, I joined him outside, where he handed me an orange. While I peeled it with my pocketknife, he explained that he wanted me to see the Peace Cave, where Cudjoe had signed the treaty and where a lot of English soldiers had died. And I believed him—even though Carey Robinson had told me otherwise, that no one knew exactly where the treaty had been signed, and even though I knew that the so-called Peace Cave had been referred to in several journalistic accounts of visits to Nyamkopong as the "so-called Peace Cave," for who, indeed, could believe that these barely literate country folk could know their own history? I, for one, believed. And I was rapidly coming to believe that they alone knew it and further that they were struggling to tell it, but no one would listen, for it never seemed to come out "right." There were all these jumbled accounts of flying Ashanti warriors and female generals with magical powers, stories about Sir Francis Drake and Julius Caesar and the Arawak Indians, Ananci tales and religious beliefs from the African gold coast, anecdotes of recent events in the lives of local personalities, obsessions with decapitation, golden tables, mermaids, and the spirits of the dead—and all these were as true as the tellers of their history as what we others had placed into our versions of their history: so, indeed, how could one trust them to be able to get it "right"?

I followed Terron across the yard and into the bush, along a path I could not see, west from the village a few miles where we had not walked in our travels before. We were quickly out of sight of houses and soon could not even see the smoke curling up from the kitchen fires. Here and there we broke out of the woods and crossed the burned-over and hand-tilled side or basin of a cockpit, the red earth open to the milky white morning sky.

It was going to rain soon, Terron observed, and we walked faster, in silence. My headache was gone now, thanks probably to the orange, and I was no longer aware of my fatigue, thanks surely to the beauty of the yellow-blossomed ebony trees, the rose apple trees here and there, the blood red soil ready for planting, and the turbulently rippling hills of the Cockpit stretching to the horizons. By now I could name a dozen of the trees and as many of the herbs, and as we passed each it was as if we were passing another dear friend, so I said the name of each as we passed, as if to bless it and receive a blessing back. To you, cross-my-heart. And to you, touch-me-not. To you also, cerasee, as we walked swiftly, mile after mile, into the country of the old Maroons.

Before long, as if we had reached the center of the entire island, the land looked the same in one direction as in another. The high ridges of the cockpits seemed to flow out from us toward the horizons, as we circled first one deep socket and then another, on and on into country that, if I had not been following Terron, would have been pathless. At one point we were passing through a defile from one pit into another, working our way between two huge limestone boulders that jaggedly lurched in opposite directions backward into the wall-like ridge that divided the two pits. It was necessary for me to watch my feet carefully in order to avoid slipping off the trail and sliding or falling off the side of the pit several hundred feet straight to the bottom which, from this height, appeared to be a mangrove swamp, a tangle of knobby, leafless roots and branches in a circular orb of black water. Snakes, I thought, even if I survived the fall. Then, looking ahead again, I realized that Terron had disappeared from view.

I scrambled ahead a few yards, passed between the boulders, and stared down at another pit, not as deep as the first and without a swamp at the bottom, but even so, it presented me with a drop-off of over a hundred feet of nearly vertical limestone. I took a quick step backward into the narrow cleft in the ridge between the high white boulders. Where was he? I called his name. Nothing. Again, with care this time, I stepped slowly toward the abyss and peered down. He couldn't have fallen, I thought, not without crying out—but then I realized, yes, of course he could have fallen and not cried out. I would have screamed all the way down, but Terron? Not necessarily. Praise Jah, His will.

I got down on my hands and knees and methodically searched the rocky brush-covered bottom of the pit for any sign of his crumpled body, fearing its not being there almost as much as I feared its being there. For if he had not stepped off the edge here, where was he? On both sides the wall was sheer and, except for the cleft where the path cut between the two boulders from the other side, rose to about twenty feet above my head, and there was no way he could have scaled that height and disappeared along the top of the ridge during the few seconds that I had taken my eyes off him.

Suddenly unsure of the reliability of my senses, I began to question everything. Perhaps he had been much farther ahead of me than I had thought and had indeed scaled the wall to the ridge above and had gone on to where he could not hear me call his name. Or perhaps while I was gazing down at the swamp at the bottom of the pit and thinking of snakes, several minutes had passed and not several seconds as I had believed. Or perhaps the path had suddenly turned where it had seemed to pass strictly and narrowly between the two boulders and, instead of leading to this abyss, had circled to the top of one of the boulders and from there onto the ridge where it looped along the top of the cockpit to the next.

I worked my way back through the cleft, feeling both sides with my hands and searching diligently for an obscure break or step in one or the other of the boulders indicating a sudden unseen turn in the path. But both boulders were unbroken, and I ended where I had started, looking down at the dark eye of the swamp and thinking of water snakes. I didn't want to panic or look like I had panicked, so I put off my sudden impulse to start shouting Terron's name. Though I now felt like a lost child, I didn't want to look or act like one.

I imagined Terron's walking ahead of me, reaching the impassable end of the path at the abyss, and flying magically across to the ridge beyond, leaving me here to wring my hands in despair and frightful solitude. Then, because of the image, I was suddenly aware of my solitude and the danger it proposed, and it occurred to me that the whole thing had been some kind of elaborate trick, getting me up at dawn and leading me out to the wilderness where I would suddenly be left to find my own way back, a cruel and rigorous rite of passage. He could have accomplished it easily, I realized, if that had been his intention, because my attention to him and where we were going was based entirely on a different understanding and trust as to the nature of our journey. My attention to him had been idle, passive, trusting, an innocent's attention that could easily have been exploited the second I looked back or away by simply stepping aside and then hiding and refusing to answer when I realized he was gone and began to search for him.

It would take me days to get back to the village, if I got back at all, for I was not even sure in which direction it lay, our path had been so circuitous. We had been moving east when we had left the village, but we'd soon turned north, then looped around to the south, and at times had even been moving west. To make matters worse, all morning, the sun had remained behind a milky sheet of clouds and I had rarely been conscious of our direction in relation to it, only in relation to our previous direction, the one we had most recently left off following. No. I did not know where I was or how to get anywhere else. I, whose sense of direction had so often been a source of pride that for me to ask for directions was somehow shameful, I was lost.

I knew that Mr. Mann was involved in placing me here, and I believed it was my conversation last night with him and Terron that had moved him to place me here, for I recalled his face when I had finished making my little speech about God and history, what at the time I had regarded as a "confession" of my belief and what I now saw was an arrogant refusal to believe. The old man had heard me out, looking deeply into my face while I talked, and when I was through speaking, he had smiled at me with amused tolerance and had winked playfully at Terron. Well, he said to me, you will see what you want to see. And I had laughed to hear those words again! Laughed at myself for having thought them so mysterious before and laughed at Mr. Mann for what then seemed to me his witty application of them now, a fellow intellect's rebuttal of my presumptuous view of his and Terron's heroes and gods. Terron had been staring at me in puzzlement. You don't believe in *prophecy?* he asked, as if he had misunderstood my words. I had placed a hand on his shoulder and had repeated to him what I had thought Mr. Mann had so wittily just said to me, putting, so I thought, yet another turn on the phrase. You will see what you want to see, I told him, feeling for all the world like an older and much wiser brother.

I went back to the cliff face that dropped into the second cockpit and sat down, letting my feet dangle over the edge. It was near midday and thickly humid. I was hungry and thirsty. Even though I had no control over my situation, now that I knew what it was and understood why, a great calm had come over me. I supposed that soon I would begin to walk in the direction that seemed to lead back to Nyamkopong, which, I decided, would be in the general direction of the movement of the sun. In time I would come to the western end of the cockpit region, and when I did I would know how to get to Nyamkopong. Though it had taken us only a half day to walk here, I knew it would probably take me several days to get back. But I was no longer afraid of becoming lost, for I was lost. It was the first time that I learned I had always been lost, and I was grateful to

Terron and Mr. Mann for teaching it to me. I promised myself that while I worked my way back to the village I would search for something to present to each of them, a beautiful stick or stone or feather or the scoured white skull of a tiny animal.

It began to rain on me, large heavy drops that quickly became a substantial downpour. Soon my clothes and body were soaked, for I hadn't moved from my perch on the cliff. From the pivot point of my solitude, the noise of the rain was like a hundred drums beating, and I was reluctant to start moving around in search of shelter because I would lose the unbroken flow of the sound, my thoughts and movements would stammer and stutter their way into the drumming. So I just sat there and let the noise and the falling water wash over me as if I were a rock or bush and not a conscious man.

Soon, though, a voice did start to cut through the drumming, a man's voice coming from a place very close to me, chanting, Rasta, Rasta, Rasta, rhythmically tied to the rush of the rain, a bass-toned voice that was not mine at all, even though it seemed to come from inside my own head. Rasta, Rasta, Rasta, the voice continued, and soon I realized that it was coming from outside my head, was actually a part of the real world. Rasta, Rasta, Rasta. I looked around me, for now I knew it was Terron's voice, his calm speaking voice, not a shout or cry, and was either a total hallucination or else was located practically beside me. Rasta, Rasta, Rasta, he went on, invisible to me, though he spoke as if no more than three feet away from me.

Terron! I cried out. Where are you, Terron?

In the Peace Cave. Unmistakably his voice had come from the huge boulder on my left—it was the rock itself speaking to me!

Disbelieving, I scrambled to my feet and walked carefully back through the cleft, looking for a way to enter the rock. At the back, where the room-sized boulder seemed to be extruded from the ridge, there near the ground was a narrow wedge of darkness barely two feet high. I crawled over to it and saw that, yes, it was an entry to a cave. Calling his name into the hole, I heard Terron's laugh, and so I squeezed my body into the hole, and entered the Peace Cave.

The huge boulder was indeed hollow. Once through the entry, I stood and saw that I was inside a rock-walled chamber. Light flowed into the room from five or six openings strewn across the wall and ceiling, holes that were the size of a finger where they broke through to daylight, too small and insignificant to be noticed from outside, but that opened widely inside the room, scattering a soft milky light throughout the interior, like that of an ancient stone church or mosque. I looked up and saw all across the damp ceiling and high on the walls ocher and black paintings and marks, stick figures of human beings, mostly males, and animals, mostly doglike beasts, and also markings that resembled writing but that were not anything like letters in the Phoenician alphabet. Sanskrit, perhaps, or secret tallies or coded notations for ritual speeches.

The Arawaks made these pictures and messages, Terron announced from where he sat at the far, dim end of the cave. And the old Africans who hid out here and killed the British, he added. Then he motioned for me to come near, which, sopping wet and now shivering with cold, I did. He showed me two peepholes, higher outside than a man's head but from inside located exactly at eye level and aiming slightly down, so that I could peer out one of the holes and see where I had stopped to stare down at the swamp and think of water snakes, and out the other hole and see where I had sat dangling my legs into the further cockpit. A man inside the cave could fire a rifle or musket through these holes, the man outside on either side would be shot dead, and the men following along behind single file would never know where the bullet had come from. Terrified, they would flee back to where they had come from.

I squatted down on a ledge, and when Terron saw how cold and wet I was, he swiftly gathered some sticks

and charred chunks of wood left there by others and
built a small fire in the middle of the chamber. For a few
minutes the gray smoke swirled around us, then caught
a draft and headed for a fist-sized hole at the top. We sat
close to the fire and in low voices talked of the people
who had been here before us, the Arawaks hiding from
the Spanish slavers, then the Ashanti warriors helping
Ysassi against the British, then Cudjoe's Maroons in the
long war against Guthrie's men, and after them the St.
James Maroons in the Second Maroon War against the
British, all of them emerging from the cave eventually
but only when it finally appeared that the enemy had
either left the island altogether, like the Spanish, or had
been defeated and thus, presumably, could be trusted,
as at the ends of the wars against the British. That was
why it was called the Peace Cave, Terron explained.
Because they never gave it up until they knew peace
would follow. From here Cudjoe and his chiefs had
walked back along the path to where the old village was,
and that's where he had met with the British colonel,
and they had sat down together and signed the peace
treaty that Mr. Mann kept. Soon, he promised, I'll take
you to where they signed the treaty and where the old
village was located.

It was a promise he would keep that same afternoon,
on our way back to Nyamkopong. But before we could
leave the cave, we first had to honor the dead Indians
and Africans and Jamaican Maroons whose cave it was.
In a visible way, visible to us if not to them, we had to
acknowledge their claim to the place, and the forms
were simple, as all sincere forms of decorum usually
are. Terron drew from his pocket a half pint of rum, and
on each of the four more or less distinct walls of the
cave we sprayed rum from our mouths across the drawings and marks, first Terron and then I. We burned the
rest of the rum, a few ounces, in the fire, then put out
the fire. Afterward and before departing, we gathered
some sticks of wood from outside and stacked them

neatly in a corner of the cave. And then, walking single file, we started back to Nyamkopong.

The rain had ended and islands of blue sky were floating overhead as we crossed back through the cockpits the way we had come. Doctor birds hovered near the pathway, their tails swooping gracefully down like slender black seed pods. Above us, the old John Crow birds looped slowly in their endless search for death. The red ground and the foliage steamed in sunlight, and soon we had removed our shirts and tied them around our heads like turbans.

An hour from the cave, Terron suddenly left the ridgepath and strode through waist-high grasses downhill along a slow slope to the right, entering a gentle, broad cockpit that from the ridge had appeared to be surrounded by a set of smaller, deeper, steeper pits. The soil here was fertile and not eroded away as in most of the pits, and the place was spacious in a way that I had not until then seen in the region. Yes, this must be the site of the old village, I thought, and as quickly, Terron confirmed it by pointing suddenly to our left at a hole in the ground between several large limestone outcroppings.

That was the well, he said, and we got down and peered into the hole. We could see nothing. After a few seconds Terron dropped a small rock into the darkness. We waited, and heard the splash.

A way beyond the well we entered a grassy, high-walled canyon, and here, I knew, was where they had built their houses. A half dozen soaring cotton trees stood in isolation from one another in the canyon, but otherwise the ground was smooth underfoot and, except for the yellow grasses, still remained clear of the tangled brush and macca bushes that covered most of this uninhabited, uncultivated region. We stood silently for a while in the middle of the space, peering up at the ridges that surrounded three sides and out into the sloping, meadowlike fourth. Crops had grown out there, I knew, near the well, where the soil was fertile and the drainage, though constant, was not so fast as to tear away the soil from the limestone underneath and swirl it downhill against the houses and storage buildings here below. Those carefully tended crops and gardens had amazed the British when, finally, exhausted, filthy, half-starved, and out of water, they had filed out of the jungle and gathered here in the crowded village to make peace with Cudjoe. And the huts where the children peered out at the motley group of white soldiers with their order and tidy domesticity, had also amazed the British. All this time they had thought they were fighting an army, not a whole people.

This settlement had been only one of seven or eight such settlements here in the west, with perhaps another dozen in the east. Three or four hundred souls had lived here, the precious treaty in their care, and then sometime, when no one was paying attention, no one, that is, who kept records, they had left and moved across the cockpits to where Nyamkopong was now. Or so it seemed. I couldn't be sure. Terron said they left when there were too many dead here, which made sense. After a few generations there would be more dead than living in the vllage, and it would have become too crowded, so the living would move on. They were the only ones who were able to move, to relocate, for the dead cannot move, any more than can the unborn.

The gigantic gray cotton trees spread their branches against the sky, and the grass gave way beneath our feet. Here the dead lived even now, and the thought made it impossible for me to imagine those who had been alive here, their talk, fires, quarrels, work, children, dogs, crops. It was not a place where a people had lived once; it was inhabited still. I could not sentimentalize it.

It was the same with the cave. Once we had performed the ritual that acknowledged the dead's continued possession of the cave, I could no longer imagine its being possessed, except as in a silly movie, by the old Maroons and Arawaks. It was a world where people die but do not conveniently disappear, so I could not people it with memories or imagined history, Carey Robinson's or my history. I had to give it over to the dead, or risk the moral consequences of lying about deep matters.

When we had returned to the ridgepath and were again walking toward Nyamkopong, I called ahead to Terron. He stopped, for something in my voice must have told him that I had an announcement and not conversation to make.

Terron, I said, if today you asked me what you asked last night, Don't you believe in prophecy? I would answer you differently.

Ah, he said.

Remember, I repeated to you what Mr. Mann had told me, You will see what you want to see.

Yes, he remembered, sadly, it seemed.

Now I wouldn't answer that way. Some other way.

Do you know what you would say?

No.

Ah, he said again and, smiling, he turned and walked on, back toward Nyamkopong.

IT WAS MY LAST NIGHT IN TOWN, SATURDAY. AND EXCEPT for two events, it was like every other night in Nyamkopong. We bathed in the Black River, ate chicken backs and rice and afoo yam, Mr. Mann and I eating first, alone, at the long table, the youngsters serving us from the kitchen outside where Devina and Mr. Mann's daughter-in-law toiled in the heat and smoke. After we had eaten, the boys cleared our plates away and washed them for the others in the house to use—Devina and her son and daughter-in-law, the three grandsons, and anyone else who happened to be there at the time. At first I had tried to impose my own etiquette on them and had suggested to Mr. Mann that the others eat with us, but he had said no with great emphasis, and after a few days, when I had a more developed sense of the inventory of their household articles, I realized that there were but a few dishes, forks, knives and glasses, and that Mr. Mann and I were using most of them.

After our meal we smoked cigarettes, and then in the dusk, with the sky turning scarlet in the west and the palms black in silhouette along the road, we walked up to the shops and made the rounds—a drink or two here, a seven of dominoes there, a serious philosophical discussion in one place about the "reality" of the American moon landing, and in another a serious political discussion about the relative danger to Jamaicans from the CIA on the one hand and Cuban-trained revolutionaries on the other. There was never anything like small talk when I was with Mr. Mann, and, despite Terron's capacities as master of chat, or perhaps because of them— since sufficient irrelevancy will draw one's attention straight to the relevant—there was no small talk with him either. Neither man revealed anything embarrassing or denigrating, what we call gossip, about anyone I knew, Mr. Mann simply by refusing to elaborate on his absolute judgment that this one or that one was a monkey—which forced me to supply the evidence on my own—and Terron by yakking on endlessly about the details and idiocies, mistakes and bad luck, foolish self-centeredness and greed of people I could never meet, so that he ended by presenting me with an ongoing morality play, a narrative that used characters to illustrate moral forms of behavior and the consequences of that behavior.

So, after bathing, eating, drinking, playing dominoes, and working up some serious talk, by midnight our evening was over, and Terron went to his bed and Mr. Mann and I to ours, and that was how all my nights in Nyamkopong were spent. This one, however, was my last night in town, and, to me at least, that made it different from the others. In the morning I would be leaving with Terron for Kingston, and from there our plan would carry us east and gradually north around the island to Port Antonio, where we would stay with Terron's younger brother and visit the three remaining Maroon villages, which were all located back up in the Blue Mountains behind Port Antonio. Then it would quickly be over the ridge from north to south, where I would take off from Kingston and return to the States, New England, home.

Though I did not then know if I would ever return to Jamaica, everyone around me seemed to take my quick return for granted—Mr. Mann, Terron, Rubber, Juke and the guys, even the Colonel—and all of them for several days now had been placing orders with me for U.S. goods, as if I were merely flying over for a few days in Miami to shop. Mr. Mann wanted books, in particular an herb book that a Canadian journalist had shown him one afternoon in 1938 and the writings of Henry Kissinger, whom he called his beloved brother Secretary of State. Terron wanted a Japanese battery-powered portable TV that he had seen advertised the previous January in a copy of *The New Yorker,* brought down to me from the States by my mother-in-law, and he would not answer me when I explained that the battery needed to be recharged after only a few hours of use and that the only way to recharge it was to plug the TV into an electrical outlet and run it for several days and nights. He merely changed the subject, as if I were talking nonsense, until later, when he would remind me to bring back one of those battery-powered TV sets he saw in the magazine in my house in Anchovy. It would be good for his kids, he explained. Rubber wanted two pairs of American Levi's and a knife like my Buck belt knife, which, along with instructions not to kill anyone with it, I simply gave to him. He accepted my instructions with sweet reluctance, because in an important way I had withheld a crucial function of the knife. Juke wanted a tape recorder and some blank cassettes so he could tape and listen to some "pure" music, meaning the all-night drumming and chanting of the Rasta I-rations, and not that "soul-boy" music the radio told him to listen to. Devina wanted soap, cakes of Ivory soap, the white soap that floats, she told me. Terron's woman wanted me to bring her cloth for clothing for the children, and she gave me three scraps of cotton—one pink, one tan cordoroy, one purple flannel—as samples. And Colonel Martin Luther Phelps wanted a flashlight, just like the one Mr. Mann brandished about the village now. Beyond these requests from my friends, every few hours those last days in town someone I barely knew, usually a man in his twenties, would grab me by the arm and ask me to bring back a Polaroid camera for him. "Then I can go down to Montego Bay and Negril and take pictures of the tourists and make lots of money," he'd explain, his eyes glazing over with the dream, the dream of coming home to his woman and children with money in his pocket.

How could I answer honestly to most of these requests? With some it was not that difficult; with others impossible. To Mr. Mann's request for the herb book, for instance, I responded by assuring him that I'd seek it out and mail it to him as soon as I returned to the States, and I might even be able to find a collection of Henry Kissinger's speeches. But I could not promise him that it would be autographed and personally enscribed to Mr. Mann as he had instructed: "To my beloved brother State Secretary of the Maroon people of Jamaica in Nyamkopong, keeper of the Blood Treaty and protector of the rights of the Maroons forever. Your friend, Henry A. Kissinger." When I had arrived in Nyamkopong the previous Monday I had presented Mr. Mann with a copy of Carey Robinson's book, *The Fighting Maroons of Jamaica*, and on the flyleaf had written, "To my dear friend, Mr. Wendell O. Mann. With fondness and gratitude," and had signed my name. He had accepted the book graciously and that night had gone into his bedroom and come back out with his own copy of Robinson's book, tattered and dog-eared, with angry corrections written into the margins where Robinson had either overlooked an important event, like the eruption of Mount Vesuvius, or person, like Julius Caesar or Theodore Roosevelt. Placing his own copy of the book onto the table before me, Mr. Mann had taken his pencil and had written on the inside cover and flyleaf for several long minutes, and when he had finished he passed the book across the table to me and said that he wished me to see that Mr. Henry A. Kissinger received it. This is what he had written:

Statements: Trelawny Town, 1738–1739. I must begin to say we as Maroons our thoughts are 100 percent promulgated by Jesus. We are originated from Africa. Our predecessors namely: Ashanti, Nina, the religious "Good Lady," Nonny, Cudjoe whose title was General Lisrimo Cudjoe. They were brought out here, Jamaica, by the Spaniard as slaves. It was good for them.

Ashanti.

When Ashanti came out and observed the situations, his versions were: Veni Vidi Vici—I came, I saw, and I conquered. It was mighty encouraging to his people that when a war broke up with them and the English, they would conquer:—for we the Maroons are the heart of Jamaica and the skin, though black, is the English people's skin. The English peoples know that this is a true fact. We as Maroons are still on our oaths to live peacefully not only with the White British people but with all the nations throughout the Globe. I can remember if my memory serves me well that it has being said in the house of Buckinghamshire by M.P.'s that any creed or nation who does not hold our Blood Treaty to be sacred are not worthy to be called a race.

Jesus sent Jonah to Nineveh: to warn the Ninevites to have peace with his brethren and his friends: the writer of these words Sincerely, saying without thressonic or no domandate, that I am the State Secretary of the Maroons of Nyamkopong, Trelawny Town, according to the form/tenure of our Noble Treaty that was being signed between the two Sovereign Powers in the year of Our Lord 1738–39.

This old boy Wendell O. Mann, as the State Secretary, writes now to the young man, Henry A. Kissinger, as the State Secretary in the U.S.A.: His Excellency— May the good Lord of the Heavens bless and keep you, as I have noticed that you are going around the Globe to make perfect peace with the nations. May the Good Lord help you to continue to do so, for such is the Kingdom of Heaven. God bless, and keep the land of Uncle Sam the land of liberty continually.

Whole heartedly, I make these feable remarks to: my brother friend of me and my family to carry to you and the people of the U.S.A. as a whole. We the Maroons loves the American republic a whole lot. Good night.

Loving suggesting,
Wendell O. Mann,
State Secretary
Written in the name of Our Lord, April 12th, 1976.
Amen.

I DID NOT SEE HOW I COULD CONVINCE HENRY A. KISSINGER to respond in kind. And Terron would not hear from me that after a few hours of use the battery-powered TV would grow dim and die. Nor would he hear me tell him that the machine cost over a hundred and fifty dollars, anymore than Rubber heard what I was really saying when I told him that Levis cost from ten to fifteen dollars in the States. Instead he had grinned with delighted amazement at how much cheaper they were than in Jamaica, where they cost at least twenty-five dollars. And when I confessed to Juke that I didn't think I could find the kind of tape deck he wanted for less than a hundred bucks, he too was amazed at how cheap such things were in the States. Mr. Mann's wife Devina, as always, asked only for what she knew she could get from me, a dozen cakes of Ivory soap and another five dollars for her church; and I knew I'd be able to send Terron's woman some cloth and even some clothing for her children. It seemed that the women knew something the men generally did not, or rather, that the women's suffering from deprivation was different from the men's. Preferring the tiny possibility to the impossible dream, they were, therefore, more "realistic" than the men. Except for Mr. Mann, of course, who was beyond the dreamings of a young man and cared little about soap or clothing or making church contribution quotas.

In the end, to those requests for goods that I knew I would indeed purchase and mail back to Nyamkopong—Devina's soap, Terron's woman's cloth, Mr. Mann's herbal, the Colonel's flashlight—to these I responded with a definite promise to deliver, and then with shock realized that I was not believed. They all smiled politely and thanked me in advance, but I could see in their eyes that they did not believe me. They were being polite because I was being polite. To those other requests—Rubber's Levi's, Terron's TV, Juke's tape deck, Mr. Mann's inscribed copy of Kissinger's speeches, and the dozen pleas for Polaroid cameras—I said only that I would try but the costs might be prohibitive; and to my surprise, this vague declaration was taken to mean that the goods would be coming within a week or two following my departure from the island. Instantly everyone concerned himself with the technical problems of mailing packages to Jamaica from the States, advising me to remove all labels and price tags to fool the customs inspectors and to be sure to wrap the articles carefully so they didn't come undone in mailing and get stolen by someone in the post office at Whitehall.

AT SUPPER THAT LAST NIGHT IN NYAMKOPONG, MR. MANN had again brought up his desire for Kissinger's book. It would help him, he said, to solve certain difficulties he was having here among the monkeys. Tightening his crisp face with anger, he pushed his chair from the table and strode into his bedroom, returning quickly with the ledger book he always carried with him when he left the house. With great, delicate care, he set the book down on the table in front of me and, as if lifting the lid of a treasure chest, opened the book to the middle, where, wrapped in cracked and battered plastic, lay the treaty. The parchment, or paper, was brown with age and stained from handling and moisture, but it was in sturdy condition nonetheless.

Lowering his voice almost to a whisper, the old man said that *this* was what the monkeys wanted him to deliver over to the government, Bulkley and that Labour crowd. Mr. Mann had come around the table to stand next to me, leaning over my shoulder and pointing in the dim light of the kerosene lantern to the florid signature of Colonel Guthrie and the thick X made by "Captain Cudjoe" and the date, 1 March 1739.

I could not believe that this was the original treaty or even a particularly old copy. As with the Shroud of Turin, there was no scientific reason for it to exist. Not in this climate, not with this kind of safekeeping. And of course I knew that the treaty existed on microfilm in the National Archives in Spanish Town and had been transcribed numerous times. I myself had read a neatly typed transcription in Boston, Massachusetts. The contents of the treaty, its legal power, such as it was, depended not in the slightest on this document before me, which I supposed was a clerk's copy made in the late nineteenth century at the instigation of some colonial functionary who, for whatever greedy reason one might wish to imagine, had wanted to flatter and aggrandize the then Colonel of Nyamkopong. Riding out to the Cockpit to hand over a few sheets of parchment was no pleasure in those days, so there must have been some kind of exchange of goods or services when the treaty was "returned" to the Maroons. The ruse had worked, though. In ninety or a hundred years the copy had become the original, so thoroughly that now the government was trying to get it back so it could be copied and the "original" preserved and exhibited behind glass at the Institute of Jamaica. What then would be returned to Nyamkopong would be a copy indeed, known as such and for that reason no treasure at all. To exchange a treasure for its counterfeit—only a monkey would be willing to be so foolish and believe it was clever for having done it.

How can Mr. Kissinger help you? I asked, looking into his eyes, those blue and brown concentric pupils that were like wells that led not downward into the ground but upward into the sky, through blue and brown to black enormous space.

Just as the American people with their powerful navy protects Jamaica from the Cuban, he explained, so will Henry A. Kissinger with the power of his name protect Wendell O. Mann from the mischief of the monkeys. When the main monkey sees that Henry A. Kissinger has learned that I am the keeper of the sacred blood treaty, then he will tell all the other monkeys, and soon they will believe that it is their duty not to steal the treaty and give it over to the government. Instead they will start to argue and fight among themselves over who shall be the one to help me most in my completion of my duties as State Secretary of the Maroon peoples and protector of the sacred blood treaty. Right now the government of Jamaica has convinced the monkeys that their duty as Maroons is to steal the treaty and turn it over. They think in return they'll get paved roads, electric power, and a health clinic, like the Moore Town Maroons got. Instead, if they steal the treaty and turn it over to the government, all they'll get is a land surveyor and a tax bill. And when they can't pay the taxes, the government will come and take over their lands and bring people from Kingston to farm their lands the way the government wants, not the way the people of the village wants. And then will come the paved road, all right, and the electric power and the health clinic, but it won't be for the Maroons of Nyamkopong. The Maroons of Nyamkopong will all be gone from here, down on the streets of Montego Bay or else slaving for a stranger on Maroon land. *That's* what the government wants. Not the treaty. If they get the treaty, they'll put it in a book somewhere or forget about it or else they'll just lose it on purpose someplace in Kingston. The important thing to them is to get treaty out of Nyamkopong. Because they know it's the treaty that keeps us strong against them.

Then suddenly he lowered his voice and began practically to whisper into my ear. I want you to tell all this to

Henry A. Kissinger when you see him. And so he'll know he's dealing with a monkey judge and not a monkey, tell him this too—but tell no one else, he warned, not even your brother Terron.

I promised I would tell no one but Mr. Kissinger, that other monkey judge, and the old man went on. For two years and seven months now, I've walked out with this ledger book under my arm, like so, and whenever I talk about the treaty, I tap on this book, like so.

He had grabbed the book, stuffed it under his arm, and was demonstrating his seemingly absent-minded tap, when I heard a moaning or groaning from somewhere outside, rising and then falling away.

Mr. Mann apparently hadn't noticed, because he went on with his revelation. So, for two years and seven months people have known that I have been carrying the treaty around with me, and now most of them believe that the treaty is the same thing as this book. Because what I don't tell them is that the treaty is *inside* the book, he grinned.

Ah, I said, with admiration. And then I heard the moaning again, a man's voice calling incoherently across a great distance.

Wait, you don't understand. I'll tell you my trick, he said, as he flipped the pages of the ledger back toward the front. Every night before I go to sleep, he whispered, I write from the treaty into the ledger book, and soon I'll have copied the whole thing out word for word. That way I'll be able to hide the real treaty from the monkeys. And then let them give that one to the government, he said triumphantly, because the *real* treaty, the blood treaty that our ancestors died to bring to us, will still be in possession of the Maroons of Nyamkopong! Let them send up a land surveyor and a tax man then, and I will bring out the true treaty and read to them how they must cease and desist and get themselves *gone* from the Maroon lands!

With my fingertips I tenderly grazed the green-lined pages of the two-column ledger where the old man had carefully, slowly inscribed, night after night, sentence by sentence, the long, tricky text of the document that the British had used to subdue the wild Maroons when their armies could not do the job for them. To be sure, there was the clause giving freedom from enslavement to Cudjoe and his people, and there were the descriptions of the two parcels of land that were to be their domain, the parcel of fifteen hundred acres taken back fifty years later when the truculent and literal-minded Trelawny Town Maroons got shipped off the island to Nova Scotia and Sierra Leona, and the one-thousand-acre parcel granted to the Maroons of Nyamkopong. There was the clause that permitted them to grow and sell on that land whatever crops and livestock they saw fit to grow and sell, and also the right to sell their produce anywhere on the island. And the clause granting them the right to hunt anywhere on the island as long as they stayed three miles away from any settlement or pen. And, too, the clause that placed two Europeans, appointed by the government, in their midst as "superintendents" who were supposed to "maintain a friendly correspondence with the island." And yes, there too were the clauses requiring the Maroons to "kill, suppress or destroy . . . all rebels wheresoever they may be throughout the island, unless they submit to the same terms of accommodation granted to Captain Cudjoe and his successors . . . ," and, "If any negroes shall hereafter run away from their masters or owners and fall into Captain Cudjoe's hands, they shall immediately be sent back to the Chief Magistrate of the next parish where they are taken; and those that bring them are to be satisfied for their trouble as the legislature shall appoint." These were the clauses that had divided the Maroons forever against themselves and, by turning them into bounty hunters, had divided them against all their racial brethren.

The groaning was now distinct, a chant almost, sounding like cries of, "Oh, woe, woe, woe!" over and over, rising slowly in volume and pitch and then falling away to garbled words that sounded like a man giving orders, but with pebbles in his mouth. Do you hear that? I asked Mr. Mann, who was folding the treaty back into the middle of the ledger.

Picking up the ledger, he walked to the door and peered outside to the silvery, moonlit yard. The Warner, he said, then turned and disappeared into his bedroom, presumably to place the ledger back inside whatever drawer or box he kept it in.

One of the grandsons had come into the room and was clearing the table of our supper dishes. Do you hear that? I asked the boy.

He stopped and listened a moment. Full moon. The Warner's out, he said, and went back to wash the dishes so he and his brothers and grandmother, aunt and uncle could eat their meal.

I got up from my chair and stepped outside to the yard. The moon rode like a cold sun above the black, shivering palms, and everything here on earth cast dark blue, sharp-edged shadows in its silvery glow. More clearly now came the Warner's cry, and it was still as I had heard it inside. "Oh, woe, woe, woe!" rising to the high call, then tumbling as if into specifics. Who is he warning? I asked myself. And if they call him the Warner, why aren't they paying attention to him? Why aren't they trying to protect themselves?

Mr. Mann, the familiar ledger under his arm again indicating that he was ready to head up to the shops, had joined me in the yard. He passed me a lit cigarette and commented on the full moon, how it never failed to please him.

What's he warning us against?

Sometimes fire, sometimes flood. It depends on what's coming.

And does he know?

Oh yes. When the moon is full, if fire or flood is coming, he knows. Otherwise, he's silent, a dummy. Just smiles and does the work his mother sets him to.

An idiot. Then, if the moon is full, sometimes he's like this. It depends.

On what?

On what's coming.

What's he warning us about tonight?

Can't tell. We'll find out later, though. Soon, he said, tolerant of my impatience, patting me gently on the arm. You'll see what you want to see, he said gently, a father to a son.

Yes. I will.

Well, shall we see if anyone's foolish enough tonight to play dominoes with us?

I put my arm around his shoulder and we walked slowly from the yard toward the center of the village, where the others had already gathered.

MORNING MISTS, FROM THE FLATLANDS BELOW, SLIDING UP the long slopes to the ridge, cast a moving shadow beneath them that grayed the iridescent green of the treetops. From above, where I stood by my car next to Terron's hut while he gathered his gear together, the mist was snow white in the sunlight, and as it neared the ridge and the village that clung to the ridge, it spread out and quickly dissolved into the cooler air. Mr. Mann sat inside the rented yellow Toyota, enjoying his first cigarette of the day. He had ridden with me from his house to Terron's so he could say good-bye to both of us at once. To wave my sons off, he said.

Finally Terron appeared at the door of his house, his arms wrapped around baskets and bundles of cane, coconuts, yams, cho-cho, coffee beans, kalaloo, and Ethiopian apples. These were gifts for the Kingston relations, a sister of Terron's woman and her children, with whom we were going to stay for a day and two nights before heading on around the eastern nose of the island to Port Antonio. Walking along behind Terron came his woman, shorter than he but three times as bulky, carrying his blue and white plastic airlines bag, his transistor radio, and his cook pot. A good Rasta never travels without his transistor radio and his cookpot.

We threw the produce and gear into the trunk and back seat of the car. Then we each gave Mr. Mann a hug. Terron turned to his four small children, two boys and two girls, who had trailed their mother out of the hut, and he touched each of them once on top of the head, then swiftly ducked into the car. Well, I said to Terron's woman, I'll be in touch . . . I'll send you the cloth.

She mouthed a silent thank you and turned away, scooting the kids back to the house.

When I had got into the car and started the motor, Mr. Mann came slowly around the front to my open window, reached in, and placed his crinkled hand on my shoulder. You don't know that you'll return to us, he told me, but I know that you will. So don't worry about it. Then he blew me a kiss, backed away a few steps, and waved.

3

THE OLD MAN WAS RIGHT. YOU DO RETURN—TO ANCHOVY and the house on Church's hill overlooking Montego Bay, to your brother Terron, to Nyamkopong and the home of Mr. Mann, to the Maroons, to the library in Kingston, to Port Antonio, to Errol Flynn's old haunts, to Evan Smith's cabin on the knob that watches Navy Island, to the Gordon Hall Maroons and the obi man whose powers take you over, to the Rasta men and women who become your companions and confidants as you become theirs, to the idea of prophecy and history, you come back to all of it, all the bloody, dark and gorgeous island of Jamaica that is the almost perfect reversal of your own world. You return to the ground against which you can see your own otherness, and so you go on seeing yourself as if for the first time. Against the mahogany voices filling your ears, you go on hearing your own flat, tinny voice, the thin, spiraling shapes of your sentences and thoughts; and against those lean, black, languidly moving bodies, you see your own body, parchment-colored, abrupt and thick, a body evolved in rocky northern forests under dark skies thousands of years ago; and against the versions of the past that gradually get revealed to you, in tale, gesture, kinship, dream, and document, you begin to notice the complexity of your own past, for if you can begin to grasp a stranger's past by means of his tales, gestures, kinships, dreams, and documents, your past too must stand revealed in the same way. You are becoming your own stranger, and in that way, when you return to the island of Jamaica, as the old man knew you would, you are returning to yourself.

Your departure from Nyamkopong with Terron took you first to Kingston, where you slept on the floor of a hovel in the middle of a huge, warm, desperate pack of people huddled in the shadows beneath glass and steel air-conditioned office buildings, where pigs rooted in street garbage below billboards advertising holidays at Disneyworld and a black ram-goat lay in the gutter outside the library of the Institute of Jamaica and swelled to bursting in the midday heat. At May Pen, as you entered the city, you stopped the car and got out to stand and stare back at what you had just passed through, miles of tin shanties, old refrigerator cartons, abandoned cars, buses, crates—all of the structures taken over for shelter against the rain and burning sun. You saw hundreds of thousands of people living in mud and filth, without running water or toilets or lights, a plain of alleys where gangs of wild boys and packs of starving dogs roamed at night. Smoke from thousands of cookfires joined in a hovering gray haze over the plain. Beyond the plain on one side the deep green foothills and then the mountains shouldered toward the evening sky, while on the other side the turquoise sea turned bloody in the setting sun. Clinging to the foothills and peering fearfully down at the city were small, spacious communities of multileveled homes with picture windows, wall-to-wall carpeting, terraced gardens, and high iron fences, barred window grates, uniformed security guards. You stood there beside your friend Terron and stared at this place and believed that you had glimpsed the future. And that night in a candlelit corner of the room in Trench Town where you were staying with Terron, his woman's sister, who could talk only of getting somehow, someday to the States where people don't have to live like this, and her three small children, you wrote a letter to a

friend in Boston, and you said to him that in the firma-
ment of cities Kingston and cities like it will soon replace New York and Los Angeles, which in turn will
soon replace those dying stars like London and Paris,
which in their turn will join the wholly dead suns, cin-
ders like Babylon, Carthage and Karnak. Faced with the
realities of Kingston, Caracas, Lima, Mexico City and
Buenos Aires, you wrote, we will grow nostalgic for Los
Angeles and New York, and we'll speak of their cleanliness, efficiency and beauty the way today we speak of
London's "old-world charm" and the delightful boule-
vards of Paris.

Two days and nights in Kingston, your daylight hours
consumed at the library, your nights holed up inside the
room where, according to Terron and the woman who
lives there, you are safe from being assaulted and robbed,
and then you leave the city and head east and slowly
north around the rainy, mountainous tip of the island.
You did not believe Terron and the woman, yet you did
not dare test their warnings by going out alone for a
drink in the evening or even for a drive in your car, for
when you drove in daylight with Terron through this
mazelike section of the city, men and boys shouted at
you and pounded the hood of your car in anger as they
crossed the alley in front of you. You knew there were
still sections of the city where open, friendly faces would
hail you cheerfully, where you could stroll at night and
speak with strangers about the weather; you had visited
those sections before, last winter when you first came
over from Anchovy to read the materials on the Maroons in the library of the Institute. But seen from the
swarming heat of Trench Town, those "safe" sections
of the city seem now to exist on another planet.

At Port Antonio, when you visit Moore Town and
Charles Town, you see what you expected to see, what
your reading and reason had arranged there for you to
see: two small settlements of subsistence farmers struggling to pay taxes on their land holdings so they will not
be bought out by speculators or the government, which,

they know, will send them and their children over the mountains to Kingston and the dream at the edge of the sea of going to the States and starting life all over again, the sad dream of forgetting the past. Moore Town has the paved roads, electricity and health clinic Mr. Mann told you about, and the Colonel there is a Member of Parliament who delivers the vote. Half the Maroon land in Moore Town is owned by people who do not live on that land. Close to Port Antonio and readily accessible to film companies working up travel documentaries for the tourist board, the dancers and drummers, you discover, perform practically as professional troupes, flowering into orders and symmetries at the urging of pamphleteers and public relations operations rather than at the urgings of the deep structures lying below the apparent chaos of community and tribe. Nonetheless, the grand chieftainess Nonny, you are told, lies buried here in this valley and soon the government will erect a statue to her and there will be a big ceremony to unveil the statue, with the mother of the Prime Minister and three of his cabinet officials coming over from Kingston for the occasion. Lots of dancing. Lots of speeches. Lots of foreigners. Do come. Lying, you promise you'll attend and then, depressed, return to Port Antonio, where you find yourself stumbling over traces of old tales about Errol Flynn, obeah, corruption from high places to low, that for the moment seem to reveal more to you of what you are doing here, what the nature of your growing obsession with this place has now become, than does your pursuit of the Maroons.

Then, after a few days in the Port, during which you make a perfunctory trip out to Charles Town—where you learn how it is when Maroons come to be wholly assimilated, so that you know you are among Maroons only because the guide book from the tourist board tells you so; where the old man who calls himself Colonel whines bitterly that he had to sell all the stone in his quarry to the government to pay the back taxes on the few remaining acres of land that the government and land speculators have not yet purchased outright—that done, you decide to return to the States. Heading west along the north coast to Anotto Bay and then inland. over the mountains toward Kingston, you and Terron, who has come to share your sadness of the fate of these Maroon towns, casually decide to check out Gordon Hall, which, from the map, is not far out of your way. You know by now what to expect: a typical country village in the hills, all the young men and women gone to Kingston to wait, the once-productive hillside land slipping back to bush, while the few remaining Maroons in town talk of themselves as an underexploited, potentially lucrative, tourist attraction, if only the government, instead of taxing them, would make a television film about them and build a hotel or guest house in the center of the town. And you know that at Gordon Hall the Colonel will claim the presence of Nonny's grave, just as the Colonels at Charles Town and Moore Town, and he will tell you and Terron that the others are liars and all they want are the statue and the big ceremony of the unveiling because that will make the town into the "official" Maroon village, leaving nothing for the others. Tourism, more than any other single industry, corrupts and corrodes a people's integrity and independence, you decide, as you try to locate Gordon Hall by asking in vain along the road to Anotto Bay. You no longer hate the tourists however; you view them now as victims of the same system. And, too, perhaps with a certain arrogance, you no longer fear that you are a tourist yourself. Indeed, you have at last started to ask, Who *is* this white American traveling with you and Terron? And because you have been asking that question constantly now—as you sat over beans and rice and jerked pork in Nyamkopong, as you squatted on your heels in a Kingston hovel and explained to a woman with three hungry babies why you can't take her back to the States with you or, in the whorehouse in Port Antonio, as you asked questions about Errol Flynn and a twenty-year-old murder or as you listened to a paunchy professional Maroon in his comfortable middle-class living room in Moore Town tell you how much he, as a Member of Parliament, had done for his people or as you heard a skinny old colonel in Charles Town weep about the nearly vertical land the government forced him, because he was the elected headman, to pay taxes on or as you stopped along the road and asked a pair of teen-age girls walking uphill over the mountain if they knew where Gordon Hall was—because, through everything you keep on asking yourself, Who is this white American traveling with you and your friend Terron in Jamaica? Because of that question, you are not a tourist.

You stay at Gordon Hall two whole days and nights, in astonishment and confusion, all your expectations broken in your lap. Gordon Hall is not at all like Moore Town or, worse, Charles Town; it is closer to Nyamkopong in character, and in certain ways closer to the Nyamkopong of a century ago: independent, suspicious, scornful and proud. There are Ashanti passwords, rites, songs, gestures, lore—you stand in the center of a circle of men, you and your brother Terron, who is no less a stranger to these people than you are, for though he is a black Jamaican and claims to be a Maroon from Nyamkopong, he cannot understand their questions. They are firing questions at him in another language, a foreign tongue, these glowering men with their powerful arms folded across their chests, and Terron starts to stammer, his childhood affliction returns, and the master of chat finds his tongue stumbling. He cannot understand what these angry, suspicious men are saying to him, and he can't make them understand him because he is stammering. When, as if working it up with his fingers, he forces an inappropriate smile onto his face, they see his fear and his embarrassment, and to punish him, divide you from him, call him a nigger who can't speak his own language. To you they speak in Jamaican patois, proud of their ability to speak your language, and one of them, a stub of a man with a pipe in his mouth and a voice like a bull's, brags that he can speak Spanish English and

French English as well as American English, but not Italian English. Having watched them humiliate and dismiss Terron, you realize that they can be dealt with only in complete sincerity, so when they begin to address you with the questions designed to reveal if you are either ignorant and honest or ignorant and a liar, you answer as honestly as you can. No, you do not know the Ashanti passwords, and you do not know the names of the gods, and you do not know the names of the thirty-six herbs and where they grow, and you do not know who their Colonel is or what his powers are. You do not know anything about these people. You have come here this great, long, and difficult way because you want to know yourself, and yes, you are afraid. And when they ask you what you're afraid of, the dark? you answer, "No, the light." But because you are not, like Terron, a black Jamaican professing to be a Maroon, and because you do not, as he did, claim to know the names of the thirty-six herbs and then, when challenged, fail to name more than twenty-three and at that name them with painfully stammered words, smiling falsely throughout the broken speech, that you are greeted with an embrace from each of the four men and taken to meet the Colonel. Terron they send back to the car, but he has already gone there.

The Colonel is a gigantic man, and the first thing you see is that his eyes are the same as Mr. Mann's, blue and brown concentric rings for pupils, lizard-lidded, and his skin is satiny black, ageless like Mr. Mann's. But in temperament this man is opposite to Mr. Mann, for he is fierce, blunt, omnivorous. Taller than you by three inches, and several times as large through the trunk and shoulders, he draws you forcibly to him by grabbing your forearm, until your face is yanked up close to his and you can feel his breath on you, can see into his unblinking eyes while they search the eyes of that white American who is traveling with you. Long seconds pass while you permit the man to see whatever he sees there, when finally he releases your arm and lets you step away.

For two sleepless days and nights you and the Colonel, whose name is spelled Bowra and pronounced Bowray, sit there on the porch of his two-room cabin, and while people come in and go out, women, children, henchmen, sons and daughters, cousins, aunts and uncles, and food is brought forward to you and the Colonel, roast afoo yam and jerked pork, beans and rice, a chicken, and rum is always there in a quart bottle between you on the table, as the sun goes down and bats dart in the darkness, and as the sun comes up again and the heat of the day passes over you, and as the sun goes down again and the valley passes into darkness again, and then as the sun rises again—you go on talking with the old man, one mad speech after the other, first he speaks and then you speak, on and on, as if there will never be an end to it: stories from your childhood, all the history you can recall, your impressions of the city of Kingston, of Nyamkopong, detailed descriptions of people you have come to love, Mr. Mann, Terron, whom you praise and praise until Bowra relents and sends for him to come up from the car and be fed; and Bowra tells you his stories and the history he believes, gives you his opinions of the other Maroon villages, and yes, he has heard of Mr. Mann and he knows their eyes are the same, but his and Mr. Mann's lights are not the same, he informs you, and it's by his lights that you know a man—until at last you find that you have come to an agreement with the old man: you will transport him and his wives and henchmen, his "cabinet," nine people in all, from Gordon Hall to Nyamkopong for the celebration of Cudjoe's birthday next January sixth; and then you will transport Colonel Martin Luther Phelps, Mr. Mann, and up to seven more from Nyamkopong to Gordon Hall on the following August first, when they have their feast day and celebrate the victory over the British; so that through your good offices, if you are somehow able to be in the country at those times, the Maroons of the two villages can come to know each other and together can make themselves stronger against the government than they are alone. You have agreed to be their agent, but the old man does not believe you will keep your part of the agreement, so more hours of discussion and chant and obeah follow, until at last you both believe that you will keep your part of the agreement: in return, he has promised that he will teach you to fly, and even if you cannot learn to fly because you are a white man, still, you will see him fly: you will see what you want to see, he promises, and now you believe that he will keep his part of the agreement too, so you are free to go.

THEN, WITHIN A WEEK OF YOUR RETURN TO YOUR HOME IN New Hampshire, you learn that a large private foundation has awarded you sufficient funds to enable you to return to Jamaica for a full year. The grant is supposed to enable you "to continue your work in the writing of fiction," the endless, unfinished novel that has languished in a file cabinet since last January. And by the end of August, your affairs are in order and you have again arranged to rent from the Churches the same house in Anchovy that you rented the previous winter. Then, with your wife content with her work and friends in Anchovy and Reading, and your children enrolled in a Franciscan school in nearby Montego Bay, you quickly drop back into your old, easy routines—writing on the unfinished novel in the mornings, wandering through complex questions of prophecy and history all afternoon with Terron and various of the Rasta brethren, and mastering the futher intricacies of dominoes in the backroom of Barrett's shop in Anchovy. You visit Nyamkopong regularly and relate to Mr. Mann all that you learned in your travels last spring in Kingston, Port Antonio, and at the other Maroon villages, and you make the arrangements with him and Colonel Phelps for the exchange of visits with the Gordon Hall Maroons. You confess to Mr. Mann that you have not yet delivered his message and book to Henry Kissinger, but you will, you will.

Most of your time during these autumn months, however, is spent in Anchovy, very little of it in Nyamkopong. The press of family life, and your ongoing work on the novel and the pleasures of the company at Barrett's keep you close to home. Declining all invitations to join the Churches or the Wests or the Beards for "drinks and dinner," you spend night after night and many of your afternoons yakking with Barrett, the terrier-faced proprietor who got his stake together years ago by working in London as a bus driver and now runs a taxi in Montego Bay along with his shop here in Anchovy. His dour, careful, tub-bodied wife runs the shop for him all day, while he drives his Toyota van back and forth from hotel to airport and at night holds forth at the bar. You also use up many of your hours gossiping idly with Yvonne, the barmaid, about everyone else in the neighborhood—she's your age, burly and thick-armed, intelligent, and has opinions that, after a few weeks of merely talking politely with you and angling for tips, she's begun to share with you. She's a sexy woman, and you enjoy flirting with her, though you know also that she's the mistress of a man named Bush who lives in Anchovy and is a cop in Montego Bay. The idea of your daring to do anything to make him angry is so far-fetched that no one, least of all you, Bush or Yvonne, takes your flirting seriously. In fact, in November Bush himself presents you with a ticket to the Policeman's Ball, to be held in early December at the Royal Caribbean Hotel and Beach Club, and asks you to join his table with Barrett and his wife, Yvonne, Barret's brother Frank who runs a dry cleaning business in Montego Bay, and three or four other men and women you've never met. Though flattered by the invitation, you tell yourself that you're curious, you've never been to a Policeman's Ball, and besides, you'd like to see more of these rising black entrepreneurs like Barrett and his family and the cops like Bush and his friends, especially in what you know will be a highly self-conscious setting, a ball, with bands and big-name entertainers from Kingston, everyone dressed to the teeth and spending as much money as possible.

The night of the ball you all ride out from Anchovy to the Royal Caribbean together in Barrett's taxi, with the radio speakers front and back blaring Barrett's favorite tape, Diana Ross and the Supremes. The women are wearing brown, wavy-haired wigs and sherbert colored gowns and shoes with matching handbags, and you men are wearing your best dress suits, straw hats, gold watches, shined shoes. Bush has a toothpick stuck in his mouth and takes it out only to grab a slug from Barrett's bottle of rum as it gets passed up and down the van. Bush is cool, never says much more than what's minimally required: he specializes in a yes or no that makes you feel like apologizing for having asked. Tonight, however, he's more gregarious, is even smiling, and is recalling to the others last year's ball when Barrett had to be carried into his house and dumped into his bed fully clothed. Mrs. Barrett laughs at the memory, as does Barrett himself. His brother Frank has a story to top that one, and then Yvonne has one too. You've never seen Barrett drunk, or any of the others—their capacity for drink has continued to astound you: Yvonne, Mrs. Barrett, Bush, all of them seem to be able to drink straight white rum hour after hour, and when finally you have to leave for the night, dizzy and sick, to avoid making a fool of yourself, you always leave them behind, coherent, comfortable, wondering why you want to go home so early. So you listen and laugh along with the others at the tales of foolish drunkenness.

Barrett parks the van in the huge lot outside the glass and tan concrete structure. Fountains burble and royal palms clatter in the cool evening breeze. The lobby is jammed with gorgeously dressed people, most of them looking muscular and compressed in their clothes, as few of them fashionably thin as unfashionably fat. Their faces are mostly tough, smart, determined and confident— these men and women are the winners in a terrible contest—and the lobby of the Royal Caribbean is where they've come to be seen and acknowledged by each other, and only by each other, for no one else can know and respect the grit and sacrifice and deep selfishness it's taken for them to be here. For a moment you yourself forget what the obstacles are, and you search the noisy, perfumy room for Indian, Chinese or even white faces, but when you realize that the only non-African face in the room belongs to you, you remember.

Inside the ballroom, the crowd is thinner and quieter as parties settle themselves around their tables and order drinks, flashing digital wristwatches, pinkie rings, bracelets and necklaces, lugging out fist-sized rolls of bills to pay when the waiter arrives with the tray of drinks. After a few rounds, with the band playing, a five-piece rock-and-roll band from Miami, if you believe the Day-Glo lettering on the bass drum, people's voices start to lift, and the ballroom has suddenly become crowded, and there are a dozen couples dancing. Not all that skillfully, either, you notice. Men move gregariously from table to table, shaking hands and slapping upholstered shoulders, cops and small businessmen and petty bureaucrats and politicos, while the women remain seated and talk to each other about people at other tables. And everyone drinks feverishly.

You are having a loud, wonderful time, a hell of a guy. You dance with Yvonne and she shows you a few new moves and compliments you besides. You even dance with Barrett's wife, and eveyone laughs good-naturedly. A hell of a guy. Bush tells you how he's going to become a sergeant next year but to get any higher he'll have to come up with a thousand dollars, which isn't bad because as a lieutenant he'd make that much back in a month. Barrett asks you if you'll write a recommendation for his teen-aged son to a business college in London, and if the boy is accepted by the college, will you write a character reference to help him get the visa? Sure, sure, great kid, happy to be able to help him out, you say, slapping Barrett on the back. And good luck, Bush, on that sergeant thing.

A witty, bass-toned emcee has taken over the mike, and after introducing the members of the band, has started to introduce himself as a singer. He mentions the hotels in Kingston he's worked and with much flattery compares this hotel and crowd to the Kingston hotels and crowds, so that everyone looks at everyone else and smiles proudly. He praises your good-looking women, your fancy clothes, your long, sleek cars parked outside in the lot, and he praises Montego Bay, the gold coast, the beaches and hotels as if these too were yours. Then he starts to sing, voice and diction like Lou Rawls', songs from the repertoire of Tony Bennett. You approve, and you applaud each song furiously, stamping and whistling after "I Did It My Way" and "Chicago."

The emcee takes a break, inviting you to drink and dance and have a good time before the floor show starts. By now you are feeling drunk, so you excuse yourself from the table and head out toward the lobby to find the men's room. At the end of a long, tiled hallway a group of men has gathered to smoke and talk at the entrance to the men's room, and as you pass through the group you nod and smile familiarly. Inside, though, there are mirrors and bright fluorescent lamps, and fifteen or twenty men washing hands, buttoning and zipping flies, straightening neckties, and when you have peed and have come to stand in front of the bank of mirrors to check out *your* tie and hair, you suddenly see your white face and pale hair, your shockingly blue eyes and pink hands. My God, you had almost forgotten how weird you look! And now that you can see it again, you realize that everyone else can see it too, and then you notice how all the men are trying not to be seen staring at you.

You hurry from the men's room, reel past the crowd outside without a gesture or word, and rush back to the ballroom, where you seat yourself in the rear of the room and as far from the others as possible. The emcee has returned to the mike and is now introducing the floor show, an act, he says, that brought down the house at the Jamaica Hilton, blew them away at the Pegasus, knocked them off their seats at the Playboy Club—it's the Fighting Maroons of Jamaica doing their world famous War Dance!

Amplified drums, and then a dozen brown showgirls leap onto the dance floor, strutting and bending in an old Las Vegas routine to the beat of the drums, which are quickly joined by rattles, cymbals, marimbas, until what you hear is a version of a Trinidadian steel band that would sound right on the Johnny Carson show. After the girls have gone through their cheerleader routines and have tossed a few good-natured humps to the laughing audience, each hump accompanied by a loud thump of the bass drum, a man, young and small with a dancer's body and wild dreadlocks flashing, leaps into the middle of the circle, and he begins a cheaply erotic dance routine with the showgirls that causes the audience to start laughing and clapping in time. The man dances up to one, then to another of the girls, pretends to reject one after another, until he comes to the lead dancer, whose glittering bikini is bright green, in contrast to the others' which are gold. The man is wearing only a sequin-covered loincloth, also bright green, and he slashes at the air with his locks, swirling his tan body around the girl he has chosen. She has gone all modest now and crouches submissively beneath him in the center of the ring, which has opened in front to give the crowd a better view of the action that will surely follow.

You rise from the table, and no one notices as you leave, or at least no one asks you where you are going. In the lobby you find yourself alone, the shouts and cries of the crowd behind you, and slowly, your head reeling from the drink and noise, you walk through the glass doors to the parking lot, where there is only the sound of the royal palms chattering against the silence of the star-spiked sky.

When finally you find Barrett's white Toyota van amongst the hundreds of cars, you open the side door and make your way clumsily to the far corner in back, where you curl up like a question mark and try to fall asleep. You try and try, but you can't, and you are still wide awake when, hours later, Barrett, his wife, Bush, Yvonne, the brother Frank and the others come laughing drunkenly back to the car. They stumble into the van, giggling and poking at one another, and they think you are asleep. You go on lying there in the corner, pretending to sleep, and all the way home to Anchovy the people in the car talk to one another as if you weren't there, and they never once mention you or any other white man.

OBI

Again, I believe that all that use sorceries, incantations, and spells, are not Witches, or as we terme them, Magicians; I conceive there is a traditional Magicke, not learned immediately from the Devill, but at second hand from his Schollers, who having once the secret betrayed, are able and doe emperically practice without his advice, they both proceeding upon the principles of nature: where actives aptly conjoined to disposed passives, will under any Master produce their effects. Thus I think a great part of Philosophy was at first Witchcraft; which being afterward derived from one to another, proved but Philosophy, and was indeed no more than the honest effects of Nature: What invented by us is Philosophy, learned from him is Magicke.

SIR THOMAS BROWNE, *Religio Medici*

1

THE AMERICAN AND THE RASTA TOSS THEIR BLUE AND white plastic BOAC flight bags onto the middle seat of the blue Mazda van. Then the American starts the engine, and the two men wave good-bye to the American wife and two children and depart from the compound. The American takes care to avoid potholes as the blue crackerbox of a van hurtles down the narrow lane from Church's hill toward Anchovy and the Rastaman leans out the window on the passenger's side and in Rasta-talk hails goats and chickens and townspeople stepping off the lane to avoid the car. They bump across the railroad tracks, pass the standpipe where a group of boys are filling buckets and wash basins with water piped from Montego Bay, and make a right turn onto the main road. Nearing Barrett's shop in Anchovy, the American slows the van and the Rasta calls out to the late-afternoon drinkers inside. Halloo, Barrett's! he yells, peering into the cool gloom of the place where a half dozen shadowy figures stand at the bar.

Recognizing the van and the bearded horse face of the Rasta at the window, Yvonne calls out his and the American's names, and immediately one of the shadowy figures at the bar rushes outside, where, swinging his huge arms, he directs the van to stop at the side of the road a few yards down from the shop. As he rushes up to the side of the car, two more men drift from the bar and follow him. The first, shirtless and powerfully built, an extremely handsome man in his late twenties who looks like Curt Flood, the baseball player, slaps the Rasta on his shoulder and plucks the spliff from his fingers. Taking a deep draw, he passes it back to his two followers, also men in their late twenties, though not as large, muscular and handsome and not shirtless.

So, Rasta, where you two trampoosing today? he asks, passing the spliff back through the window.

The Rasta's voice starts low and rises swiftly as he develops the subject. He and the American are on a journey to the Maroon city of Gordon Hall in the mountains of the east, he tells the man, there to deal with the African ascendants and their chief, and then to transport the chief and his officers and drummers forward from Gordon Hall to the ancient Maroon capital of Nyamkopong in the Cockpit, for the high purposes of holding discussions between the chiefs and officers of the two cities and of celebrating together with days and nights of dancing and drumming the feast day of Cudjoe, that old Ashanti father of the Maroons who led them against their enemies, the slavemasters of Jamaica who stole us out of Africa into Babylon.

The shirtless man looks across at the driver. Truth? he asks.

Truth, the American answers, smiling.

Plenty of beef there?

The Rasta scowls darkly at his lap, and the American answers, Yeah, man, too much beef. Wear you out, man. Even you.

The shirtless man laughs and yells, *Never!* His coal-colored skin shines dully in plates of orange sunlight that drift through the leaves of a tall breadfruit tree across the road. A loaded bus careens past, and the young man, still yelling, *Never!* spins away from the side of the blue car and dances, tossing pelvic humps at the air. *Never* too much beef! *Never!* His two followers stand away and laugh with him.

The American puts the car in gear and says they have

to go, they're supposed to be in Gordon Hall by midnight. That's the agreement.

Suddenly somber, the shirtless man grabs the window ledge next to the Rasta as if to hold the van back. Wait! he tells them. Those old Africans up there in the mountains, he says, dropping his voice and placing himself so that his followers can't hear or see what he's saying. They're friends of yours, right? You're up there a lot now, up in Nyamkopong and that other place, Gordon Hall? The man appears to be talking more to the American than to the Rasta.

Yeah, I guess you could say that, at least about Nyamkopong. We've only been to Gordon Hall once, though, last April. But the Colonel there, Bowra, seemed to like us and I think he basically trusts us.

That man trusts no man, the Rasta corrects him.

True, the American admits. True, but he trusts us as much as anyone else he can't control. We have an agreement with him, sort of a contract.

Fine, fine. What about that other one, the man in Nyamkopong? What about him?

Colonel Phelps?

A monkey, the Rasta grunts. Pure monkey.

No, the other man you told me about. You remember. Mr. Mann.

Yes, that one. Is he still your friend?

Yes, the American says. The Rasta nods agreement.

All right then. I need some help. Do you think he would help me, since I'm your friend too?

How?

My mother, the man says. She's sick. She's almost dead. He motions with his head toward his cabin beside the road. She's so sick I can't go any further from the house than Barrett's. The pain is so bad sometimes she can't even recognize me. She calls me my Daddy's name. Would your friend give me something for her? You know what I mean.

The men are silent for a few seconds. The hospital in

the Bay won't take her? the American asks. Can't you get her over to Mount Salem?

Not now. They sent her home to die. She's got the cancer. So they gave her back to me.

I don't think Mr. Mann can help her, if they couldn't do anything at the hospital, the American says.

Sure he can. Those old Africans know things. They know things. He'd do it for you. You know what I mean.

What?

Put her out of her misery. Kill her.

Kill her?

I can't! I'm her *son!*

Don't deal with the dead, the Rasta grunts. Jah lives. Jah lives. Never no deaders.

Why don't you come along with us? the American suggests. Then you can ask him yourself.

I can't, the man replies, his broad shoulders sagging. She needs me. I have to wash her and take care of her piss and shit and talk to her. She needs me. Anyhow, no one else can do it, I'm the only one still here. All her other children have gone off to Kingston.

All right, the American says. I'll ask Mr. Mann if he wants to help you. I'll explain it to him. But it'll cost. That old man doesn't help people for nothing, you know that.

How much?

I don't know. Twenty, thirty bucks, maybe.

The man's shoulders sag still further. Then he brightens. *You* pay him! And then when she's dead, I'll be able to get some work and pay you back. Because then I won't have to stay here at the house all the time. If you want, I'll work for you and pay you back that way. All right?

All right, man. I'll talk to him, I'll tell him your story. It'll be a few days before we get back, and I'll try to have something for you then. But she may be dead by then anyhow.

I hope not! the man exclaims.

Why?

She's my *mother*, man!

Right, the American says. Well, okay, then, I'll see you when I get back. Then he lets the clutch out and moves the car back onto the road as, behind them, the three young men head back to Barrett's.

2

IT'S NOT QUITE MIDNIGHT WHEN THEY ARRIVE AT GORDON Hall. A full moon floats between five-thousand-foot-high peaks and glazes the Maroons' terraced crops with silver light, as the blue van works its way through the valleys to the town. They pass huts and houses scattered alongside the narrow, unpaved road, but no signs of life—the windows are shuttered and doors closed. Occasionally a dog barks as they pass, but no one calls out or pokes his head through a doorway to see what a car is doing this far off the main road at this time of night. A car coming through during the day would be unusual; one coming through at midnight ought to be alarming. Especially a van capable of carting out a half ton of ganja, with two strangers, one white, the other a Rastaman.

The van turns off the road onto a crumbly lane that loops around the base of a mountain. Below the lane on the right a narrow stream heads noisily through the darkness for the Flint River and northward, where it eventually joins the Wog Water River and enters the sea. Above the van on the left the side of the mountain seems to leap straight up for the sky. As the van curls around the mountain and has come almost full circle to the road again, there is a break in the side of the mountain, a cleft that opens to a yard and a house with a porch running along the front. Behind the house the ground rises a few hundred feet above the lane to a cleared plateau and then disappears into the bushy side of the mountain, which keeps on rising steeply until half the sky is blocked from view. The van pulls off the lane and onto the packed dirt yard before the house and stops. The engine at the back ticks as it cools in the night air.

Ashanti! a man's voice cries from the darkness of the porch.

Ashanti baba! the white man answers loudly.

Johnny, that you? another, deeper voice calls from the porch.

The same! calls the American, as he leaves the car and walks in silvery moonlight toward the darkened house. The Rastaman too has stepped from the car and is standing on the other side, pissing into the bushes.

When the white man, the one they call Johnny, steps onto the porch, he is greeted by a half dozen men and women, blocky, dark figures illuminated only by cigarettes and the low flame of a candle guttering in a saucer on a small table in the corner. Next to the table, his back to the wall, Colonel Bowra is seated in a folding plastic and aluminum chair. The others are standing and leaning in the small space, filling it almost completely and with difficulty moving back so Johnny can make his way toward the Colonel. Behind him, standing off the porch, is the Rastaman.

You got Rasta with you, Johnny? barks the Colonel from his chair in the corner.

Yes.

All right, then you come forward too, Rastaman! Come on here!

As the Rasta pushes through the crowd and joins his friend, the old man, with difficulty, rises from his chair and takes a step toward them. I saw you coming, he says, and he wraps the two men in his huge arms and pulls them to him, the white man they call Johnny and the short, horse-faced, black man they call Rasta.

Ashanti, he says to each in his gravelly voice, and,

Ashanti baba, they answer. Then everyone else on the porch comes forward and slaps the two on their backs and shoulders, offering drinks, food, chairs to sit on. They appear greatly relieved that the two have come. If they had not come, the Colonel would have lost face, for he was the one who made the agreement with the white man and the Rasta from Nyamkopong. On his assurance that the strangers would show up as they had promised, Bowra's people came to his porch tonight with their drums and the abeng, wearing their suits and dresses and good shoes, with food for the trip and money and bottles of rum. If the white man and the Rasta did not appear with the van to transport them across the island all the way to Cockpit Country, they would all feel foolish, and they would all be forced to blame their Colonel for their feelings. For he alone insisted that the two men, Johnny and Rasta, would actually come to Gordon Hall at midnight tonight, January fourth, as they had promised back in April.

I saw you coming, Bowra says to the two. They have taken seats, Johnny and the Rasta on the porch rail, the Colonel in his lawn chair. He is wearing a Kelly green, double-knit, short-sleeved suit, is shirtless, and has a tan pith helmet on his head. The others on the porch are also dressed in clothes they probably take out and wear only once or twice a year—a long, purple taffeta dress on one old lady and on another a white dress that must have been someone's wedding dress. The woman in the white dress is the Colonel's wife Regine. She is powerfully built and, like the Colonel, tall. But where he moves slowly, ponderously, and with a certain care, as if he suffers from arthritis or the gout and it causes him pain to set his feet down, she moves with swiftness and power and a kind of recklessness, even in a crowded room, as if she were the only person in the room. Other people make way for her. The woman in the purple taffeta dress is called Aunt Celia. A singer, the Colonel tells Johnny and Rasta. She is old, probably much older than the Colonel, and it is difficult to imagine her voice having much force. She too is tall and, though thin, is broad-shouldered. Deep lines loop across and around her face, and when she smiles the lines seem to whirl. At the door that leads from the porch into the darkened house, a pair of old men hold onto each other as if to prop each other up. One man, large and toothless, wears a white shirt and scarlet necktie and on his head a battered black Homburg. Called the Captain, he is Bowra's younger brother, and in one huge pawlike hand he holds the abeng, the Maroon horn. The man next to him, dressed like an undertaker, is smaller and older. His toothless face is ridden with tics and twitches, and he continually gulps, *Ay-yup!* like a Yankee farmer. Gondo is his name, and he and the Captain hold onto each other and embrace almost as if they were lovers. The Captain is the chief when I am away from the city, Colonel Bowra says, but since he is the abeng man, he will have to travel with us this time. Another man, one of the lieutenants, is to take over in the Colonel's and the Captain's absence. Gondo, Bowra explains simply, is the best Maroon dancer in the world. There are four other men in the group—Harris, a pipe-smoking, deep-voiced man—My mouth-man, Bowra says—has the same blue and brown eyes as Bowra and Mr. Mann in Nyamkopong; Charles, who is tall and lean, claims to have an invisible black bird sitting on top of his head, even when he wears a cap, he insists; Pie, a fox-faced drummer—the best in the world, Bowra says—and Steve, Pie's apprentice, a large, muscular youth wearing a silver and yellow flowered rayon shirt with billowing sleeves, tight black pants, patent leather shoes, and a Levi cap set on his head at a precisely jaunty angle.

There are nine, then, who will be carted across the island to Nyamkopong, ordinarily a five-hour journey. There is the Colonel, who has moved off the porch and has taken the front passenger's seat. Then his wife Regine, Aunt Celia the singer, the Captain with his abeng, Gondo the dancer, Harris the mouth-man, Charles and his invisible black bird, Pie the drummer and Steve his apprentice. And of course Johnny, who will drive, and Rasta, who knows the way. While the Colonel from his seat in the front gives orders, the others lug to the side of the car the round gombay drums, different from the Nyamkopong gombays, which are square, and the two joints of thick bamboo, which the apprentice Steve will beat on, the head-basket of cooked food for the journey, jerked pork and pieces of chicken, mostly, and several bottles of white rum. For a few moments they argue over whether they should lash everything to the roof, to make more room inside, but finally they decide to keep their goods and drums inside where they can get at them whenever they want, and everyone climbs inside, carrying and pushing pork and chicken, rum, drums and bamboo stick. The drummers and tall Charles and Rasta jam themselves together way at the back; Harris, the two women and the Captain are in the middle; and Gondo, as small as a twelve-year-old boy, is between Johnny and the huge Colonel in front. The car is loaded and stuffed. They are ready.

Blow the bugle! Bowra barks at his brother, who is next to the open window behind him. The toothless old man in the Homburg sticks his head out the window, puts the cow horn to his lips, and starts to blow—at first a weak, wetly sputtering tootle, then a stronger and clearer and more sustained hooting tone, like an owl's, and finally a loud, lovely, warbling cry that echoes through the dark valleys.

Now, give me the rum! The rum! Bowra commands, and a hand, Harris', passes the bottle from somewhere in back. People are complaining, arguing, chattering all over the car, as if the Colonel were their father and the others, including Johnny and Rasta, his quarrelsome children. Johnny hollers back to Rasta for directions. Do we head south toward Castleton and then straight for Kingston and Spanish Town and go up from there, or should we go along the north coast to Montego Bay and head inland from there? The Rastaman can't hear him so he shouts for him to say it again. Steve the apprentice is trying to score some ganja from the Rasta, and Pie is drumming lightly across the worn skin of his gombay. Charles argues with Harris in front of him about the best route to Nyamkopong. Harris has seen a map of the island once and claims that Charles couldn't possibly know how to get there because he can't read. Charles reaches out and grabs the much smaller Harris by the throat and shakes him like a doll, and Harris screams with laughter. Aunt Celia has already started singing, a high-pitched gospel singer's voice singing an African song that repeats, repeats, repeats a single musical phrase. And next to her Regine scowls and yells at her husband the Colonel, telling him to hurry up and get finished with all this monkey business so they can reach Nyamkopong before the entire celebration is over and forgotten. Next to her the Captain is talking to his abeng, blowing the spit from it and chiding it for its weakness. In front, Gondo twitches and jumps every few seconds and gulps, *Ay-yup!* The Colonel unscrews the cap of the rum bottle, fills his mouth, sprays the ground outside his open window. Then he passes the bottle to Johnny, Gondo making a spastic grab for the bottle as it goes by, and orders Johnny to do the same. Filling his mouth with the fiery stuff, Johnny sticks his head out the window and splashes the rum on the ground, then passes the bottle back to the Colonel, who takes a pull from it and places it on the seat between his legs.

They have been jammed into the car for fully ten minutes and haven't left the Colonel's yard. There are still more preparations. The Colonel draws from a jacket pocket a tiny glass vial and hands it to Johnny. Drink that! he orders.

Unscrewing the top, Johnny sniffs the contents and winces. What is it?

Never mind. Just drink it. All of it. You're the driver and you have to be protected so you can get us there safely. Drink it.

Obediently, Johnny empties the vial into his mouth, grimaces, and swallows the oily liquid. Are we ready now? he asked Bowra, starting the engine. At the sound of the engine, everyone in the car suddenly goes silent.

The Colonel starts to sing, a high, slightly off-key, chanting song that is quickly taken up by the others in the car. Aunt Celia's voice comes in at the top, an ancient, keening sound that gives the chant a timeless quality as it rises and rolls on and over itself. Pie's drum and Steve's clattering bamboo come in under the song and start to drive it, and in a moment even Johnny's tenor and the Rasta's deep bass have caught up and joined them, and as the car sits there in the moonlight with its motor running, the choir of voices and drums lifts it off the ground and, as if on the hand of a god, carries it through the air. Hurriedly, Johnny slaps the rising car into gear, flicks on the headlights, and now, as if steering a boat, spins the wheel and guides the vehicle above the yard to the lane and above the lane to the rutted, unpaved road that curls through the narrow valleys to the road to Castleton. As they leave the settlement of Gordon Hall, the old Captain sticks his head out the window and blows furiously on the abeng, a long, clear, rising note that finally breaks and fades away, and they are gone.

The valleys are again silent and dark. A light wind moves up from the river below and ripples the leaves of the banana trees on the terraces, making them glitter coldly in the moonlight. A dog barks once, then goes back to sleep. Someone somewhere in the village tosses an empty bottle over a cliff, and after a few seconds it smashes lightly against a limestone outcropping far below near the river. Another dog, startled by the tinkling sound, barks. Then silence. And moonlight and wind and shadow.

3

THE TOWN OF CASTLETON IS CLOSED FOR THE NIGHT, BUT then the blue van crosses the ridge that spines the island from east to west, and they start the switchbacking descent to Kingston, the car leaning dangerously on the sudden curves as it descends to the lights below. Halfway down, they come to the crossroads town of Stony Hill at the outskirts of the sprawling city, and Bowra, shouting everyone into silence, instructs Johnny to stop the car in front of the only shop in town still open for business.

Bowra enters the bar first, his entourage coming along close behind. Except for the Rasta and Johnny, the group is well known here. The bartender hails Bowra, and the half dozen late-night drinkers at the bar greet the several members of the troupe cheerfully, and soon everyone is drinking and talking together. Harris controls the attention of several of the men by explaining elegantly and elaborately why they are out this late. We are on a peace mission to our brother Maroons in Nyamkopong, he begins, and then goes on to tell how for generations they have been lost to one another, but now they are going to extend the hand of Ashanti brotherhood and join forces. His voice rises and he begins to sketch out for his audience a scenario in which the Maroons deal with the PNP and Michael Manley the same way the old Maroons dealt with the British slavemasters. His gift is a preacher's gift, and this is evidently what Bowra means when he calls him his mouth man, for Bowra's gift is different. Bowra controls Harris the mouth-man, and Harris controls the words for him.

At the end of the bar, Charles and Gondo and Pie have gathered around a bulky young woman in a tight T-shirt and cutoff jeans and high-heeled shoes. Charles seems enormous, nearly seven feet tall, because of the black bird that sits on top of his head, and he flirts with the woman, while Pie and Gondo affirm the truth of what he is telling her, that there is a beautiful bird on his head. She says over and over in a tired voice, You crazy, man, ain't no bird up there. But soon she starts to believe them. It's invisible, Charles tells her, but you can see it if you want to. As she reaches delicately up to touch it, Charles warns her that it may bite. It does, the woman yells and yanks her hand back as if from a flame and jams her finger into her mouth and starts to suck on it. Gondo laughs wildly and then breaks into hiccups; Pie smiles like a fox and takes a swallow from his glass of rum.

Near the door the Rasta and Steve are rolling joints, tapping and tightening them, lighting up, inhaling deeply, dreamily. In a corner, the two women are sitting at a table and drinking Heineken from the bottle, waiting impassively for the men to finish their usual mixture of business and foolishness. Aunt Celia smiles cordially but inwardly, as if at a remembered holiday pleasure, while Regine, with a somber, slightly impatient expression on her face, watches the yakking men at the bar. Her husband the Colonel and his brother the Captain have moved purposefully through the bar and have disappeared into a room beyond.

Johnny! Come forward, Johnny! Bowra's voice booms out, and the white man crosses into the back room, where Bowra and the Captain are seated at a table with a third man. The stranger looks Syrian or Lebanese, is tall and thin, his black hair slicked greasily back in a pompadour. He is about forty and well dressed in a tan

bush jacket open to the waist. His chest is covered with
a pelt of black curly hair, and around his neck he wears
a half dozen fine gold chains, each bearing a different
emblem—a cross, a Star of David, a fertility symbol, a
small gold coin, a Maltese cross, and a caduceus.

Johnny, meet Doc. Doc's the M.P. for Gordon Hall.
The whole district belongs to Doc. Right, Doc? Bowra
asks, smiling broadly.

The man says nothing, extends his hand limply toward
the American, without looking up at his face.

Sit down, Johnny, sit down, Bowra says. Have a
drink. Want a drink?

No. A beer, maybe. I've got to drive all night, he
says, sitting down opposite the one they call Doc.

This here's Johnny, Doc. He's the one I told you
about. We call him Johnny. That's what we call a good
white man, Johnny. What's your *real* name, Johnny?
Tell Doc here your real name. Go ahead.

Johnny tells the man his real name, and the man nods,
his face expressionless. Then the Captain, who had gone
out to the bar for a few seconds, returns with a bottle of
stout and sets it in front of Johnny, who reaches into his
pocket as if to pay.

My pleasure, Doc says, waving a long bony hand at
him.

Thanks.

My pleasure.

The four men drop into silence. From the bar out
front comes the noise of Harris and Charles, Gondo's
hiccupping, the blat of raggae from the juke box and the
roll of the Rasta's reasoning with Steve.

Are you Labour or PNP? Johnny asks the man.

He looks up. Labour.

Oh.

The whole district belongs to Doc, Bowra adds.

Gordon Hall too?

Gordon Hall too, Doc answers.

They go on drinking in silence. Stacked high against
the walls of the room are hundreds of beer cartons, Red

Stripe and Dragon stout, mostly, and the place smells of stale beer. Windowless, the room is lit by a single bulb near the ceiling, and there seems to be no exit from the room except through the bar in front.

Is this your office? Johnny asks.

Doc laughs lightly, as if Johnny is stupid. No. I own the shop.

He owns the whole building, Bowra adds. And lots more too.

I bet he does, Johnny says, getting up from his chair. Well, Colonel and Captain, we'd better keep moving if we want to get to Nyamkopong by sunrise.

Good, good, the Captain says suddenly and he rises and departs quickly without saying anything to Doc or his brother.

The Captain's not a Labour man, Bowra tells Johnny, as if to explain his abrupt departure. But he's not the Colonel, he adds. Then he slaps Doc on the back, bids him good-bye and follows his brother out the door.

Thanks for the beer, Johnny says to Doc, and then he leaves too. By the time he reaches the van, everyone has already packed himself in. The noise of argument and teasing, complaint, song and boast, has returned, as everyone shouts, sings, talks, whines, and brags at once. Again Bowra starts to chant, and again the others soon join him—Pie on the drum, Steve on the bamboo stick, and the high voice of Aunt Celia keening over the top— and again the van floats into the air and is quickly flying down the long winding mountainside into Kingston. This time, though, the Captain keeps the abeng in his pocket and instead merely sings the rollicking, repeating chant along with the others.

FROM STONY HILL AT THE NORTHSIDE EDGE OF KINGSTON the road slips and slides rapidly past middle-class suburban homes, grows smooth and is suddenly lit by street lights. By the time the road reaches Constant Spring, it has become a boulevard with shops, department stores, shopping centers, and drive-in restaurants along both sides. In the nightlight, the city resembles Los Angeles. Then at Mary Browns Corner the road levels and begins the run for Half Way Tree and from there quickly into downtown Kingston and the waterfront.

It's raining now, and the road glistens. Traffic is light— only the cop cars and the cars of the night people flit past like shiny insects. And among the night people tonight come the Maroons of Gordon Hall, drumming and chanting their way to Nyamkopong to celebrate the birthday of their Captain Cudjoe. The blue van sails through the city to Half Way Tree, turns right and heads for Spanish Town Road, then right again toward Spanish Town itself, past the rows of warehouses and factories, then past the lands taken over by the squatters, the homeless ones who have come in from the country to huddle at the edge of the city in tiny patched-together shanties, where they wait to be removed by bulldozers, so the land can be developed in what developers call an orderly way. But the Maroons and Johnny and the Rasta see none of this—like Dorothy and her cronies on their yellow brick road, they fly past the disorder and rubble of the world without seeing it, because all they can see tonight is their goal tonight, Nyamkopong, the African city where their ancestors signed the treaty with the British and where Cudjoe ruled.

Spanish Town, built mostly of bricks, is an old city, the first British capital of Jamaica and before that the main Spanish settlement on the island. It's also where Marcus Garvey was jailed, and when he prophesied that the walls of the prison would fall and the doors open wide for him, he was talking about this high-walled prison, dark and silent and wet as the van passes by. In the back seat the Rasta groans, Marcus, oh Marcus. Marcus, oh Marcus. The others, as if out of respect for the Rasta, fall into silence.

Marcus Garvey was a great man, Johnny finally says.

No! Bowra bellows back. A great *African!* And then begins a long, screaming argument between Bowra and the Rasta on one side and Harris and the Captain on the other as to whether or not Marcus Garvey was an African. Harris and the Captain insist that Garvey was a Jamaican because he was born in Jamaica, and Bowra and the Rasta yell back that he was an African because he was a black man, and at least according to Bowra, a Maroon. Bowra and the Rasta agree that the only true Jamaicans were the Arawak Indians, but since none of them exist anymore, having all been slain hundreds of years ago by the Spanish and the British, then no one is Jamaican. Everyone is either African or Indian or Chinese or British or American or Canadian, the Rasta explains.

Or Syrian! Bowra adds.

Or Syrian.

But they don't win the argument. It just gets lost in Gondo's sudden, angry explosion of words, incoherent, disconnected words, as if he were having a fit or were possessed by a demon. He leaps in his seat between Bowra and Johnny, thrashes and angrily shouts a wild mixture of English and Ashanti words and expressions. Johnny, clearly frightened, slows the van, draws it over to the side of the road, and hollers at Gondo to shut up and sit still so he can drive. To the Colonel, he cries, Shut him up, for Christ's sake! Hold him still, I can't drive with him like that!

From the back of the van comes the thrumming sound of Pie's hands against the goatskin, and then the high wail of Aunt Celia starts the song, *Ah-ya-ya-ya-oh-h-h! Ah-ya-ya-ya-oh-h-h!* Bowra, ignoring both Johnny's plea and Gondo's fit, joins in with his heavy voice, and the others swing in behind, until in a moment everyone but Johnny and Gondo is singing, the drum and bamboo stick shoving them along and shoving them faster and faster, smoothing their voices out and bringing them into formation. And then Gondo too has caught up and has joined them. His body ceases to leap about and settles back into its normal quiet twitchings. Finally even Johnny relents and hurries into line with the others and he too is singing, *Ah-ya-ya-ya-oh-h-h!* The van pulls back onto the road, speeds up, and lifts off again, rising smoothly over the coastal flatlands west of Spanish Town, heading through the darkness for May Pen.

ON THE OTHER SIDE OF MAY PEN, BEFORE THE LAND STARTS to rise toward the Mocho Mountains in Clarendon, they pass through a village called Denbigh, where the Colonel spots an open shop. He directs Johnny to slow down and pull into a lane on the left that leads them between a pair of cinderblock warehouses to a tiny shop fronting the lane. Three or four women with small children racing around them have set up charcoal braziers in front of the shop, where they are cooking and selling fish and hot peppers and onions. There is a small group of people—cops, prostitutes, gamblers, a few "soul boys" off the road from Kingston—at the bar and standing around outside, drinking and eating fish and peppers off sheets of brown paper.

Fish and peppers! Johnny says, and he draws the van over to the shop and parks it. All the men climb out of the van and head for the bar. Behind them, Aunt Celia and Regine stretch out in the emptied seats and close their eyes for sleep. Johnny and the Rasta buy Dragon stouts and step outside for the fish stands, while the others gather around their Colonel at the bar, order rum, and commence describing the purpose and significance of their journey to the barman and the men and women standing around in the small three-sided room.

We are the Maroons from Gordon Hall! the Colonel announces, when everyone has been served and he has spat the first sip on the dusty ground and has swallowed the second.

A tall, gaunt, rat-faced cop with buck teeth, a redstriper in uniform, leans against the juke box and takes in the group with an amused smile on his lips, a cold critical look in his eyes. He glances swiftly out at Johnny and the Rasta, then back to the Colonel, whose Kelly green bulk dominates the room.

What about those two? Are they the Maroons from Gordon Hall too? he asks.

The Colonel tells the cop that the short one, the Rasta, is a Maroon from Nyamkopong, and he's helping the taller one, the white man, Johnny, carry them across the island to Nyamkopong, where the chiefs of the Maroons will celebrate together and have a big conference. Then he barks at the two men outside, instructing them to come forward and present themselves to these strangers, which they do, with apparent reluctance, both of them unsmiling and stepping warily into the presence of the cop, for he has made himself the center of the group of habitués and soul boys in the bar. They watch him as if waiting for his reaction to these loud country people claiming to be Maroons from the mountains beyond Kingston. Then, depending on how the cop takes them, they will react.

You a Maroon? the cop asks Johnny.

No.

Where are you from?

Anchovy. In St. James.

Long ways from here.

Yes.

And you, Rastaman. You a Maroon?

I-and-I am the son of a son, and I-father as well, back there to the ancient times when the Africans came into their captivity, and since those among them who cast off the shackles and chains of slavery came to be known amongst the people of the world as Maroons, so the ascendants of I-and-I would have I be also. Sar, the Rasta adds with a smile.

The cop turns to the barman. Give the Maroons a drink, he says. All of them, even the white Maroon, he adds good-naturedly, nodding toward Johnny. The Rasta too. The I-man's a Maroon too. At least tonight he is.

Johnny feeds the juke box and the Rasta punches the keys, and soon the alley is filled with music and the noise of men shouting over it to each other. It's a good juke, with forty or fifty of the newest songs on it, the sign of a critical and demanding and political neighborhood. Johnny and the Rasta nod and jog in place to the heavy beat of the records, Pie drums along on the countertop, while the cop and the Colonel try to ignore it and talk over it to each other about the government and other weighty matters appropriate to their respective positions. Charles is trying to dance with one of the women, but she wants to sit on a beer carton and watch, so he dances alone in front of her, trying to impress and seduce her with a shuffling, intricate step that seems slightly out of time. Harris, his pipe clenched in his teeth, is at the Colonel's shoulder, his mouth at the ready. The Captain has stepped outside for fish and a chat with the women at the smoky stoves.

Gondo, though, after starting slowly, has begun to dance faster and faster, in perfect time, with increasing grace and lightfootedness, a tiny old man who soon seems to have left the ground to dance a few inches above it, whirling like a dervish in the crowded room, forcing everyone to clear a space for him in the middle. His unbuttoned black suit coat flares out around him like a skirt as he spins and dips, leaps up and drops through his own circles to the bare ground, while the music pounds along behind, his only perfect partner. The women and children leave the fish stands and come to stand at the open front of the bar to watch the old man, and everyone in the bar, even Charles, stops what he is doing and stares happily at Gondo, for the brittle, nervous, tiny man with the chirping voice has become liquid and weightless, has turned his old body wholly into music.

It seems that they remain for hours at the bar in Denbigh, drinking and eating fish and peppers, dancing and watching Gondo dance, full of brag, shout and argument, until at last the Colonel, on some schedule of his own, orders his people from the place, and they climb back into the van. Gondo has switched places with the Rasta and falls swiftly into sleep in the back. The others are soon asleep also, and then only Bowra, the Rasta, and Johnny are awake, the Rasta and Bowra talking in low voices about crops. Bowra complains that the land in Gordon Hall is too hilly and difficult to farm and wants the Rasta to tell him what kind of land the other Maroon villages have, for he has not traveled before to any of the other three villages.

Charles Town is the worst of the four, the Rasta tells him. All rock and hills and not much water. Moore Town is better than Gordon Hall because it's in Portland, where the rain always falls and is situated among gentle river valleys with plenty of deep rich soil. But Nyamkopong in the Cockpit, the Rasta tells him, has the best land of the four villages for farming. The water and the soil settle into the bottoms of the cockpits, and, where the sun reaches the bottom, there are beautiful gardens.

Johnny aims the van into the night, driving easily, comfortably, while the two farmers talk. He smiles as the car leaves the ground again and flies.

THE ROAD CLIMBS TOWARD MANDEVILLE, AND THE SMALL engine at the back of the van begins to labor, and soon Johnny is shifting gears back and forth to keep the vehicle moving. With the others sleeping, except for the Rasta and the Colonel, the load seems to have tripled in weight, and though the car remains airborne, it flies slowly and low over the road.

At Mandeville, when they pass the Alcan processing plants and where the yards, buildings, and equipment are protected by eight-foot-high, chain-link fences and arc lights on aluminum poles, the people in the back seats start to wake. First Charles, whose low talking with his bird wakes Harris, who tells him to shut up. Then Gondo, who tells Harris that Charles needs to keep his bird happy or it will leave him. And then Pie, whose light drumming wakes Steve, and then the two women, both of whom start to sing quietly, Regine singing one line and Aunt Celia the answer, an Ashanti riddle song in which the questions change and the answers remain the same.

Bowra grumbles that he is cold and goes to work on the second bottle of rum, passing it to the people in back now and then but quickly demanding its return. Compared to the coastal flatlands, it is cold now, and dry and dusty along the road from the red clouds of powdered bauxite surrounding the huge dump trucks that haul the ore night and day into Mandeville from the mines at Williamsfield and Myersville and other, smaller outposts in the hills. West of Mandeville, though, the road starts a long descent, and in seven or eight miles, by the time it reaches the town of Spur Tree, the road has returned almost to sea level, where it is warm and humid again.

Spur Tree is a small agricultural town whose largest building is an open-sided banana packing plant, basically a large corrugated tin roof on poles. As the blue van cruises through the village, the place seems wholly asleep, but Bowra knows better. He says he knows of a shop in this town that belongs to a "big man," the head of security for the Alcan plant in Mandeville, and he's so big he's able to keep the place open all night long if he wants to and the cops never bother him for it, even though he's only got a tavern license and legally is required to close by eleven at night. Bowra's never been to this shop himself, but he's heard of it from a cousin who used to drive a truck over here for one of the bauxite companies.

Suddenly everyone is excited again and full of energy— Gondo jerking spastically and gulping, *Ay-yup!*, Harris and Bowra yammering rapidly in Ashanti, the women singing, Pie and Steve drumming away, Charles feeding his bird so it'll be strong, the Captain arguing with the Rasta that the Gordon Hall abeng man, meaning himself, knows the old African codes, and the Nyamkopong abeng man, he'd heard, only knows how to blow it as if it were a toy trumpet. The old Maroons could send messages with the abeng, he tells the Rasta, and they used a code whenever they played it, a language, to make the horn talk. They didn't just stand up and toot on the thing, he points out scornfully. They *talked* with it.

Out of this babble Bowra suddenly cries, Stop! and Johnny obediently pulls the van off the road to the left into a lot where a half dozen cars are parked in front of a darkened cinderblock building that from the outside resembles a pink bunker—windowless, squat and ominous-looking. This is it! the Colonel announces. Let's go get a drink and dance with the girls!

He swings his bulky body out the door and the eight other men follow, the women once again slumping back into the vacated seats to sleep. Bowra marches straight for the door at the center of the building, yanks it open and strides down three steps into a dimly lit, low-ceilinged room with a bar at one end and a dozen small tables scattered along the sides. The walls are painted garishly yellow and are decorated with Day-Glo posters of American pop figures like Jimi Hendrix and Bob Dylan.

In one corner is a juke box, but no one is playing it, and the place is silent when the Maroons enter. Not silent, however, for long. A few drinkers have gathered in a knot at the far end of the bar and seem to be engaged in private conversation with the barman. Scattered along the bar are three solitary drinkers, not farmers but apparently locals, in khaki work clothes, and then there are the usual bored, tired prostitutes in tight Levi's, psychedelic T-shirts, and wedge-heeled plastic sandals. The men talking to the barman—there are four of them, and the barman is the fifth—are not farmers either but look more like truck drivers or machine operators. They're all wearing the same dark gray uniform with their names on their left shirt pocket, as if they all work for the same company. They are hard-working men who have jobs that pay them well for it. They also look mean and very sure of themselves.

Rum! Bowra shouts down to the barman, as his entourage scatters itself along the bar in various groupings—Charles and the Captain heading as usual for the women, Steve for the Rasta, Harris for his position at the shoulder of the Colonel, and Pie, Gondo and Johnny for the juke box—making a sudden clamor of their presence, causing the group of uniformed men at the end of the bar to turn and stare at them without amusement.

The barman moves slowly toward the Colonel. He's a thick-bodied man, below average in height but powerful looking in a tight, dark green, GANJA OIL CO. T-shirt. Stopping in front of the Colonel, he crosses his arms over his beefy chest and says one word, Closed. Then he returns to his friends in the gray uniforms.

Bowra raises his eyebrows in mock astonishment. Closed? he asks Harris. Closed? With all these people drinking, he says, waving his hand grandly in the direction of the three solitary drinkers at the bar and the pair of prostitutes reaching tentatively for the bird they can't see on top of Charles' head. With all these people here, the man wants us to believe he's closed?

Harris' response is in rapid-fire Ashanti, a harsh, bass-toned, sputtering line of syllables that brings the Maroons and even Johnny and the Rasta, who don't know what he has said, to attention and draws them quickly over to the Colonel's side.

Come here, Bowra says to the barman, who looks up, surprised. Come here, man. The Colonel's voice is not loud but is emphatic and utterly sincere. It is the voice he would use with a misbehaving child, as if he were more disappointed in the child than angry.

Me? the barman asks, pointing at his chest.

Yes. Come here. Come here, man.

Obediently, the man comes forward, while Harris chatters in Ashanti into the Colonel's ear.

When the barman has come to stand before the Colonel, he is told to look into the Colonel's eyes, which he does. Harris goes on talking in that strange, intense language as if the language in his voice were a drum in his hands accompanying Bowra's confrontation with the barman.

Lifting one of his huge hands, Bowra points an index finger directly at the barman's heart, and the man lurches

backwards, clutching his heart and howling with pain.
Then Bowra brings his hand down, and the pain apparently ceases, leaving the barman gasping.

You all right, Larry? calls one of the men in the group
at the end of the bar.

The barman doesn't answer. He is staring into Bowra's
eyes as if fascinated by the blue and brown concentric
rings. Two of his friends have taken a step toward the
Maroons and are looking at the barman in puzzlement.
Hey, Larry, you all right, man?

Charles answers them. The man is learning who the
Colonel is, he explains. He's all right.

Rum, the Colonel says calmly. Eight glasses and two
half pints.

Silently the barman fills the order. When he has set
out the glasses and the rum, the Colonel says, Thank
you, and dismisses him with a little wave.

Johnny and the Rasta stare after him as he walks back
to his friends, while the others grab for their glasses and
pour out the rum. The barman and the Maroons too
behave as if nothing unusual has happened, as if the
barman merely changed his mind and decided to serve
the group after all, since that would be the reasonable
thing to do anyhow. They clearly are on the road and
have stopped in for a quick, single drink.

Johnny looks at his friend the Rasta, who lifts his
eyebrows and purses his thick lips. Then they each
reach for a glass, and for the first time since Johnny has
met the Rasta, he sees him drink off a glass of rum, and
it is Johnny's turn to raise his eyebrows and purse his
lips.

Smiling sheepishly, the Rasta shrugs his shoulders,
and Johnny slaps him affectionately on the back. Terron,
this here's Oz, and we're on the yellow brick road, he
says, laughing. I guess we can expect just about anything to happen. Jah will forgive you one drink of rum,
my friend.

The others are heading for the door, apparently without paying for their drinks. Johnny turns to the barman,

who seems to be ignoring them and is immersed again in his conversation with the truckers. Hey, friend, how much? Johnny calls to him.

He looks up slowly and seems not to know what Johnny's talking about. What?

How much for the drinks?

Oh. Forget it. It's late, he says. We're closed now, he adds and goes back to his conversation.

Okay by me, Johnny says, and he and the Rasta turn and move for the door.

Outside, the two men stand for a moment and savor the cool air. The others have packed themselves back into the van. The eastern sky is a dark, silky gray color, but in the west it's still night-dark, and the stars flash across it in belts and blankets. A light breeze is stirring and carries the smell of a cookfire. Somewhere in the distance a truck is shifting gears as it hauls its load of bauxite uphill to Mandeville.

The wizard of Oz, the Rasta says in a low voice. The wizard of Oz.

They're silent for a moment, while a rooster crows.

The wizard of Oz was a fake, Johnny says. Remember?

The Rasta says he never saw that movie, he just heard about it.

Well, he was a fake wizard, Terron. A phony.

No. It couldn't be. Or they wouldn't have called him that.

What?

A wizard. A wizard is a wizard, he explains.

Yeah, I guess so, Johnny says, and the two walk to the darkened van, where everyone is sleeping. The Rasta slides in between Johnny and the snoring Colonel from the driver's side, then Johnny gets in and starts the engine. One or two in the back stir and mumble, then slump back to sleep, as the van bumps onto the road, turns left toward Santa Cruz and Maggotty, and builds speed.

*   *   *

FOR THE REST OF THE JOURNEY THE AMERICAN AND THE Rasta remain silent, and the others sleep. Now and then, with a casual wave of the hand, the Rasta tells the American he should turn right or left, as the van works its way slowly west and then north toward Cockpit Country, through Santa Cruz, Lacovia, and Newton, until they are in the valley of the Black River and nearing the town of Maggotty. The sky behind them has gone to a silvery white and ahead of them has turned to zinc, and the stars have disappeared. Smoke from cookfires curls up from kitchens behind the shanties and cabins alongside the road. Here and there an early-rising farmer walks from his cabin to his fields, or a child sleepily carries a tin of water from the standpipe near the road back to the house.

A few miles outside Maggotty, the American says in a low voice, It's all right, I know where I am now. He enters the closed-up village, passes the shops and stores, the doctor's office, the ESSO station—familiar territory at last. They cut through the Appleton factory grounds, pass by the men coming in for the first shift, pick up an unpaved road on the other side, swing past the rows of worker's cabins and start the long run through the deep green cane fields. As they pass the river where Johnny and the men and boys from Nyamkopong used to come to bathe, the sun cracks the horizon behind them, splashing sudden waves of golden light across their backs and over the motionless stalks of cane. In the distance the hills of Nyamkopong above the rapidly rising haze are flooded with sunlight.

The Maroons are awake. They know where they are, even though they have never been here before. Pie brings his drum to life, Steve joins in lightly, and Aunt Celia starts a mournful song full of the ancient grief and happiness of coming home, the cry for time found and lost forever. Regine's powerful voice wells up, and then Harris and the Colonel, Charles and the Captain and Gondo are singing also, a wailing song that Johnny and the Rasta cannot join, and in silence, their faces washed with awe, they listen and stare straight ahead at the winding, rising road to Nyamkopong.

At Whitehall Johnny stops the van, for this is where the land of the Maroons begins, and the Captain blows the abeng, a cry, a wail, a plea, three separate blasts on the horn—and they enter Cockpit Country slowly, ceremoniously, in the pathetic little blue Japanese van, the ancient sounds of the abeng preceding them, as the sun springs free of the horizon, shudders a second, and ascends into the sky. Now they come unto Nyamkopong, the African city of Cudjoe and his fierce Ashanti warriors. Now comes the Colonel from the brother city of the Maroons in the east, now come the chief of the brethren from Gordon Hall and his captain and lieutenants, his women and drummers and dancers, bearing gifts and offerings for their beloved brethren and the gods and a deep desire to exchange views and wisdom with their wise and ancient brethren of Nyamkopong. Now comes the heart of Jamaica to embrace itself and to know itself in the presence of its counterpart here in the east. Let the others stand away, let the sons and daughters of the slaves and the sons and daughters of the slaveholders and all those who came after—let them stand away on this day and honor the sons and daughters of those who waged war against the slaveholders and slew the slaves who aided their masters, who endured the wilderness of the Cockpit and learned to survive and thrive there, who kept alive the dances and songs and the knowledge of the sacred herbs and the names of the gods and also kept alive the memory of an African language—who kept their powers. This remnant of a remnant, honor it.

4

THEY PULL UP BEFORE THE PINK STUCCO HOME OF COLONEL
Martin Luther Phelps. The town is still pretty much
asleep, a half dozen cookfires burning, some sleepy-
eyed children stumbling around carrying water, a tall
man stretching in his doorway like a lion. When the blue
van chugged uphill into the town, abeng blowing from
the window, drums and people inside wailing away as if
celebrating the end of a long and mournful war, the few
people who were up and about merely stared after the
van in puzzlement. Some small boys carrying water on
their heads saw the van and, recognizing it, called out
the name of the American who owned it. But that was
the only sign of recognition or welcome they received,
until they got to the Colonel's house and shut off the
motor, opened all the doors of the van, and let the
Captain blow and blow on the abeng, making it howl in
hurt and anger at the Colonel's closed door.

At last, Colonel Phelps opens his door and peers out
at the people gathered by the road before his yard—
Bowra, huge and glowering in his pith helmet and bright
green suit, and the two old women, their arms folded
across their chests, and Harris and tall Charles and even
tiny Gondo staring darkly at him, while the drummers
pound away and the Captain blows on the abeng. Colonel Phelps is clearly rattled, surprised, embarrassed—he
must not have believed the American and the Rasta

would actually do what they said they were going to do, carry the Maroon Colonel and his officers and musicians all the way from Gordon Hall in St. Mary's so they could join the Maroons of Nyamkopong in their celebration. How else to explain Colonel Phelps' surprise, his lack of preparation and ceremony, the fact that when they arrived at six in the morning the town is half asleep and even the Colonel of Nyamkopong himself has to peek out his closed door and wonder who is making such a racket out there?

Agitated, hopping tentatively forward onto the porch, then rushing nervously across his yard in his bare feet, wearing only his undershirt and beltless pants, Colonel Phelps embraces his brother Colonel, gushes over the stern-faced women and the scowling men, apologizing all the while for not expecting them this early in the day, he believed they were coming, he knew they were coming, of course, of course, but he thought they wouldn't arrive until tonight when the celebration actually begins. He is a tiny, nervous man next to Bowra, fawn-colored and brittle before the black-skinned, implacable, bearlike man from Gordon Hall.

Did Johnny tell you we would come this morning? Harris demands. Johnny knew what to do, he tells Phelps. He knew to arrive at Gordon Hall at midnight on the fourth of January and carry us to Nyamkopong. He knew to bring us here safely so we could sit and have consultations with you and your officers on this day and tomorrow concerning important Maroon business. Did he tell you this?

The drums have gone silent, and the Captain has shoved his abeng back into his pocket. Colonel Phelps looks confused. Johnny? he asks. Johnny? Who is Johnny? Do you mean Nonny?

No, you *idiot!* the Colonel shouts down into the man's narrow, frightened face. *Johnny!* he says, and points over at the American.

Oh, yes, yes, now Colonel Phelps understands. Johnny! Yes, yes, Johnny did say he would arrive this day with the people from Gordon Hall, yes, indeed he did say it, but it didn't seem possible to the Colonel that it could be accomplished—after so many generations of separation and so much distance . . . It seemed too good to be true, he says to Bowra, his voice oily and in control again, and he takes one of the man's paws in his hands and leads him to the porch.

Seating Bowra in one of the plastic lawn chairs and the women in the other two, he pulls the American aside and draws him into the living room. Working rapidly, he grabs glasses and a nearly full bottle of rum from the sideboard and orders the American to take the drinks outside while he gets dressed and his wife prepares food. Tell the Colonel I'll soon come, he says, almost pleading. Then he says the American's new name, as if trying it out. Johnny?

Yes, Colonel.

Can you help me out?

How do you mean?

I mean—can you let me have some money? How many of them *are* there?

Nine.

Yes, yes. Nine. Well . . . I should feed them and give them plenty to drink, you know. I mean, they came all this way . . .

Truth, Johnny says flatly. Truth. And he fishes in his pocket, draws out his money, and hands the man two tens. That's all I'll be able to give you, Colonel.

The man folds the bills and stuffs them into his pocket, then pushes Johnny outside and, as the American steps onto the porch, starts hollering for his wife in the bedroom, shouts several quick orders at his son, demands to know where his uniform is, he needs his uniform, get the fire started, kill a chicken, the red one, the red one, you idiot!

Outside on the porch the group is silent. It has started to shower and everyone has crowded onto the porch for shelter. Johnny sets the rum and glasses in front of the Colonel and steps to the side where the Rasta stands, while the others grab for the bottle. *Water!* Bowra bellows, and just as Johnny moves for the door, Phelps' son, a boy of about twelve, comes running out with a Mason jar of water, sets it carefully down on the low table next to the Colonel, and rushes back inside.

Martin Luther Phelps don't got no manners, the American says to his friend in a low voice. The others are gulping angrily at their drinks and whispering among themselves. The sudden shower has become a rainstorm and has grayed out everything beyond the yard. The doors of the van are standing wide open, but the rain is so heavy that no one seems willing to cross the yard and close up the car.

"The man's a monkey," the Rasta declares and starts to work rolling a spliff.

GRADUALLY, HOWEVER, COLONEL PHELPS GETS MATTERS under control. The rain lets up and the day becomes merely a cloudy, cool one. Under the woolly gray sky, trees drip loudly and run-off water from the tin roofs trickles into rain barrels. By the time the Maroons have emptied the first bottle of rum, Colonel Phelps' son, also named Martin, delivers a second, and the smell of chicken frying and yams baking in the coals has started drifting around to the porch from the kitchen in back. It is then that the Colonel of the Maroons of Nyamkopong finally appears, and it's a different man this time from the one who an hour before was skittering confusedly about in his undershirt and bare feet. This man is straightbacked and walks like a graduate of West Point. He wears a pith helmet that's cleaner than Bowra's and unbattered and a uniform that must have belonged originally to a British policeman—dark blue with a Sam Browne belt across his chest, a crisp white shirt and dark blue tie underneath, and glossy black shoes.

His son comes stumbling out behind him, carrying a heavy straightbacked wooden chair, and when he sets it down before Bowra, Colonel Phelps sits and ceremoniously pours himself a glass of rum. It looks perfect now: the

two Colonels, both men in full regalia, facing each other
with raised glasses, the Gordon Hall entourage standing
back quietly while the smell of a feast being prepared
encircles them and sunshine breaks through the clouds
and brings the brilliance of the green hills and cockpits
into sharp focus for miles—so that, with apparent relief,
Johnny and the Rasta, who have been glumly mopping
out the van, walk smiling back to the porch to stand
with their friends from Gordon Hall and enjoy this
moment.

There is a brief speech from each of the Colonels: first
Colonel Phelps toasts his beloved brethren from Gordon
Hall and their common ancestors; then Colonel Bowra
prays for peace and prosperity for all Maroon people.
They each dribble a bit of rum on the floor of the porch
for the dead and empty their glasses in a swallow. As if
on cue, Harris starts to sing and Pie and Steve go to
work on the gombay and bamboo stick as the women,
Charles, the Captain, and Gondo come shrieking and
bellowing in. Finally both Colonels, having refilled their
glasses, join the song, their face wide open and happy,
for it is a song that Colonel Phelps evidently knows as
well as his counterpart does, a song that goes back over
two hundred years to the slave ships and for hundreds of
years before that to West Africa and the Empire of the
Coromantees, a jubilation song that leaps and jumps
about disjointedly, so that a person who has not heard
its words and tune hundreds of times cannot sing it.

The two men stand and throw their arms around each
other and kiss each other's cheeks. All is forgiven. The
Maroons of Nyamkopong and the Maroons of Gordon
Hall are one—two of the chambers of the heart of Jamaica have been joined, and the world seems stronger,
purer, more lucid for it. Terron the Rasta, the serious
man, smiles sweetly, and the white American's eyes are
wet with tears.

Suddenly clattering over the rise and skidding to an
abrupt halt behind the blue van there comes a green-and-
cream-colored Toyota Land Cruiser with four uniformed

cops from Maggotty inside, a round-faced sergeant driving and three dour patrolmen carrying shotguns. The Sergeant, a dapper, mustached man with a broad smile and a trim but soft-looking body, steps out and strolls languidly across the yard to the porch. The other cops remain inside the Land Cruiser, holding their shotguns between their legs like umbrellas.

The Maroons have gone silent and, except for the two Colonels, have all taken a single step backward, even Johnny and the Rasta, opening an alley for the Sergeant, who strolls through the group straight for Colonel Phelps, extending his hand as he nears the man and smiling even more broadly than when he left his vehicle.

Martin, he says, as if greeting an old family friend. All dressed for the celebration, I see. You're a day early, though, aren't you? It's tomorrow, isn't it? The celebration?

Now Bowra too has taken a step backward and away from his position at the side of Colonel Phelps, and, like the others, he has covered his face with a curtain, as if he were not himself but an actor playing himself. No one looks at anyone else. Everyone is watching the police sergeant's hearty black hand shake Colonel Phelps' limp brown one.

Yes, yes, that's right, the celebration *is* tomorrow, Phelps says rapidly, averting his eyes from the steady gaze of the smiling sergeant. Yes, tomorrow, January sixth. For the birthday of Cudjoe . . .

But look at you, all dressed up in your dancing suit!

Well, yes . . . yes . . . but . . . it's because of my friends here, he says, waving his hand weakly to indicate the nine from Gordon Hall. This is the Colonel of the Maroons from Gordon Hall . . . and these are his officers . . .

Ah! the sergeant exclaims and reaches out to grasp the big man's hand. Colonel . . . ?

Bowra. Sergeant . . . ?

Kemp. Quickly he turns back from Bowra's mask to Colonel Phelps', which has a thin, nervous smile trickling over its lips. Well, then, Colonel, may I? he asks, nodding in the direction of the half-full rum bottle.

Yes, yes, of course, just a moment while I go get a glass, he says, scuttling from the porch and quickly returning with a clean glass, pouring off three fingers of rum and handing it to the man. There you are, Sergeant, he says uselessly, turning away and refilling his own glass and abruptly emptying it into his mouth.

The Sergeant lifts his glass with ceremony and toasts the health of the Maroons of Gordon Hall. They nod acceptance, and then he too empties the rum into his mouth and sits down, taking Colonel Phelps' wooden chair as if it had been set out for him alone.

Phelps stands opposite him like an eager waiter. The others have begun to collect into a tight knot behind their Colonel. Johnny and the Rasta, as if they too were Gordon Hall Maroons, have fallen into formation with them. An outsider viewing the scene would surmise that the thin man in the pith helmet and dark uniform was petitioning his chief for some favor and that the group of people behind the big man in the bright green suit was waiting its turn to present its petition. Doubtless the Maroons, at some point, perceive how they look, or would look, to a stranger, because as one they take a few steps randomly away from the porch, and the group disperses. Brooding alone and in pairs, they walk off— Johnny and the Rasta returning to the job of mopping out the blue van, the others wandering around as if investigating the yard and immediate neighborhood. Everyone makes a large circle around the police car and looks through or past it, as if it were invisible or not there at all. Things have clearly gone wrong again.

The Sergeant and Colonel Phelps go on talking in low voices on the porch, the Sergeant pouring himself a second drink, the Colonel quickly following. Then the Sergeant stands, waves to the three inside the Land Rover to follow him, and steps inside the house after the Colonel. Carrying their shotguns familiarly under their arms, as if they have been out bird hunting, the three red-stripers stroll across the yard and enter the house, where through the window they can be seen standing around a table, filling plates with chicken and rice, beans and yams.

The rain is falling again, lightly but steadily, as if settling in for the day. In a few moments Bowra and the others have arrived at the van and are climbing wetly, grumpily inside, for the first time seeming uncomfortably crowded in the van. They are tired and bad-natured, arguing crossly with one another in low voices.

Harris reaches forward and pokes Johnny on the shoulder. Where's their abeng man? Don't they have an abeng man? Tell me that!

Yes, they have one. I've heard him play it. He's an old man, older than the Captain. But he plays it well.

Hah! he said and lit his pipe. Where is he, then? Tell me that.

I don't know.

Bowra turns his bulk in his seat and stares at Johnny. And where's this Mann you told about? This Secretary of State or whatever they call him. Is he the mouth-man?

I don't know . . . I don't know where he is.

Entering the conversation as if waking from a nap, the Rasta in a thick voice says simply, Mann won't deal with that monkey Phelps.

Does he know we're here? Johnny asks the Rasta. Maybe we should go to his house . . . ?

No, Bowra answers.

He's not the Colonel, Harris adds, explaining patiently the protocol of the situation. He's only the Secretary of the Maroons of Nyamkopong. This man down here, this monkey with the police all around, he's the Colonel, and it's his duty to make all the preparations. Your Mr. Mann knows all this, and if he's not here to welcome his brother Maroons, and if the abeng man isn't here to call out our arrival to the rest of the people, and if there are no drummers and no one to sing with us and no one to sit down and eat and talk with us about matters of great importance, no one except that monkey of a Colonel and his friends from the police, then it's because the Colonel has not done his job.

Why don't they kill him? inquires Bowra, his brow wrinkling in apparent puzzlement.

What?

Why don't they kill him? Cut off his head.

Kill him? Johnny asks.

Kill him. And make your friend Mann be the Colonel. That's what you've got to do. Especially now, explains Harris.

The rest joyfully agree. Kill him! Chop him up! Throw the pieces to the dogs! Kill the monkey! Kill him! Kill him!

Johnny looks at the Rasta, who has a light smile on his face. Should they kill him? he asks his friend.

Who?

Colonel Phelps.

No, I mean, should *who* kill him?

Oh . . . well, you . . . I mean, the Maroons of Nyamkopong. You know, like Harris says, kill the Colonel and make Mr. Mann the Colonel. Should they?

Sure.

Johnny turns away. I thought the Colonel was elected, he say quietly.

He is, Harris explains. But sometimes you have to kill him to get rid of him. Then you have an election so you can have a new Colonel, because when you become Colonel, it's for life.

That's not the way it's done here in Nyamkopong, Johnny says proudly. Here we have elections every couple of years. We don't have to kill a man to get rid of him, he points out defiantly.

You do if the man keeps winning the elections, the Rasta answers, and everyone laughs, especially Bowra.

Looks like the monkey man wants us to come in, Charles suddenly says.

Indeed, for there he is, standing on the porch and waving for them to come to the house. Johnny cranks down the window and cups his ear with his hand, and Colonel Phelps calls out for them to come and eat.

Babylon had his fill, the Rasta observes. Our turn at the trough.

Slowly, almost reluctantly, they climb from the van and trudge across the muddy yard to the porch and one by one enter the living room, where the Colonel's wife has set out platters of food on a makeshift table, an old door laid across chairbacks. Most of the platters are empty, however, and all that remains are a dozen chunks of yam, some cold rice, the back and wing of the chicken, and a handful of red beans. The Colonel's sour-faced wife enters the room with a plate stacked high with sliced white bread and places it in the center of the table. Then she quickly disappears into the bedroom, closing the door tightly behind her. Beyond the living room, Sergeant Kemp and his men are standing in the back doorway, smoking cigarettes and picking their teeth and peering through the rain at the hills.

Soon I'll have more food, Colonel Phelps promises, as the group studies the remains of the meal. I've just sent my boy to the shop for more rice and tinned beef. There will be plenty for all, he assures them. Plenty.

Harris once again takes over. He grabs a plate and swiftly ladles the rest of the food onto it, all the rice and beans, the few cold chunks of yam, and the bits of chicken. Then he matter-of-factly presents the plate to Bowra, gives him a fork, and steps away. As if attending a church supper, the Colonel carries his plate outside to the front porch, sits wearily down there and begins, almost sadly, to eat. The others stand around in the living room, silent and alone. After a few moments, Colonel Phelps moves jerkily toward the back door and joins Sergeant Kemp and his men. They edge aside and make room so he too can stand and watch the rain fall grayly against the green hills.

5

THINGS GET WORSE AS THE DAY GOES ON. COLONEL PHELPS'
son returns from the shop, and the Colonel manages at
last to feed the rest of Bowra's party, but not before
Sergeant Kemp and his men have left the house and
walked to a cabin a few hundred yards further down the
road and have beaten and dragged from the cabin the
young Rasta named Rubber, who is Terron's friend and,
until today, his partner in the cultivation of about five
acres of ganja plants. This is not, however, why they
haul Rubber out to the road and crack his skull with the
butts of their shotguns, bind his hands and tie an inch-
thick length of Manila rope around his neck and lead
him like a captured animal back to their Land Cruiser in
front of Colonel Phelps' house. No, they take Rubber
because he is well known in town, especially now, when
tonight and tomorrow he will be operating one of the
two diesel generators and sound systems in Nyamkopong.
By making a show of capturing and controlling Rubber,
the police can send a message to the people of the town.
It says: Behave yourselves in the next few days. We are
in charge.

To his guests, Colonel Phelps merely says, The Rasta
youths are troublesome here. That one maybe stole something in Maggotty. You never know. You just never
know.

Sickened, the Rasta and Johnny leave for the Rasta's

cabin, where, wordless, they fall down on the mattress that practically fills the cabin and immediately leap into sleep. The Rasta's woman and children tiptoe around the sleeping men, and when one of Mr. Mann's grandsons comes to tell the American and Terron that Mr. Mann would like to meet and talk with his Gordon Hall brethren, the woman sends him away, crossly instructing the boy to inform his grandfather that Terron and the American have been away in Montego Bay and Kingston on important American business and have just got back from driving all night and are now sleeping. And besides, she never heard of any Gordon Hall brethren anyhow. The boy shrugs his shoulders and leaves.

All day long the weather too is dismal. It rains steadily, heavily, falling straight down in ropes. After Sergeant Kemp and his men have carted Rubber off to Maggotty, Bowra and Harris berate Colonel Phelps for more than an hour, until, disgusted with the man, they stalk from his house and go looking for Johnny's van. The others—Charles, the Captain, Gondo, Pie, Steve, and the two women—have already found the vehicle where Johnny parked it, next to Terron's cabin, and they have all crawled wetly inside and, in various, cramped postures, have gone to sleep. When Bowra and Harris arrive, there is no more room for them in the van, so they step out of the rain into Terron's cabin and flop onto the mattress next to Johnny and the Rasta. At this point, despite the downpour, Terron's woman gathers her brood and heads for an aunt's house down the road.

Around noon they start to wake. The rain is still coming down, and the sky is low, heavy and gray. Outside the cabin the ground is squishy with red mud. Johnny stands and peers out the door and sees that the others are apparently still sleeping in the van. Then stretching, yanking and scratching at his clothing, which clings to him at the crotch and under his arms, he finally sighs heavily, as if remembering a painful obligation, and asks the Rasta what they should do now.

The Rasta laughs. He is sitting on the edge of the bed, barefoot and shirtless.

"What's funny?" Johnny asks glumly from the door.

The huge Bowra, like an overturned green boat, lies on his back crossways on the bed, his hands behind his head, staring somberly at the underside of the tin roof, as if studying the progress of an ant. Next to him lies Harris, on his side and propped on an elbow, deep in pipe-smoking thought and, for once, silent and with no opinion.

The Rasta goes on laughing, which is highly unusual. Terron never laughs. He smiles sometimes, but that's all. He's a *serious* man.

What's funny? Johnny asks him again, crossing around him in the cramped, cluttered space to the small, square window on the opposite side of the room. He stares out the window at the broad, sopped leaves of a banana tree. Then the acrid smell of urine drifts up to him from the muddy ground just beyond, and he wrinkles his nose and steps back.

When he turns around, the Rasta is building a spliff and smiling broadly, as if at a suddenly remembered joke. No, really, Terron, what's so funny? This whole thing was supposed to be such a big deal, but it's all turned out like shit. You know that.

Heh, heh, heh, the Rasta chuckles. Now we know, he says with a sly expression on his long face. Now we know. Now we know.

Know what?

We know who is the wizard of Oz.

Unsmiling, Johnny crosses slowly to the door. You said you never saw that movie. A wizard is a wizard, you told me.

That doesn't mean one or two of the wizards can't be fakes. Phonies. Oh no, the Rasta explained, just because a man's a fake doesn't mean he can't also be a wizard. And this fake here, this Martin Luther Phelps, he's the wizard of Oz. Understand?

Johnny understands. He takes a hit off the Rasta's

spliff. Then he asks Bowra and Harris what they want him to do now.

Take me to see your Mr. Mann, the Colonel orders.

Harris starts to say something, evidently thinks better of it and instead merely shrugs his shoulders. He's only the mouth-man. The Colonel is the Colonel.

Standing, the Colonel brushes off his suit and squares his pith helmet. Get the others out here, he says to Harris, and Harris scrambles out the door into the rain. Banging on the car windows, he rouses the others and starts shouting and gesturing for them to leave the car and come to the cabin.

We can drive over, Johnny suggests. No sense getting wet. It's a ways from here.

No. We'll walk.

Johnny looks at the Rasta, and they both, like Harris, shrug their shoulders helplessly. The Colonel is the Colonel.

By the time Bowra exits from the tiny cabin, the others have left the shelter of the van and have angled toward the cabin door, as if hoping to enter and get out of the rain. But the big man blocks them at the door and they are forced to stand and listen. The American and his friend listen from inside the cabin.

We are going to walk through this city of Nyamkopong, he says grimly. We have seen their Colonel and we have seen how he is with the police from outside. We will see a little more of this city and then we will leave it.

The others somberly nod agreement, and as the Colonel strides to the road in front of the cabin, his people fall in behind him. Johnny, get up here! he commands. Rasta, you too! and the American and his friend jog to the front.

The road is deserted, mucky, crisscrossed with rivulets darting like snakes for the gutters. No one calls out or hails the group until the marchers reach the center of the town, where a pair of shops face each other across the road. From the dark shelter of the shops come the cries of a few who recognize the American and who are friends of the Rasta. Oy, oy, oy, one heart, one love! they cry. Irie, Rasta! Love, man. Dread, Rasta!

But no one acknowledges the cries. They simply march along in the rain, slogging through the mud, past the shops, turning right and down a grassy lane to a blue house at the end where the hand-lettered sign over the door proclaims, TRELAWNY TOWN 1738-39, and a small spotted dog stands at the doorway and barks furiously at the strangers.

After a few moments, while they stand outside in the downpour, Mr. Mann's wife appears at the door. The American steps forward and, putting on a cheerful face, asks her where her husband is. An important man wants to meet him, he adds.

The tiny old woman crossly points with her chin back down the lane. "Look in one of the shops if you want him," she suggests and abruptly turns and goes in, slamming the door behind her.

Smiling weakly, the American tells Bowra that Mr. Mann must be in one of the shops they just passed. Let's go have a drink with him, he urges. Then he adds, He must not have been told you were coming today. Not so early anyhow. Something . . .

For a second the others glare at him. Even the Rasta gives him a hard look, and then they turn and slog back the way they just came, leaving him to run and catch up.

MR. MANN IS AT THE SECOND OF THE TWO SHOPS. AT THE first, when the American asked for him, the proprietor had merely pointed in silence across the street to his competitor's shop, then had gone quickly to a hushed conversation with an old woman at the counter.

At the second shop, dark as a cave, Mr. Mann is seated at the far end before a domino table, playing an idle two-handed game with another old man. At the sight of the American and behind him the Rasta and the entourage from Gordon Hall, all of them sopping wet and scowling as they crowd into the place, Mr. Mann rises from his chair and comes quickly to embrace the white man with affection.

Johnny makes the introductions, his voice soft with fatigue, then steps away to the bar where three or four local youths with dreadlocks, Natty Dreads, have been standing and talking with the barman. Apparently penniless and loitering here inside because of the rain, they are not drinking. One of them, the slender, sweet-faced boy named Benjie, is a true Rasta and will not drink alcoholic beverages anyhow. He refuses even to wear leather or eat anything that doesn't grow above or below ground. Strictly Ital, man.

Drinks for everyone, Johnny tells the barman, who sets out two half pints of white rum and a dozen glasses. Behind Johnny and the youths at the bar, in an almost British accent, Mr. Mann is talking loudly in his public way. With polite and elaborate circumlocutions, he expresses his delight at meeting the famous Colonel Bowra of the Gordon Hall Maroons, and though his beloved American son had some time ago told him that the people of Gordon Hall would send a delegation to Nyamkopong for the celebration, he himself did not dare believe it, for he was aware of the great distance that lay between the two towns, having once traveled to Kingston himself for the Queen's jubilee, there to dance the old African dances in honor of Her Majesty's visit to the island of Jamaica.

Confronted by this tiny, eloquent man, whose blue and brown eyes match his own, Bowra backs off a step and grimly swells his bulk. With his thick arms folded across his chest, he resembles a tree, and, after a second of silence, he simply grunts down at Mr. Mann, which brings an even wider smile to the little man's face and yet another ornate speech from his mouth, this time a swift recounting of their common Maroon heritage, their common descent from the grand chieftain Cudjoe here in the west and his sister the great African sorcerer Nonny in the east and their shared one-hundred-year war against the British slavemasters, for, as is well known among all the peoples of the civilized world, he concludes, we the Maroons are the heart of Jamaica.

Again, Bowra's reaction is to huff himself up and utter a grunt. And Mr. Mann smiles and launches a third speech, this time one that welcomes the delegation from Gordon Hall to Nyamkopong and leads to a courteous and precisely framed question as to whether they have been made comfortable by Colonel Martin Luther Phelps? In the manner befitting your high offices and emoluments and the extraordinary occasion of your visit, he adds, still smiling innocently at the big man.

At the bar, the American almost chokes on his drink, and Harris whips around angrily, while the others look at each other and sneer. The Rasta, who has been standing at the door smoking a spliff and studying the rain, turns and watches. For several long seconds the gloomy, dark room is silent. Then Bowra explodes.

This Colonel of theirs, this Martin Luther Phelps they call a Colonel, this man is a whore to Babylon! This whore who calls himself a Colonel feeds the police while his brother Maroons go hungry! This man who calls himself a Maroon smiles and bows and licks the hand that beats him!

Mr. Mann has raised his eyebrows in what could barely pass for surprise in an amateur theatrical production. Then, shaking his head from side to side in a show of sympathy, he takes Bowra's hands in his and leads the big man to the bar, nudges a glass to him, and picks one up for himself. The man is a monkey, he says almost sweetly to Bowra. They raise their glasses, dribble a bit onto the ground, and empty them.

How can you have a man like that one stand forth as your Colonel? Harris wants to know.

Kill him, says Charles.

Chop him up, Pie suggests.

The youths, who up to now have merely been standing in out of the rain, have brightened considerably and are elbowing each other and casting knowing looks at the barman.

Bowra takes in the three boys slowly. They are in their late teens and, though dreadlocked, are farmers, dressed in dirty T-shirts and mud-spattered pants and wearing knee-high rubber boots. All three are carrying machetes. *You!* he says, and they suddenly dissolve their grins and stare at him. How is it that you let such a man stand forth as your Colonel?

They smile sheepishly and shrug their shoulders.

Count! he orders.

They don't understand and look at one another, puzzled.

Count! Don't you know how to count? Don't you know your numbers?

One of the three nods.

Then count!

The one who nodded, Benjie, gulps and begins. One. Two. Three. Four. Five. Six. Seven. Eight . . .

Enough!

Mr. Mann has been following the exchange between Bowra and the boys carefully and with a sober expression on his face. When Bowra is clearly about to speak to them again, the smaller man places a hand on his arm and stops him, although Bowra does not take his eyes away from the gaze of the boys. Before you go any further, he says, in a light but quite serious voice, as if he were speaking to someone he did not wish to alarm, Yes, before you go on with these lovely young men, let me tell you a story. Very briefly. An interesting story that might lead you to an understanding of our life here in Nyamkopong.

By keeping his voice moving, he keeps Bowra from interrupting as he proceeds to tell a story about a man who left his beautiful wife and young son and went to work in Cuba where the United States Marines taught him to be a welder in a school they ran there at Guantanamo Bay. The man worked in Cuba for seven years, and when it came time for him to return to Jamaica, he drew all his savings from the bank, over three thousand dollars, and packed his suitcase. On his way to the airport for the ride home to Jamaica, he stopped into a bar for a last drink with a friend, and his friend, an old and wise Cuban man, told him about a dream he'd had the night before. In the dream the Jamaican man went home to discover that his wife had a new boyfriend living with her and that she and her new boy friend got together and killed the man and kept the money he had been saving all these seven years in Cuba.

The Jamaican man laughed and said good-bye and went on his way. But when he got back to Jamaica, he started to remember his friend's dream, and by the time he got to his village way up in the hills, he was a very worried man. It was early in the morning when he arrived at his house, for he had been traveling all night, and when he opened the door of his house and walked in, no one was up yet. Very quietly, he looked into the room where their bed had always been, and he saw his wife, as beautiful as before, lying asleep. One of her large breasts had fallen from her dress, and he looked at her with all his old feelings. Then he realized with horror that lying next to her was a handsome young man, and he knew that the Cuban's dream had been right about everything. To save his money from them, he pulled out his knife and stabbed first the young man and then his wife. And then, with shock, as he looked down at the bloody bed, he realized that the young man was his own son, probably the same age as these boys here before us, who may well still sometimes sleep with their Mommies when they have no other place to go to sleep. Am I right, boys? he asks the three.

They nod, almost with gratitude, and turn away.

Bowra glares down at the old man, who smiles peacefully back.

He's yours, then, this Colonel you call a monkey. Bowra turns to his brother the Captain and Harris. Where's Johnny? Where is he? Johnny!

The group steps away from the bar and uncovers the American standing at the end. His eyes are dark with fatigue. Here, he says in a low voice.

Johnny, we're ready to leave! Get your vehicle! he commands.

Now?

Now.

But . . . the celebration . . . It's not come yet.

Nothing here to celebrate.

The past, says Mr. Mann, almost to himself.

Nothing here to celebrate, Bowra repeats.

All right, I'll bring the car around. The American is exhausted and trudges toward the door and into the rain outside as if he were pulling a cart loaded with stone. The Rasta, Terron, has already gone on ahead.

6

THEN YOU AREN'T COMING? THE AMERICAN ASKS HIS FRIEND. They are standing inside the Rastaman's cabin, both men soaked and staring out the door at the rain.

No, the Rastaman will stay here in Nyamkopong, he explains, because he has to watch over the fields of ganja he planted with Rubber. Otherwise, when he returns they will have been stripped bare and half the youths in town will be wearing new clothes and carrying around new tape decks and transistor radios. Some of them will be in Kingston on new Hondas. The Rasta is stuffing a change of clothes into a seed sack. He'll take his machete and move into the bush, he tells his friend, where he'll live until he can harvest the crop or until Rubber is out of jail and can relieve him. If one of the youths from town tries sneaking into his field, he'll be found dead in the morning. The Rasta swings his razor-sharp machete like a samurai. Chop, chop, chop! A dead man! Dead in the morning, all chopped up and flies on the face! Chop, chop, chop!

The American jogs from the cabin to his car. Starting the engine and flicking on the windshield wipers, he backs the vehicle onto the road, chugs up the muddy road to the shop, where he stops and toots the horn to signal Bowra and the others that he is ready to take them home to Gordon Hall. It's almost dark and the rain is still falling. Unshaven, his hands trembling from fatigue,

244

the man lights a cigarette and raps again on the horn. The interior of the car smells sourly of stale smoke, old rum and sweaty bodies. The man looks at his face in the rearview mirror, grimaces, and raps the horn a third time.

Finally his passengers troop outside and climb into the van, arranging themselves as before, except that now, with the Rasta gone, there is a little more room. As if somehow relieved, Bowra says to the driver, So the Rastaman will stay here this time?

Yes. He has work to do. The cops took away his partner . . .

I know that, snaps Bowra. I know why the Rastaman is staying here.

You do? The American turns in surprise, and Bowra smiles, the first time since morning that he has smiled.

Mr. Mann has come to the driver's side of the car, where he taps lightly on the window glass, drawing the driver's attention away from Bowra's curiously smiling face.

The American cranks down the window and tells the old man he'll be back in a week or two. After he's taken Bowra and his people home, he'll have to go to Anchovy and check on his family, he explains, but then he'll come back, and they'll talk. I want to have a long talk with you, he says.

The old man looks worried, as if he has misplaced something crucial. Silent at first, he suddenly announces, God will protect you, son, and quickly he turns away from the car and steps back inside the darkened bar.

Drive, Johnny! Bowra orders.

And Johnny drives. Down from the Cockpit to the cane fields outside Maggotty, through Maggotty and over the hills south and east toward the coastal plain he drives, like a machine, silent and relentless, beyond exhaustion, his body operating on its own or as if it were a stranger's. The others in the car sleep and now and then mumble something to one another and reluctantly turn and shift position to make room or relieve a cramped muscle, while outside the rain pounds down endlessly.

He stops once outside Spanish Town for gas and no one bothers to wake, even to see how far they have come.

It's almost midnight when, at last, the blue van turns off the road and enters the narrow valley of Gordon Hall. As if at a signal, or as if he had not been sleeping at all, Bowra wakes and quickly calls out to his brother the Captain. The abeng! You got to blow the abeng! Johnny, he says, stop right here!

The driver slows the car and pulls to the side of the road. The rain drums heavily against the tin roof and washes across the road in shiny skeins. Now the others are awake—Harris swiftly repeats the Colonel's order to the Captain, who in turn is struggling to untangle the horn from the cloth of his pants pocket, and Charles, who strokes his bird and coos to it, while Gando begins to gasp and jerk and irritate the women on either side of him, as Pie and Steve dutifully reach for the drums.

Finally the Captain opens his window, and sticking his head out, he puts the horn to his lips and rips a blast from it. Then a series of blasts—strong, sustained, high notes— and the drums start up and the women start to sing, their high-pitched voices laying out a new song, a happy, relieved and thankful song, as Johnny puts the car in gear again and drives the final half mile to Bowra's house in Gordon Hall. When he turns off the lane into Bowra's muddy yard, the Colonel places a heavy paw onto his right shoulder and says to him, You're a good boy.

Johnny switches off the ignition and slowly turns and looks across at the big man. Thanks. He is silent for a second. No one in the car has moved to leave yet. Thanks, thanks, thanks, thanks, Johnny says. Thanks for *everything*. He speaks in a low, cold voice.

Moving heavily, Bowra opens the door and steps from the car, and everyone else scrambles to get out. As he leaves, Harris reaches forward and taps Johnny on one shoulder. *Now* you will see what you want to see, he promises.

Thanks, the white man answers. Thanks, thanks, thanks. Slowly, with trembling hands, he lights a cigarette.

Come, Harris says quietly. Come with us.

7

THE RAIN HAS STOPPED, AND THE SKY, SUDDENLY SCRAPED
clear, sparkles darkly with stars, and the trees and hills
drip in the new silence. Colonel Bowra, his lieutenant
Harris, and the white American sit alone on Bowra's
porch around a small table. On the table are a pack of
Craven A's, a quart bottle of white rum, and a smoke-
smudged kerosene lantern. The three men are smoking
and drinking straight from the bottle and talking in low,
intimate voices about the Colonel of the Nyamkopong
Maroons, Martin Luther Phelps, a man they believe
deserves to die. Or so they say. They agree that the man
is a traitor, like Juan Lubolo, who went over to the
British and ended his life chopped to bits by his betrayed
brethren. They agree that Cudjoe would have killed any
of his people who had gone over to the slavemasters'
side, even one of his own brothers. Too many of the old
Africans suffered and died for the treaty, they say, to let
someone today get away with treating it like a scrap of
paper. That's why the Maroons call it the "Blood Treaty,"
that and because it was signed in blood by the Maroons
and the Englishmen as well. Let the Englishmen violate
the treaty if they will—they are so many that not much
can be done to them for it. But when a Maroon Colonel
himself violates the treaty, when a Maroon Colonel himself invites the police to breakfast and lets them seize
and take off Maroon land any man they wish, when he

lets them beat that man in the street and tie him up like an animal and then makes excuses for them—when all that happens, you kill him for it. And there is no way on this island to escape death when the Maroons have decided that you must die. You can smile and beg and bow down and lick boots, but your head will drop off. You can surround your house with police and guns, but in the morning your wife will wake up next to a dead man. You can run into the bush and try to hide out there, but the Maroons will track you down and stick you like a pig and carry you back tied to a pole, with your head banging in a bucket hooked to the front of the pole. You can run into the city and try to hide in a white man's house, but the white man will go out on business, and when he returns, he will see your blood streaming across his tile floor. You can run to Negril in the west or Morant in the east, and you will come to the sea, and in the morning your head will come bobbing in on the waves.

A boy, shirtless and barefoot and sleepy-looking, comes out of the house carrying a white chicken by its feet. The bird lifts its head like a snake's and gazes steadily at Bowra. Harris gets up and goes inside the house, returning in seconds with a blue plastic bowl and a kitchen knife and a bronze statuette the size of a human hand, an eagle with its beak open and wings spread. When the boy gets the chicken upside down and in front of Bowra, the man stabs the bird in the throat and bleeds it into the bowl. Bowra speaks in a low, rumbling voice, no longer using patois, and Harris joins in. When the bird has been bled dry, the boy leaves, taking the carcass with him, and Bowra swiftly mixes rum and, from his jacket pocket, seeds and crumpled leaves into the blood, chanting in a low voice while he stirs the mixture, then suddenly drinks off the mixture, emptying the bowl. The eagle that was a bronze statuette flaps its wings, screeches, and flies off its pedestal, flutters for a few seconds in the lamplight near the porch, then soars into the night sky. The three men rise at once off their chairs as if to follow the bird. In a second, the white man has fallen back to his chair—then, a few seconds later, Harris. But Bowra has gone on rising, like a great puff of smoke that hovers over the lamp, dimming it, then moving away from the cluttered tabletop, off the porch to the yard, where he floats in the shadows cast by the lower branches of the breadfruit trees, and, silently, he rises and disappears into darkness.

At the table, Harris and the American stare coldly at each other. In a harsh voice, Harris barks a string of unknown words into the American's face, and the American bellows back in English, Shut up! I don't know what the hell you're saying! A vicious sneer slowly curls over Harris' mouth, and he picks up the knife and draws the edge of the blade across the underside of his left wrist. The black skin parts and blood bubbles into the cut, swiftly running into the cupped palm of the hand. Then he extends the knife to the American, who with his right hand draws the knife slowly across his left wrist and lets the blood spill over the white skin into his cupped palm, which the black man suddenly clasps in his, mixing and splashing the blood down their arms. Again, Harris shouts at the American, and again, the American tells him to shut up, he doesn't know what the hell he's saying!

Harris smiles, stands, and quickly walks from the porch, leaving the American alone in his chair, the lamplight flickering over the empty rum bottle, the blue bowl, the knife, the bloodied arm. Bats dart across the yard beyond, doves huddle and coo at the feet of the trees, and a large tan moth flashes toward the lamp and dives erratically at the glass chimney, as if there could be light without heat and this cone of light were somehow a hole into day.

Slowly, moving his body like a man moving chains, he gets up from his chair, blows out the lamp, and enters the darkness. He walks to the end of the porch, steps down to the muddy ground and crosses the yard to his car. Opening the side door and closing it behind him, he then locks all the doors, after which he carefully stretches himself out on the middle seat, as if he were handling the body of an invalid, and sleeps.

In the morning, he will be wakened by the sound of children playing on the roof of his car. He will wash himself in the stream below the road and will eat jerked pork and yams with Colonel Bowra on the porch, and then he will drive back along the north coast to Anchovy. When at sunset he arrives at his home on Church's Hill and has hugged and kissed his children and his wife, he will discover that the Rastaman, his friend Terron Musgrave, has been waiting there for him since midday, waiting to give him the news that Colonel Martin Luther Phelps has been killed.

Dread

"Know thyself." As if it were so simple! As if only good will and introspection were needed. An individual can compare himself, see himself and correct himself wherever an eternal ideal is firmly anchored in closely knit forms of education and culture, of literature and politics. But what if all norms are shaky and in a state of confusion? What if illusions dominate not only the present but also all generations; if race and tradition, blood and spirit, if all the reliable possessions of the past are all profaned, desecrated, and defaced? What if all the voices in the symphony are at variance with each other? Who will know himself then? Who will find himself then?

HUGO BALL

1

EVERYONE CALLED HIM JOHNNY NOW, EVEN HIS WIFE. IT
had started the previous April with Bowra on his first
visit to Gordon Hall, and when later he had tried to
correct Harris by repeating his real name, Harris had
said that they knew his real name fine but Johnny was
what they called all nice white men. Then Terron had
picked it up and started referring to his friend as Johnny
whenever he moved among the people down at Barrett's
shop, with Yvonne, Bush, Barrett and his wife and the
half dozen or so regulars, all of whom, though they
thought of themselves as friends of Johnny, knew that
Terron's position was closer. After all, the Rastaman
practically lived with Johnny and his family up there on
Church's hill. Eventually, with everyone else calling him
Johnny, his wife too began to use it as his name, at first
as a joke, then gradually as if it were in fact the name he
had been born with. By January, if a stranger asked him
his name, he answered with Johnny, unless the person
happened to be white, in which case he answered with
the name he had been born with.

Terron's name, of course, had not changed. In spite of
Bowra's and the other Gordon Hall Maroons' fondness
for calling him Rasta, he remained Terron to everyone
else, except perhaps in Port Antonio, where he had been
a child and where he was still commonly known as
Stammer. Tonight, out on the terrace with Johnny, as he

struggled to tell Johnny what had happened in Nyamkopong in the twenty-four hours since Johnny had left with
Bowra and his people for Gordon Hall, his childhood
affliction had returned. Terron's tongue, teeth and lips,
instead of making their usual dance, tonight bumped and
stumbled against one another, so that Johnny couldn't
make out what the man was trying to describe to him.
The only other time he had seen Terron turn into Stammer had been back in Gordon Hall last April, when
Bowra had challenged him to name the thirty-six sacred
herbs and Terron had been able to name but twenty-
three. Then, as now, Terron's huge and serious face had
lost all its balance and proportion and had come to
organize completely around his mouth—his brown eyes
wildly struggling to see what was the matter with his
mouth, his broad, flat nose seeming to pull itself flatter,
to give the lips more room, his cheeks, chin and forehead drawing back and away fearfully.

Placing a hand on his friend's shoulder, Johnny silenced Terron and drew him over to the edge of the
terrace. Below them in the hazy twilight lay Montego
Bay, and the Caribbean, silvery gray near shore where it
fell in the shadow of the hills of Anchovy, scarlet-streaked
out near the horizon, where the last light from the setting sun spread across water from the red western sky
beyond Negril.

Slow down, man, and tell me from the beginning,
Johnny said. The children, two girls aged eight and ten,
had followed their father and his friend out to the terrace, and they too were trying to tell him what had
happened during his absence from them, only forty-eight
hours, more or less, but in this strange land, enough had
occurred in their daily lives to make them eager to
report it to him. Johnny's wife stood at the sliding glass
door of the living room and watched her husband ignore
her children.

Benjie's dead, Terron finally got out. Johnny's wife
went back to the kitchen and hollered for the girls to

come and eat supper, and reluctantly, the girls left the terrace for the kitchen.

Dead? Why? How? Johnny ran his hand through his greasy hair. His clothes were rumpled and dirty, and he looked exhausted, with deep, dark circles around his eyes and a three-day beard on his face.

Terron drew close to him, and even though they were now alone on the terrace, talked in patois in a hushed voice. He was shot, Terron explained. Five times. Then they scalped him, he said, using that word, *scalped*.

Who, for Christ's sake?

The cops. Babylon.

Johnny sat down slowly, like an old man, on one of the pink wrought iron chairs. Benjie was shot by the cops? Jesus. And scalped! What do you mean, scalped? Like Indians? He shuddered.

Yes, like Indians. They cut off his locks, his dreadlocks. With scissors. They brought the scissors with them from Maggotty in the Land Cruiser, Terron said. They cut the locks of a *deader,* he said, repelled and amazed. No Rastaman no deal wi no deaders. Praise Jah, Jah lives— and then he was off on a singsong chant about the impossibility of death so long as God, Jah, lives in every man, and no man, who knows that, can fear death—I-man who know I-self cyan deal wi no deaders—rolling on and away from what Johnny apparently thought was the subject, for he quickly interrupted him.

Why did the cops shoot Benjie? He was just a *kid,* for Christ's sake!

They shot him because they found his gun. The cops had gone into the House of Dread this morning, Terron explained, had routed the brethren there out of bed and had found Benjie's gun. They had simply picked it out of his bed, where he kept it when he slept, and then they shot him for it. Five times, twice in the head and three times in the body. His "structure," Terron called it.

But he didn't have any bullets! Didn't they see the gun was empty?

It was empty then, Terron explained, but they could

tell by the smell that it hadn't been empty long. The gun had grown bullets and had fired them not long before the cops kicked in the door of the House of Dread and started laying about at the sleeping Rastas with billyclubs. And when they yanked Benjie out of his bed, they saw the gun, and then the Sergeant, Sergeant Kemp, sniffed the barrel, and he knew.

Knew what?

Knew that the gun had been out shooting. And he figured Benjie was the one who had been shooting it. So they shot him.

Who the hell was Benjie supposed to have been shooting at?

Colonel Phelps.

Phelps! Did someone shoot *him?*

Benjie's gun shot him, Terron answered. It grew two bullets and it shot him. Bang, bang! he said, pointing with a finger at his friend's face. In the eyes, one bullet in each eye.

Johnny looked away and lit a cigarette. Inhaling deeply, he leaned back and, letting the smoke drift from his mouth, made little ohs with his lips. After a few seconds, he said, Okay, let me get this straight. Someone, using Benjie's gun, shot Colonel Phelps sometime last night. When the cops from Maggotty busted into the House of Dread, they found Benjie's gun in his bed, saw that it had been fired recently, and so they shot him, in cold blood, and then cut off his dreadlocks. How do you know Benjie *didn't* shoot Colonel Phelps? Maybe Kemp was right. At least about that, I mean.

Terron explained that the boy couldn't have done it because when Colonel Phelps was killed, sometime around midnight, Benjie was in the bush with Terron, helping to watch over his and Rubber's ganja patch. He was going to be my new partner, Terron said. Then he told Johnny that Benjie had spent almost the entire night out there, smoking and reasoning with Terron, and by the time he left, it was almost dawn. A few hours later, Terron had been awakened by his cousin Juke, who had been inside the House of Dread and who'd come to tell him about Benjie's murder.

Did Benjie have his gun with him when he was out in the bush with you? Johnny asked.

No. He was worried that someone had stolen it. According to Terron, the gun had disappeared from Benjie's bed the night before.

How was that possible? Johnny wondered. No one can steal a gun from the bed you're sleeping in.

It probably just got invisible for a while, Terron explained.

Oh.

According to Terron, the problem lay not in the disappearance of the gun but in its reappearance in Benjie's bed. Otherwise, the cops wouldn't have shot him. Another problem, apparently, was that the police had now practically taken over the village, and the celebration had been cancelled. The Colonel was a monkey, Terron pointed out, but an important monkey, especially today. So the police had forbidden the people to dance or sell food or set up the sound systems, and they had sent everyone home. Then he, Terron, had got nervous, and he'd hitched a ride out of town with a Rasta from Montego Bay and had come straight here, to warn his friend Johnny.

Warn *me!* Of what?

The police.

What are you talking about? I was in Gordon Hall last night!

Terron knew that. Everyone knew that. But apparently Colonel Phelps' wife had told the police all about the visit yesterday from Colonel Bowra and the Gordon Hall Maroons and, until they found Benjie's gun and shot him, she had claimed that Bowra had gone around town threatening to kill her husband and that the white American, who owned a gun, had gone around with him.

I don't own a gun! Johnny shouted.

Terron said nothing, merely raised his eyebrows in mock surprise.

Johnny stood and was pacing nervously from the edge of the terrace back to the sliding glass doors by the living room, as if eager to lock up his house but not sure of where to start. So you think the cops'll be coming here now. Because they think I have a gun.

You're a white man, and a foreigner. They'll make you go back to the States . . .

But I don't *have* a gun!

Terron ignored him and went on explaining how he should handle the situation. He should cover the gun with heavy grease and wrap it in plastic and bury it in the bush where he can find it again. Also, he should get rid of all the ganja he had in the house. There was no problem with the several dozen plants they had been cultivating since November in the flower gardens—Terron had yanked them up and burned them this afternoon as soon as he arrived from Nyamkopong. Then, when the cops can't find anything illegal going on here, they'll leave you alone again, Terron explained, because you're a white man and a foreigner, the same reasons they bothered you in the first place. They'll probably expect something for their troubles, of course.

You mean a bribe.

This house is a rich man's house, Terron reminded him. They'll see how you live.

Johnny grunted. Okay. I'll get rid of my stash, it's not much anyway. As far as the damned gun goes, that's no problem. It doesn't exist.

Terron raised his eyebrows again, this time with high admiration, as if his friend were saying that the gun was now invisible. His stammer gone, he was able to speak smoothly again. Jah will protect you, he said. Bowra and Mann have arranged it. Your family will be safe, and you'll be able to continue with your work, he said matter-of-factly, as if giving a knowledgeable opinion of tomorrow's weather. He knew the signs.

My work? What work?

Terron sat down in the pink wrought iron chair, stretched out his short legs and crossed them elegantly at the ankles, and was rolling a spliff. Your work as a wizard, he said.

I'm no wizard, for Christ's sake. And what the hell are you doing, rolling a spliff? I thought we were supposed to clean this place out.

We are, we are, he said, smiling and lighting up the spliff. Jah will protect. Don't worry, Jah will protect.

Shaking his head, Johnny went into the house to get his stash, a few ounces of lamb's breath that he kept in his shaving kit. As he crossed the living room, his wife called him from the kitchen. Are you going to eat?

Yeah, yeah, in a minute! he answered impatiently, heading for the bedroom.

TERRON STAYED ON AT THE COMPOUND FOR ANOTHER WEEK,
spending his time more or less as Johnny spent his—in
the morning leisurely attending to trivial housekeeping
chores, then in the afternoons going to the market in
Montego Bay. Afterward he usually stopped by to visit
and reason with various Rasta brethren in the mud-yard
neighborhoods of Mount Salem and Albion and along
the gulleys of Jackson Town, where thousands of tiny
one- and two-room shanties had been tossed together by
the people who, starving, had come to feed off the
carcass of the tourist industry. There was Rasta Speedy,
a handsome half-Chinese pimp who could hold forth
eloquently for hours on the social, moral and theological
necessity of repatriation, so that the idea of returning all
Caribbean and American black people to Africa became
an eschatology. There was old, gray-bearded, gray-locked
Bongo Johnson, who in the 1950s had been a disciple of
Prince Edward Emmanuel, "Repairer of the Breach,"
and had gone to prison with him after the police had
raided the Prince's African Reformed Church headquar-
ters in Kingston and had discovered a huge weapons
cache—detonators, shotguns, handguns, and dozens of
sheathed machetes sharpened on both sides like broad-
swords. There were Rasta sculptors, poets, cooks, gamblers, clockmakers, beggars, carpenters, auto mechanics,
athletes, farmers, musicians, men and women and

dreadlocked children, their huts and shops papered with old rotogravure pictures of Haile Selassie seated on his throne in full imperial regalia or Haile Selassie in military uniform seated on a white horse or Haile Selassie on a balcony blessing the multitudes. The people who were Rastafarians—at least the ones Terron knew and who, therefore, Johnny had come to know—were all poor, but except for that and their devotion to the God in Man, Haile Selassie, their love and admiration of their uncut locks, that "pure African hair," and their belief in the spiritual clarity provided by the wisdom weed—the herb, grass, hemp, ganja in all its forms, from kali weed to lamb's breath—they were as varied in their approach to Rasta as the poor of any religion are. Though the exterior forms and rites, because they grew so naturally and syncretically out of their culture, were easily kept by all whose culture it was, the intensity and rigor of their belief moved up an extremely high ladder so that, as one ascended the ladder, the forms and rites deepened, grew elaborate, and became increasingly difficult to keep. At the bottom steps loitered the punks, mostly teen-age boys and girls, alley cats with dreadlocks and ganja habits and evil hearts; and near the top clung full-blown mystics, monks, and nuns keeping vows to God and each other and the several holy texts, which they analyzed, annotated and applied like Chassidic rabbis at work on the Cabala. Recently and increasingly, middle-class youths, some even students and graduates of the University of the West Indies in Kingston, had started the climb up the Rastafarian version of Jacob's ladder. But the old-timers, most of them with a lifelong habit of regarding their religion as an expression of God's love for the down-trodden, "the sufferers," and His hatred of the "I-pressors," viewed the newcomers with deep mistrust, calling them "risto-Rastas." There were also a few white converts, probably not a dozen on the island, all of them women and foreigners. Though they were doubtlessly sincere in their belief in the divinity of Haile Selassie and kept all the rites devotedly, it was as difficult for the poor black Jamaican Rastas to believe in the authenticity of their conversion as it was for their parents and friends back in Arlington, White Plains and Grosse Point. These white Rastas were, in a sense, attempting the impossible, and to attempt it with sincerity, they had to be practically schizophrenic, which made them, however assimilated into the Rastafarian daily life they seemed, pathetic. Try as they might, they came, for example, to Rastafarian speech by way of a written language, conventional English, and thus they could only, with varying degrees of skill, ape what the black Jamaican Rastas in the act of speaking were creating. It was not the same as learning to speak patois, a "pidgin" that had evolved several hundred years ago to deal with the needs to communicate between masters who spoke European languages and slaves who spoke African languages. Necessity had brought that about, a more or less English vocabulary tacked on top of a more or less African grammar and syntax, and though there were ways of representing it phonetically by means of the Phoenician alphabet, the language resisted visual representation and existed solely and fully in the speakers' mouths and ears. Now, because patois was the "slavery language," just as the walls on the Errol Flynn estate, to Terron, had been "slavery walls," the Rastafarians had begun aggressively to modify and reshape it, building with the stones and blocks of patois a Coptic house, a structure that had domes, minarets, towers and rooms filled with mansions. Created by the historical experience of centuries of racist slavery, the old language in the mouths and ears of the Rastafarians, with their vision of a black African God and Redemption, was in the process of being radically transformed from inside. Coming at it from the outside, trying to "learn" it, as if it were a foreign language or an argot, was at best pathetic, as in the case of the white American converts to Rasta, and at worst racist, as in the case of American college students and chic dope-smokers who, after seeing the film *The Harder They Come* in Harvard Square for the third time and spending a few weeks in Strawberry Fields Campground or on the beaches of Negril, start to call themselves "I-and-I" and try to grow their hair in dreadlocks that keep coming out like Shirley Temple's ringlets.

USUALLY TERRON AND JOHNNY SPENT THEIR EVENINGS DOWN at Barrett's in Anchovy. Sometimes Johnny's wife joined them for a few hours, but she didn't play dominoes, so most of the time she either stayed up at the compound or spent the evening with friends, a different circle from Johnny's friends—a Swedish engineer and his wife whose presence in Jamaica was part of Sweden's foreign policy in Third World countries; a young woman artist from Philadelphia who had lived in Montego Bay for seven years and with whom Johnny's wife was preparing a Jamaican cookbook for publication and sale in the States; a psychic from Miami, a woman eccentric in ways related to the fact that she was enormously fat, who lived in a condominium across from Doctor's Cave with her invalid mother and skinny Jamaican boy friend and gave tarot readings to local politicians and businessmen. Most of the time, Johnny and his wife went out separately, so that they were seldom in the house on Church's hill at the same time. Their children saw one parent or the other, rarely both, and, more often than either, saw Caroline the housekeeper.

At Barrett's Johnny seemed happy and relaxed. The night after his return from Gordon Hall he showed up with Terron around seven and stayed until two in the morning, even though the place was legally closed at eleven. When he arrived, strolling in the golden twilight through the wide door, the place was quiet, almost somber. Yvonne was behind the bar studying an Archie comic, and Barrett on the other side of the shop was chopping pork with his machete. Beside him on the counter was his tumbler of white rum. An old man named Cap, a toothless rumhead whose drooling obsequiousness always angered Terron and repelled Johnny, was slumped over the bar a few feet down from Yvonne. Catching sight of the old man, the two spun on their heels, flashed a smile and a wave at Yvonne and Barrett, and headed next door where the man named Big Ron lived with his dying mother. Along the roadsides for a hundred yards beyond Barrett's both ways, most of the villagers had clustered in the cooling evening breeze to talk and watch—familiar faces and sometimes friends who responded to the sight of the American and the Rasta out for a stroll with cheerful waves and went quickly back to their conversations.

As the two stepped off the road and entered Big Ron's yard, Johnny snapped his fingers with irritation. *Shit!* I forgot to ask Mr. Mann to help Ron with his mother!

Some things take care of themselves, Terron said quietly as they stepped up onto the unpainted, collapsing porch and came face to face with Big Ron, barefoot and shirtless as usual, standing in the door, filling it from jamb to jamb.

A broad grin spread across his handsome face, and he stepped forward and embraced the two men at once in a single enveloping hug. Then suddenly serious, he said to Johnny, Oh man, I have to thank you! The same night you left, man, right after that morning when I talked with you out here on the road . . . His voice drifted off as he went back inside the house.

What? Johnny called.

Wait a minute! Sit down, sit down out there, it's cooler! I got to get my transistor!

In a minute, he was back, his radio blaring from one huge hand, a half-smoked spliff cradled in the other. Sit down, sit down, make yourselves homely, he said, as he himself flopped his long body across the board floor of the porch. He handed the spliff to Johnny, who took a leisurely hit and passed it on to Terron. No, a serious thing, man. I got to thank you.

Johnny sat down, and Terron, spliff dangling from his lips, strolled out to the road, crossed to a group of three sullen Rasta youths who operated a vegetable stand there and immediately entered into intense conversation with them, gesturing grandly with his arms to describe enormities and miracles.

The man never stops preaching, Johnny said.

Prophecy. Revolution. The fire next time, Big Ron recited. Next time comes the fire, when seven meets against seven. Then must Babylon fall, he promised, and drifted dreamily away, his eyes half closed and a light smile on his lips.

What's happened with your mother, man?

Oh! the big man said, popping to attention again. That's what I've got to thank you about! She just went to sleep that night, and around midnight she woke up cured. The cancer was gone, man. She's perfect!

Perfect?

Yeah, just like she used to be. She got up, and I heard her moving around, so I lit the lamp, and there she was, standing out of bed, looking in the dark for her clothes, as if she'd never been sick a day. Man, those old Africans, they know things.

Where is she now, your mother? I'd like to see her.

She's down the road visiting friends. But she'll be around plenty now, so you'll see her. She's even cooking for me again and sweeping the house, washing clothes. Everything. I spent last night in the Bay rocking all night long with some beef, and when I came in this morning she already had my breakfast cooked for me! I really want to thank you, man.

I didn't do anything.

Sure you did. How much do I owe you?

What? Johnny was staring morosely across at Terron and seemed not to be paying attention to Big Ron.

How much do I owe you, man? For the old African. What'd he charge?

Oh. Nothing, nothing. Listen, Ron, I didn't . . .

Nothing! C'mon, man, I can work it off for you up there in your yard. I'll dig you some gardens, cut back some bush, wash your car. Don't worry. I'll pay you back.

No, man, you don't owe me. I never asked that man to help your mother. I forgot, it got so busy and crazy, I just forgot. I had to keep track of so many things . . .

No, no, no. You can tell that to some dummy, but not Big Ron! I *owe* you, he said emphatically, placing a hand on Johnny's shoulder and shaking it affectionately.

C'mon, let's go see Barrett and Yvonne, Johnny said.

Yvonne. Yes, man. That beef wants you, man, he said, leering.

Naw, we're just friends. He got up slowly from the porch and stepped toward the road.

Friends! Hah! the big man laughed and leaped to his feet and came bouncing along after. *Friends!*

The old drunk Cap was still at the bar, but asleep and snoring. Yvonne smiled broadly when Johnny and Big Ron and, a second later, Terron came in. Crossing around to the bar, Barrett greeted them easily and asked if they wanted some dominoes tonight, some "serious" dominoes, which meant for money. Two of his friends were coming from the Bay to see if the boys up here were good enough to play them.

Sure, Johnny said. I could use a night of dominoes, he quietly added, then with a gesture ordered a round for Barrett, his two friends, and Yvonne herself. Barrett gave Big Ron some change for the juke box and went back to clean up his machete and the counter where he'd been chopping the side of pork.

We'll have us some pork tonight, too! he called over to the group. Barrett's jerked pork was admired for miles around; people drove all the way from Montego Bay to sit around gnawing on the crusted, succulent meat, and the terrier-faced man was proud of it.

Ital! Terron answered in his booming bass voice. I-man cyan deal wi no swine world!

Hah! Barrett said, and laughed. More for us!

Yvonne put her hand on Johnny's. You look weary, she said to him in a soft voice. The juke box had started to blast the chugging sounds of this week's hit, "Sipple Out Dere," and Big Ron was dancing in front of the box, mouthing the words and studying the names of the songs, struggling to read them. Like most of Barrett's customers, though, it was easier for him to remember the songs by their numbers than to read the titles, and after a minute he called out a title to Yvonne and got the number, B–4. Then another, "A Whey Mi Do." G–8. He dropped a second nickel in and got three more numbers from Yvonne, who seemed to have memorized the entire selection.

The blat from the juke box had drawn a few kids off the road to the open door of the bar, and they were bopping in the orange light outside, their heads bobbing and fingers snapping, feet moving in a tight, precise, shuffling step. A few adults, men and women who had been standing by the road chatting, had also moved closer to the door of the bar, and they too were soon moving to the music, with one of them every once in a while breaking free of the group and swinging off on a step of his or her own for a minute or two.

Johnny admitted to Yvonne that, yes, he was weary. Strange things were happening to him, he explained, and he was losing track of his life. He smoked at a cigarette and drank Dragon stout. She drank white rum, and every few minutes picked the cigarette from his hand and took a drag, then carefully replaced it. Yvonne was a handsome but not pretty woman, in her mid thirties. Her regular boy friend was the cop named Bush, who lived in Anchovy with his wife, supposedly a nasty-tempered fat woman, and a crowd of children. Yvonne lived upstairs over the shop with her children, two boys and a girl, in a small apartment rented to her by Barrett. The father of her three children, she said, was a Bahamian who had worked for years as a waiter in one of the hotels in the Bay, until the government had thrown him out and given his job to a Jamaican. Though she'd never married him, she claimed she loved him still, even without having seen him once in five years. She knew there wasn't much chance for her to get together with him again, she explained, because the Jamaican government

wouldn't let him come over here and the Bahamian
government wouldn't let her go over there. She'd tried
once to get a visa, and they'd found out that she'd spent
a year in jail for stabbing a man, so they had refused to
let her into the country. If she had enough money, she
knew, they'd change their mind and let her in, and then
she and her boy friend could get married and bring the
children over, and she'd be happy. When Johnny had
asked her about the stabbing, she had brushed him off,
saying, That—oh, it was nothing, man. He beat me up a
couple of times, and I got scared, so one night when he
started up again, I just juked him. Three times in the
chest, and it still didn't kill him! But I had to go to jail
for a whole year.

Who was it you stabbed? Johnny had asked.

My boy friend. The Bahamian.

As the evening progressed, Johnny's conversations
with Yvonne grew more intimate and, in a way, confes-
sional. He stood, usually alone, at the far end of the bar,
while Yvonne moved swiftly back and forth from her
post next to him to serve customers, mostly regulars
from the neighborhood stopping in to exchange views
and listen to the juke box. Big Ron came and went, as
the urgent business of arranging and keeping appointments with girls and women dictated, and Terron too
came and went as his business, the business of Rasta,
dictated. Barrett drank and yakked and argued with the
regulars and waited for the arrival of his friends from the
Bay.

What was passing between Johnny and Yvonne was
an ancient, coded form of flirtation, in which the man
and the woman, by complaining about their respective
mates, manage to communicate their mutual sexual attraction to one another. Yvonne admitted that she was
using Bush, the cop. She hoped that, because he was a
cop, he would have the connections that would get her,
eventually, to the Bahamas and the arms of her true
love. Somehow, all the many kinds of authority and

officialdom were interconnected, so that if she could gain access to one of them, she'd have access to the others. To illustrate, she cited her conversation with a customs officer she'd met in December at the Policeman's Ball, which she never would have been able to attend in the first place if she hadn't been Bush's girl friend. She'd asked the customs officer if he could help her get a visa to the Bahamas, and he'd said it was possible and he'd drop by Barrett's one of these days to talk about it. He hadn't shown up yet, but she knew he would. Johnny wondered if there was any way he could help, but she said no, probably not, he was an American. The only kind of power he had access to came from his being rich. We both have to buy what we need, she said smiling.

He pondered that one, while she ran to refill glasses. When she came back to him, she brought with her a long-legged stool and set it down so that she could sit with her back to the wall and keep her eye on the bar. She was tired and dropped her powerful body heavily onto the chair. She was a short woman, broad-shouldered and muscular, built like a female shot-putter, but slick and black, and she moved with precision and power. Her hair was cropped close to the skull and her face was broad and flat with high cheekbones and eyes that were almost oriental. Her mouth was thick, sensual, and, even when she wasn't talking, always busy—chewing gum, nibbling, sipping, upper teeth with a gap between the two front teeth biting against her full lower lip, pink tongue flicking the corners of her mouth, washing across her lips, rubbing against gums. It was the clear, animated center of her face and made her seem more accessible, more warmly sociable and sexy than most of the women Johnny had dealt with. Except for Dorothy, the woman he'd spent the night with last April in Port Antonio, most of the women he'd met kept their mouths closed and still or else posed them self-consciously in what they thought, or hoped, were cute little pouts, as if they were trying to look like the blonde, tanned, Anglo

beauties they'd seen in American magazines advertising
the comfort and beauty of Jamaican resorts by revealing
how comfortable and beautiful they were as they lounged
around the pool or ran gaily along the beach or delicately held frosty piña coladas in the cocktail lounge and
enjoyed a brilliant conversation with an elegant, rich,
silver-haired stranger in cummerbund and white dinner
jacket.

For most of the evening so far, Johnny had complained about his wife, how she didn't really understand
him, the usual complaints, and Yvonne had complained
about Bush, how selfish and insensitive he was, how he
used her as his "outside woman" and would never leave
his wife for her. But now they had reversed themselves,
so that Johnny was talking about Bush, politely, indirectly, inquiring into the nature of his claims on Yvonne,
his tendency to be possessive, jealous, violent, and,
with equal politeness and indirection, Yvonne was inquiring about the same aspects of Johnny's wife's character and claims. According to Johnny, his wife knew
that he would occasionally sleep with another woman,
but it didn't really matter to her, he said, so long as it
was only occasionally. She was more afraid of his falling
in love with another woman than of his sleeping with
one, he told her. So far, so good. Yvonne seemed to
understand what that meant, even if she did raise her
eyebrows in surprise. But when she told him, with scorn,
that Bush was like all Jamaican men, and if she slept
with another man and he found out, he'd try to kill the
man and he'd probably cut her up, too, Johnny looked
at her strangely, as if he didn't understand what she was
trying to tell him, as if he couldn't read the code any
longer. Even so, he couldn't resist taking one more step,
and quickly he made the conversation incomprehensible: Well, then, he said, smiling broadly, we'll just have
to keep Bush from finding out, won't we.

She laughed, as if he had just told her a joke, jumped
from her stool, and ran to serve a pair of customers
who'd just walked through the door. Johnny looked

around, located Terron, who was in deep conversation on the grocery store side of the shop with Barrett's wife, and Big Ron, who was dancing next to the juke box with a friendly-looking woman in her forties, a good dancer and very fat, just the type of "big beef" Ron was always saying was irresistible to him—huge hips, belly and breasts moving up and down and side to side in soft waves as she danced and Big Ron, shirtless, barefoot, handsome as a movie star, chugged along in front of her. Slowly, Johnny left the bar, walked around the side of the building, zipped open his fly and peed onto the ground. The moon was still almost full and floated overhead—more like a smokehole in a tent that opened to the outside than a solid sphere riding an orbit around a second sphere.

He heard his name being called. Johnny! Where's Johnny? Where the hell's Johnny? It was Barrett's sandy voice. He quickly zipped himself up, stepped back inside the bar, and saw Barrett about to go into the back room with two men in their fifties, strangers, the same two that Yvonne had rushed off to serve a few moments earlier. Barrett saw him and motioned for him to follow. It was ten o'clock. The place would close at eleven, and Yvonne would climb the stairs to her rooms above the shop, where she'd sleep—alone, if Bush didn't drop by. Otherwise, not alone.

Give me a Dragon, Johnny said to her, and she handed it to him, quickly and not even looking at him, as she rushed to fill the orders of several other men standing at the bar. Then he walked out back, to play dominoes until two in the morning with Barrett and sometimes Terron and Big Ron and anyone else who happened to walk in and pair off with him against Barrett's two skeptical friends from the Bay.

3

SOON THE POLICE STARTED COMING AROUND. NOT, HOWEVER,
as Terron had predicted and as Johnny had probably
expected—a pair of Land Cruisers and a dozen or more
cops armed with shotguns kicking in the doors at three
in the morning, terrorizing him, his wife and children, as
two officers interrogated him while the others ransacked
the place looking for ganja so they could toss him and
his family out of the country. No, they came politely, in
midafternoon, a pair of slender, articulate, upwardly-
mobile, brown-skinned sergeants at a time. Within a few
days of Phelps' death and Johnny's return from Gordon
Hall, the first of them showed up. They asked to see his
visa and seemed more interested in the person from
whom Johnny had rented the house than in anything
else. In fact, if Johnny hadn't known better, as he told
his wife, he would have thought they were investigating
not him but the Churches. A week later a second pair of
sergeants showed up right after lunch, and asked politely if they could walk over the estate and "check out
the gates." There had been some robberies in Reading
lately, so they were looking after what they called "the
better neighborhoods," making sure they were secure.
Johnny, slightly stoned, giddy, demonstrated Church's
amazing lighting system. You oughta see this place at
night! he shouted, flicking switches. You'd think it was
a fucking shopping center! When a third pair of ser-

geants showed up a few weeks later and accomplished essentially what the first two pairs had accomplished—a measure of the extent and condition of the Church estate—Johnny conceded that his wife was right, they weren't after him, they didn't give a damn about Phelps' death, probably had never even heard of it, and had no reason to think he owned a gun. They probably weren't even interested in getting him out of the country. In fact, they were more likely to be trying to figure out how to get him to stay. What they *were* worried about, as she had told him, was money, Church's money in particular and how to keep it in Jamaica. That was the problem. *Your* problem, she told him, is that you think you're important to anyone other than yourself. Your little melodramas don't count for *anything* in the real world, mister. You can't tell the difference between a country's economics and your personal experiences. That's your problem.

You're right, he said, walking out the door for Barrett's. Absolutely right. Absolutely.

ONE AFTERNOON IN LATE FEBRUARY, THE CHURCHES' GRAY Mercedes appeared unannounced outside, Mr. and Mrs. Church had come to call. Entering the house with the same appraising gaze at the pool, poolhouse, modern electric kitchen, cathedral-ceilinged living room, terrace, gardens and spectacular view of the Bay as had the police, they settled themselves finally out on the terrace and immediately made the purpose of their visit known.

We want to sell you the house, Mr. Church said. A large man, his nose and cheeks swarming with broken veins and his belly swollen from alcoholism, his blotched hands trembling for a drink while his voice strove to present him as still the man-in-charge he once had been, he alternately sat back casually in the wrought iron chair and leaned forward with sincere desperation, as if he couldn't hold a point of view for longer than ten or fifteen seconds.

His wife, if less direct, was more focused. Perching

herself on the edge of her chair, she crossed her tiny feet, smiled at Johnny and his wife and explained to them how, if they wanted to, they could buy a hundred thousand dollar house for thirty thousand dollars. She and Mr. Church were leaving the island for Canada, she explained, to join their son and grandchildren and because of Mr. Church's health. But because of the socialists, all they could take out of the country was a "pittance." She grew angry. After all these years, a lifetime of building this country up, and now they're told if they leave they can't take out more than ninety dollars apiece!

Johnny said, Surely that can't be true. But he had heard hundreds of times by now of this "capitalist" or that leaving the country owing the Jamaican banks hundreds of thousands of dollars, after having for years smuggled an equal amount out by courier and mail, stashing it in banks in Miami, New York, or Toronto, until either they couldn't borrow any more here or else simply became too frightened and harassed by audits, regulations, and paperwork to keep it going and had, at last, on tourist visas, deserted their real property and debts here and fled to join their money, Canadian and American currency, if they were lucky, or jewels, as the Jamaican dollar kept on being devalued to comply with the conditions set by the International Monetary Fund.

Oh yes, Mrs. Church said, it *was* true. Ninety dollars! Of course, she herself planned to carry a whole lot more than that when *she* left, even if she had to hide it in her hair-do, she said, fluffing her thick, curly, gray hair, where at least a dozen American fifties could be hidden and pinned, if rolled tightly enough.

Do it! Johnny said, too loudly. His wife gave him a hard look.

Oh indeed she would, she declared righteously. Indeed she would. But more importantly, before they left the island, she wanted to give Johnny and his wife the chance of a lifetime. She couldn't tell them exactly *when* they were leaving, naturally. The walls have ears, she explained, casting a wary glance toward the kitchen, where Caroline was washing dishes, and then out the open doorway to the gray Mercedes, where the driver sat reading his *Gleaner*. What the Churches had to offer was legal ownership of the house Johnny and his wife were presently renting for three hundred dollars a month, which three hundred dollars a month had been sent regularly and very nicely too from Johnny's bank in the United States to the Churches' son's bank in Toronto. If Johnny and his wife agreed to transfer thirty thousand dollars from their bank directly to the son's account in Toronto, just as they had been sending the rent, then they could own the house, including the furnishings. We'd simply sign it over to you, she told them. It would be legal, completely legal. Their son apparently had signed the house over to them the same way when he had left for Canada. They loved this house, she said, and Mr. Church agreed. And this hill, too. They loved the hill.

It was nothing but bush up here when I bought this hill, Mr. Church said. I got the hill for three hundred pounds, a lot in those days, and it was pure bush. I carved this place out of the jungle! he exclaimed, and slumped back into his chair.

I don't know . . . , Johnny began. He was smiling, almost grinning, as if he did know.

Well, I should tell you, Mrs. Church interrupted, that if you don't want to buy the house, we won't be able to continue renting it to you.

Johnny stopped smiling. Wait a minute. You agreed to rent it to us until August first. I have letters from you.

No, she said firmly. No. If we can't make the right arrangements to sell the house, to you or someone else—it makes no difference to us so long as the arrangements are the right ones—then we'll just have to sell off what we can. The furniture and the appliances and so on. After all, we must raise whatever cash money we can. We're not young people, we can't start over again. She started looking at the furniture with an auctioneer's eye, the wrought iron table and chairs on the terrace, the sofa, chairs, and console television in the living room, the mahogany dining-room set, the beds and dressers, the stove, refrigerator, washer and dryer—Jamaica was a buyer's market, there were still quite a few buyers on the island for furnishings like these. No one was manufacturing them locally, and the import restrictions and duties made them prohibitively expensive to buy new from abroad, or simply not available at all.

But I have letters. You agreed.

Our agreement, she pointed out, was private and personal. *Legally,* she said, emphasizing the word so Johnny would understand, you have been our guests here. Then she was silent.

Johnny looked at his wife and shrugged his shoulders. We can't buy the house, he said to the Churches. We don't have that kind of money. He looked at his wife again, as if for encouragement, but she was looking at her lap. Besides, he said, even if we had the money, I couldn't do it. *Wouldn't* do it. Not that way. Not anymore. I feel rotten that I've been renting the house this cheaply this long by cheating, by taking advantage . . .

Of whom? Mrs. Church demanded. Tell me that! Who suffers? Who?

It's a fine point, I guess. Eventually people here suffer. They suffer indirectly from the fact that other people, people like you and me, swap foreign currency in foreign banks in exchange for services rendered here. But directly, *I* suffer. *I'm* the one who suffers directly. I take advantage of myself. And I end up losing. Of course, that's only important to *me*. But it *is* important to me, now that I see it.

What are you talking about? Mrs. Church wanted to know.

Her husband was leaning forward in his chair again. They're not interested? Hmm, not interested. Really.

It doesn't matter, Johnny said to Mrs. Church. The important thing, for me, is to say no to you. And then to find out how long we can stay on here as your "guests." After all, you wouldn't want simply to evict us. Not after having enjoyed such a financially rewarding relationship with us for so many months now.

Mrs. Church laughed at that. *Squatters!* That's what you'll be, squatters! Fine. Stay as long as you like. We'll sell the furniture out from under you, young man, and then we'll be gone! And then you'll have plenty of other squatters up here right alongside you, she warned. Once we're gone from this hill, with our dogs and my husband's hunting rifles and shotguns gone, how long do you think you can stay up here without getting yourself chopped up? Those people down in Anchovy have been looking at these houses and this property for years, years, just waiting for the chance to take it over!

The place was pure jungle, Mr. Church explained.

You'll see, his wife warned and she rose to leave. The trouble with people like you is that you don't understand this country. You come in here and six months later start telling us how we ought to behave here. You think you understand Jamaicans, but you don't. They're our Jamaicans, and we understand them. You'll see. After we've gone, you'll learn what we already know. And it'll be too late to do you any good. C'mon, she said to her husband, and trotted on her tiny feet to the Mercedes, her husband following loyally along behind.

THERE WERE NO FURTHER DEVELOPMENTS FOR THE NEXT FEW weeks. Johnny and his wife and, when he was around, Terron speculated on when, exactly, the Churches would put their plan into action. They would probably move down a list of prospective buyers for the house, Johnny guessed, a necessarily short list, if they wanted to keep their imminent departure from the island a secret from the authorities. They'd sound out the few foreigners that they thought were rich enough and naive enough to be willing to deal with them—friends of theirs or friends of trusted friends. If they came up empty-handed, they'd let it out to their trusted friends—trusted only because they were in a boat like theirs if not the same boat altogether—that they were willing to sell everything in the house. And then people would start showing up at odd hours in pickup trucks to cart off the furniture and appliances piece by piece, until the house was as empty as the abandoned house over on the ridge, where, Terron informed him, a group of young Rastas had recently taken up residence. Johnny had walked out there many times that fall and winter along the overgrown, potholed road that the hurricane of 1967 had ripped up, but, he said, the place had begun to depress him. Duppies, Terron had explained. The restless, homeless spirits of the dead, more angry than mischievous, more like bad-tempered leprechauns than ghouls, duppies, when their presence was sensed, were to be avoided. But beyond that, on his last walk over there to the house on the ridge, Johnny had seen scrawled on the wall the usual Rastafarian graffiti, BABYLON MUST FALL AND PROPHECY MUST FULFILL! and out on the terrace had seen the remains of several campfires. He hadn't gone back after that, nor had he mentioned the graffiti and the campfires to his family or Terron.

Then, late in February, Johnny's friend from New Hampshire, the filmmaker Upton West, telephoned. He was in Jamaica, at his parent's home in Reading for a few days. I'm helping Mother and the Captain put their affairs in order, he said in that nasal, overarticulated voice of his. Upton always managed to sound as if he were being interviewed.

Oh? Johnny said. Why, what's happening?

Ah, yes, Mother mentioned she hadn't seen you folks in months, so naturally you wouldn't know. She and the Captain are leaving the island. I've found them an apartment in Cambridge, where I think they'll be content. Mother has family there, you know, and the Captain's always enjoyed Cambridge. Though he still thinks of the States as one of the colonies, Upton joked.

Ha, ha, Johnny laughed. When Upton was silent, he asked him why his parents were leaving. It'll be much harder for them up there, he said.

Yes, in a sense, but they're frightened now, because

of all the violence and the robberies and so on, and of course it's more and more difficult for them financially. It's a new Jamaica, he sighed. And they can't be expected to adjust. They knew the old Jamaica.

So they're selling their house and everything?

No, no, they can't, really. It's difficult to explain, he said, hesitating. It's . . . it's the same as with the Churches. Which brings me to my reason for calling, he said, swinging back into his usual, smooth way of speaking in whole sentences and paragraphs. I learned just this morning from Mother that last month the Churches made you a certain proposition and that you'd declined it, ostensibly because of a lack of ready cash. As you know, I'm quite familiar with the . . . item, and therefore I know its true value. And frankly, I wanted to urge you to reconsider and perhaps let me explore a few possibilities for raising the cash for you in the States. In fact, I'd be willing to lend you the money myself, as long as it were a short-term loan that you could repay when you got back to the States in August.

You don't understand . . .

There's great opportunity here right now, Upton interrupted, for those of us who live in the States. We just have to wait a few years and all this economic chaos will blow over. It's a buyer's market, my friend. All we have to do is sit tight for a few years in New Hampshire. People like my parents and the Churches, because they're Jamaican nationals, can't come back once they leave. Unless they take what they can get for their property now and turn that over to the government, which forces them to leave with nothing. Which is why they make "other arrangements." Naturally, those "other arrangements" are what make it difficult if not impossible to return. But what else can they do? Most of them are quite old and can't make a decent living in the States.

Will you be taking care of your parents in Cambridge? Johnny asked.

Yes. Just as you, if you agreed to accept their proposition, would be "taking care" of the Churches.

So you think this new Jamaica is just a phase, that the old Jamaica will come back in a few years. That it's safe for people like us to speculate?

Right. Oh, of course there's a certain risk involved. People here are terrified that the chaos will produce another Cuba, but you and I know how unlikely *that* is. The U.S. would never permit it. Neither, for that matter, would the International Monetary Fund. Seriously, though, I'd like to lend you the money. I have to fly out in the morning, because of commitments in New York, and then I'll be in L.A. until the end of March. But you could come up anytime in the next three or four days, and we could sign the papers in my office in New York. I could have my lawyer draw up an agreement as soon as I got back. You could fly in, sign it, and be back in Jamaica in a day. The banks up there would take care of the rest. What do you say?

No.

What?

No. The whole thing makes me sick to my stomach. I've done enough of this shit. No more.

I didn't realize you were so principled, Upton said coldly.

I'm not. It's not *principles* that're making me sick to my stomach! It's what's in front of me every day here. It's what I see when I wake up in the morning and my housekeeper tiptoes out to the terrace with my coffee and tries not to rattle the china cup against the china saucer so as not to disturb my important boss-man morning thoughts. It's what I see all day long and all night long, no matter where I go on this island. So, no. No more. I'm not going to help "take care" of the Churches, no matter how much it benefits me in your upcoming new version of the old Jamaica. I think you're right about that, by the way, or I should say, *accurate*, though it may take ten or even twenty years for the human suffering to get so bad that this chaos, as you call it, blows over and Jamaica becomes a seller's market again. Unless, of course, you believe in prophecy. In which case, old friend, Babylon must fall, and you'd be better off buying into tin mines in South Africa.

Oh, well, yes. That. Well, he said, I'm sorry you feel that way. But do let's get together when you get back to the States and we can talk about all this then. I'll be in New Hampshire in the fall for a few weeks. I love being up there when the leaves turn. We'll have to get together then. All right?

Right. Oh, say, I almost forgot. I did get up to Nyamkopong. I go there regularly and have friends there.

Really?

And the Colonel you once referred me to, Colonel Phelps?

Yes.

He's dead.

Oh?

Yes. Shot. A bullet in each eye. Bang, bang.

Well . . . who shot him?

Circumstantial evidence pointed to a local Rasta youth, a kid. So the cops shot him. Dead.

Killed him?

Five times. Twice in the head and three times in the chest. Twice in the stature, thrice in the structure. Bang, bang. Bang, bang, bang.

Well . . . , Upton said, clearing his throat. Well, I really must go, I've got hundreds of things to take care of.

The kid had an alibi, though.

Really? Well. So who killed Colonel Phelps, then?

It's an interesting question, Johnny said. Then he let go and politely said good-bye to his old friend and hung up. When he set the receiver down, he saw that his hands were shaking.

4

IN APRIL THE STRANGERS IN PICKUP TRUCKS AND VANS AND large cars started showing up, usually in the company of Mrs. Church, whose view of the house now seemed to be that it was a used furniture store. She treated Johnny and his wife and Terron as employees, hired hands who were there to lift and carry out the dining-room table, chairs, and sideboard, and then, a few days later, the end tables and lamps in the living room and the dresser from the room the children slept in. Most of the customers were white, but a few were not. An East Indian doctor and his sari-wrapped wife came up the hill one afternoon and had Johnny and Terron load the dryer onto their U-Haul trailer. Another Indian, a dentist who'd trained in Iowa and was now attached to the Mount Salem Hospital, bought the sofa and matching easy chairs and coffee table, and the Chinese manager of an auto parts store in Montego Bay bought the equipment used to clean the pool. It's gotten impossible to buy this stuff new, he said, as he stuffed the hose for the vacuum cleaner into the trunk of his BMW.

Finally, one night Johnny came in from Barrett's alone—Terron had gone back up to Nyamkopong to relieve his new partner, his cousin Juke, who had been out in the bush for the previous two weeks guarding their rapidly maturing ganja crop—and he found his wife waiting up for him. She was out on the terrace smoking cigarettes and drinking beer, and from the empties in front of her, was on her fourth by the time Johnny strolled out and saw her there.

She had made a decision, she told him. She was going back to the States, to their house in New Hampshire, and she was taking the children with her. There was no reason to explain. He could come with her, if he wanted . . .

I *can't!* he interrupted. I've got to stay here till August first, you know that! I gave my word.

None of that mattered to her, not anymore. He could come back with her and the children now or he could come back in August and they'd figure it out then.

Figure out what?

Figure out what to do with this thing we're still in the habit of calling a marriage, she said evenly. Then she informed him that she'd made reservations for tomorrow afternoon's flight to Miami and Boston. She'd phoned a friend in New Hampshire, who would meet them. And she'd told the children.

Told them what?

That we're leaving tomorrow. They were very glad to hear it, by the way. They asked if you were coming too, naturally, and I said no. I thought it was safer telling them that than having to disappoint them if you decided to stay. Which I guess you have.

Well . . . I *have* to, he said weakly.

You have enough money here to take care of you until then, if you're careful with it, she pointed out. And there was enough in their account at home to carry her and the children through the summer. Especially now that he'd written the bank in New Hampshire to stop paying the Churches, something he'd done back in February, as soon as they had learned that they were guests here.

It's the best thing to do, he said quietly. He knew the girls were growing frightened and confused, especially as the house was rapidly being stripped of furniture and appliances, and he knew that she no longer had any good reason of her own for staying on. It was only a little more than three months that they'd be separated, and, by then, he told her, they'd both know better how to deal with this thing we're still in the habit of calling a marriage, he said, quoting her.

She rubbed out her cigarette and stood up. I'm going to bed. I'm sleeping in the girls' room, she informed him, almost as an afterthought.

Oh. Yes . . . well, that makes sense. He seemed relieved and walked slowly to the kitchen and got himself a bottle of beer, opened it, and, when he returned to the terrace, she was gone and the door off the living room to the large bedroom where the children slept was closed. He walked to the edge of the terrace, sat on the wall, and stared down at the glittering lights of Montego Bay. Sipping thoughtfully on his beer, he sat there for close to an hour, before he left the terrace and went into the bedroom he had shared with his wife. In the dark he undressed and climbed into the big, hand-carved, four-poster bed that Mrs. Church was asking five hundred dollars for. It was a genuine antique, she had explained, made in the 1700s for the first Church on the island by one of his slaves, and every Church since then had been born in that bed. It's irreplaceable, she said. You can't get anyone to make a bed like that today. I don't care how much you want to pay for it.

THE NEXT DAY, AFTER LUNCH, JOHNNY DROVE HIS WIFE AND daughters to the airport and stood up on the waving deck as the plane taxied away from the terminal, turned at the western end of the main runway, then rushed past him, lifted off, and roared into the eastern sky, where it banked slowly around to the north and soon disappeared. He had waved frantically at the darkened windows of the plane as it passed the terminal, even though it wasn't possible to see any of the passengers at that distance. As soon as the plane had disappeared from sight altogether, he walked quickly down to the main terminal, out to his car in the lot, and then drove directly back through Montego Bay to Anchovy, and Barrett's.

He parked the blue van in front of the shop and walked in, found the place empty, except for Yvonne, who, as always, was happy to see him, and started drinking. By six, he was drunk. By seven, he had made an appointment with Yvonne to sleep with her that night after she got off work. Assuming, of course, that Bush didn't show up first. No way, she assured him. Bush was in Ocho Rios for the week. At eight, he told Yvonne that he was going up to the compound to take a shower and try to get himself sobered up. At nine, he left Barrett's to do so, but at five after nine, he smashed his Mazda van into the concrete and stone gatepost at the entrance to the compound.

At the crest of the hill, the road forked into two driveways, the one on the left leading out to the point, where the Churches were still in residence, and the other, on the right, looping slightly downhill for fifty yards to the house where Johnny was now in residence alone. He'd come over the top a little too fast, had spun the wheel hard to the right and had been unable to keep the car from whacking head-on into the pylon there. He'd walked, somewhat dazed, down to the house, where he discovered that during the afternoon Mrs. Church had sold off the wrought iron furniture on the terrace and also the beds the children had slept on.

After taking a shower, he ate, while standing in the kitchen, a half-pound chunk of orange New Zealand cheese and a quarter pound of sliced smoked marlin. Around eleven, he left the house again, walked past his car, where he saw that the front bumper, grill, headlights, windshield and steering arms, column and wheel would have to be replaced, and saw also that the gatepost was undamaged, and then walked down the long hill in the dark to Barrett's again, where he broke his appointment with Yvonne.

She said, Okay, not to worry, and he answered, No, it wasn't okay. She said she understood, and he said, No, she didn't understand. My life is coming apart, he told her, and I don't know how to stop it from coming apart.

I'm not even sure I *want* to stop it. One thing I do know, though, is that I can't trust my judgment right now, and unless I'm very careful from now on, he said to her, I'm likely to get myself killed. If not by Bush, then by smashing up my car. And if not by smashing up my car, then by some lunatic gunman from Nyamkopong. Or maybe by some Rasta crazies with double-edged machetes who think I'm sitting all alone up there in that empty house on a chest of gold, just waiting for the chance to smuggle it out of the country. Or maybe the cops will do it some night because I know my friend Benjie didn't kill Colonel Phelps. Or maybe the Churches will have me knocked off because of what I know about them. Or maybe the government will think I'm a CIA agent, now that my family has left and I've no clear reason for continuing to stay here myself. But one way or the other, he said, unless I'm careful and start acting like I'm scared, then I'm going to be killed. I'm starting to behave like a *tourist,* he said, shuddering at the word. That's why I've got to break our date. But if I ever end up living on this island of Jamaica, he said, suddenly smiling and flirting again, I'll come around here and try to take you away from Bush, fair and square. It's the sneaking around in the nighttime while you're still Bush's woman that I can't stand. She asked him if he meant that, and he said sure he meant it. Did he think he would end up living on this island of Jamaica? she wanted to know. He smiled and turned to leave. Not up there, in *that* house. I can tell you that much, he said as he strode from the bar.

He slept in that house that night, however. And the next, and the next. And every day the process of stripping the house and outbuildings and yard went on—the chaise longues next to the pool, the refrigerator, the telephone table, the dresser and chairs in the bedrooms, the lamps and end tables, even the wall-to-wall carpeting. Johnny continued to pay Caroline, who no longer had any work to do but come in every morning at seven anyhow and stayed around until he woke around nine and sent her home. One morning he tried to use the phone, to call the garage in Montego Bay, where his car had been towed and where, if the parts could be located, it would be fixed, and found that the phone had been disconnected. He continued to sleep in the big mahogany bed. Then one afternoon a woman drove all the way from Savanna-la-Mar, an attractive fawn-colored woman with a permanent, to buy the sheets, blankets, and towels. Carefully, meticulously, she boxed all the linens in the house and placed them into the back of her new, red Volkswagen van. They were for her sister, she said, who was getting married. When she started for the sheets on Johnny's bed and the towel in the bathroom, he had protested, until finally he managed to convince her to sell him the pair of sheets and towel for ten dollars. She didn't particularly enjoy doing it, and she told him so. I'm no higgler, she pointed out to him. And you can't buy sheets like these anymore. You have to go to Florida for them. And really, what would Mrs. Church say? He shrugged and smiled through his beard. I don't think she'd want me sleeping on her bed *without* sheets, do you? No, she said, as she got into her van and started the engine. But I really don't think she wants you sleeping in her bed at all. He laughed. Tell Mrs. Church that I'm guarding her house for her! he called, as the woman drove quickly away.

He kept only fresh fruit in the house now and ate at Barrett's or at Big Ron's in Anchovy, so when one night he came back to the house and all the pots, pans, dishes, and silverware were gone, he didn't seem to mind. He simply observed their absence and went into the bedroom and slept. His clothes were dirty and piling up in a corner of the bedroom, where he'd stacked the contents of the desk after it had been sold—his papers, notes, financial records and correspondence, his portable typewriter, several hundred manuscript pages of the novel that once he had tried to write but now hadn't even looked at in almost six months. He used his suitcase for a dresser, and next to it on the floor there were a half dozen books, borrowed in the fall from the Montego Bay public library and growing a skin of mildew from lying on the damp uncarpeted floor. When the electricity was shut off, he bought a packet of candles from Barrett's. And when two workmen in a flatbed truck disconnected and hauled out the gas stove, he stopped drinking tea in the mornings and gave the mug and saucepan he'd borrowed from Caroline back to her. Almost apologetically, she used the occasion to tell him that she couldn't come in anymore; her new job was down in Reading and the lady wanted her there early. With clear relief he paid her a week's wages and thanked her for all she'd done. With the electricity off, the pool circulator no longer worked, and in two days the water was green and slimy, so Johnny opened the gate valves and emptied it. Though he still had running water to bathe in—the cistern was uphill from the house and didn't require a pump—and, when he ran out of clean T-shirts and jeans, could use the kitchen sink to wash his clothes, he was forced to bathe himself and his clothes in cold water. The water heater, sold now, had been an electric one.

The last thing to go was the mahogany bed, and Mr. Church himself came for that. Apparently, no one would pay him what he thought it was worth, so he had decided to ship it to his son in Canada and claim to the customs people that it was his gift to his son, a family heirloom. Because that's what it was, damn it! A family heirloom! It's a shame you have to lie, though, he said to Johnny, who had been standing at the kitchen sink washing out his underwear when Mr. Church drove up in a company pickup with a pair of laborers squatting in back. Following Church's loud instructions, they quickly dismantled the bed and lugged the pieces—headboard, footboard, sideboards, slats, boxspring, and mattress—out to the truck. I had to have the boxspring and mattress custom-made in North Carolina, Church said admiringly, as the pieces were carted past him. Johnny kept silently at his wash. You know what that bed would cost today? Church asked him, still looking at it in the back of the truck, admiring it in pieces. Johnny shook his head no, but Church didn't see him. Hell, he said, you couldn't even get it made today! No matter how much you wanted to pay for it. Times have changed. Most things worth having you couldn't even buy anymore. He was angry and yanked his lips tight to his teeth. After a few seconds, he turned to Johnny. Well, what are your plans? I understand your family has returned to the States. My maid told me.

Oh. Right. Well, I'm not going back till August. I have some business . . . some work to do, up there with the Maroons.

Well, I can't let you stay here any longer. I'm closing this place up. Everything's gone from it, so there's no longer any reason to keep it open. If anyone needs to see the place, you know, to buy it or maybe rent it, my wife and I can let them in. We're going to be up here on the hill for a while yet . . . You understand. I want to lock it up tight.

Oh, okay, sure. I'll get my stuff out today, this afternoon, if you want. He wrung out his underwear and emptied the sink. Out on the terrace he spread his shorts and T-shirts along the wall to dry in the sun and called back to Church, who stood at the open front door, his yellow Ford pickup truck behind him, the two shiny black laborers sitting in back with the bed, expressionless and still, sweating in the hot sun.

The keys are on the hook there, next to the door! Johnny said. Why don't you just take them now? I'll leave as soon as these clothes are dry. And I'll be sure all the doors and windows are closed and locked before I leave, he promised.

Without answering, Church grabbed the keys, stepped outside, and drove away, leaving Johnny alone in the house. He showered, packed his papers, and, when his underwear on the terrace wall had dried, packed his clothes into his suitcase. Then he too left the house. At Barrett's he hitched a ride with Barrett himself into Montego Bay. Barrett in his white Toyota taxi-van was on his way to the airport, but Johnny asked to be left off near the market, where the buses left for the interior.

Where you going, Johnny? Barrett asked him as he stepped down from the van and hauled out his heavy suitcase and typewriter.

Nyamkopong.

What about your car.

I think it's dead, man. No parts on the island to fix Mazda vans, and no more coming in. I'll probably have to sell it for junk and it'll end up providing parts for someone else's Mazda van, someone who smashed up the back end of his.

Barrett laughed. Too bad, though. That van was worth a lot.

I'll get alone without it, Johnny said, and waving good-bye, he picked up his gear and made his way through the loud, bustling market crowd to find the Maggotty bus, which, he knew from Terron's travels back and forth, would be leaving the Bay around four o'clock, arriving in Maggotty by seven. It would still be daylight and he could hitch a ride at least as far as Whitehall, and from there he could walk the rest of the way to Mr. Mann's house.

5

HE WASN'T GREETED WITH MUCH ENTHUSIASM AT MR. MANN'S.
The old man's difficulty in following Johnny's explanation of why he was in Nayamkopong now, at the end of
May and without a car, seemed deliberate. And he seemed
almost not to believe him when Johnny said that the
reason he was staying on in Jamaica without his wife
and children was because he had promised Colonel Bowra
that he'd transport the Nyamkopong colonel and his
entourage across the island to Gordon Hall for the celebration there on August first.

That's a full two months off, the old man observed.
He was seated outside his house on the top step of the
stoop, with Johnny seated next to him, his suitcase and
typewriter on the ground below where he'd dropped
them a few moments before.

Things had changed. Mr. Mann was now Colonel Mann.
Colonel Phelps' widow had moved in with Colonel Phelps'
cousin, the man who drove the Ford van back and forth
between Maggotty and Nyamkopong. A rich man, Mr.
Mann told Johnny. And a widow-maker, he added in a
sly voice.

Johnny looked quickly at the old man. Really? A
widow-maker?

Mr. Mann changed the subject. Put your bags inside
my house for tonight, he said. You can sleep here, and
tomorrow, if you want to stay on here in the village, I'll

find you an empty house you can rent. Ordinarily, the old man assured Johnny, he'd have him stay here in his own home for as long as he'd like to stay in the village, but when he was made the Colonel, two of his daughters had come up from Kingston to live with him, and now his house was crowded. They think, because you're Colonel, you're a rich man, he said, sighing.

Johnny tried nudging Mr. Mann back to the subject of Phelps' widow and cousin. He told the old man that he'd heard Terron's version of how and why Phelps had died, but it didn't quite make sense to him. Terron's version was that the gun belonging to the Rasta youth Benjie had done the killing all right, but that Benjie himself was innocent.

The gun was in his bed. He tried to use it on the police and they shot him for it.

That's not what I heard, Johnny said in a low voice.

Well, you hear all kinds of things, Mr. Mann said, brightening. Things about lost guns and reappearing guns, about obi and science, and I even heard one story that was about you, my son. But I didn't once believe it. Not for a minute.

Me?

Yes, you. The widow Phelps put it out. She said that you and the Colonel from Gordon Hall killed her husband, but then they found Benjie with his gun, so she forgot about you and the Colonel from Gordon Hall. For her, one story was as good as another. One story served her purposes as well as any other.

And what were her purposes?

To marry the bus driver. Who, as I have already mentioned, is a rich man. She'd been his outside woman for several years, he explained to Johnny, and then, the night before the January sixth celebration, she learned that her husband, as the Maroon Colonel, was arranging through Sergeant Kemp to have the bus driver's license revoked and given to a friend of Kemp who lived in Whitehall. She realized if that happened, her boy friend would no longer be a rich man. She argued bitterly with

her husband, but after a while he lost patience with her
and beat her up. So she ran to the bus driver and told
him everything. He was the one who hired Benjie, Mr.
Mann said, and Benjie was the one who shot Phelps. It
was early in the morning, and Phelps went out to the
privy, where Benjie was waiting for him. And he shot
him with his pants down, Mr. Mann chuckled. Afterward, according to Mr. Mann, the boy had run back to
the House of Dread and pretended to sleep, until the
police came. Then he had panicked and pulled out his
gun, which is what got *him* shot. Simple, he said, smiling. No obeah. No mysteries. Simple.

Why didn't Kemp arrest the bus driver and Phelps'
wife? Johnny wondered. Then his friend in Whitehall
could get the license for the bus service between
Nyamkopong and Maggotty. Besides, if what you say is
true . . .

Of *course* it's true!

. . . then they're as guilty as Benjie was.

Well, my son, you can know things in this world and
not be able to prove them in a court of law. Some things
you must leave to the judgment of a Higher Court.
Besides, the bus driver has lots of money. The police
won't bother him now, not with Benjie dead. It's more
profitable this way. Every once in a while Sergeant
Kemp goes by and says things to Phelps' cousin and
widow, things that make them nervous, so they take
care of him and he goes away. Why would he arrest
them? Mr. Mann asked, laughing as if in admiration of
Kemp's intelligence. That Kemp is no monkey, he's a
fox, he said.

You're reminding me of a man I knew in Port Antonio, Johnny said evenly. His name was Evan Smith, and
he thought Errol Flynn was a fox.

Oh yes, yes, yes. Errol Flynn. The old man pondered
the name for a few seconds. Yes, well, he *was* a fox. A
fox in the henhouse, as the saying goes, heh, heh, heh.
Then, abruptly, he got up and instructed Johnny to carry
his suitcase and typewriter into the house and place

them in the room behind his bedroom, the alcove back there with the cot where Mr. Mann himself had slept last April when Johnny had stayed in his house for a week. The old man apologized for the inconvenience, explaining that because so many people lived in his house, now that he was Colonel, he was unable to receive guests adequately. The government ought to build us a hotel, he said, or at least a guesthouse. He himself, however, was going to move into Colonel Phelps' house soon, just he and his wife Devina, and leave this old place for his children and grandchildren. He'd already arranged with Phelps' widow to rent it to him. For a pittance, he said, winking. A pittance.

JOHNNY SLEPT ON THE NARROW COT IN BACK OF MR. MANN'S own bedroom, where now, or at least for this one night, Mr. Mann's two daughters from Kingston and their babies slept. In the morning, after a breakfast of oranges and hard-boiled eggs, Mr. Mann informed Johnny that he could use Rubber's house for as long as he wished to stay in Nyamkopong. Forever, if you like. He told him where the house was located, a one-room cabin like Terron's that was alongside the road about two hundred yards beyond the Colonel's old house.

I know where it is, Johnny said. I was here when Kemp and his boys dragged Rubber out to the road and hauled him off to Maggotty. Where's Rubber now? he asked the old man. He's not still in *jail*, is he?

Oh yes. Certainly.

Why?

Well . . . you never know. With these Rasta youths, I mean. He probably did some serious robbing. But don't you worry, the old man assured him. You can use his house as long as you want to. I'm the Colonel, and it's *my* decision, he proclaimed. He could keep Rubber in jail *forever*, he bragged.

Johnny's mouth was open, as if he were about to shout. But he remained silent, except to thank Mr. Mann for his hospitality. Then he grabbed his suitcase and typewriter and walked straight for Rubber's house. As he passed Terron's cabin, he stepped in, greeted Terron's woman and was told, vaguely, that Terron had gone away and wouldn't be back for a few days. He thanked her, said he'd stay in town until Terron came back from wherever he was, and then went on to Rubber's.

6

FOR THE NEXT FEW DAYS, JOHNNY KEPT PRETTY MUCH TO himself. Rubber's cabin was furnished with a double bed and blanket, a small oilcloth-covered table and two straightbacked chairs. There was a cookpot, but because Rubber was a Rastaman, Johnny went out that first morning and bought his own pot at one of the shops. You can take over a Rastaman's pot, but you can't borrow it. At the same time he bought some rice, gungo peas, tinned beef, cheese, eggs, condensed milk, Milo, and candles, and also a bottle of Appleton overproof. Behind the cabin Johnny saw and identified a breadfruit tree, a pair of orange trees, a half dozen yam plants, and some ripening corn. There were also the usual soot-blackened kitchen and a leaning, doorless privy. Next to the cabin were two full barrels of run-off water. If Rubber had ever owned any clothes, shoes, or a transistor radio, or anything else of value, they had, in his absence, been removed from the unlocked place. What remained was merely what every other adult in town already owned or simply could not sell and therefore would not steal.

The cabin was clean and airy, with two windows and two doors, one in front facing directly onto the road, the other opposite it in back facing the endless Cockpit. The bed was under one window and the table and chairs were under the other. Once he had his supplies in,

Johnny seemed content to stay there and did not move in the evenings toward the shops at the crossroads and did not visit the homes of any of the numerous people he knew there. Once a day he cooked outside in the kitchen. Though he had found plenty of deadwood for his fire stashed under the cabin and in back below the trees, he couldn't break the long branches of mahoe into small chunks without a machete, so on the second morning he went back to the shop and, to the shopkeeper's amusement, bought a machete and a rabbit file to sharpen it with. From then on he spent several hours a day gathering and chopping firewood.

No one came to call. Not Terron's cousin and partner Juke, who, if Terron was guarding the crop, was probably here in town, and not the Rastaman Bongo Smith from the House of Dread, not Terron's heavy woman or any of his kids, not the schoolteacher who last year had been so eager to show him the new Canadian schoolhouse, not Devina to extract another five-dollar pledge for her church, and not Colonel Mann. It was as if Rubber's house were still vacant.

Then one evening, when he had been in the house six days, the colossally bearded and dreadlocked Bongo Smith showed up. They sat together in the doorway that faced the Cockpit and burned a spliff and cursed the injustice of Benjie's death at the hands of Babylon. Colonel Mann's explanation for Phelps' and then Benjie's deaths Smith thought ridiculous. He spat angrily at the ground. Then in a whisper he asked Johnny who in this town got the most out of Phelps' death. Say that name, Smith commanded, and then he would know who had killed Colonel Phelps.

Johnny didn't bother to say anyone's name. Instead, he asked Smith if Terron agreed with him.

Maybe. He didn't know. Terron is still friendly with Mann, but he has to be, because of the cops. Especially now, with his crop coming in, he added and flashed a knowing wink.

Johnny just said, Oh. I didn't know.

Right. Right. Smith smiled lazily and took a long hit from the spliff, and then stood up to leave. He took a step away, turned back and asked Johnny if he'd heard about Mann's daughters yet.

No. What about them?

Smith laughed. The daughters are fighting over you, man, he said. A few nights ago one of them, according to Smith, had stabbed the other.

Over *me?* C'mon, Smith. I barely met them. I don't even know their names.

That doesn't matter, Smith explained, grinning. These Jamaican women will kill another woman to keep her from controlling a rich man. What the rich man wants or doesn't want makes no difference. Dem wan fe mash de nex oman down, he said. Dem ras im, dem chop im, no matta fe de mon im long gone.

Johnny shook his head slowly. Is she dead, the one who got stabbed?

No, but she had got her face and shoulders rather badly cut. Apparently Colonel Mann had rushed between them and stopped the fight in time. He probably would have liked to see them get on with it, Smith added, until one was dead and the other had to go back to Kingston and hide out. But he was more interested in keeping things quiet now, Smith told him, at least until Johnny was gone.

What the hell does *that* mean?

Smith just smiled and stepped away. You're not invisible, man! he said, laughing. You think so, maybe, but you're not! And then, still laughing, he was gone into the darkness.

Things moved rapidly then. The next morning Colonel Mann himself appeared at Johnny's door. He stepped in, took a seat on one of the chairs, and announced that he had come to collect the first week's rent, ten dollars, and also to tell Johnny that he would not be able to go with him to Gordon Hall on August first. I want you to be my personal emissary, however, he told Johnny. I want you to present my humblest apologies to my brother

Colonel of the Maroons of Gordon Hall and to give him an important message. Tell him that I have taken it upon myself to direct the Member of Parliament from this district, the Honorable Mr. Bulkley, Esquire, to make or have made three copies of the sacred Maroon treaty, and then to mail one copy to each of the remaining Maroon cities in Jamaica, Moore Town, Charles Town, and Gordon Hall. The original, of course, will remain here in my personal possession, he said, tapping his chest as he used to tap the ledger he carried when he was Secretary of State.

Did you give the Honorable Mr. Bulkley, Esquire, the copy in the ledger book? Johnny asked as he drew a ten-dollar bill from his wallet and passed it over. Or did you give him the other copy?

Colonel Mann took the money, folded it without looking at it, and shoved it into his shirt pocket. Then he smiled, that crisp quick smile of his. He has the old original, and I have the new one, he said. Then, suddenly serious again, he expressed his disappointment at not being able to travel to Gordon Hall with his musicians and cabinet, but he had discovered a prior commitment that could not be broken.

Declining to press him as to the nature of that prior commitment, Johnny simply agreed to be his emissary and told him that as soon as Terron returned, he would leave for Gordon Hall.

Colonel Mann thanked him and, with no further conversation, departed.

Then, that same evening, shortly after sunset, Terron himself finally showed up, exhausted and angry. Juke, he claimed, had stolen his crop and was in Kingston. According to Terron, both the crop and Juke, who was supposed to be guarding it, had disappeared, and Terron, following hunches and gossip all the way to Kingston, had learned that the ganja, six hundred pounds of it, was still up here in the Cockpit, hidden in or near the village somewhere, while Juke tried to make arrangements in Kingston to sell it. But, Terron said, because everyone

in town now believed that he, Johnny, had come to
Nyamkopong to buy the ganja from Terron and was
staying around here now expressly for that purpose, his
hope was that whoever had stolen the crop with Juke
would get Juke back up here so that Juke would try to
sell it to him. Then, Terron explained, Johnny could
play along with Juke and in that way could lead Terron
to the ganja and whoever was storing it for Juke here in
town. He looked over at Johnny's new machete lying on
the floor by the bed and, for the first time since entering
the house, smiled.

Listen, Terron, I should get the hell out of here.

What about my crop, man? How am I going to get
back my crop?

Someone's going to get killed over that grass!

Juke! Juke's going to get chopped.

Maybe. But maybe you too . . . maybe me. Maybe all
of us.

No, Terron said soothingly. You're protected, man.

Because I'm white. No, Terron, not now, not anymore. Not when everyone out here, including the cops
and Colonel Mann and Bongo Smith and even Mann's
daughters, for Christ's sake, thinks I'm a big dealer up
here to make a buy. They probably think I have a plane
coming in from Miami that'll land down there some
night on the road that cuts through the Appleton cane
fields. They probably think I have a two-way radio under my bed here to tell my pilot when to fly in for the
pickup. And everybody in town wants a piece of the
action. Mann keeps Rubber in jail so he can rent me this
house for ten bucks a week. His daughters are cutting
each other up so they can keep each other from sleeping
with me. Juke and whoever his secret partner is are
being sucked into a trap where they'll probably get
chopped to bits by you and Smith, because you know
Smith will help you jump Juke and his partner if he
thinks he'll get part of the action for it. Tomorrow morning the cops'll probably show up at my door, and I'll
have to slip Kemp fifty or a hundred bucks just to keep

them from breaking my head with their billy clubs and tossing me in jail. I'm the misfit here, man, and my presence is screwing everything up. If I just leave, get the hell out, things'll quiet down and maybe no one will get killed or cut up or bribed or tossed in jail.

No way, man. Terron had picked up Johnny's machete and file and, laying the flat of the heavy blade across his thigh, was expertly sharpening both edges, turning it from a simple chopping tool into a razorsharp, double-edged broadsword. No way. Babylon will go on without you, my brother. Babylon will go on the same as before you came. But you don't have to bust your brains, man. You're protected.

How? Tell me that, Johnny demanded.

You're a wizard, man. No one can hurt you. No one except I-self and Jah. And I-man can't run from I-self or from Jah.

What's that mean?

It meant, Terron explained, that Johnny shouldn't leave because of fearfulness. No more fearfulness. Jah lives. Terron gently laid the machete on the rickety table and stood and placed a hand on his friend's shoulder. Don't bust your brains, man. Only prophecy can bring Babylon down. It won't fall because you leave. So you shouldn't leave because you think your departure will bring prophecy to fulfillment. Prophecy needs no man for fulfillment. Man needs prophecy. And you shouldn't leave because you are afraid. No one you can fly from can hurt you. So free up your heart, my brother. No more fearfulness. Jah lives.

7

AT SUNRISE, WITH THE MIST DRIFTING TOWARD THE RIDGE, Johnny packed his clothes and papers back into his suitcase. He lashed the sharpened machete and his cookpot to the outside of the suitcase with the piece of clothesline from behind the house, lifted his bag and typewriter and stepped outside, closed the door carefully behind him, and started walking, downhill along the road to Whitehall, descending through the cool mist, and after an hour, emerging below it, where he caught a ride on a flatbed truck heading for Maggotty. By the time he reached Maggotty, the sky was clear, endlessly blue, and the heat-browned hills behind him lay precisely carved against the sky. A higgler sold him an orange for ten cents, and before he had peeled it, the Kingston bus, leaning and wheezing, had pulled in. He got on, paid, and then was gone from Nyamkopong.

8

AT VICTORIA PARK IN THE CENTER OF DOWNTOWN KINGSTON, Johnny stepped from the bus and joined the throng— higglers and musicians, gray-bearded Rastas haranguing passers-by, nuns cruising in silent, quick pairs, gangs of huge laborers and hard-hats munching meat patties and watching the office girls strut past, cops, beggars, cripples, slit-eyed Natty Dreads nodding stoned in the midday heat to the beat of transistorized reggae, goats, dogs, wandering pigs, Chinese bankers, Indian women in saris, white businessmen in their drip-dry suits, backpacking American teen-agers looking extraterrestrial, people screaming at one another in the sweltering heat, people weeping, people shouting the names of angels and lost children, people yelling out the price of what they've got to sell—hot meat patties, mangoes, kalaloo, roast corn, ganja, shoes, radios, cocaine, hats, transportation, ideas, salvation, *everything*—because if you can't sell it then you have to buy it, and into this throng Johnny pushed his way, stopping only to buy a red, green and gold Rasta tam to protect his head from the sun, a man as human and peculiar as any other man, bearded, long-haired, skinny and becoming scrawny, thirty-six years old but looking ten years older now that his brown hair and beard had grayed away, dressed in jeans and a green T-shirt that had the words *Seit Ya*, meaning "Legalize it now," printed on it, as he lugged

303

his heavy, battered suitcase with machete and cookpot tied to it and his portable typewriter case through the whirling traffic of North Parade to the Orange Street side of the square, where he got onto a bus headed north out of town to Constant Spring, which is where the suburbs begin and the buses loop back downtown again.

Hitchhiking now, with rides from several people—a Rasta on a Honda who tried to sell him cocaine and took him as far as Stony Hill, a cabdriver on his way to the Playboy Club in Oracabessa on the north shore where he hoped tonight to pick up a rich American drunk who wanted a black woman in Kingston and was willing to pay to be driven fifty miles for it, and a third ride from a kid in a new Ford pickup truck, a soul boy with an American-style Afro and wraparound sunglasses and a billowing rayon shirt. This ride was from Castleton, where the cab driver had dropped him, all the way in to Gordon Hall. The kid explained that he worked for the M.P., Doc Semmell, a man Johnny met briefly in the back-room of a shop in Castleton last January, and the Doc, as the kid called him, was in Gordon Hall today, campaigning for reelection. As the kid tooled the truck skillfully through narrow passes and around hairpin turns, double-clutching and sliding the pickup as if it were a Formula One racecar, they talked politics, until it came out that the kid was PNP, Michael Manley's party, not JLP, his boss' party, the leader of which—a man named Edward Seaga, a Harvard-educated economist of Syrian extraction—had promised to halt the leftward drift toward communism and restore Jamaica's faith in Jamaica. Those Communists ain't the ones who made Jamaicans poor, the kid said to Johnny, whipping the truck up the sides of mountains. The only people in Jamaica who want to bring back the good old days are the ones who were rich in the good old days! he yelled, as the truck leaned out over the Flint River a thousand feet below.

In less than an hour they were in Gordon Hall, bumping along the lane toward Bowra's yard. On both sides of the lane, half in ditches and half out, cars and small trucks and

Hondas had been parked, and the kid had to thread his way through them with care, as people, most of them with rum and beer bottles in their hands, staggered in small, straggling groups down the lane toward the Colonel's place.

Doc does this every election, the kid explained. He brings in a couple cases of Red Stripe, a couple of Dragon, and a couple cases of overproof, and the chief up here gets out his dancers and drums and has a big party for him. Doc's a big man up here with these Maroons. And the chief loves it. Makes him a big man with his people. All Doc cares is that the old guy delivers the vote, and he does deliver the vote, let me tell you. They'll be voting Labour up here for the next hundred years! the kid laughed. And all it costs Doc is a few cases of rum and beer. A hell of a lot less than it costs the Labour guys over in Beverly Hills or Montego Bay. In Jamaica, the kid said, when you're out you got to pay to get in, and when you're in you got to pay to stay in. He laughed and drew the truck directly into Bowra's yard, parting the crowd and coming to a halt before a knot of about twenty-five people, mostly old people, dancing in a thick circle.

From the cab of the truck, Johnny could see Pie and Steve on the ground in front of the porch banging frantically on gombay drums, another man beating on the bamboo stick next to them. In the crowd of dancers he could see the Captain tootling on the abeng and stamping along in time, and there were Charles and Aunt Celia and Bowra's wife Regine, and, near the center, Gondo, leaping like a dervish, while on the outer edge of the circle, Harris, with a rum bottle in one hand and a batch of green herbs in the other, swooped and staggered, moving counter to the slowly clockwise spin of the dancers. At the center of the circle, like a hub, was Bowra, not dancing but turning slowly in place, glowering into the faces of the people moving before him. He brandished a stick over his head and every few seconds extended it and touched on the chest or top of the head of first this dancer, then that, causing the dancer to go suddenly rigid and fall and thrash blindly at the ground, when Harris, immediately alert, would shove his way through to the fallen one and apply his handful of greenery to the person's black face and then spray a mouthful of rum onto the person's lips, which would bring the fallen dancer back to life, would raise him or her, dazed and wobbly, and slowly move the dancer back into time with the drums, back into the circle. Then Harris would stalk the edges of the circle again, until another dancer, touched by Bowra's stick, would fall.

The kid stayed in the truck, smoking a cigarette and watching, a superior smile on his lips, but Johnny got out, grabbed his suitcase and typewriter from the back and made his way toward the porch. As he passed the drummers, Pie looked up and, after a few seconds of not recognizing him, probably because of the wool tam and beard, suddenly realized who he was and nodded sweetly and went back to his drumming. The porch was crowded with people watching the dance, one of whom, taller than the others, was Doc, the politician, a bottle of warm beer in one hand, a chunk of jerked pork in the other. He was surrounded by women, mostly girls in their teens who were standing as close to the politician as they could get without quite touching him and without losing their place to the girls next to or behind them, and when Johnny tried to step onto the porch with his suitcase and typewriter, he disrupted the precise positioning of the crowd there, forcing people to nudge and bump and squeeze against each other in ways that confused them and in seconds brought them all, even Doc, to stare at him, this peculiar-looking stranger pushing his way onto the Colonel's porch, saying, S'cuse me, sorry, sorry, as he shoved people off their carefully chosen and tightly held pivot points, making chaos of a structure he hadn't perceived until after he had disrupted it and it was too late. A heavy hand grabbed his shoulder from behind, and Johnny turned to face a large, muscular youth—a stranger to him—with the size and physical force of Big Ron, shirtless, and angry, extremely angry, who yanked Johnny backward off the porch and tossed him, as if he were old clothes, against the side of the building. His suitcase and typewriter clattered to the ground, and the cookpot and machete broke loose, the pot rolling downhill toward the dance ground and the machete falling flatly between Johnny and the other man, who went for it, reaching down with his right hand as if to snare a bird. Johnny kicked at the man's hand, knocking it away, and grabbed for the machete himself, reaching it first, closing around the wood handle, lifting it in a swooping arc that hit the man's right hand at the wrist, severing it cleanly and continuing the arc to a point high above Johnny's head, where it stopped.

It was Harris who took the machete away from Johnny. He appeared out of nowhere, while people screamed and the cut man moaned and fell bleeding backward into the bushes where three or four men grabbed him and one of the men ripped off his shirt and tied a sleeve around the cut man's elbow, wrenching it to stop the jets of blood spurting from the stump, slowing it immediately to a bubbling that another man staunched by wrapping his shirt around the stump. By now the cut man was limp and dazed, in shock; someone hollered for a car, and the group of men administering to him led him away.

Meanwhile, Harris had simply walked through the screaming tangle of people surrounding and pointing and yelling at Johnny, and when he saw Johnny and recognized him, hollered his name and bellowed a chain of words in Ashanti, which caused the crowd to back away a few steps. Then the man walked up to Johnny, who still stood with his back to the building, the machete raised above his head as if he were hanging from it by one hand, and took the machete out of his hand. Then Bowra was there, holding the man's severed hand as if it were a dead lizard. He held it out to Johnny a few inches from his face.

Spit on it! he ordered.

Johnny looked at the thing and shook his head no.

Spit on it, Johnny! If you don't, the other hand will kill you!

Johnny spat on it, and swiftly, as if rushing to save the hand, Bowra wrapped it in a batch of herbs and hurried onto the porch, pushing past Doc and the others there, and disappeared into the house.

Grabbing Johnny by the arm, Harris brought him into the house behind Bowra. Inside the dark room and hunched in a corner, Bowra was mumbling and dousing the severed hand in rum and carefully wrapping it, after which he deposited it inside a wooden Royal Jamaican cigar box. Johnny sat down on the double bed. On a table across from him perched the brass statuette of the bird.

I have a message to give you, and then I have to leave, Johnny said in a high, thin voice. Outside, the drums had started up again, the screaming and shouting had stopped, and people were starting to sing the African songs again, Aunt Celia's keening voice taking the lead, as usual, and the others falling in behind with growing volume and enthusiasm.

Bowra came and sat next to Johnny. Harris stood at the open door, as if keeping guard. That's right, Johnny. You have to leave here.

Colonel Phelps is dead.

I know that, the old man said.

Yes, and Mr. Mann is the Colonel now.

I know that.

And he won't be able to come down here on August first to join you in your celebration.

I know that too.

And he is having a copy of the sacred Maroon treaty sent to you.

Yes, that has already arrived and Harris has read it to the people.

All right, then. I've delivered my messages, Johnny said.

And now you have to leave.

Yes. I've seen everything I wanted to see.

No man can see more, Bowra said tenderly. Then he shouted at Harris to find Doc and ask him to come forward for a moment.

Harris ducked out and returned instantly with the tall politician in tow.

What is it, Colonel? he said, staring hard at Johnny, as if trying to remember when he had met him before.

The Colonel asked Doc if he was going back to town soon, and Doc said yes. Now, in fact.

Will you take this white man out of here with you in your truck?

How far you going? Doc asked Johnny.

The airport.

I'll take him, Colonel. For you. But he'll have to ride in the back. And I want your people to know that this man does not work for me and he is not my friend.

Oh sure, Doc, don't worry about that, I'll tell them, the Colonel assured him.

Let's go, the politician said. Then, in a cruel voice, he said to Johnny, I want you out of the country. That's why I'm taking you to the airport.

Johnny nodded and followed him out of the room, with Harris and Bowra coming along behind. The crowd parted for the politician and called out to him, Doc! Hey, Doc! Don't forget us, Doc! We're voting for you, Doc!

At the side of the truck, Johnny turned, as if to say good-bye to Harris and the Colonel, but they weren't there. The Colonel had returned to the dance, and Harris was again stalking around the circle of dancers, guzzling rum and sucking at the handful of herbs.

Get in back, Doc said and got in on the passenger's side and slammed the door. Johnny flung his suitcase and typewriter in ahead of him and climbed over the tailgate. The kid in the wraparound sunglasses peered through the rear window at him and grinned. Then he backed the truck slowly out of Bowra's yard to the lane, dropped it into first, and headed out.

THEY LEFT HIM AT THE AIR JAMAICA TERMINAL, WHERE HE bought a one-way ticket for the six-fifteen flight to Miami. It was then five-forty-five, and he had to run. He passed through the gates quickly, routinely, despite his appearance, and went aboard a few minutes before departure time.

About the Author

Russell Banks is the author of THE RELATION OF MY IMPRISONMENT, FAMILY LIFE, SEARCHING FOR SURVIVORS, THE NEW WORLD, HAMILTON STARK, and TRAILERPARK. He has won Guggenheim and National Endowment for the Arts fellowships, the St. Lawrence Award for Fiction, and Fels, O. Henry, and Best American Short Story awards. He lives in Brooklyn, New York.